Becoming the Devil

Bargain with the Devil series – Book 2

Alessandra Vu

BECOMING THE DEVIL

Published September 5, 2025
Copyright © 2025 Alessandra Vu.
ISBN: 979-8-9906682-4-9

Written by Alessandra Vu.
Book cover design by Alessandra Vu

Author's Note:
Regarding content

This is a paranormal fantasy romance that includes explicit sexual scenes. Some scenes include light BDSM. BDSM should always be performed with a partner who has had clear conversations revolving around trust, consent, and boundaries. If not practiced with clear communications, participants may endanger themselves.

There is violence on page. There is reference to sexual assault on page. Hell is a cruel place to live and it is depicted as such.

These characters are also not depictions of the healthiest, safest romantic partners to have. I do not condone nor promote their behavior. I write characters that match and fit each other well, but that does not mean they are healthy representations.

In simple, blunt words: depiction is not endorsement.

For those who wish to continue on with reading, I hope you enjoy.

Thank you.

The Seven Circles of Jeznia

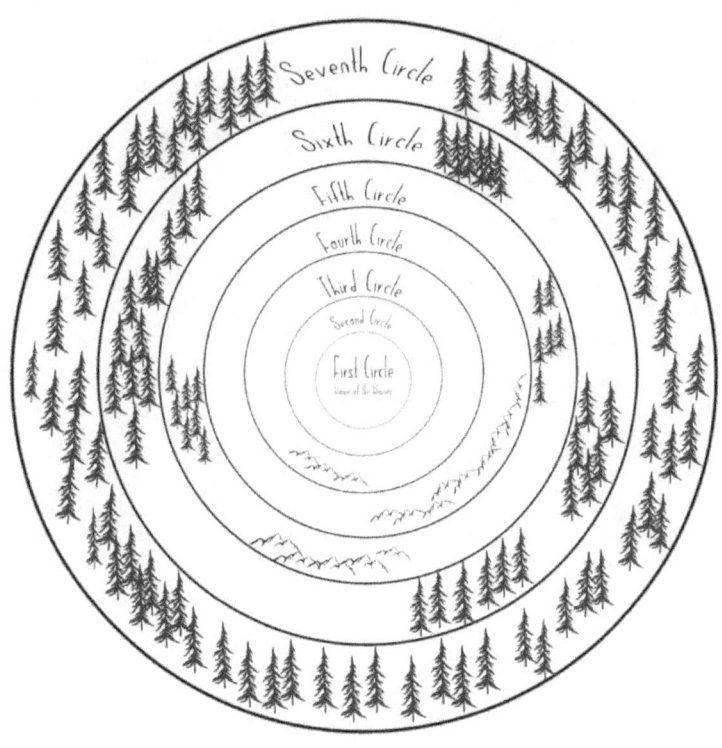

THE WASTELANDS

Prologue

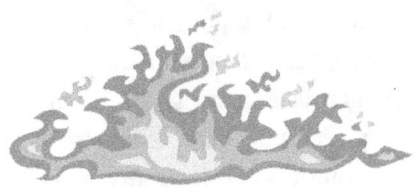

SLOANE SLEEPS DEEPLY beside me, not a care in all the worlds as she curls into her pillow. My eyes catch on the curve of her bare shoulder, down the length of her arm before said arm disappears beneath the pillow. She's exquisite. Every inch of her perfection. Yet, it was never her looks that drew me in.

It was her intellect.

So elegant. So sharp. So quick. She never hesitated in her decisions, her brain a frenzied machine analyzing her options in seconds. Not much escaped that beautiful mind of hers and I found myself revealing secrets of Jeznia that would doom a devil if she used her hand correctly.

She didn't disappoint.

A small, nearly invisible smile grabs hold of my lips as my hand reaches out to caress her face. She twitches at the cold sensation my fingers bring, but she does not wake from her slumber. I study her face; the shape of her lips, the arch of her cheekbones, the slant of her nose before my gaze wanders up to those magnificent horns. So dazzling with gold streaks of lightning contrasting against pitch black. The Lords of Jeznia would have slaughtered her for the threat she now poses, destroying that spectacular quick–witted intelligence, had I not been able to secure the Records Keeper for my trial. It had been our salvation, but it came at a high price.

Unease wraps its cold tendrils around my throat as I stare at her. The Records Keeper had required a secret worth damnation for the request I made. I readily gave it despite knowing how dangerous departing with such a secret could be. I confessed my secret because Sloane's worth that cost. She's worth every bit of risk thrown my way. It doesn't matter that the Records Keeper now holds the power to destroy me should the need ever arise because *she's worth it.* I can no longer live my life without her. Without that sharp tongue, without that extraordinary smile, without that natural born domination. I need her more than I need the air to breathe or the secrets that hold my freedom.

The tingles darting down my spine alert me of Umbra's impending arrival. I spare Sloane one last longing look before slipping out of bed. She moans her disapproval, her body further curling into the pillow as the heat vacates with me. It takes every ounce of willpower I possess not to climb back in bed with her. Instead, I settle for heating the bed with my magic so she doesn't miss my presence and quietly close the door behind me as I exit the bedroom.

Umbra appears in a swirl of black shadows in the center of the living room. The Boston apartment is rather grotesque in its drabness, but Sloane is not yet ready for the acquired taste of Jeznia. She's taken in stride what little she has seen, but her queasiness and her disturbance of Jeznia is not lost on me. Thankfully, I have seven years to prepare her.

As the black shadows clear, Umbra turns her head towards me. Her ashen grey skin, as dehydrated as a mummy's, absorbs the shadows whenever she calls them forth. The lids of her eyes have been sewn shut, forcing her to rely on her other senses the way a Shadow Seer should. If one cannot move smoothly, quickly, and deftly through absolute darkness, then I have no use for them as a Shadow Seer.

Her ears extend upwards past her scalp and come to a point, allowing her greater hearing than most. Those ears are meant for eavesdropping, for hoarding the secrets of my enemies, and are her greatest assets as a Shadow Seer. If I truly wished to wound her, to destroy the bond that connects us, I would slice those ears off without remorse.

She's roughly the same height as Sloane but with a stronger build. Umbra must climb and slink her way through the Houses of Jeznia to retrieve her intel. I could have used my magic to build her a body perfect for the job, but then she would never truly understand her physical limitations should my magic ever fail her.

Instead, I threw her to the monsters and put her through Hell before allowing her to partake in the House Primis House Aide trials. I made it known that if she wanted to serve me, she would be befitting of my reputation. For my goal is much more intricate than inheriting a seat at the table with all the Lords. I must ally myself with those who are strong enough to endure the long battle ahead of me.

I pop open the whiskey decanter, pouring myself a rather generous glass as I keep my back to my Shadow Seer. A show of how little I think of her as a threat.

"Correct me if I'm wrong, Umbra, but I thought I made myself rather clear not to disturb me until I returned to Jeznia."

"Zagon is on the move," she answers, her voice as quiet as a thousand whispers. Another intended attribute to her purpose as Shadow Seer.

I toss back the whiskey, briefly wondering what the burn feels like that so many humans speak of when drinking before I place the empty cup onto the counter. The glass clinks against the marble as my eyebrow arches up.

"What of it?" I ask.

Zagon is often on the move. How is this any different? My eyes glance down at her mangled hands and I contemplate removing both ring fingers as punishment for disobeying an order.

"He has a Blood Reaper in his midst."

My lips push out towards the side of my mouth upon hearing the news. Blood Reapers are House Aides to House Aranea. Lord Taron. An... *interesting* choice of an ally for Zagon Primis when he puts such a large emphasis on combat and strength. Not only is House Aranea ranked *sixth* out of seven, but Blood Reapers are not known for their combat skills. They're sly creatures who require only a sliver of blood in order to control the body. The more they drink, the longer their control lasts. If Zagon has a Blood Reaper within his circle, I must assume he already has a target in mind for the Blood Reaper to go after. That begs the question: who is the target and what promises did Zagon make to Lord Taron in order to obtain a Blood Reaper?

"Where has he taken the Blood Reaper?" I ask, keeping my tone casual.

"I lost them within the shadows. Caelum is still the better Shadow Seer."

"Of course he is," I sigh out as I pinch the bridge of my nose. "He's been Zagon's House Aide for over a thousand years. You have two measly years."

"My apologies, my Lord."

"What good are apologies when you have nothing to show for it?" I snap at her, my rage manifesting into fire igniting down my horns. She does not move or flinch as she remains expertly indifferent. "Find out where Caelum took that Blood Reaper. I presume Zagon has promised Lord Taron a favor that may come to harm Sloane. Let me know if you hear any whispers of her name. I don't care from where or from whom. You let me know every time you hear her name within another's mouth or I will make you eat your heart before you die."

Not a difficult threat to enact when my magic would allow me to keep her alive long enough to enjoy her heart. Umbra knows it too. She bows her head slightly, her mutilated hands coming to rest atop her stomach.

"Of course, my Lord. I will protect her with my life, for she is peccatum tuum."

Rage overwhelms me as the fire consumes the top of my head, darting down my spine and washing over my shoulders. I only ever uttered those words while being intimate with Sloane, not wanting anyone to know the true weakness she is to me. For Umbra to know... it would mean she's slinking where I have not given her permission too.

Umbra smiles, her lips cracked and bleeding as rotted teeth come to view. "I will protect your secret, my Lord. I trust in the choices you make."

The flames immediately flicker out as I stare at Umbra with uncertainty. Trust is not so easily garnered in Jeznia, yet the bond we share makes it impossible for Umbra to lie to me. She may not understand the choices I am making, but she trusts in them. That will have to be enough for me.

I lightly bow my head as I utter the words quietly, "Descendere in flammas."

"Descendere in flammas, domine mi," she repeats back.

There's a silence that falls between us as my head lifts back to its normal position. With our mutual understanding that Sloane is to be protected, there is nothing left for us to discuss. I pour myself another glass of whiskey, tossing it back with a refreshing 'ah' before starting my trek back to the bedroom where Sloane slumbers.

"I expect an update on that Blood Reaper upon my return to Jeznia. Find it, Umbra, or be prepared for the consequences," I throw over my shoulder.

Tingles shooting up my spine notify me of Umbra's departure just as I enter the bedroom. As quietly as I'm able to, I slip back into bed, removing the magic that heats the empty space I now occupy.

Sloane shifts, her eyes blearily blinking open a few times before closing shut.

"Where did you go?" she asks, her voice groggy and heavy with sleep.

My arms wrap around her as we do our best to ignore the cold creeping halfway up my forearms. She easily settles her head upon my chest, snuggling deeply into the warmth I offer.

"I went out for a nightcap," I answer, not a lie but neither the whole truth.

I'll tell her about it when the time comes. For now, she must concentrate on honing her powers and hiding the kind of magic she holds.

Her head pops up from my chest, eyes squinting at the clock on the bedside table. "It's three in the morning."

"A dry throat cares not for time, Sloane," I hum the words as I push strands of brown hair behind her ear. "Forget about it and go back to sleep."

She stares at me, her brown eyes darting back and forth between mine, and I bite back the smile that begs to be let free. Even in her sleepy state, I can see the wheels turning inside that head of hers. How I love that analytical, domineering, sharp brain.

My fingers delve into the soft tresses of her hair before I pull her towards my lips.

"Sleep Sloane," I whisper against her lips.

She grunts, offering a quick kiss before dropping her head back to my chest. My fingers trail up and down her spine as she snuggles deeper into me. Not five minutes later, her soft, rhythmic breathing informs me she's wandered off to dreamland.

As I stare up at the ceiling, pondering what Zagon is scheming, I decide none of it truly matters so long as it doesn't involve Sloane. Whatever Lord Taron wants, whatever Zagon promised, if Sloane is left out of it then I don't care.

She is my future now.

Everything else is dust.

I

"CHANGE THE COLOR of the pigeon," Balthazar instructs as he sits languidly on the bench in Boston Common.

I stand roughly five feet from him as pigeons peck and waddle between us. Balthazar has both his hands draped along the back of the bench, his long legs spread out in such a classic man spread that it mildly irritates me despite how attractive he looks.

He's in casual clothes instead of the classic suit he wears when bargaining for souls. He picked the perfect outfit for the cooler weather. Grey cashmere sweater with fitted dark jeans and brown leather boots. My first thought is he's sweating underneath his layers, but then again, with magic at the snap of his fingers, he's probably pleasantly comfortable.

Balthazar's thick black hair is uncharacteristically not styled. Instead, it's pushed back with a thin black headband. It gives him a youthful look, like he's fresh out of college and not in his mid–thirties.

His olive skin is a little tanner than when we first met. I suspect that's due to the amount of time he's been hanging outside with me these past few days. Black eyes sprinkled with red specks stare at me in observation as sunlight manages to cut through the canopy above and bounce off his glossy black horns.

Overall, the entire air surrounding him screams casual, relaxed, and maybe even the tiniest bit bored. I do my best to ignore that last part as I focus on the reason why we're here.

"What color should I change it to?" I ask as I look at the group of pigeons.

Today is my first magic lesson. Crazy how only three short weeks ago, Chad shot me, nearly killing me. If it hadn't been for the fact that I still had a wish to make, I'd actually be dead, rotting in the walls of Hell – Jeznia, according to the locals.

Thankfully with my wish, I saved my life while simultaneously finding a loophole that prevents me from being tortured for my afterlife. I wished to become a devil for all *eternity*. Balthazar granted it without hesitation.

He later confessed he never intended on turning me into the powerful devil that I became. Apparently that happened because of the old magic I possess. But old magic is a dangerous thing to have. If the Lords of Jeznia find out I have old, deep magic, they'll either kill me or do unspeakable things to get access to it. To prevent that from happening, Balthazar insisted he teach me normal magic; the kind of magic every devil uses. I agreed to his lessons because the other option wasn't really an option.

So here we are, our first lesson of teaching me how to use normal magic and Balthazar wants me to change the color of a pigeon.

"Any color you want," he answers without a care in the world.

I stare at the multi–colored bird and consider that making it all one color is probably the easiest way to go about this. Although technically that means I'm changing 4+ colors at the same time. Maybe it would be easier trying to just change one color. Though that would mean focusing on a smaller area on the bird instead of the bird as a whole. If I really think about it, both scenarios are *equally* difficult because they require a different set of focus and intent.

"Sloane," Balthazar says my name, his voice laced with mirth, and my eyes snap up to him.

He's smiling a crooked grin, the right side of his lips pulling up as he stares at me in open amusement. How does he get more handsome the longer I know him? Shouldn't I become immune to it as time goes on?

"You're overanalyzing the task," he states and a heat floods my cheeks at his call out. I didn't realize I was so easily read.

"Do I change *all* the colors or just one?" I ask despite my embarrassment. "This is the first time I'm attempting something like this. I don't know which one is easier."

His eyes glance down at the birds as he studies them before he answers. "Make it all the same color."

I frown, not too pleased with his answer, but trusting him all the same. Afterall, he's the expert here. He should know what he's talking about.

"Ok. I'll change it to brown."

He nods his head and I stare at the bird closest to me. It's minding its own business as it pecks the ground for any leftover seeds. It's a chunky bird and I can't help but smile. The bird pecks mere inches from my feet, not at all alarmed or bothered anytime I move.

"Sloane, peccatum meum, as much as it pleases me to watch you, focus on the task at hand."

A glare settles on my face as my attention darts up to Balthazar. I'm not purposely stalling. I literally have no idea what to do. He said to change the color of the bird, but he didn't tell me *how* to do that. Does he expect me to know what to do without ever having done this before?

I don't hold back from letting him know my thoughts. "You're a shitty teacher, you know that? You haven't given me any advice on how to actually *use* magic."

His jaw juts back and forth, a displeased look crossing his features as he strums his fingers along the back of the bench. Looks like I've stumped him and a flash of satisfaction courses through me. I manage to suppress the smug smile that's begging to be let out. That smugness would only cause tension between us and get me nowhere with my first lesson in magic.

"You've got that clever brain inside your head, why don't you put it to use?" he challenges after a few moments in silence.

Irritation zings down my spine at his lack of accountability. Why did he even bother suggesting he'd teach me how to use magic if he's not going to do that? Seriously. I get teaching may not be intuitive for him since Jeznia is all about taking care of yourself and no one else, but it's infuriating that he offered to help if this is how he's going to teach.

"What's the point of having you for a teacher if you aren't even going to help?" I protest, arms crossing over my chest as all my weight shifts to my right leg. I'm not going to let him off easy just because of his upbringing. But if I want his help, I need to offer him a little motivation. This question should do the trick. "Do you secretly want the Lords to find out about me?"

"Not in the slightest," he answers without hesitation as his attention wanes, eyes drifting up towards the leaves whispering in the wind. "I have faith in you, Sloane. You're smart. I know you'll figure it out."

That backfired really fast, I internally grumble to myself. His statement is a double edged sword. I can't even put into words how his confidence in me makes me feel. Lightheaded? Weightless? Over the moon? No one has ever seen me the way Balthazar does. I'm not just a pretty face to him. He sees my intellect and *likes* it. His simple acknowledgement of my intelligence has a smile nearly breaking the surface.

Yet it's easily squashed at Balthazar's reluctance to help me. I don't *want* to be doing this on my own. I want help. I want his input and suggestions. I want us to figure this out *together.* That's how I was able to figure out my wish and that's how I want to do it with my magic.

"Friendly reminder that you supplied information to me about Jeznia," I tell him. "Your help and information is how I figured out how to word my wish. I didn't come up with it out of thin air and completely on my own."

"Fair point," he muses as he leans forward onto his knees, eyes catching my own. He's contemplative for a few moments before saying, "Very well. Draw your magic forward."

A couple of seconds pass by as I wait for him to offer more feedback, but he remains mute. I flail my arms out in annoyance. "What does that even mean?"

"Exactly how it sounds," he states in mild exasperation. "Draw it forward. Pull it forward. Reach out to it. It's about intent—"

"That!" I shout as I point at him. "Saying it's about intent is way more informative than 'draw it forward." I use a mocking tone as I say *draw it forward* to emphasize my point.

"Sloane, do not test my patience," he says as he pinches the bridge of his nose.

"Oh yeah?" I ask, hand resting on my hip. I can't resist the natural urge to do the opposite of what he's asked. "What are you going to do about it?"

His eyes flash white, his jaw clenching and unclenching. He's so predictable that sometimes it's laughable. Any time I challenge him, no matter the time or place, it drives him crazy, but the *good* kind of crazy. He loves it. The back and forth, the threats, he even enjoys degradation. It makes him putty and, over these past three weeks, I've learned how to use that to my amusement and entertainment.

"You wanted this lesson," he reminds me as he sits back against the bench. It's irritating how calm he appears when just seconds ago, I was pretty sure he was ready to lunge at me for a kiss. "*I* wanted to bury myself deep inside you over and over again, but you requested this lesson instead."

Mortified, I quickly glance around our area, my face flushed as I worry someone walking by might have overheard what he said. It's my own stupidity for playing with fire in such a public space.

Thankfully, no one meets my gaze so I hope that means no one heard him. Feeling a little reassured no one is paying attention to what we're talking about, I turn my attention back to Balthazar. He's smirking, more than pleased with himself.

"I'm going to get you back for that," I promise him and his smirk deepens.

"I look forward to it. Truly."

My heart skips a beat at the lust I see swimming within his eyes. We're too compatible for our own good. How are we going to get anything done? Right now, I sort of regret asking for this lesson instead of doing what Balthazar had suggested. We could be in the throes of passion instead of arguing over how to change the color of a pigeon's feathers.

Balthazar must sense my waning attention because he pulls our focus back to the issue at hand. "Draw your magic forward with the intent to use it. Change the pigeon to brown."

I stare at him for a few moments, too drawn in by how handsome he is. My eyes soak in his plump lips, his toned body, his menacing presence. Memories of him pounding into me from all kinds of angles has a slow heat coiling in my stomach.

A sly smile spreads across his lips as if he knows *exactly* what I'm thinking. *Cocky bastard,* I think and hate the fact that he has every right to be. Rolling my eyes, I use all my willpower to turn my attention to the pigeon standing roughly a foot from me.

It's now or never. I shake my arms out as my weight shifts back and forth on my feet. For good measure, I take a couple deep inhales. Hopefully that'll help center and focus me.

It's time to use some magic. My heart pounds against my chest and I try to quell the nauseating nervousness that eats away at me. I don't want to hurt the pigeon or even cause it distress, but how else can I learn magic? *Oh god, if I kill it, I won't be able to use magic ever again,* I think. The anxiety barrels into me, bile sitting in the back of my throat at the thought of accidentally ending the pigeon's life.

"Sloane," Balthazar urges me as he stands up from the bench.

"Let me go at my own pace," I order, shaking out my arms one last time before I close my eyes.

Draw the magic forward with intent, Sloane. Nothing to be afraid of. Just let normal magic come forward nice and gently. Hair along my arm rises and prickles as electricity thrums in the air. Simultaneously, I can *feel* magic flowing through me, starting at my feet and working its way up. It's different from the last time I used magic. When I killed Finthorn it felt too heavy, too thick, too ancient. This magic is lighter.

It's also slipping through my fingers every time I try to grasp it. I could grab the old magic and it did what I told it as soon as I thought it. This normal magic is like smoke, swirling away every time I reach for it.

"You'll need to open your eyes to try the magic out," Balthazar's voice cuts through my concentration.

"I can't grab it," I tell him, eyes still shut as my hands grab at empty air.

"That's because it's outside of you," he says.

Upon hearing those words, my eyes fly open. Lightning the color of rich, shimmering gold streaks across the space surrounding me. Despite the sunny and bright day, I can see a thin layer of lavender smoke swirling around me where the lightning resides. My hand reaches out, the purple smoke billowing around my fingers before a lightning streak zaps my hand. It stings worse than a static shock, but less than a paper cut.

"Is this… normal?" I ask, completely captivated by the small lightning flashing through the purple smoke.

"I have never seen magic work this way," Balthazar answers.

Panic darts through me and the words fly out of my mouth, "Won't the Lords be suspicious when they see my magic working like this?"

"Sloane," he breathes my name like an ode. "You're a human who was born with a Jeznian soul that has now become a devil. They won't expect normal from you because there's nothing normal *about* you. Just know this kind of magic might bat an eye or two due to its peculiarity, but it will not draw attention the way the old magic will. This magic is safe."

My panic eases. Inhaling deeply, my lips press into a thin line as I refocus my attention on the magic swirling around me. So… my magic is *weird* but everything about *me* is weird which makes it ok. This strange kind of magic won't draw much attention. I won't attract the Lords curiosity or worse, Zagon's. This is good, it's ok.

"Try turning the pigeon brown," Balthazar calmly repeats, snapping me from my thoughts.

I nod my head, turning my attention to the pigeon. It's now walking around the leg of the bench, pecking at the ground for any leftover seeds. I concentrate on using my magic to change the pigeon from gray to brown. As my thoughts intensify, the lightning increases, crackling like a firecracker as it darts around the air in rapid succession.

The more I focus on holding on to the magic, the wilder it feels. Desperate not to lose it, I act impulsively. I mentally reach out to the pigeon, a booming *BROWN* echoing within my mind, and the lightning streaks out at the bird. There's a brief shriek from the pigeon as it's zapped by the magic before it flutters its wings to escape. Balthazar stops it, using his own magic to keep the bird in place, and we watch as the bird transforms. Not gray to brown but into a white duck.

Balthazar clicks his tongue as the duck quacks, stumbling on its feet as it gets used to its new body.

"Interesting choice, Sloane."

"I didn't do that on purpose," I argue as I watch the duck flop down before scurrying to its feet. "I just… It felt like I was losing the magic."

"So, you hastily reacted before you lost control."

"Yeah," I answer shamefully, my attention dropping to the pavement and I wince as the duck quacks again.

"Truth be told, I'm impressed you were able to use magic on the first try," Balthazar states before snapping his fingers. The duck changes back into the pigeon in an instant.

My eyebrows pinch together as I turn towards him. "You are?"

"It took me a year before I could use my magic on purpose," Balthazar confesses, his eyes lingering on the pigeon as it stands motionless. Like the poor bird is going through a midlife crisis after being changed twice.

My heart drops at hearing Balthazar's words as worry burrows its way into my heart at the implications of what his confession means. That I'm *better* at magic than he was. That it comes more naturally to me than it did to him. Will that make him resentful?

I can't hold back my question as anxiety drives the word forward out of my mouth in a meek voice. "Really?"

"Yes," he answers simply. He continues on, talking as though he's discussing the weather and not revealing intimate information about himself. "My mother started teaching me about magic when I was two years old. It wasn't until I was five that I finally felt it, six when I was able to use it with intent, and ten when I took on my first job."

"Wait, you didn't feel your magic until you were five years old?" I ask in genuine surprise.

"Correct."

I nibble on my lower lip as I watch Balthazar. His hands are in his pockets as he watches the pigeons peck around us. The expression on his face doesn't give away what he might be feeling inside. *Is* he jealous that I can use my magic right away? He said he's impressed, but is that just to mask his envy? The urge to tell him that our circumstances are different overwhelms me. He was a boy when he started practicing magic. Maybe the fact that I'm older gives me a better advantage.

"Maybe magic doesn't manifest until you're five years old," I suggest, hoping that it'll ease any potential resentment he might be feeling.

He glances at me, his expression indifferent as he says flippantly, "I wouldn't know. I've never met any devil children."

Something about that statement cuts me deep, his words a visceral reminder of how cruel and unforgiving his life has been from the moment he was born. I take a step towards him, my hand reaching out to grab his arm. My fingers wrap around his forearm and I'm shocked at the cold seeping through the thickness of his sweater. The cold has crept up to his elbow. He's spent too much time on Earth. He should head back soon to recharge before the cold sets in even more but I can't let him go home without clearing the air between us.

"Are we... ok?" I ask and his eyebrows furrow together as he tilts his head.

"Why wouldn't we be?"

"It's just that…" I trail off as I think of the best way to say what I want to say. "Does it bother you how quickly I've used my magic in comparison to yourself?"

He chuckles as his hands slide out from his pockets and he grabs me possessively around the waist, pulling me flush against him. "Not in the slightest, peccatum meum."

Concern morphs onto my face as I stare up at him, my hand resting against his chest. He says that, but is he being honest? Most men would feel inferior, incompetent even, if the woman they were dating easily excelled at something that took them years to accomplish. Doesn't he feel the same way?

"Are you sure?" I ask. "Because I would totally understand if you felt that way."

He dips his head forward to rest his forehead against my own. "I assure you, Sloane, I have no feelings of envy or jealousy towards you. If anything, I'm relieved. You'll learn magic much quicker and will become a formidable opponent much faster than I anticipated."

"Promise me you'll tell me if your feelings ever change?"

He pulls his head away from mine, a frown marring his face as his hand on my waist slips beneath my shirt. I hiss and shrink away from his freezing appendage, goosebumps flaring along my skin, but I quickly adapt to the cold and settle back in place.

"Why is this a concern for you?" he asks as his fingers continually squeeze and release my waist.

"Because," I breathe out as my head tilts forward and I focus on his chest instead of his eyes. "I know you're not human, but most guys have a hard time when the woman has more power in a relationship. You're a Lord of Jeznia, heir to the most powerful House, but then comes along little ole me who learns magic like it's nothing. Most people would be resentful."

Balthazar's ice cold fingers dive into my hair, gripping it hard enough to force my head backwards so I'm forced to look him in the eyes.

"Rid yourself of these foolish thoughts," he demands as he firmly holds my gaze. "I expect my owner to exceed me, to exceed the strength and power of Lord Balthazar of House Primis, heir to High King Zagon Primis. I will not settle for less."

"But isn't that just for, like, sex? You don't really mean that, right?" I sheepishly ask.

We've never really talked much about how we view our relationship. For the past three weeks, we've been coasting along and doing what feels natural to us, but we've never defined the relationship. I have no idea whether we're on the same page or not, but I've been ok with the way things have been going. I haven't felt the need to have "The Talk" with him, but right now it seems like we should. It'll be good for both of us to know what the other expects.

He arches up an eyebrow, his fingers still holding my hair as he stares down at me. "You wish to *partially* own me?"

My mouth opens and closes as I stare up at him, not entirely sure what my answer is. Do I want to own him? In a way, yes. I want him to be mine and only mine. But I don't want to strip him of his freedom or will. I want us to be as equal as we can be. I enjoy dominating him in the bedroom, commanding him and watching him fight against himself to obey me, but he isn't a *thing* for me to keep. He's his own person. I don't ever want him to feel less than me or objectified by me.

"No one owns you, Balthazar," I answer. "You're strong enough to be your own person. I want us to be equals. I want us making decisions together, communicating with each other about our wants and needs. Do you... not want that?"

He squints his eyes at me, his lips puckering to the side of his face, and I can't refrain from smiling at the face he's making. He looks confused and perhaps a little put off by what I've said. Like I just told him that in order to grow up big and strong he has to eat the vegetables he doesn't like.

"Sloane," he says my name with an utter seriousness that it causes my stomach to drop.

He's going to reject me, isn't it? Of course he is. I'm learning magic easier than he did. I'm a threat to his status in Jeznia. It would be dumb of him to keep me around. The Lords will think of him as a joke if he stays with me. Never mind what his father, the High King, will think.

"You were born a human with a Jeznian soul," he says as he affectionately pushes hair behind my ear. "When I used magic to turn you into a devil, the magic *inside* you took over and made you what you are. Your innate magic is more powerful than you understand. The magic the Lords collectively possess, myself included, is child's play compared to your own."

He pauses for a moment, his eyes darting back and forth between mine before he offers a gentle, almost invisible smile. "I'm under no illusions of who is the more powerful one between the two of us. I don't care about that. *You* own me, Sloane, through and through. It is not just a 'sex thing'."

Something clicks into place after hearing his words. Like I've been waiting for him to give me permission to truly grow and embrace this powerful magic inside of me. He's given me the freedom to become whatever I need to be, regardless of the power disparity that might grow between us. I can go forward now without fear, without anxiety, and without hesitation. Balthazar will support me through it all because he embodies the ideology that a success for *me* is a success for *him*. I could not have met a more perfect equal than him.

My hand reaches up to his horn as I personify the role of master he has graciously given me and I tug the horn down so we're eye to eye. He doesn't resist, the hand playing with my hair dropping away as the hand gripping my waist holds me tighter in excitement.

"Ok," I breathe out as we lock gazes. "I own you, Balthazar, so you better not break my heart."

He smirks wide and eagerly. "I wouldn't dream of it, peccatum meum."

II

"Y OU SHOULD HEAD back to Jeznia," I tell him as I release his horn, my hand sliding down his freezing arm. "The cold's gone too far up."

"We've only just begun your lesson," he replies, a sly smile spreading across his lips.

The corner of my mouth pulls up in a weak smile as I roll my eyes and shake my head. "It can wait. I'd rather not lose my teacher to something preventable."

"We've got time," he insists as he pulls me flush against him, hand dropping down to slip into the back of my jean pocket. The coldness of his hand seeps through the material, causing me to frown. "I'd say I have about ten more hours before I'm at risk."

"Balthazar," I breathe out sternly as I push against him. It's fun and games to him, but this is the safety of his life we're discussing. It's not a joke to me no matter how cavalierly he talks about it. "Go back to Jeznia."

"But we haven't even had any fun," he says with a pout.

A soft glare settles on my face as annoyance creeps its way in. He's pushing the boundaries and I'm not amused. "Keep refusing to listen and we'll have even less fun."

He openly rolls his eyes as he shakes his head. "No sense of adventure."

"And yet, I still managed to get myself turned into a devil," I quip airily, my eyebrows raising up towards my hairline as if to further my point.

"Fair point," he yields with a slight bow of his head. "If you insist I return to Jeznia, so be it. Now that you have a feel for how your magic works, it's up to you to practice."

That's how he's going to play it? If he doesn't get what he wants, I don't get what I want either?

"But–"

"Trust in yourself, Sloane," he interrupts me. "You know what you're doing. Practice will refine the talent you already possess. I'll help when I'm able to, but I have my obligations as a Contract Liaison and Lord of House Primis. That's not including the time constraint placed on me by the cold. You will have to be responsible for your self–study."

"What if I hurt someone?" I ask and can't suppress the slight fear in my voice. I don't think I'd ever feel comfortable practicing magic ever again if I hurt someone in the process.

He tilts his head, fingers diving into my hair as his thumb caresses my cheek. When he speaks, his voice is gentle but firm as he holds my gaze. "I assure you if that happens, it will be on purpose."

"You promise?"

"You have my word," he answers before pulling his hand away and taking a step back. "I'll be back in time for dinner. Should you require any assistance from now until then, ask for Umbra."

I force a smile to my lips as I nod my head. There's no way in Hell I'm asking for Umbra's help. She already doesn't like me; I don't want to make it worse. Besides, how can she help me with magic? She doesn't have magic of her own. I keep that obvious flaw to myself, prioritizing his trip home over the accuracy of his statement.

"Donec tunc, peccatum meum," he says with a light bow, his right hand resting atop his heart.

"What does that mean?" I rush out the words before he has the chance to snap his fingers and disappear.

He smirks as he looks at me with a heated gaze. "It's my little secret."

Snap.

He's gone from sight and I'm left alone with the birds. *Asshole,* I can't help but think as my attention shifts to the pigeon I accidentally turned into a duck. It hasn't moved from its spot. Frowning, I crouch down and gently poke it in its chest. That snaps it out of its hazy state and after a moment, it takes flight.

A heavy sigh blows out of my mouth as I rise to my full height before I plop down on the bench Balthazar had been sitting on moments ago. He wants me to practice magic on my own, but I have my reservations about it. I don't know much about magic, but I have enough intelligence to deduce my magic looks volatile. It manifests as literal lightning *outside* of my body. What if it gets out of hand when I try to use it and he's not around to make things safe? What if it explodes? Could I die using magic?

Despite the questions, doubts, and concerns I have, I can't ignore the fact that Balthazar has enough confidence in me to recommend that I train by myself. Then again, he grew up in Jeznia. His mother probably used very questionable methods to get him good at using magic. He's probably using those same exact methods with me. Except the difference is I grew up on Earth. I care about harming others while he was taught to find joy in it. He had the freedom to practice his magic without concerns of harming others while I'm the exact opposite.

I heave out another heavy sigh. He may not be the best teacher to have, but he's the *only* teacher I've got.

"Screw it," I breathe out as I lean over and grab a twig from the ground.

I twirl it in my hands for a few moments before getting up from the bench and walking out onto the grass. About ten feet in, I plop down, cross my legs, and place the twig on the ground in front of me. I figure it's best to be away from people on the off chance I lose control of my magic and it lashes out. And you know what? A prayer can't hurt either.

I press my palms together as my index fingers rest against my nose and I squeeze my eyes shut.

"Please don't explode," I whisper three times in rapid succession before opening my eyes again.

I can do this. Balthazar believes I can do this. Like he said, it's all about intent and I've got plenty of intent! Levitating the twig off the ground should be easy with all the intent that's running around inside me. I may not have changed the *color* of the pigeon, but I did change it. That's proof enough that there's hope for me.

Exhaling loudly, I shake out my arms before closing my eyes. *Let the magic fill you up, Sloane.* I concentrate on that familiar feeling, on the magic filling me from the feet up. It's light, wispy, and electric. Now I understand why. I inhale deeply as I try to calm my nerves, getting a little bit more familiar with the way my magic feels and reacts. *I can do this,* I think and I'm happy to admit I actually believe it.

My eyes snap open and, even though I expect to be surrounded by a light mist of lavender smoke and gold lightning, it still amazes me that it's there. The lightning streaks out, zagging through the air in elegant lines. I wonder if my magic will always look like this or will it change as I become more adept at using it? I hope it doesn't change. It's beautiful the way it is.

I raise my hand up to the smoke and lightning zaps my knuckle. It hurts, but not like the sting I anticipated. It's more like a strong pinch. Either way, if it can hurt me, it can definitely kill me. I need to be wary of it. Respect the danger of it. If I don't, I'm sure I'll end up dead.

That leaves me feeling uneasy. If something goes wrong, no one is around to save me. I really shouldn't be practicing magic without Balthazar. He's the only failsafe I have.

I briefly wonder if he had to overcome this same exact hurdle. If he did… then so can I. It's a silly belief with zero proof to back it up, but I grab hold of it. If Balthazar can master his magic, *so can I.*

I exhale a deep breath as I focus on the task at hand. Levitate the twig. Control the magic. Don't reach out in desperation. *You can do this, Sloane. Just move the twig.* I remain seated with my legs crossed and my hands gripping my shins. Lavender smoke swirls around me as the golden lightning flashes become more frequent and longer. The magic solidifies inside me as if the smoke is changing into mud. It's heavier, stickier, like my hands have been smeared in cake batter that I can't shake off.

My eyebrows pinch together as I stare at the twig half a foot from where I sit. *Levitate* repeats on a loop inside my head. Excitement courses through me as the twig begins to vibrate. I lean forward over my legs as I beg the damn twig to lift up into the air. It's close. I can see it. It's almost there. Just a hair more and it'll be off the ground completely.

Lightning abruptly crackles next to my face, hot and bright as it flashes across my eyes. I lose my focus and the twig stops its movements completely.

"Damnit," I shout as I slap the ground and immediately jump back as a minor explosion blasts beneath my hand.

I shriek as I roll away from the small hole I created.

This is exactly what I was worried about! How is Balthazar so confident I'm not going to hurt myself in the process? *Maybe he expects it and thinks it'll help me learn faster*, I think, irritated. That's probably how his mother taught him. Why would he be any different?

More than aggravated, I flop onto my back and stare up at the green canopy of tree leaves above me. I need a break. It'll help me recalibrate and relax for when I try again. It's *not* me procrastinating. I swear.

The leaves above me billow in the calm wind. The sun shines brightly as small white fluffy clouds lazily drift by. The air is crisp and clean. A little on the cooler side for the beginning of September, but that's New England weather. It never knows what it's doing.

As I lay there, a calmness settles in and my well–guarded feelings slink their way through the cracks of my armor. Feelings I've been working hard to suppress. Fear. Anxiety. Anger.

So much has happened in my life in such a short amount of time. I died twice – the day Balthazar met me and the day Chad shot me. I was almost killed too many times to count. I technically no longer have any family or friends left. I'm isolated and alone with Balthazar as my only support. It's a lot to process and I've been doing my best *not* to process it. Ignoring it is so much easier.

I don't want to think about how angry I still am that my life was taken from me. I don't want to think about how most nights I wake up in a cold sweat, gasping for air thinking someone has their hands wrapped tight around my neck. I don't want to think about the Lords discovering the truth and crucifying me when they do. It's too much. All of it is too much.

What I need to focus on is learning magic. In becoming stronger. Once I become powerful enough, no one will be able to fuck with me ever again. Balthazar said it himself. He *expects* me to exceed him. *Him.* The devil that *six* Lords walk on tiptoes around. Yet he believes I'll be more formidable than him.

If I can just focus on that, on the future he expects me to have, I can push down everything else that happened to me. What good is there in thinking about the past? I can't change anything about it. I can't change how Matt tied a piece of cloth so tight around my neck I passed out. Or that if it wasn't for Balthazar, Matt would have successfully killed me.

I can't change the fact that Chad shot me because he was too angry the devil let me live despite killing me in all other senses. Or that if Balthazar hadn't shown up *again*, I would have died, *again*. I can't change that it was pure luck I still had a wish to make and was able to save myself.

"Fuck," I breathe out, vision blurring as my emotions threaten to overwhelm me.

I'm *not* supposed to be thinking about this. Who cares what happened to me? No one. No one cares because I'm *dead.* I'm not even in the news anymore. People have moved on and have much bigger concerns to worry about than some basic white girl who got chopped up into eight pieces. No one cares about the torment I went through. About how hard I fought to figure out a loophole. How I never gave up even when it seemed hopeless. And now that all that stress is gone, no one cares about the emotional drop that comes afterwards.

Balthazar probably doesn't care, but I haven't allowed myself the opportunity to find out. I haven't bothered to talk to him about it because, realistically, he wouldn't understand what happened to me. He grew up in Hell. *Literal* Hell. The worst place anyone could be born and raised.

The chances that he's dealt with far worse than what I've gone through are very high. It would be stupid of me to expect sympathy, empathy, and compassion from him. He'd be more likely to tell me to get over it or to get used to it than he would be to offer a comforting embrace. Afterall, I'll be living the rest of my afterlife in Jeznia where devils rip arms off each other for stealing. What I went through was a cake walk in comparison. I need to get over it, to get over *myself*.

My cheeks puff out as I try to rid the tears from my eyes. The leaves above me warble in my vision but when I blink my eyes, clearing away the tears, they become crystal clear. This is so pathetic. I need to harden up. The things that Chad and Matt did to me were nothing. They don't deserve the time and energy I'm giving them. They're both dead so why am I shedding tears over what they did when I've already got my revenge?

Inhaling and exhaling loudly, I sit back up and turn my attention to the twig. Better to ignore my feelings and focus on my magic. I need to be able to defend myself from the Houses. I can't rely on Balthazar forever. There might come a point in our future where we break up and he could become an enemy. Forever is a long time to live. A lot could happen. I need to prepare. I need to make myself strong and independent from him. The thought of us breaking up has a visceral reaction shooting through me, but preparing for it is the smart thing to do.

"You can do this, Sloane," I whisper to myself as I stare at the twig.

This time, I pull the magic forward but I keep my eyes open so I can see what's happening. I need to start small with my practicing. One step at a time type of practice.

My first step will be pulling my magic forward faster and faster. To the point where I'll be able to use it with a snap of my fingers. I can work on moving the twig later. For now, I'll practice pulling my magic forward, releasing it, and repeating the process until I become comfortable pulling it forward like it's second nature.

For the next two hours that's all I do. I remain seated on the grass, my legs crisscrossed, my eyes focused on the twig as I let the magic fill up before releasing it and starting the process all over again. Within those two hours, I can tell I've improved. I've gotten used to how my magic feels, how it starts at the little toes before exploding up into my core, how the smoke may be light and airy, but that there's always something firm for me to grab within the smoke. All I have to do is locate it.

Releasing the magic is easier than I anticipated. All it requires is me mentally letting it go. As soon as I release my hold on it, the magic disappears. Case in point, the purple smoke disappears as soon as it appears and I smile at how easy it's become for me to do.

"Move the twig," a quiet yet firm voice orders from behind me.

I yelp as I whirl around, my heart in my throat as I stare at Umbra less than three feet from me. She stands stoically, her hands resting at her sides, and is dressed in the familiar black form fitting clothes. Her box braids are pulled back in a low ponytail and her golden eyes aren't staring at me, but at the twig half a foot from me. Her sepia brown skin glistens as the sun bounces off it and I notice a light sheen of golden glitter across her cheeks.

She looks out of place in The Commons not because of her outward appearance but because of the vibe she gives off. Lethal. Dangerous. Fuck around and find out. I think if she were to smile, it wouldn't look friendly, but instead threatening. Nothing about her is approachable. And yet, here she is, *purposely* talking to me as she orders me to move the twig.

"I was going to try that later," I confess as I turn away from her.

"Do it now."

"I'm not ready," I protest, though it doesn't sound as stern as I'd like.

"Do it now," she repeats herself in that quiet voice that holds no room for arguments.

My hands curl into my palms as my lips press together in irritation. It's so easy for her to demand I do that when she doesn't even have magic to practice with. She must think it's like breathing, that I should just be able to do it as easily as Balthazar does. Newsflash, it isn't. I couldn't move the twig two hours ago. I can't move it now. I need to practice more with pulling my magic forward. Continue getting a better feel of it so I can understand it more. Once I have that down, I'll practice moving the twig.

Umbra doesn't say anything as she walks past me and picks up the twig. I watch as she expertly twirls it in her calloused hands before flicking it into the ground. It makes a light thud as the tip digs into the dirt and the stick remains vertical. She's an excellent shot and I can't help but glare at her as the stick barely misses nicking my shin.

"Move the twig," she orders, her golden eyes devoid of emotions as she stares at me.

Angry and annoyed, my fingers curl around the twig before I yank it out and toss it roughly five feet away.

"Happy?" I ask with all the attitude of a haughty teenager. "I moved the fucking twig."

"Yes," she answers monotonously, which immediately deflates my sails.

I wasn't expecting her to agree. If anything, I expected her to snarl or glare at me. Maybe even do something to make me flinch. The reaction she gave me instead... I'm not sure what to say or how to respond to her simple yes.

Umbra's attention shifts to the twig before her gaze slides back to mine. "There is no correct way of doing anything."

Her statement surprises me, my back going straight as a board while embarrassment floods me. It's such a simple statement, loaded with truth and fact, yet it never crossed my mind. I've been approaching my magic by how Balthazar would because he's the only real frame of reference I have. But Umbra spies on devils and Lords as part of her job. She's probably seen her fair share of magic in action and cataloged the different ways it's been used. Balthazar is a good frame of reference for me to use, but I shouldn't let it pigeonhole me in how I use my magic. Especially considering how differently my magic works from his.

My gaze flits down to the grass in shame as my cheeks go hot. I pray she doesn't notice the sudden pink coloring of my face.

"Thanks," I mumble.

"Don't fear getting hurt," she says. "You'll always heal. Fear the consequences of inaction. *That* will get you killed."

Her words strike true and, despite the shame I feel for not figuring it out on my own, her message motivates me. She's right. Even if I break all the bones in my body from using my magic, I'll heal. I have to change my mentality around this. I should learn how to take a punch. It'll make me stronger, more resilient, and less afraid. The more familiar I become with the pain, the easier it'll be for me to push through it. My magic *won't* kill me because *I* control it. Even when it's volatile, wild, and lashing out, *I* still control it.

With renewed determination, my magic appears rapidly, almost as soon as I think to call it forward. I inhale nice and deep, turning my entire focus on the twig five feet from me. I can feel the magic slinking over to the twig and I quell my excitement as best I can. I need to remain focused. As soon as I think of the twig shooting to my hand, it does. The lavender smoke pounces on the twig as the golden lightning shoots it to my hand.

My palm burns as I hold the twig. I glance down and see small lightning bolts streaking out from my enclosed hand. It hurts. More than what I want to endure but I force myself to hold on. The pain will eventually subside. The more exposure I get to it, the less it'll hurt and the less I'll fear the pain. I can do this. I *will* do this.

I catch black smoke swirling out of the corner of my eyes and leap out towards it.

"Wait," I shout as my fingers touch Umbra's shoe.

The smoke disappears as she stares down at me, no emotion flitting across her face.

"Thank you," I say as I stand up so we can see eye to eye. "I couldn't have done that without your help."

She says nothing and I realize it's probably because my words mean nothing to her. She doesn't care that she's helped me or that I've succeeded. Which begs the question: *why* is she doing this?

"Why are you helping me?"

She doesn't miss a beat as she says, "Because you are Lord Balthazar's peccatum. Because it's important for him that you get stronger."

Again with the word I don't understand. It must be something really important if both of them are using it. What if it's something bad? No, it can't be. If it were bad, they wouldn't bother helping me learn my magic. Still, the not knowing is driving me crazy. Does it count as cheating if I ask Umbra for the definition when Balthazar said it was his secret? *Whatever. I don't care.*

"What does pecca–whatever mean?"

She stares at me long and hard while I stare right back. She'll either answer me or leave. That's just the way she is. If she does leave, it means I'll have to torture the definition out of Balthazar. On second thought, that actually sounds kind of fun.

"Peccatum translates to the English word sin," she finally answers.

My eyebrows furrow together as I process what she's said. "Pecca...tome means sin? And you're helping me because I'm his sin?"

That makes absolutely no sense.

"Yes," Umbra answers.

"What does that even mean?" I ask in complete and utter confusion, my arms gesturing to emphasize my bewilderment.

"Ask him."

Without another word, Umbra disappears in a cloud of black smoke, leaving me confused, alone, and mildly irritated, but better at wielding my magic.

III

Balthazar arrives at the condo shortly after 6pm. I've already ordered Indian take out and have placed the food containers on the kitchen island for us to pick at.

He's clearly agitated when he arrives, his hand combing through his hair *three* times before he even glances at me or the food.

"Ah," he finally says as a handsome smile spreads across his lips and he walks over to grab an empty plate to fill with food. "This looks delicious."

"These are extra spicy," I tell him, pointing to the lamb vindaloo and aloo gobi.

"Perfect," he purrs as he dumps the food onto his plate while taking a separate bowl of rice.

I watch him as he moves about the kitchen and notice that, despite his best efforts, he can't completely hide the tension in his shoulders. Something must have happened today that upset him.

Curiosity has me practically opening my mouth to ask him what went wrong, but I bite back the words. Balthazar typically hands over information when he's ready to. If he hasn't told me yet, there must be a reason.

Yet as he sits down beside me, his shoulders nearly touching his ears from tension, I can't help myself. Whatever has him so worked up must be important. Maybe important enough that it involves our little secret. If that's the case, I *need* to know.

Gently twirling my fork in my hand, I ask, "Anything worth mentioning that happened today?"

Balthazar doesn't hesitate in his response. He rips the metaphorical band aid off in one go.

"The Houses want you to start attending meetings," he answers so nonchalantly that it takes me a moment to understand the gravity of what he's said.

My fork clatters against my plate as my head whips toward him. The steady thrum of my heartbeat thuds heavily against my chest. Why on Earth do they want me at the House meetings? They *hate* me. It makes no sense they'd be willing to let me around sensitive information. Besides, I'm not even a Lord of a House. I have zero rights attending House meetings.

"Why?" I is all I'm able to ask, confusion deep in my voice.

Balthazar doesn't immediately answer. Instead, a soft sigh blows out his mouth as he stares down at the steaming food on his plate. My stomach drops at his hesitancy. Is there something larger at play here? Are they trying to use the meetings to get access to me? Maybe one of them will attempt an attack on me. They certainly wouldn't need a good reason to do attack me, but Balthazar gave them one when he turned me into a devil knowing they wouldn't approve.

Why would they want me at the meetings? Their House meetings are basically government meetings. Spouses of government officials aren't usually allowed in these kinds of meetings, so why would they want me there?

"I don't think I should go," I declare when he doesn't answer my question.

It has to be some kind of trap, some kind of scheme to kill me. There's no way I'm going to put myself at risk like that. Balthazar can make up a lie for why I can't go to the meetings. It won't be a problem.

"You have to go," Balthazar counters, but there's no bite to his words.

My blood runs cold and a split second later, the words are pouring out of my mouth, no filter or consideration to be heard.

"Why?" I ask bitterly. "Because they said so? Since when do you do what they tell you to?"

He clicks his tongue in disdain as he snaps his fingers. A moment later, a whiskey glass appears beside his plate and he takes a sip before offering his reply.

"I am not complying because they've ordered me to," he practically growls out. "The simple fact is that you, Sloane, are a Lord's spouse. Therefore, it is expected that you will attend just as all the other Lords spouses attend. It's suspicious you're the only spouse that isn't in those meetings. They assume you're spying on them while their entire House is preoccupied. They won't stand for it."

My lips part as I process what he's said. Other spouses attend the House meetings? Other Lords of Hell — of Jeznia are *married?* That makes no sense! Jeznia is a world that fosters hatred, manipulation, screwing over anyone and everything to get a leg up. Love doesn't exist in Jeznia. Lust, sure, but love? Yet these Lords have supposedly bound themselves to another devil for all eternity? Maybe not eternity, maybe for a set period of time, but still, it's hard to believe.

Balthazar is the exception to the cruelness of Jeznia. Honestly, when I *really* think about our situation, I find it nearly impossible that he's capable of love. Jeznia doesn't foster love, vulnerability, or trust. What little information he's shared of his upbringing is filled with cheating, lying, and scheming. Yet somehow this magnificent devil found it in him to fall in love with me. A human. And the only plausible answer I can land on as to how that happened is prolonged exposure to humans.

He's been around humans since he was ten years old. In the three weeks that we've been together, it's become abundantly clear to me that Balthazar has his favorite spots in Boston that he likes to go. That means he spends time in the city even when he's not making deals.

He's spending time around humans, observing them, taking in their daily lives, and even interacting with them. Yes, the humans he makes deals with are usually the scum of the Earth, but the woman and child he sits next to in the café, the elderly man who insisted Balthazar buy me a bouquet of flowers just because, the married couple celebrating their anniversary, and the family vacationing in Boston all show him what love can look like.

Through exposure to these kinds of humans, Balthazar has been taught vulnerability. He's capable of falling in love. It may not always fit or look the way I'm used to, but every day he shows me he loves me. But the other Lords of Jeznia? Married? Why would they do such a thing?

"Married," I say, voice flat as I level him with a look to match.

"Yes. Married. The chair on the right is reserved for their respective partner. The chair on the left is for offspring," Balthazar informs me.

He's referring to the throne room. Every throne is located at the top of seven steps. On the fifth step there are two additional chairs for each House. I've always wondered if there was a specific reason why some devils sit in the right or left seat but never got around to asking about it.

"Ok," I drawl out as I mull over what he's told me. "So, they want me there to make sure I'm not spying on them?"

"Yes," he answers before taking another sip of his whiskey. "With you in attendance, all major members of House Primis will be accounted for."

"But what about your father?"

"Zagon is High King. As far as he's concerned, all the Houses belong to him. And as far as the other Lords are concerned, so long as he thinks that he owns them, they see no problems with him going off and doing his own thing."

"What happens when he expects them to comply with something they don't want to do?" I immediately ask.

Sure, the Lords can pretend and go along with Zagon to make life easier for everyone involved, but what happens when pretend becomes reality? I can't imagine they agree that Zagon actually *owns* their House.

"From what I've witnessed, they typically go along with him because they believe he has Jeznia's best interest at the forefront. Afterall, there's a never ending war with Odantha going on in the background."

Right. I forgot about that. Once upon a time, Jeznia, Odantha, and Earth mingled together without any deadly time constraints put on them. But then Jeznia got too greedy, took advantage of humans and Odantha stepped in. Jeznia lost the fight and as consequence, the Creator created the cold, forcing all Jeznians back to Jeznia withing 48 hours. Jeznia's been pretty bitter about it ever since.

I blow out a heavy breath as I process everything he's said. So... the Houses want me in attendance at their meetings. Meetings about Jeznia. Basically, *government* meetings. I'm not qualified for that. Do I need to be? Does Balthazar even want me there? Or is he agreeing to appease them and prevent them from looking where they shouldn't?

"I guess I'll start attending the meetings," I say but it comes out sounding more like a question.

"Yes," he agrees, though he sounds less than pleased about it. Like he doesn't want me there.

I can't bite back the words of insecurity. They leave my mouth in an instant. I need to know what his stance on this situation is but I hate the way it makes me sound and feel.

"Do you want me there?"

His gaze snaps to mine, his facial expression hiding his true thoughts. His black and red speckled eyes look back and forth between mine, a slight narrowing to his gaze as whatever thoughts shooting through his mind remain unknown to me. I hold his gaze, slight nerves bundling in the pit of my stomach at the possibility he might say what I don't want to hear.

"Yes," he answers simply. "I do want you there."

"It's ok if you don't," I rush out, unsure if I'm trying to convince him or myself that it's ok for him to hate the idea of my unqualified ass going to these meetings with him.

I know nothing about running a government. Especially not one so cruel. What good am I going to do? Should my job be just to look pretty and stay mute?

Balthazar reaches out his hand to mine, his fingers already ice cold as they curl around my hand.

"I want you there, Sloane."

"I'm useless at these meetings."

"No, you're not," he immediately argues as his face scrunches in slight anger. "It will be beneficial to me to have another set of ears and eyes in the meetings. That's the exact reason why the Lords marry in the first place. Spouses are loyal to their Lords. They would rather die the worst death imaginable than betray their Lord."

My eyebrows pinch together as confusion overshadows everything else I'm feeling.

"That makes no sense," flies out of my mouth. "I've been under the impression this whole time that Jeznians are the *opposite* of loyal. If that's true, why would any Lords spouse be loyal?"

Balthazar bites back a smile but he can't hide the slight twinkle in his eyes. I've amused him and I haven't the slightest clue what's done it. His hand leaves mine as he reaches for his whiskey glass, taking a quick sip before he answers.

"You're not wrong, Sloane," he says. "Jeznians *are* the opposite of loyal. They backstab, cheat, and plot betrayals so grand it's actually an artform. However."

He pauses as he peers at me out of the side of his eyes. "Lords are very specific about who they choose to marry. The spouse is usually someone who knows how to keep their head down so that they can get by in life. They're not powerful enough to change their own life, but they're smart enough to not get themselves killed. A Lord needs someone who can pay attention, who can observe the other Lords that aren't speaking and report back what they've observed.

"In return for being a dutiful spouse, they get to live a luxurious life, one incomparable to what they could achieve on their own. They would never betray the master that spoils them."

"A spouse has seriously never betrayed a Lord?" I challenge because honestly it's a little hard to believe. This is Hell we're talking about.

"Not that I'm aware of," he answers before taking a bite of his food.

"But what if the third House tries to lure the seventh House's spouse with promises of an even more luxurious life?"

Balthazar cocks up an eyebrow as he offers me a sideways glance.

"No one's that stupid, Sloane," he answers, his tone full of mirth as he bites back a smile. "It's a miracle they were selected to be a partner in the first place. They're not going to risk everything on what is most likely a lie. I supposes it's not completely impossible but, as I've stated, I've not heard of it happening. Once you become a part of the House, you *become* a part of the House."

It takes a moment for me to understand what he's saying. *He's talking about being magically bonded to the House.* The words spill from my mouth as soon as I think them while my eyes watch his every reaction.

"Does that mean you became a part of House Primis?" I ask.

According to Balthazar, Zagon Primis's offspring are brought to House Primis when they're three years old. But that's not what happened with Balthazar. His mother hid him from Zagon and raised him on her own. She taught him how to use magic even though she had no magic of her own.

When Balthazar turned 30, his father discovered his existence and immediately killed Balthazar's mother for her dishonesty. Balthazar was brought to House Primis and given the title Lord Balthazar.

So, does that mean on the day he became a Lord he also became a part of House Primis? Is that why, despite everything, despite his hatred towards Zagon, he's never retaliated against his father?

"Yes," he answers as he blows out a heavy breath. "I did."

My stomach tightens upon hearing the news. If he's magically bound to the House, what does that mean? What kinds of limitations does he have? How much freedom does he have to disobey House Primis?

"If you're bound… does that mean you'd kill yourself over betraying House Primis?"

It's a dangerous question to be asking but I need to know the answer. I need to know where he stands. Even with all the hate he has towards his father, if he's bound to his House the way Umbra is bound to him, he won't have a choice in defying Zagon. Magic will make him obedient even if it destroys his soul to do so. So if Zagon orders me captured or killed… Balthazar will *have* to do it no matter what.

"I will always make choices that benefit House Primis, but let me be clear, Sloane," he says as he catches my gaze. "Those choices don't often benefit Zagon himself. Zagon is *not* House Primis."

My heart skips a beat at the look he's giving me. It's as if he can read my internal thoughts and worries. He washes them away before they can fester into something bigger. Every day he amazes me at how well he can read and understand me.

My lips part to shower him with verbal affections but he continues speaking.

"He's outlived his rule and I will not allow him to sully you. No matter the cost." He turns his body towards me, his hand reaching out to gently grasp my own. "You are safe with me and you are safe in House Primis."

Balthazar, the amazing devil that he is, knew exactly what I was thinking without me explaining. He heard the question in between the words I spoke. *Will you kill me if Zagon orders it?* No. He won't. Because Balthazar is the master of loopholes and he will do whatever he must to protect the House. *Not* Zagon.

God, how did I get so lucky? I act without hesitation, leaning across the gap between the high stools we sit in, and kiss him. His fingers clench my hand as he kisses me back before he leans his forehead against mine.

"I will do everything in my power to protect you, Sloane."

Sliding off the stool, my hands turn Balthazar's swivel stool towards me. I push myself between his legs, settling my hands on his thighs. He gladly makes room for me, his hands coming to rest firmly on my hips as he pulls me flush against him.

"You won't always need to protect me. I promise. I'll get stronger," I whisper as our foreheads rest against each other. "I was able to move a twig today with my magic. I'm already getting stronger."

"Umbra informed me," he replies as he starts placing kisses along my face and neck. "You did more than move it, Sloane. You called it to you."

My hands comb through his thick hair as my head falls back, giving him more access to my throat. He greedily takes it, lips leaving searing hot kisses down the column of my neck. It's been a few days since we were last intimate. Balthazar has been busy with securing deals and the Houses while I've been busy adjusting to my new life.

"It won't be long before you rule Jeznia," Balthazar declares, his hands slinking down to my ass and gripping it possessively.

"You really don't want to rule, do you?" I ask in amusement as I pull his head back.

He growls his disapproval at being forced away from my neck, but he obeys. His heated eyes stare down at me, endless depths of black and red. He truly is magnificent. More than I could have ever bargained for.

"I'd rule if you demanded it," he answers plainly, his hands slipping around my front and unbuttoning my jeans.

Heat pools in my crotch as anticipation for what he plans on doing fills me with excitement. Our gazes remain locked as he pushes the hem of my pants down just far enough to allow him to slip his hand in. I inhale sharply as his cold fingers slide down the front of me, slipping between my folds and pushing inside.

"I'd do anything so long as you asked it," he breathes out heavily, eyes hooded, as he pumps me smooth and slow.

My hands tightly grip his shoulders as my hips rock against his hand. I love the way his palm creates that delicious friction against my clit. His touch is intoxicating. He barely has to brush up against me and I burn with desire for more of him.

"What if I demanded you renounce your title?" I ask because I can't help myself.

The amount of power I have over him makes me greedy. Just how far would he truly go for me? How much would he sacrifice just to please me?

"For you... I'd willingly walk into The Wastelands," he growls as he finally breaks eye contact, leaning forward to sink his sharp canine teeth into my shoulder.

I moan my pain, but it's pleasantly mixing with the pleasure he's giving me as he finger fucks me. My legs tighten up as he slowly builds the climax, slipping in two more fingers to stretch me out.

His words aren't lost on me. I remember what he's said of The Wastelands. How not even his father, the most powerful being in Jeznia, would dare venture out there because if he did, he'd become lost for eternity. That's quite a sign of devotion, but it lacks a certain bite to it. I want something more profound than that.

"What if I made you bow down on your hands and knees, forehead pressed to the floor in front of all the Lords?" I ask as my heartbeat quickens and the lust inside me comes alive.

Balthazar groans as he plunges his fingers in rough and hard. *Oh, he likes that,* I think as a greedy smile spreads across my lips. I'm learning just how much humiliation Balthazar truly loves and it's exhilarating the way he responds to it. He's an exquisite creature and he's *all mine.*

I grind my hips against him signaling him to pick up the pace. He does as he's silently told, his palm rubbing against me in smooth, firm strokes as his fingers plunge in and out in rough, quick thrusts.

God this feels too good. All of it. His fingers inside me, his palm against me, the way he loves being owned and dominated, yet I crave more of it. I pull his head back just far enough so I can whisper in his ear.

"I'd have you wearing a collar with my heeled foot on your back while I held a leash in my hand for all the Lords to see."

"Fuck, Sloane," Balthazar groans as he rams his hand against me.

My legs weaken as the pleasure overwhelms me and Balthazar easily holds me up with his other hand.

"Do it," he begs as he expertly edges me closer and closer to my release. My breath hitches in my throat as I squirm against him, unable to contain my eagerness. I'm close. So close. "Make me grovel at their feet. I will. Demand it of me and I will."

This. This is true submission and power. He'd do anything for me, consequences be damned. All I have to do is order it. Not even ask. He *gives* me that power. No one else but *me.*

The truth slams into me at the same time as my orgasm and I curl into him as a deep moan leaves my mouth.

"Balthazar," I whisper against his collar bone, my legs clenching against his hand as the feel good chemicals flood my body.

He holds me close as he gently removes his hand from my pants, his fingers wet from my desire. My face flushes as he greedily sucks his fingers clean before my eyes glance down at his crotch. He's sitting in the high stool and his pants are bunched around him, but I can see the hardness resting against his leg.

I take a step away from him, my attention shifting to the kitchen island where our dinner lays forgotten. We've had a few bites, but nothing that put a dent in the amount of food I bought. To be completely honest, though, food is the least of my concerns right now. I might have had my fun with my orgasm, but I haven't had my fill of Balthazar. His fingers are nothing compared to his cock or the weight of his body on top of me.

If this were any other relationship, I'd cut straight to the point. Take him to the bedroom and have my way with him. But I've learned Balthazar prefers things a little differently. He enjoys a good old fashion fuck, but he goes insane whenever play is involved.

While I've been relatively confident in dominating him, there are other parts of his desires that I want to explore. It's still a learning process for me, but I want to be good at it because he's *amazing* to me. Our pleasure should be reciprocal.

My eyes shift back to Balthazar and I take a step away from him. He's watching me like a hawk, trying to anticipate my next move, but I honestly have no idea what I'm going to do. I did a basic search on kink play two days ago but ended up on a lot of porn sites that didn't help much. The one good takeaway I got was needing a safe word. We don't have one. Pineapple is the most commonly referenced one but I can't picture Balthazar agreeing to something like that.

"Sloane," he says my name like he's trying to pull me from my thoughts.

I'm overthinking this. *Trust your gut. At the end of the day, he'll be grateful he got to fuck you.* The thought eases the tension out. I'll try things out and if they don't work, they don't work. Next time, I'll try something else. It's not the end of the world. Right? Right.

"Strip," I order him.

A smirk flashes across his face before it disappears as he complies. Balthazar stands up from the stool and slowly lifts his hand to snap his fingers. When I don't object, the *snap* echoes throughout the room. He's left standing stark naked and I let my greedy eyes roam over his body.

My eyes catch on the tattoos across his chest, on the inverted triangle they make as they end just above his navel. They're made of swirls and text, but I can't read the language. One of these days I need to ask him what the meaning of his tattoo is but that's not today.

I inhale deeply as I sink into the dominant role he loves so much. It's an entirely different persona that takes over. A secret, hidden part of my personality that had always been there, but I had suppressed because women are supposed to be submissive. Because women are emotional and don't have what it takes to lead. I regret to say that I catered to society. Even so, that dominant part of me fought hard, rearing its ugly head from time to time. I could never fully suppress it, which is why I threw that damn drink in Chad's face in the first place.

But Balthazar... Balthazar graciously gives me the freedom to be domineering, to be rude and crass without fear of retaliation, to let me put him in his place. He begs for it, lives for it, and craves it. He responds so well that I can't help but give in to him more. Dominating him, receiving his submissiveness... It's healing the parts of me that Chad destroyed when he wished me dead. I'm taking back my power even if Balthazar is willingly giving it to me.

"Lay down on the counter," I order and Balthazar cocks his head to the side.

A moment of hesitation. Irritation flashes down my spine.

"Did I stutter, Lord Balthazar?"

His upper lip twitches at my condescending tone, but he doesn't object. He hops up onto the counter, a displeased expression grabbing hold of his face as he sits on the cold marble.

"Lie down," I order firmly, not shying away from showing open frustration at his lack of cooperation.

He resists and a *tsk* falls out of my mouth. He wants more domination than what I've currently given. Fine if that's what he wants, then so be it.

I cross my left arm just beneath my breasts, resting my right elbow atop my arm as I inspect the nails of my right hand. The message is clear: my nails are more important than the naked man in front of me.

"I've had my fill, Lord Balthazar," I breathe out in a bored manner, eyes glued to my fingers. "I don't need to entertain you. I'm perfectly fine walking away and taking a nice, long, leisurely bath all by myself while you remain hard as a rock, wishing you'd listen to my commands so I'd let you cum. So, what'll it be?"

"Your way," he answers as he lays down on the counter, withholding the hiss at how cold the marble feels against his back. "It'll always be your way."

I walk up to the counter, combing my fingers through his hair as I smile down at the most handsome devil to exist. "Good boy. You know your place well."

He leans into my touch, eyes sliding shut as he sighs in relief.

"Have you had a difficult day?" I ask, fingers still raking through his soft tresses.

"There's nothing difficult about making deals with humans," he answers and his eyes remain shut.

I watch as his body relaxes onto the counter, how some unknown stress eases out of his corded muscles as my fingers comb through his hair. There's something hidden beneath the surface that he's not telling me. It bothers me that he's keeping me out of the loop, but if I demanded he tell me now, it would feel like I forced it out of him against his will. I want him to tell me because he wants to, not because he likes being ordered around and being submissive.

It'd be so easy to force the information out of him too. So long as we remained in this space with lust and sex in the air, he'd comply. I know he would. But I can't – I *won't* do that to him.

My fingers slip from his hair as I study the planes of his chest.

"You have such disdain for humans, yet look at you," I say as my index finger circles around a nipple.

His pectoral flinches beneath my light touch and I smile. All this power within him succumbs to my will. It's incredible when I really think about it. My magic is but a fraction of his. He could put me in my place in a heartbeat. *I* would be the one naked and sprawled out on the counter if we went by who truly held the power in our relationship.

It's indescribable knowing the clear power imbalance means absolutely nothing to us.

My finger flicks his nipple as my eyes glance back up to his face. He peers at me from half hooded eyes, the black so inky it hides any flecks of red.

"If any one of those humans you've made a deal with were to see you now, they would never fear you. What's there to fear when you're sprawled out on the kitchen counter butt naked?"

He parts his mouth to retaliate but the words die on his lips as I grab his cock in my hand. It's stiff, hot, and a little slick from the bit that's leaked out of him. My fingers hold him tightly around the head before I pump down once and he inhales sharply, eyes fluttering shut as his muscles strain against me. He's forcing himself to remain still. I haven't given him permission to move.

Seeing him obediently comply ignites my desires on fire. How did I end up so lucky to meet a man – a devil who so willingly *listens* to me? Especially when so many of the guys my age *tell* me what I like and don't like.

Girls don't like dad bods. If you don't have a six pack, they want nothing to do with you.

Girls *say* they want a nice guy, but all they date are assholes.

Girls won't date a guy who is shorter than them.

Girls won't date a guy if he doesn't make more money than her.

Girls would rather date the hotter guy for clout than date the nice friend who's always been a shoulder to lean on.

It's *infuriating*. Yet here is Balthazar, naked and laid out on the counter all because I told him to. But it's *more* than that. It's more than him submitting just because he enjoys it. He views me as his equal. He wants to hear my opinion. He readily admits when I've made a smart and fair point. He isn't embarrassed to be "owned by a girl". He *welcomes* it.

"Sloane," Balthazar says.

His voice snaps me out of my thoughts and I offer him a small smile as I lean down towards his face.

"There's nothing to fear about you," I whisper as I pump his cock again. "Imagine what the Lords would think if they saw you right now. Imagine the disgust on Ivy's face when she sees the way you let me touch you. Do you think she'd still want to sire your child?"

"Fuck," he sharply breathes out, his pleasure clear as day as his cock twitches in my hand, his hips flexing as he stops himself from thrusting into my hand.

"She'd rather have a child with me when she sees the way I *own* you."

His eyes snap to mine, a snarl on his face, and he can't help as his body moves on its own. He thrusts up into my hand and I let him because the absolute feral look on his face is worth the disobedience.

"That's her problem though, isn't it?" I ask as I release his cock and he growls his frustration. "She doesn't realize you've been wanting to be owned. You never wanted this position of power. You were happy living your life as a Contract Liaison, weren't you? You *want* to be told what to do. But would you let Ivy own you the way you let me?"

"Never. She doesn't have what it takes," he answers. And then he begs. "Sloane, touch me."

A sly smile spreads across my lips as I reach out, trailing my fingers up his sternum. His frustration feels nearly tangible as he lightly thrusts his hips into empty air. He wants my hand wrapped back around his cock, but he doesn't call the shots. *I do* and I'll touch him however I want.

"Why doesn't Ivy have what it takes?" I ask as I twirl my finger around his left nipple.

His jaw clenches and unclenches as he glares at me, then down at his raging erection. I splay my hand across his chest before dragging it down towards his belly. He inhales in anticipation and nearly roars when I circle back up towards his chest.

"Sloane."

His voice is layered, sounding like multiple people are talking at once, and it sends a tingle darting down my spine. *Oh, he's pissed*, I think and it delights me how desperate he's become for my touch. But we're not done here.

I wrap my fingers around his horn and jerk his head sideways as I lean down towards him. His eyes find mine, feral and wide, as his lips twitch to hold back a snarl.

"Remember your place, Lord Balthazar," I murmur in a low, quiet but menacing voice. "If I want to walk away right now leaving you unsatisfied, I will. You belong to me and I'll treat you however I want to. You want a reward? Then be a good boy who answers when he's asked a damn question."

This feeling of utter superiority is electrifying. I can feel it thrumming in the air. Balthazar wasn't wrong when he said I was a born natural. Maybe that's why my soul is red. Maybe I was always meant to be this wicked, cutthroat, dominant bitch. Maybe that's why Balthazar was brought into my life, to help me see the truth.

"I want you, Sloane," the words rush out of him in one quick breath. "I need you. Fuck, look at what you do to me. Let me have you."

I pull back to stand at my full height and allow my eyes to drink in the sight of him. His fingers have dug into the marble countertop, leaving imprints and cracks from the sheer force of his restraint. His cock, so swollen and red, has leaked out precum on his hip. He's flushed in desire, his pupils dilated. He's entirely gone. I've tipped him over. When I let him have me it'll be wild, rough, and otherworldly. Exactly what I want.

My body vibrates in eager anticipation.

"I'll let you have me when you tell me why Ivy doesn't have what it takes," I tell him as I cruelly trail my finger around and near his erection but never touch it.

His muscles twitch beneath my fingertips and I can see how difficult it is for him to think straight. *I made him like this,* I think in amazement.

"She doesn't… have what it takes because she'd never defy me. She'd do everything I'd tell her to, hoping it's what I'd want, but you. Fuck, *you,* Sloane, will *take* from me and say *'you're welcome'* as you do it. Now please, I need you Sloane. I might lose it if you don't let me have you."

I smirk, knowing full well he might actually lose control if I play with him any longer. I don't mind ending early. My underwear is practically soaked through with desire. I don't want to wait any more either. It's time we both have our fill.

"Then lose it," I whisper into his ear. "I'm all yours."

A split second later, he snaps his fingers. Gone are my clothes and gone is he from the counter. I barely start to turn around to look for him when his cold fingers curl around the back of my neck and he shoves me forward onto the cold, unforgiving marble. An actual shriek expels from me at the sudden onslaught of coldness against me, but I'm given no time to adjust as Balthazar slides himself in.

My hands are splayed on the counter as the edge of it digs into me just above my hips. Balthazar holds my left hip in a vise grip while his right hand curls around the curve where my shoulder and neck meet. He's pushed in as far as he can go and I shift my legs to a wider stance to help accommodate his girth. He feels too good inside me.

"You might want to hold on," is all he says before he starts fucking me.

His hard cock slides in and out with every powerful thrust of his hips. He's never hurried, never too fast, in his actions. He's always precise and purposeful with how he uses those thrusts.

The edge of the counter rams against me with each slam of Balthazar's hips. Such a delicious mix of pain and pleasure. He grips me tight around my neck, those cold fingers pressing in hard enough that I know they'll leave a bruise.

"Sloane," he grunts as he fucks me smooth and hard. "You feel so good."

My nipples, stiff and sensitive, rub against the cold marble in perfect rhythm with Balthazar. They'll be chafed and it'll suck later tonight, but in the moment the rubbing only deepens my pleasure.

I reach behind with my right hand, my nails digging into his powerful, muscular thigh as I moan my approval.

"More," I beg as I move my hips against him.

He yanks me up by the back of my neck, his hand coming around to slide under my arm, up in between my breasts, before he wraps his fingers around my throat. With his other hand, he lifts up my leg, settling my knee on the stool, and my body acts on instinct, arching my back to deepen the new angle.

He lets go of my leg on the stool as his hand slips around my thigh to my clit. He continues to pound into me in rhythmic thrusts as he uses his fingers to rub against me. Cold fingers against my heated clit is the *perfect* combination. I loudly moan my approval as my head drops back against his shoulder.

Balthazar rubs me with purpose, building and edging me towards my orgasm. My hands reach up, gripping his forearm that's settled between my breasts as my breath comes out in quick whines. The pleasure is too much. My legs tremble in anticipation. I have difficulty staying on my feet as his cock penetrates me over and over again.

I feel Balthazar's hot breath on my ear before he says in that sinfully low voice, "Cum for me, Sloane."

A few vigorous rubs later, my orgasm slams into me hard and furious. I crumble in his arms, grateful he holds me up as I clench around his cock.

His deep throaty moan vibrates down my back as the *slap, slap, slap* of our bodies echoes in the room. I feel his cock stiffen just as his hips lose their even pace. Then he's jerking inside me, fingers wrapped tight around my throat while his other hand grips my thigh as his release comes.

Our mutual labored breaths fill the silence of the room, Balthazar still buried deep inside me. My body is nearly limp in his hold as he rests his forehead on my shoulder. His hand finally lets go of my throat, dropping down to splay against my bare stomach.

We stay like that until our breathing calms. Then gently, he removes himself from me only to turn me around and kiss me like a parched man deprived of water. His tongue sensually flicks against mine, his hands ghosting against my skin only to grip me in a death grip in the places where I curve. His kiss is deep, passionate, and slow. Like he has all the time in the world to get me drunk off such a lazy yet addictive kiss.

"I will drown in you, peccatum meum," he whispers against my mouth while grabbing an ass cheek.

Peccatum. *Sin.* I pull away from him, my hands resting atop his chest as my eyes dart back and forth in his gaze.

"What does that mean? Peccatum meum."

He regards me quietly for a few moments, his index finger trailing up and down my spine as he holds my gaze. Finally, after what feels like an eternity, he answers.

"It means *my sin*."

My eyebrows furrow together in confusion. Why would he call me that? Isn't being a sin a bad thing? But maybe it's a good thing since he lives in Jeznia. Afterall, of the three worlds that exist here, Jeznia would be the one to embrace sins.

"Do you curse me or worship me when you say it?" I ask him, wanting to know with certainty how he uses the term.

He smirks that devilishly handsome smile, eyes twinkling in delight as his left hand drifts up to my bare breast and his thumb circles my nipple in a tantalizing tease.

"Shall I show you what I mean when I say it?"

"Yes, you shall," I answer with a coy smile. "On the bed this time and with your entire heart put into it. I want to really see how you mean it."

"As you wish," is his simple answer before we disappear down to the bedroom where he fucks me raw and tender.

IV

"HOUSE MEETINGS ARE rather dull," Balthazar states from the bedroom while I finish the last touches of my makeup in the connecting bathroom.

My eyes are done up with a simple smokey look with sparse red glitter highlights and medium sized fake lashes. Not overstated or understated. The right amount for the part I'm playing. I've styled my hair in dual bubble braids with wisps of hair pulled out to frame my face. A dark plum colored lipstick sealed in clear gloss pulls the look together.

Once I'm done, I walk out of the bathroom into the bedroom. Balthazar's sitting in an oversized chair in the corner of the room, basking in the sunlight that streams in through the windows. My heart flips in my chest at the sight of him and I'm briefly amazed that someone I find as attractive as him is coiled so tightly around my finger.

"What do you guys talk about in House meetings?" I ask to refocus my thoughts as I walk over to the outfit laid out on the bed.

It's a black bodysuit with a black long sleeved sheer dress to wear on top.

"Why is everything I wear always black?" I ask as I hold up the fabric.

Not even Balthazar wears black clothes when he goes to House meetings. It's always some variant of a deep, dark color like maroon or navy. Never black.

"Do you prefer another color?" he asks from his spot in the corner of the room.

I glance at the material in my hands, my lips puckering side to side. "Yeah, actually. I like the outfit but can you change it to champagne instead of black please?"

He smiles as he links his hands together in his lap. "You do it."

The order catches me off guard before excitement replaces it. He's absolutely right. This is a perfect opportunity for me to practice magic.

I toss the clothes back onto the bed and draw my magic forward. It appears almost immediately, the lavender smoke a deeper, more vibrant purple, causing the gold lightning to contrast even more against the smoke.

I concentrate on my intent, on the exact color I want the material to change to before I grab hold of my magic and send it out to the fabric. I see the exact moment the magic hits when gold lightning streaks out. The fabric changes from black to pewter grey. Not even close to the color I wanted.

Frustrated, I try again. Lightning strikes the materials a second time and it changes to khaki green.

"What the hell?"

I turn around to stare at Balthazar for guidance.

He stares right back at me, unblinking, and says simply, "You're changing the color."

"Yeah, but it's not the color I want."

"I understand, but you haven't changed anything else about the outfit. Only the color."

"Duh, I don't want to change the outfit," I say, my voice dripping in irritation as my arm gestures wildly to further emphasize how I'm feeling.

"Yet when you tried yesterday to change the color of a pigeon, it turned into a duck."

"Yeah, well, that was yesterday. This is today."

He lets out a heavy sigh as he stands up from the chair and walks over to me. A frown pulls at my lips, a certain tightness to the corners of my mouth as my eyebrows pinch together.

Balthazar gently cups my face, his hands freezing beyond comprehension, but I don't pull away. Instead, I raise my hands up to tenderly hold him around the forearms, a little bothered by how cold those are too.

His eyes hold my gaze firmly as he speaks in a soft, low voice.

"The rate at which you're improving is unheard of, Sloane. You're too impatient, wanting to see results right away. Your impatience is blinding you, making you miss out on what you're accomplishing. I've watched Contract Liaisons struggle with their magic despite working with it for decades. What you've just accomplished," he says as he nods his head towards the green clothes on the bed, "Zagon will be trembling in his skin when you reach your true potential."

My eyes glance down to focus on his neck, my emotions a whirlwind of excitement and anxiety. It's too much holding his gaze, seeing the look on his face. The pride and joy at what I'll be one day. Is it really that simple? Will he really be proud and happy when I become stronger than him? Won't he come to resent me for it?

"Doesn't my power scare you?" I ask in a quiet voice, the doubts overwhelming my mind.

So often men claim they can handle a powerful woman, but it's a misconception. Too many feel emasculated. But with Balthazar being Jeznian, I'm not worried he'll feel emasculated, I'm worried he'll feel *threatened*.

"Sloane, we've been over this," he says and he doesn't hide the exasperation in his tone as his hands fall away from my face.

He pinches the bridge of his nose while taking a step back from me. When he looks at me again, his gaze is hardened, the red speckling growing within the black and threatening to take over as his irritation grows into anger.

"You need to shed yourself of these doubts and insecurities. I am not like those pathetic excuses in your old life that would rather tear you down for their own benefit. I will benefit the best from you when you're at your most powerful. I have no intention of chiseling away at your confidence until you're wholly dependent on me. That does me no good. Your magic doesn't scare me, it *excites* me.

"You're perfect in the bedroom," he states in a low timbre, eyes flashing a brief red. "Exude that. Live, breathe, eat that. Otherwise, Jeznia will eat you alive even with your magic at full power."

Tears blur my vision at hearing his harsh words. I know what he's attempting to do, but that doesn't mean I have to like it. This is his fucked up way of offering me comfort, but all he's done is make me feel like shit.

"And what if I don't eat, breathe, sleep that person I am when we fuck? What then? Are you going to abandon me?" I ask with a trembling bottom lip. I hate how upset I am over this but I push forward. "You talk about this like it's a walk in the park, like I haven't been living my entire life being beaten down by messages telling me to make myself smaller, make myself more appealing to men, never talk too loudly, never share my opinion. You're expecting me to change at the drop of a hat, but I need a grace period."

"You have it in you, Sloane," he insists, letting loose a bit more of his irritation in his tone. "You show it to me every time you call me Lord Balthazar. Just let it out."

"Fuck you," I snap at him. "If it's so easy, then why don't *you* show *me* more compassion? I know you have it in you! I see it when you touch me gently, when you say my name like I'm the most important person in the world. If it's so easy to change that quickly, then you do it. Be more understanding of where I'm coming from, of the life I've lived. You talk about how long it takes devils to learn their magic, that I shouldn't be so impatient, yet *you're* impatient with who I am as a person. Am I supposed to just all of a sudden start acting like I've lived in Jeznia my whole life because that's what *you* want? *Fuck you.*"

The silence that follows is very telling. At least he knows he's being a hypocrite. I honestly don't know what I would have done if he argued back, if he tried to defend his behavior while also critiquing mine. At least he's smart enough and logical enough to see the point I've made.

I tilt my head backwards as I blink away the tears, not wanting to ruin my makeup. Balthazar continues to remain silent as I pat under my eyes and surrounding area to dry them. When I'm satisfied, I shift my head forward to its normal position, but I pointedly ignore him.

Balthazar says nothing as I walk over to the khaki green outfit and get dressed. I try to squash the anger swimming beneath the surface. It won't do me any good to stay mad at Balthazar, especially when he's aware of how hypocritical he's being. It's easier said than done, though.

The only sound that fills the bedroom is the rustling of my clothes as I put them on. He continues his silence as I walk over to the closet and pick out a pair of thick heeled black sandals. I quietly buckle the shoes on before flattening out any creases on the sheer khaki dress.

My outfit is finally complete. I hate the color of the clothes, especially since it clashes with the red glitter eyeshadow I have on, but I'm done trying to change it. If I look like an idiot to everyone in the room, screw it, I don't care.

"Ready?" I ask as I finally look at Balthazar.

He's already staring at me, a hardened expression on his face. He clenches his jaw in a slow rhythm before he snaps his finger and the clothes I wear change to the champagne color I had wanted.

I inhale deeply, feeling mixed emotions about his help, before I begrudgingly mutter, "Thank you." A moment later, I ask a smidgen louder, "Shall we go?"

"Peccatum meum…"

I *tsk* as I turn my attention away from him. Now he wants to get all lovey dovey? He knows he was being too harsh so now he's trying to sweeten me up so I'll forgive him. *I'm not that easily manipulated.*

"You asked me what it meant," he says in that low, quiet timbre.

I concentrate on the entrance of the room instead of looking at him as I cross my arms over my chest. I'll hear him out but I'm going to make a show of how mad I am at him.

"It means you'll bring out the best of me and the worst of me," he states evenly. "It means you'll bear witness to all that I am and all that I can be. The good, the bad, the abhorrent and atrocious. It means I cannot escape you nor do I want to.

"Peccatum meum," he breathes the words gently as he steps to me, hand firmly but tenderly holding my face.

I can't keep refusing to stare at him when he's holding my face. I finally look him in the eyes. There's emotions swirling within those black–red depths. Conflicting emotions that I don't quite understand, but they speak to my heart and soul. It weakens my anger and I lean into his hand as he speaks.

"We are destined to forever clash and embrace each other. I wouldn't dream of anyone else taking your place."

"Why can't you just say 'I'm sorry' like a normal person?" I ask in mild exasperation. "You're saying everything but the words 'I was wrong. I'm sorry.'"

A crooked smile spreads across his lips as his thumb caresses my face. "Moments ago, someone expertly pointed out how difficult it is to abruptly change behaviors and patterns you've been living all your life."

"Well, that someone can suck it," I gripe childishly.

Balthazar chuckles deep and warm and it pulls a smile from me against my wishes.

"I have something that person can suck on if it pleases you," he quips and I don't miss the heat in his eyes.

My mouth drops open in shock and I slap his chest as a laugh tumbles out of me.

"Bastard! You say that like I didn't give you a blow job last night!"

"You were the one who proposed the idea, not me," he replies smugly.

"Screw you."

The words don't match my tone or smile as I shake my head. He chuckles again, arm slipping around my waist as he pulls me close. He snaps his fingers and we transport out of the room. When we arrive in Jeznia a moment later, Balthazar's outfit has been replaced with the one he always wears in Hell. Dark harem pants, no shirt, golden circlets around his bicep, smokey eyeliner, and no shoes.

I glance around the room and realize that even though it's not my first time here, it's my first time taking a moment to study the room. It looks like an office. There's a desk made out of black stone, a comfortable leather chair in the corner, a bookshelf, and a fire chandelier in the center of the room.

"Is this your office?" I ask as I step away from Balthazar.

"It is."

"Why do you need an office?"

"I am one of seven rulers of Jeznia. Why do you think I wouldn't need one?"

He makes a fair point, but I really can't wrap my head around seven devil Lords each having their own office. It strikes a little too close to home and goes against how I view Jeznia being ruled. Not that I have any idea of how Jeznia is ruled, but still. Who thinks of Hell and envisions a devil sitting behind a desk?

"Do you do, like, paperwork?" I ask as I walk over to his desk to inspect it.

He does nothing to stop me from investigating the space. There are a few pens on the surface, but no paperwork, not even paper to write on. My finger trails the edge of the desk and my eyes catch sight of something carved in the upper left corner. Dates. Two of them.

August 15 and August 22. Two weeks and three weeks ago. My heart skips a beat. Those dates are seared into my mind, body, and soul. August 15th was the night Balthazar and I met – the night he came to fulfill Chad's wish and kill me. The 22nd, a full week later, was the day I was forced to make my wish – the day Chad shot me. Balthazar carved these dates into his desk… because of me?

"Sometimes I do paperwork," he answers from the middle of the room.

My eyes snap up to him before I glance back down at the desk. I want to ask him about the dates, but I'm distracted by the idea of Balthazar sitting here, signing off on laws and policies. It's absurd. This is Hell. Isn't it chaos down here? I thought the only real law and order was that the strongest and or most cunning come out on top.

"What kind of paperwork do you do?"

"This and that," he answers vaguely.

"If it's classified information, you can just say that," I reply as I give him a mild glare.

"I mostly keep notes on the meetings," he answers and I'm a little shocked by what he's said.

"You do?"

"Mhm. I keep track of how the Houses interact or avoid each other, which direction they rule in, who seems overly invested or not invested enough. Most times, it's the things that they don't do or say that is very telling. I keep record of it all in case it ever comes in hand."

"Aren't you worried someone will steal your records?"

"I don't store them here. In truth, Umbra is the only one who knows where they're kept. I write my notes and when I'm done, she retrieves them."

"You trust her that much?" I ask in shock.

He's never treated Umbra particularly kindly. He's threatened to remove one of her limbs for disobeying an order. He doesn't talk to her like an equal but like someone beneath him. He once became infuriated with me when I implied that he relied on her for help. To hear him say he gives her important documents to file away surprises me. It sounds a bit unlike him.

"Umbra is my Shadow Seer. If I'm unable to trust her with confidential classified tasks, what is the point of her?"

"I mean… that's a valid point. It's just you don't treat her very well so that's why I'm surprised."

"According to whose standard?"

His words are sharp as he asks them and I don't miss the anger within his gaze. He makes another valid point. The way he treats Umbra is atrocious to Earth standards, but not Jeznian standards.

I default too frequently to Earth standards. But can he blame me? We were literally arguing minutes ago about my upbringing being different from his. I don't mean to offend him with my viewpoint the same way he doesn't mean to offend me. But just because I'm a devil now doesn't mean I can switch my beliefs and standards on a dime. It'll take time. And I'll *need* to change my perspective if I'm to live in Jeznia for the rest of my eternal life. I have to play by their rules, not mine.

Quietly, I walk around the desk and close the distance between us as I come to a stop in front of him.

"You make a fair point," I concede. "By Jeznian standards, you're pretty nice to her." My lips quirk up as I can't hold back a little teasing. "But don't blame me if she decides working for me is better than you."

He openly scoffs but there's clear amusement on his face. "You're mistaken if you think she'd ever trust your kindness."

"We're immortal," I remind him. "She'll eventually trust me."

"Perhaps by then, you'll be Jeznian through and through."

Hearing him say it out loud causes my stomach to churn. I know if I'm to live a long life in Jeznia, I need to become more like them. It's a fact. But all my life I've been striving to be a good person, to continually expand my empathy, and to fight for the betterment of humanity. Yet now I'm supposed to go to the other side of the spectrum or else I'll die.

It's a heavy pill to swallow. One I will force down if necessary. I have no intentions of dying anytime soon.

"Come," Balthazar says as he extends his hand to me, drawing my attention away from my morbid thoughts. "The meeting awaits."

I glance down at his hand, a brief frown flitting across my face. I'll have more time to debate and think about what my future will hold. For now, I need to concentrate on the piranhas waiting for my arrival just down the hallway. It'll be life and death in that room. Being a devil with powerful magic doesn't change that fact. I need to up my game and put on my poker face.

With a heavy sigh, I take his hand.

V

BALTHAZAR AND I are the last ones to arrive in the throne room and, as we walk across the room to our seats, I take note of each House's additional chairs.

The second House, House Vespertilio, only has an heir.

The third House, House Anguis, has no heir and no spouse.

The fourth House, House Felis, only has an heir.

The fifth House, House Lupus, only has a spouse.

The sixth House, House Aranea, only has a spouse.

The seventh House, House Scolopendra, has both an heir and spouse.

How is it that the weakest House has an heir and *a spouse?* I ask Balthazar but I'm not sure if he'll hear it. I never know when he activates his telepathy but I trust that it's there. If he says nothing, I'll ask him later in the privacy of our own room.

It's because *they're the weakest House. Lord Ruulin needs all the allies he can get his hands on.*

But wouldn't it be beneficial for any House to have an heir and spouse? Why don't more Houses have both? I ask.

It depends, he replies as we walk up the steps towards his throne. *Most heirs kill the Lord to secure the House.*

Spouses are more loyal but have a tendency to die quicker. Competition to be a Lord's spouse is quite brutal.

I falter in my steps, nearly tripping up the stairs if it weren't for Balthazar's steady hand. The children kill their parents to inherit the House? After giving it some thought, it makes sense. Everyone here is immortal. If an heir wants to rule the House, they'll need to remove the person standing in their way and there aren't many ways to successfully do that in Jeznia.

I'm ashamed to admit that the thought never crossed my mind. But if that's how new Lords come into play, why have children in the first place? I ask Balthazar the question just as I sit down in my chair.

Why does anyone do anything? Power, he answers simply.

My lips pull downward in a frown. Is power really worth the threat of being murdered by your own offspring?

Are you not concerned about the other half of the statement I made? Balthazar asks.

My eyebrows furrow together as I glance at him in silent question. His lips twitch but he quickly suppresses whatever urges he has to smile.

You're a target now, he states. *I've confirmed I'm willing to take a spouse. Others will want to kill you to inherit your role.*

I roll my eyes as I turn my attention back to the room. *Who* doesn't *want to kill me?* He chuckles behind me before he addresses the Lords.

"So," Balthazar's sharp voice echoes out into the room. There's no kindness to be found in his tone. "What is on the agenda today?"

"I request that House Lupus and House Scolopendra supply a team of Feral Mongers and Hunters to deal with the fifth circle insurrection," the devil at the cat throne states.

House Felis but his name escapes me. *Lord Idris,* Balthazar supplies. His tawny brown skin is as flawless as I remember but he appears to have lost a bit of weight around his stomach. If I remember correctly, the first week I met him he had more of a pronounced dad bod than he does now. I wonder why he changed his physique.

He's sans a shirt, wearing layered gold necklaces of varying lengths and gems. He adorns a long dark skirt that reminds me of ancient Rome. His black hair is kept short and his horns extend out his temples before curling to the floor.

What are Feral Mongers and Hunters? I ask as I try to remain as stoic as possible.

House Aides.

In layman's terms, Lord Idris is requesting House Lupus and House Scolopendra send their House Aides to deal with an insurrection happening somewhere in Jeznia. This is *not* how I imagined a House meeting would go. Before I can ask Balthazar if they're usually like this, someone begins to speak.

"Are your Sentinels unable to snuff out the problem?" Lord Ruulin of House Scolopendra asks.

I can hear the amusement in his voice, like he's happy to hear Lord Idris is forced to ask for his help. Still, I have a hard time taking Ruulin seriously when I know he's the weakest House here *and* his horns look like the cosplaying horns they sell on Earth.

His horns are so small compared to everyone else's and they look a little out of place on his larger stature. He must be over six feet tall. He's a big boy, yet his horns are *tiny*. All the other Lords have substantial sized horns. Can Lord Ruulin really afford to sound as haughty as he does if horns showcase power or, in his case, *lack* of power?

"This is a House issue, Lord Ruulin, so I expect a House resolution," Idris states in an even tone, unbothered by Ruulin's inciting question. "If inhabitants from the lower circles start invading the higher circles, there will be no rule or order. But perhaps that's what you're hoping for."

Circles? What is Idris talking about? This is the first time I've heard mention of circles in Jeznia. Are they literal circles that people live in? Where are the circles? I know Jeznia is surrounded by The Wastelands. Is Jeznia a city made up of circles? Are the circles laid out in a straight line or grouped together?

I have so many questions running through my head that I barely catch what Lord Carmilla says to the left of me.

"Or perhaps Lord Ruulin doesn't have the numbers to help."

She's as impeccable as I remember. Not a single dark red hair out of place, clothes accentuating her frame, simple makeup to highlight her features. She dresses like she's attending a scholar awards ceremony but makes sure her outfit is questionably inappropriate.

My attention then glances down at Ivy, the spitting image of Carmilla except her hair is a little lighter in color. She does everything in her power to emulate her mother, but the one thing she can't do is hide her disgust of me. Even now, she's scowling as she meets my gaze. I offer a quick small smile because I know it'll piss her off before I turn my attention to Ruulin. I'm sad I can't see her bristle at my friendliness, but it's palpable. I feel it and smirk in satisfaction.

Ruulin's fawn skin flushes pink at Carmilla's insult. "Easy for you to throw around when no help has been requested from your House."

"I have no issues with sending a few Executioners down to the fifth circle," she replies in an even tone. "In fact, I think it would be best if I do. I imagine the inhabitants will lose their motivation to invade the fourth circle once a small handful of them have had their souls destroyed."

"You make a valid point, Lord Carmilla," Balthazar states from behind me and I love the way his voice sounds. Firm, confident, powerful. It is *most definitely* a distraction. "As we don't know who is leading the rebellion, a Hunter will be rather useless, don't you think, Lord Idris? I'm not sure why you would request help from Lord Ruulin when other House Aides would be more beneficial for what you're trying to achieve."

Idris smiles, but I can see that it's a restrained smile as it doesn't meet his eyes. I don't know what secret hidden message Balthazar has just said, but it looks like Idris understands it perfectly. Idris clicks his tongue, the smile frozen on his face, as he shrugs his shoulders.

"Lord Carmilla is not known for dispatching Executioners for the cause," Idris says simply, but even I can tell he's withholding information despite me not understanding the conversation at hand.

"Today is a rather lucky day for you then, isn't it?" Balthazar asks.

"What will you ask in return for your Executioners, Lord Carmilla?" Idris pointedly asks, blatantly ignoring Balthazar.

A pang of irritation zings down my spine at the disrespect Idris shows Balthazar, but everyone ignores it. Even Balthazar so I do my best to follow suit.

"Three Sentinels," Carmilla answers.

Idris's head falls back as a loud, boisterous laugh explodes out of him. "Not a chance."

"Then you'll resolve the insurrection issue on your own," Lord Carmilla states coldly. "We'll expect a resolution within the next three days. House vote?"

Everyone but Idris raises their right hand. He's glowering, clearly displeased with how the issue was handled. To be honest, I'm confused. They went from being open to helping him to very quickly leaving him on his own. Yet, they still expect him to solve the problem despite the fact that he asked for help in the first place.

How is he supposed to solve the problem if no one is willing to help him? I ask Balthazar and I do my best to refrain from glancing at him over my shoulder. I don't know if they know Balthazar can speak telepathically so I don't want to give it away if they're in the dark about it. It's difficult, though, when I don't have an expert poker face.

Sentinels, Lord Idris's House Aides, are the most versatile in combat, Balthazar answers. *A circle uprising is nothing Sentinels can't handle. Lord Idris was making a play for a Hunter and masking it by also requesting the help of Feral Mongers while pretending his Sentinels are in over their head. No one bought it.*

Holy shit.

The politics of Jeznia are going to be the end of me. Balthazar was able to discern all that in such a short conversation? I know it's a little different for him since he grew up in Jeznia and he's been a Lord for the past five years, but still. I'm a little overwhelmed at the idea of everything I need to learn about Jeznia *on top of* becoming powerful enough to protect myself from an attack. Will I even survive through my first year? *Fuck.*

Agreed, Balthazar hums. *I'd rather be fucking.*

That's not what I was saying, asshole, I snap at him.

He softly chuckles from his spot two steps behind me.

I can't believe you're thinking about sex right now, I say as I adjust my legs, crossing my right over my left. We're discussing a literal insurrection happening in their city. How can his mind be wandering during such an important situation?

I'm staring right at you. Of course I'm thinking about fucking you.

My lips turn downward and I can't withhold the annoyed *tsk* that leaves my mouth.

Friendly reminder that I'm not a sexual object that exists solely to give you pleasure. I may have agreed to enter into a relationship with him but I am more than a mere tool to please him.

He hums lowly and thoughtfully. *No, you are so much more, Miss Kensington. I won't make such a disparaging remark twice.* Before I'm able to clarify that I don't mind the spicy comments in the right context, Ivy directs her attention to Balthazar. His low hum caught her attention. She arches in her seat to look at him, purposefully drawing attention to her ample cleavage as she stares at him with hungry eyes.

"Has something caught your interest, Lord Balthazar?" She asks coyly and, honestly, Ivy knows what she's doing.

She does it well. I can't deny her attractiveness. She has a symmetrical face and a desirable body. Her surface level value is *very* high. On top of that, she's also the heir to the second most powerful House in Jeznia. That means she has powerful magic. She's not someone to mess around with no matter how coy or ditzy or weak she might portray herself to be. She's Ivy Vespertilio, *heir* to *House* Vespertilio. She'll do some damage to me if the chance arises.

Despite all that, she still misses the mark with Balthazar and I almost laugh at her attempt. She has pick me energy and I'm amazed at my own personal ability to not outwardly cringe at her very public missed shot.

"Does anyone else have any other topics they wish to bring forth?" Balthazar asks, clearly ignoring Ivy's question.

It takes everything in me not to make a sound or turn to look at her reaction. Everyone in the room heard Ivy ask a question and everyone bore witness to Balthazar blatantly ignoring it. I would die of humiliation if that ever happened to me.

"Is your wife acclimating well?"

It's Lord Taron who asks the question. If it had been anyone else asking, I would assume they were trying to feel me and Balthazar out. To see if they might discern any clues about my powers as a devil based on how Balthazar answers the question.

But Lord Taron was a relative to Finthorn. The devil I killed three weeks ago. Finthorn brought forth a case against Balthazar, hoping the Houses would rule in his favor and kill Balthazar. They almost did, but Balthazar came prepared. He proved he had acted within his rights, not only as a Contract Liaison, but also as a Lord of a House. After seeing the evidence, the Houses withdrew their votes against him and overturned the ruling. That meant Finthorn lost.

I ended up killing him for the part he played in trying to get me killed. I wish it was Chad I got to kill, not Finthorn, but at that point in time, Chad was already dead. I had to take the only opportunity given to me.

"If there is nothing else worth my time, I'll take my leave," Balthazar answers in an even tone, directly ignoring Taron's question. "I do have a more important job than this one, after all. Souls aren't going to buy themselves."

It feels as if the room visibly bristles like a living, breathing entity. He's insulted everyone — Lords, heirs, and spouses — with that simple statement. I can't suppress the amused look of disbelief that crosses my face.

Balthazar is ballsy. He holds no punches. Does he not fear retaliation? He may be powerful, but if they all teamed up against him, would he stand a chance? He has to have a solid chance at winning. He wouldn't be stupid enough to poke the lion in the face if he thought he might not be able to win. Right?

No one says anything in regard to what Balthazar said, but he also doesn't wait for a response. Instead, he grabs my shoulder and snaps his fingers. We disappear from the room before reappearing back in his office.

"Aren't you worried they'll continue the meeting without you?" I ask as Balthazar walks over to the desk and pulls out a piece of paper.

He grabs the pen, sets the tip to the paper, and walks away. I watch in wonder as the pen starts writing. The amount of magic and concentration that would require is incredible. Yet somehow, Balthazar believes I'll be *more* powerful than him.

"I expect them to," he answers from his spot beside the desk. His fingers are tracing the carved dates, but he keeps his attention on me. "They speak more freely when House Primis is not in attendance."

"Then why show up at all?"

"To remind them of our presence and power. Umbra will finish the rest of the notes and inform me of the contents."

"Sounds like Umbra should be *Lord* Umbra of House Primis," I say before really thinking it through. A moment later, my mouth drops open to clarify or to apologize, I'm not really sure, but Balthazar beats me to the punch.

"Indeed," he agrees, which takes me by surprise. "It's a shame the Lords would never allow it."

"Even if Zagon appointed her his heir?" I ask, no longer feeling sorry for the rude statement I made.

"He would never do it, which is precisely why they would never allow it."

It falls quiet between us, the sound of the pen scratching against paper filling the air. Balthazar's eyes drop to the dates beneath his fingertips before looking back at me. The silence is a little awkward. He looks as though he wants to say something but can't bring himself to open his mouth. Is he waiting for me to bring it up? But I don't even know what *it* is.

There didn't seem to be anything strange about the meeting. To be honest, it was a little surprising how normal the meeting went. I've only been to three House meetings, not including this one. The first one I barely remember, the second one Finthorn lost an arm, and the third one was Balthazar's trial. This one was tame. Very business–like.

"What are your impressions of the House meeting?" Balthazar finally asks and I give him my honest answer.

"I get why you say they're boring," I answer as I cross my arms over my chest and shift my weight to my left foot. "Are they usually like that? Talking about the circles and bartering for House Aides?"

"More or less."

I pounce on the opportunity to learn more about the circles, the words spewing out of my mouth faster than I can think them up.

"Are these literal circles we're talking about or do we just call them circles as a frame of reference? Is it common for a circle to invade another? How many circles are there? Why do you keep the circles separate?"

Balthazar chuckles at my rapid fire questions as he steps to the side of the desk and rests his thigh against it.

"There are seven circles in Jeznia. Each circle is a ring or layer around the mountain that we reside on," he answers. "Every few hundred years the fifth, fourth, or third circle tries to invade the one above it. Never the seventh or sixth circle. They appear to accept their fate at the bottom but the middle… the middle is never happy.

"The circles are kept separate because a divided world is easier to control. The citizens spend so much time trying to obtain enough merits to move up in the circles or they're plotting how to invade a circle that they never organize and turn their attention on the Lords who control everything and have a very vested interest in keeping things the way they are."

It's scary how similar their governing is to how the States are run. Except the States give the illusion of a democracy, that the people have the power through voting, and that they have a voice that deserves to be heard. At least here in Jeznia it's black and white. The Lords don't deny what they're doing or why.

"Ok, so why do you think Lord Idris was trying to secure a Hunter?" I ask as I quickly move on to other parts of the meeting, my mind running a mile a minute as it dissects and analyzes the information I've received.

"Hunters are self–explanatory," he says. "They take a scent and don't stop hunting for the origins until the target is found. You don't ever want a Hunter on your tail. They'll follow you through Ephiri all the way to Odantha if it means ending the chase."

"Even if it'll kill them?"

"Yes. Lord Ruulin boasts of their relentless determination and he has quite the track record to back it up."

I fall silent as I process what he's told me before saying, "You said you don't know who the leader of the rebellion is, so having a Hunter with nothing to smell is pointless. The Hunter would have no job."

"Precisely. Yet Lord Idris specifically requested for one."

"And you don't think he wanted the Feral Mongers?"

"Feral Mongers are brutal fighters. Their bloodlust knows no bounds. One Feral Monger is all it would take to calm the rebellion, but Lord Idris asked for a few. This was most likely an attempt to have us focus on the absurdity of his request for multiple Feral Mongers when we all know one would be overkill. Lord Idris probably anticipated that House Lupus would make a big stink about such a ridiculous request."

"If *one* Feral Monger can handle the rebellion, why doesn't House Lupus just send one?" There's slight exasperation in my voice as I ask my question. It's like every new answer he gives me just makes it all more and more confusing.

"Each House is responsible for a circle. If your circle is under threat of invasion, you're responsible for protecting it. It is not the responsibility of the House whose circle is *doing* the invading. Since the responsibility of protection falls onto individual Houses, no one will offer aid without incentive. Like how Lord Carmilla wouldn't send Executioners unless she received three Sentinels in return."

"Oh my god! You guys are a bunch of children. *None* of this makes any sense," I declare in aggravation as I throw my arms up. "You want to keep the people separated and divided so they don't turn against you, the rulers, yet when an uprising occurs, you don't help each other out. Instead, you adopt the mentality *'every man for himself'*. Make it make sense!"

"It doesn't," Balthazar freely admits as he taps his index finger against the desk. "The Lords are prideful, arrogant, and selfish. To ask for help shows weakness. To offer help shows weakness. Nothing in Jeznia is ever given without strings. Yet it is agreed upon that separate circles are best so that we may remain in power. However, we offer no aid in protecting a circle when it's under attack.

"I'm well aware that none of it makes sense. The hypocrisy runs deep within Jeznia. Most things only make sense when you acknowledge it's a dog eat dog world here and that everyone is selfish beyond comprehension.

"If you're going to be successful here, Sloane, you must start asking the questions 'what can I gain from this?' and 'what do they gain from this?'"

"Jesus Christ," I breathe out as I rub the back of my neck.

I'm expected to live here for the rest of my afterlife. In a world that doesn't make any sense. How am I going to survive?

"I assure you Jesus Christ is nowhere to be found," Balthazar states and I hate that I find his dumb joke funny.

"No shit," I lightly laugh against my wishes and he offers a smile in return.

The light–hearted moment breaks apart my annoyance. I take the opportunity to inhale deeply and refocus my attention. What was the most important takeaway from the meeting? That Idris wanted a Hunter. That means there's someone he wants found and probably killed. He *has* a target.

"You think Lord Idris knows who the leader of the rebellion is?" I ask.

"If he knew, he would have informed us. That's not something worthy of keeping a secret."

"If that's true then that means he doesn't want a Hunter to go after the leader, so… Who does he want the Hunter for?"

"*That's* the question you should be asking, Sloane."

I heave out a big sigh. I feel like I've mentally just run a marathon. I never anticipated Jeznia would be so difficult and confusing to maneuver. Death, murder, and evil shouldn't be so complicated. You either kill or be killed. But no. Jeznia has Lords and a loose form of government and there's way too much mental work that goes into figuring it all out. Why does this House want that? How did House A react to House B? What are they hiding? Plotting? Will a House make a move soon? Hell was simpler when I thought of it as a bad place. Now, it's a fucking political maze.

"This shit is exhausting," I say, shoulders slumping in defeat.

"Now you understand why it's beneficial for a House to have a spouse or an heir attend the meetings," Balthazar muses.

Especially if they have debrief meetings the same way Balthazar and I currently are. I'll need to up my game if I'm to do a good job as Balthazar's spouse. He'll need my ears and eyes taking in what he can't.

Suddenly, the pen drops to the desk and the paper disappears from sight. With the note taking done, Balthazar pushes off the desk and walks over to me, his hands sliding to grip my hips possessively.

I respond in kind as I wrap my arms around his sturdy shoulders, my fingers twirling some of his soft hair. This is a perfect opportunity to ask him about the dates carved into his desk. Will he answer? I'm honestly not sure, but there's only one way to find out.

"What are those dates on your desk?" I ask.

"You're a smart woman," he says right before he kisses me. "You'll figure it out."

I groan in irritation and say as we pull away, "I really do hate you."

He smirks as his hand drifts down to my butt cheek and gives it a firm squeeze. "My favorite kind of hatred."

I roll my eyes as I shake my head. "I've already figured it out," I confess as I stare into his beautiful dual–colored eyes. "I just wanted to hear you say it."

The smirk disappears from his lips, the playfulness gone from his face. He pulls me flush against him, closing any distance that snuck its way between our bodies as he leans forward and presses our foreheads together.

"Those dates are the worst and best days of my life," he declares.

"The worst?" I ask in surprise, my head rearing back from his.

Meeting me was the *worst* day of his life? My heart pumps rapidly inside my chest as my stomach bottoms out. I can't believe he feels that way. Have I been living ignorantly these past three weeks thinking we're both on cloud nine when it was only me? Jesus Christ. I think I might actually throw up.

His eyes flit across my face as he takes in whatever emotions I've let loose.

"Yes, worst. You almost died on those days," he states matter of fact and my mouth drops open in shock as I understand what he means now. "They're the best days because you didn't."

A breath of relief whooshes out of me. All that panicking for nothing. No, not for nothing. For the kindest, sweetest man I've ever had the opportunity to love.

A small smile makes it way to my face as I tenderly touch his cheek. "You can be such a romantic."

A moment later, my lips are sealed against his. We kiss each other passionately, deeply, and it's no surprise that the lust within my body wakes up. I can't get enough of him, always eager and hungry for more. Balthazar growls angrily, but not the good or fun kind. This is real anger, like he wants to rip someone's head off.

"What?" I ask as I pull his bottom lip between my teeth. Maybe I can distract him from his anger.

"I don't have time to indulge, Sloane," he says.

"Not even five minutes?"

"Five minutes is more than enough time for someone else to secure a deal in my territory."

"Let them," I say as I begin kissing down his neck and he tenses, a growl of frustration vibrating out of him.

"If I did that, it would be sending a message to every devil out there that they are free to steal from me."

I might only have three weeks under my belt as a new devil, but even I know that wouldn't be a good message to be sending.

I huff out my irritation as I step away from him. "Jeznia sucks."

He chuckles at my clear frustration. I get what he's saying and I understand the importance of it but I hate it. We both want a round. There should be no reason for us to skip it, but *Jeznia* is making us. His reputation is important for his role as a Lord and his role as a Lord is important for *my* safety. I get it, I really do get it, but this *sucks*. I'm horny and want to have some fun.

"Fine," I breathe out in irritation as I stop attacking his neck. "Then take me back to Earth."

"I'll make it up to you," he says as he offers me a wink.

"Whatever," I say as I pout like a five year old, but it's more for his benefit than mine.

He laughs and kisses me on the head before grabbing my hand and transporting us out of Jeznia with a snap of his fingers.

VI

THE NEXT COUPLE of days I practice my magic on inanimate objects while Balthazar secures deals across the east and west coasts of the US. My practice goes ok. I'm not improving at the pace I want to and some days, I have difficulty concentrating. My mind wanders off to memories I try to desperately bury. Memories of slimy hands, of tight cloth, of loud bangs and searing pain.

There are times I get stuck in a loop so intense that I jolt *'awake'* only to be confused that I'm sitting in The Commons and not underground in that cold, musty basement or hidden away in the alley behind the dive bar.

Unfortunately, that's exactly how today is going.

After two failed attempts at magic and nearly inducing myself into a panic attack, I've decided the best thing for me to help bury these wretched thoughts is to take a walk through the park with an iced chai tea latte. It turns out that when I concentrate too much on magic it makes me concentrate on *why* I'm practicing magic and right now, I'd rather think about something else. *Anything* else.

It's still the beginning of September, but the weather has been fluctuating rather dramatically. Summer heat one day only to be replaced by autumn cold the next. Today is one of the hot days so I've dressed lightly. A pair of denim short overalls, a short sleeved white crop top, cute floral printed shoes, and a pair of aviator sunglasses.

The Commons is as busy as it usually is, but it strangely feels empty today. People walk by me without a clue that my face and life story used to be plastered all over the news. Do they look at me and feel a vague sense of familiarity?

My story had been pretty popular. National news sensationalized how I went out on a date with Chad only for my body to be found cut up into eight pieces a few days later. A week after that, the police found Chad dead by suicide in the basement of Balthazar's apartment complex with a note explaining why he did it. The following days after Chad's confession and suicide were a mess. I couldn't turn on the TV or scroll through TikTok without seeing my story and now...

Am I really that easy to forget? Ella hasn't texted me since Chad's body was discovered. She sent one message: FUCK YEAH THEY CAUGHT HIM but it's been radio silence ever since. Is she already moving on? Are my parents?

I've contemplated dropping by their house again, but I'm too afraid I'll see them living their lives as usual. What if they're laughing and smiling? What if they're entertaining friends and family despite the fact that I've been butchered and bagged? I know the whole point of visiting them was to give them closure so they could go back to their normal lives, but I don't think I could stomach it if I saw my parents having fun only three weeks after I died.

My fingers squeeze tightly around the cup in my hand as I inhale deeply. I need to refocus my thoughts. The whole point of this walk is to stop thinking about the things I want to ignore. Like, look at how beautiful today's weather is. The sun is out, there's a nice breeze, people are laughing and smiling, having a good time out and about in the city. This sight should make me happy, but instead it makes my heart hurt. I feel empty with no one standing beside me.

I wish Balthazar was here with me. He fills the massive void that threatens to consume me. When he's gone, I have too much free time to think. Not just about me being dead, but also about the life I'm living. I have no job. I can't access my bank accounts so I have no money. What is the purpose of my life now? I'm supposed to be this badass devil, but most days that doesn't feel like me. Is it because I'm depressed? Am I grieving? Or am I just upset that Jeznia is my future instead of Odantha?

A heavy sigh blows out my mouth. All these questions and no answers. *This walk is stupid.* I force myself to concentrate on something other than my mess of a life. Let's think about Balthazar because he's the only real joy in my life nowadays. Without him, I'd be a piece of drywood adrift in the vast ocean.

I think about the dual color of his eyes, the way his lips pull up on one side of his face when he's teasing me, the way his eyes darken in lust, how he speaks my name like I'm the most important person to ever exist to him. That last sentiment squeezes my heart. I wish I could see in me what he sees. He keeps saying I have all this powerful magic inside me, but I don't know how to use it. What good is having magic when I can't do anything with it?

Meanwhile, Balthazar's natural ability in using magic is insane. I know I haven't been trying all that long, but manipulating magic is *hard*. Yet, Balthazar makes it look as innate as breathing. That everyone and anyone who has magic should just *know* how to use it.

That must be why the Lords fear him. He claims it's because of his association with his father, and to some degree he's right since magic is hereditary, but Balthazar is formidable on his own. I see it every time we enter the throne room. I feel it in how the room shifts as he walks across the floor to take his seat. If Balthazar were weaker, the Houses would eat him alive. If he were weaker, Zagon wouldn't have made him a Lord. No matter what Balthazar says or who he pretends to be, there's no denying how powerful he is.

Then there's little old me who's still trying to change the color of clothes and levitate small objects. How can Balthazar say over and over again that I'll surpass him when I can barely do anything? My magic can't be that strong, but he's convinced it is. Does he just assume it's strong because supposedly it's deep, old magic? He's admitted not even his father understands the kind of magic I have. What if the knowledge they have is wrong? What if I'm not as threatening and dangerous as Balthazar believes? Will that change anything between us?

I can't stop the nagging feeling that things *will* change if I don't live up to Balthazar's expectations. I don't imagine he'd want to keep me around if he has to protect me for the rest of eternity. It's why I'm so eager to advance my magic, but it feels like practice is going nowhere. I can never change the color to the one I want. I might be able to levitate an object to my hand, but I'm struggling with levitating it in place.

I hate how easy Balthazar makes it look. Never mind the fact that his teacher didn't even *have* magic so he basically had to figure it out on his own. For fuck's sake, he was *ten years old* granting wishes and I can't even change the color of my shirt.

Irritated, I angrily sip on my drink, concentrating on the flavorful mixture of spices. I attempt to let the enjoyment of the drink distract my insecure thoughts. Condensation droplets litter the surface of my plastic cup, wetting my hand, and the ice within the cup makes my fingers cold. I wonder… Could I increase the temperature of the drink? Make it a hot chai tea latte instead?

I stop walking as I focus on my intent. Magic immediately swirls in the air, purple smoke and gold lightning surrounding me as I think about the way a hot chai tea latte feels in my hand, of the steam that billows out the top, of a specific number to heat the drink to. When I feel confident, I send my magic to the drink in my hand and it erupts like a mini explosion.

"Crap," I shout as the cup drops away from me, my hand drenched in the tea.

I glance down at my clothes and shoes to inspect them, grateful the drink didn't get on me. The plastic cup rolls in a semi–circle before coming to a stop at the edge of the grass. I shake my hand dry as best I can before crouching down to pick up my trash.

"Well, this sucks," I exhale out loud, realizing that my entire drink has been dumped out. What a waste of money. *And it's not even your own money.*

Why can't I get this right? I think as I remain in my crouched position, the empty plastic cup crunching in my hand. I have to learn magic if I want to survive. Balthazar will drop me if I'm dead weight. He can't afford to have that kind of baggage around. I have to keep trying. That's all I can do. *But what if it's not good enough?* I wonder as tears blot my eyes. What if *I'm* not good enough?

One second.

My entire body tingles so violently that it actually hurts. *Two seconds.*

I abruptly teleport from my crouched position to three feet away on the right, the air thick in that apple scented smoke.

Three seconds.

Metal clangs loudly against the pavement where I just was.

Four seconds.

My attacker swings the sword back before lunging towards me.

Five seconds.

Tingles explode inside me, painful and violent, as my magic lashes out at the attacker.

Six seconds.

The sword narrowly misses me, some invisible force shoving the blade to the side and the sword embeds into the dirt.

My heart pounds like a jack rabbit as I realize this person before me is *very deliberately* attacking me. Fear has me frozen in my spot but then our eyes connect. Stormy dark grey eyes stare at me with such abundant hatred that it snaps me out of my trance. Who the Hell is he to hate me when we don't even know each other? I swear, it's like every turn I take there's another person who hates me for no reason! *What have I done wrong?*

A raw, ferocious rage births inside me as I rise up to my full height. Anger vibrates within me as if it were a living, breathing thing. It pulses through my veins, burning hot and fierce. I can barely contain my fury as I watch my attacker swing his sword for another strike towards me. He's trying to kill me. Someone is trying to kill me. *Again.*

"*Enough,*" I declare in restrained rage, my voice mutilated in multiple layers, and my attacker is magically thrown back ten feet.

The air is *drowning* in smoke and apples, but I can't do anything about it. My magic has a mind of its own, determined to snuff out the threat to my life.

My attacker gets to his feet and falls into a defensive stance, legs shoulder length apart as he crouches and wields his sword.

I size him up, taking in the dark steel fitted armor. Carved vines and leaves adorn the polished dark steel and is heavily accented in a deep emerald green. It's beautiful, intricate metal work. If I wasn't so pissed off and my life wasn't in danger, I'd admire the work a bit more and compliment him.

The armor fits him like a glove. I can't find any noticeable openings except for his neck and head. Strange that he'd leave the most vulnerable areas open for attack but at least it gives me a good look at his face.

He's tall. About Balthazar's height with umber skin and cool undertones. A sharp angular jaw, pronounced brow with thick eyebrows, and a diamond shaped face. He looks every part of the fierce warrior he portrays.

Silver paint darts across his face from the hairline at his temples angled down towards his cheeks before curving sharply to his jaw and neck. Two more lines are painted at the middle of his eyebrows, darting up to his hairline. The sides of his scalp are shaved bare while thick braids run along the top of his head.

A hardened glare rests upon his face as his fingers hold his sword steadily within his hand. His intent rolls off him in waves. He means to kill me.

My horns ignite as fire darts down my spine and the back of my arms. It burns and hurts but I instinctively know it won't damage me. The pain it causes me is the motivating kind. The kind where your muscles hurt the next day after a brutal workout. I embrace it as I sink deeper into my stance.

He shifts his feet slightly, probably finding a bit more stability in his new stance before he speaks.

"You are guilty of breaking ordinance 58 29 point 4 and are hereby sentenced to death," he states in an even, deadly tone.

"Jokes on you," I reply arrogantly as I watch him for any sudden movements. "I don't know what ordinance 58 whatever is and I'm *not* dying today."

"Yes, you will be," is all he says before lunging for me.

He's lightning fast, but my magic is faster. I act on impulse because that's all I have. My arm raises up and fire shoots out of my palm directly at him. He dodges to the left but my magic uses an invisible force to shove him back into the line of fire. He rolls underneath the fire stream, popping up on the other side of it and swings the sword for my head.

I'm abruptly yanked backwards by an invisible force. I stumble as I barely manage to remain standing. He lunges for me again and I yell out all my fury, grief, and frustration as I meet him head on.

We clash against each other, the blade of his sword pressing against my forearm. It cuts me, but it doesn't dig in. It's a superficial gash, blood dripping out of it like a small papercut. My attacker grunts as he pushes the sword as hard as he can, but the smoke and apple smell thickens around us as my magic pushes against him. It hurts like a bitch. I can *feel* the blade pressing against the bone and nerves. Why can't my magic do something about the pain?

"What… are you?" he asks with a strained voice.

"Your worst nightmare," I answer as I push against him, my voice equally as strained as his.

He lets up, causing me to tumble forward as he creates about five feet of space between us. He uses the newfound distance to assess me.

His gaze remains hardened, but I can tell something's up. He no longer stares at me with open hatred, but guarded curiosity. He looks me up and down while he remains poised and ready for another attack.

"Your magic," he says as he glances around the area and honestly, it's a little weird *no one* seems to care we're fighting in the middle of The Commons. I know this is Boston but come on.

He suddenly flicks his wrist and a gasp flies out of my mouth as I abruptly shift to the side by about two feet. An object whooshes past my head where I once stood. It takes me a second to realize what he attempted. He just tried to dart me! *Bastard!* Before I'm able to do anything in retaliation, he starts talking again.

"That smell," he says as he inhales deeply. His stance becomes a little more relaxed and less threatening. "It is you."

I stare at him for a moment before deciding lying is my best plan of option. I don't know who this guy is. He might work for Zagon or one of the other Houses. I need to play dumb.

"Are you saying that I smell? That's pretty rude, asshole," I state as I cross my arms over my chest and I realize the fire is no longer there. Neither is my overwhelming rage.

"Your magic still works," he states, but it's more like he's talking to himself, verbally working out everything he's just seen. "It appears to be working on its own."

"Who are you?" I ask because two can play this game. "Did one of the Houses send you?"

A harsh glare befalls his face, the wrinkles in his brow emphasized by the silver stripes painted on his forehead.

"I would kill each and every one of the Houses if The Tribunal sanctioned it."

That statement doesn't rule out High King Zagon, but I also have no clue who or what The Tribunal is. Honestly, it sounds like some sacrificial event. Like, every two hundred years or so, the people of Jeznia are given the chance to take their shot against the Houses. And then whoever defeats a House inherits it.

That sounds kind of cool, but, when I really think about it, it doesn't sound like something the Houses would allow.

"Dude, who are you?" I ask in exasperation as I gesture with my arms. "Just so you're aware, I still want to kill you for attacking me. That's not cool. I'm *sick* of people trying to kill me. I mean... Is this what my life is now? Assholes trying to kill me at least once a week? Gah, just thinking about it is getting me mad all over again."

Anger hums beneath the surface as Chad and Finthorn's choices run through my mind. Ever since my dinner date with Chad, there's been a target on my back. Maybe I should accept this as my new reality. It doesn't appear like it'll be going away any time soon. If anything, since I became a devil, my target has only gotten *bigger*.

This is exactly why I need to learn how to use my magic quickly. It's nice to learn the magic instinctively protects me while I'm under attack, but I need to learn how to use it *on purpose.* I want to be the one making the decisions, not be a bystander watching it happen as it happens to me.

My attacker doesn't say anything as he sheaths his sword. A moment later, a bright white light encases him and when it clears, he's gone. *Cool,* I think, annoyed. I got absolutely nothing from him, but I'm not surprised. Why would anyone answer questions from their enemy? Hopefully Balthazar will be familiar with The Tribunal.

A second later, just as I attempt to take a step, exhaustion slams into me. My legs give out and I crumple to the ground. My entire body is jelly. Any attempt to lift or move my limbs is futile. It feels like I climbed to the top of Mount Everest completely unprepared and now the aftermath of all that effort has me sprawled out on the ground in The Commons with no ability to get myself home.

I could shout out to ask for help, but this is Boston. It might take a while before someone actually comes over to inspect how I'm doing. Besides, I'm out on the grass away from the paved pathways. No one is going to venture this way for quite some time. Do I have any other options other than shouting at the top of my lungs?

Should you require any assistance from now until then, ask for Umbra.

I blow out a heavy breath. I have no idea when I'll get my strength back. I don't want to be stuck out here completely vulnerable for another attack. I *have* to call Umbra to help me.

Damnit. How do I do it? Telepathically? Verbally out loud? *I guess I'll try both and see what happens.*

"Uh, Umbra," I say, my voice tired. "I need some assistance. I'm in The Commons. If you could stop by when you're free, it would be greatly appreciated."

I repeat the exact message inside my mind. It feels like a couple minutes pass by but Umbra isn't anywhere to be found. Do I ask again? What if she's in the middle of something important? Balthazar said she hides the meeting notes. What else is she responsible for? She could be doing some serious business for House Primis and I'm interrupting her. *God, I hope not*, I think in dread.

A split second later, her feet come into my view about a foot from my face. I glance up at her and don't miss the deep inhale she takes. Her sharp amber eyes snap to mine but she guards her emotions well.

"You used old magic."

"Uh…"

No one's supposed to know about that. Is it ok that Umbra does? Balthazar never mentioned telling her. Am I supposed to feign ignorance? *What do I do?* I understand that she's his Shadow Seer, but there must be certain things he keeps from her. Maybe this is one of them.

"You can't move," she states as she tilts her head sideways. "Lord Balthazar mentioned immobility was a consequence of using old magic."

Balthazar *did* tell her. *Thank God.*

"I can barely move a muscle," I confess as my emotions overwhelm me. All I want is to go home and cry myself to sleep. "Some asshole tried killing me. If my magic hadn't acted on its own, I'm pretty sure I would be dead.

"Can you bring me back to the apartment please? I'll explain everything there, but I'd really like to not be on the grass, exposed for another attack anymore."

Her eyebrows furrow together as a look of deep concentration takes hold of her face. "Lord Balthazar will not be pleased."

"Neither am I, Umbra. Neither am I."

VII

A MOMENT LATER, Umbra transports us to the condo, easily discarding me onto the couch.

"Thanks," I quip as I manage to shimmy myself into a more comfortable position.

It's harder than it should be and I nearly whine in frustration but keep it together because Umbra is here. To be honest, she's the *only* reason I'm currently keeping it together. My body *and* mind are processing the events I just went through and it's not going well.

Now that I'm out of danger, the panic and fear come barreling into me like a twenty foot wave, threatening to drown me and uproot any sense of comfort I had.

I'm trying to squash the panic as best I can but my body is overloaded. There used to be a time in my life that I was afraid of walking the streets alone at night, but I never experienced *true* fear. Before Chad, no one ever attempted to murder me. I often imagined what it would feel like to be genuinely afraid for my life, but it's nothing like the reality. I'm fortunate my flight or fight response is to fight. Except once the moment has passed, all those emotions I had been suppressing – especially the sheer terror – come crashing down.

I fight it off as best I can. Umbra probably has fought for her life since the day she was born. She probably doesn't get the shakes or the rapidly beating heart or the twisted knots in her stomach that make you want to puke.

Keep it together, Sloane. Focus, I tell myself as my eyes slide shut and I breathe in deeply. *Process what happened. What were the main events?*

The act that stole the show is that someone tried to kill me. Literally said *'hereby sentenced to death.'* It sounded really official. Like he was acting on orders he received. And what was that ordinance nonsense he was talking about? Balthazar has *never* mentioned ordinances. Is he keeping information from me or is he unaware of what ordinances are?

"Umbra, do you know anything about ordinances?" I ask as I finally manage to get comfortable in my seat.

My arms and legs tremble from use but I'm grateful that I'm able to move them.

"Ordinances," she repeats the word calmly as she stares me in the eyes.

"Yeah. The guy who attacked me said I broke an ordinance and sentenced me to death."

"Describe him to me."

I do my best to give her every detail I can remember. How tall he was, the style of his hair, the color of his skin, the paint on his face, how meticulous and beautiful his armor was, and what happened during our fight. She says nothing, gives away no emotions as she absorbs every bit of information.

There's about thirty seconds of silence from when I finish telling her what happened to when she finally speaks. Her words are evenly spaced and lack any sort of emotion that might give away what she's really thinking. It's *incredibly* annoying.

"You survived an attack against a Beastial."

"Against a what?" I ask as I sit up a little more in my spot on the couch, some strength finally coming back.

"A Beastial," she answers but doesn't elaborate on what that means. She's just as bad as Balthazar.

"Ok." I grind out as patiently as I can. "*What* is a Beastial?"

"Champions selected by The Tribunal to be trained in the art of assassinating devils."

Again with The Tribunal. I have no idea who or what they are but Balthazar mentioned Champions before. What did he say they were? *Odanthians trained to fight Jeznians.* So, a Beastial is basically a Champion that was promoted to be an assassin and their specialty is killing devils. Does that mean Champions don't fight devils? Are they meant to fight regular Jeznians who don't have magic? But then why would Balthazar bring up a Champion in our conversation if a Champion would never fight a devil? This is stupid, complicated, and makes no sense.

"Umbra," I breathe out as I rub my eyes. "I can't with any of this anymore."

"You should be dead," she states and my eyes slide open.

"Thanks for the vote of confidence," I reply sarcastically, a lazy grin on my face.

She doesn't chuckle or smile back. She merely stares at me with that stoic expression. God, she must think I'm the biggest annoyance in the entire world. She's stuck here playing my babysitter. I highly doubt she had this planned for her future. She's probably plotting my death as we speak just in case Balthazar ever gives her the green light.

I need to figure out a way to smooth over our relationship. Umbra is Balthazar's trusted second–in–command. She practically runs House Primis. I have to solidify some form of allyship with her if we're both going to be around each other for a while.

"Zyvn is over three thousand years old," Umbra states and I have to assume she's talking about the Beastial who attacked me because who else would it be? "He swung his sword against you four times. That's unheard of."

"Yeah, well, it didn't seem like he was using any magic so how do you expect him to win against a devil that does?" I ask as I stare up at the ceiling, grateful that little by little my strength is returning.

I can easily lift both my arms now. My legs still feel like jelly, but the rate at which the strength returned to my arms, I'm confident I'll be back on my feet in the next 10 – 15 minutes. I'm glad the shaking has finally stopped.

"A Beastial's power negates a devil's magic," she states casually, like she's telling me 2+2 equals 4.

I shoot up in my seat as soon as I realize what she's said.

"I'm sorry what?" is the only thing that comes out of my mouth as I stare at her in open shock.

"You should be dead," she repeats. "I've never heard of a devil defeating Zyvn."

"Uh, I think it's important to point out that I *didn't* defeat him," I clarify because if word gets out that the newly minted devil *defeated* a 3,000 year old *Beastial*, I'm royally screwed.

The Houses will lose their absolute mind over this piece of information and, before I know it, Zagon will hear about it and he'll come after me. That's the *one* thing Balthazar is trying to prevent.

"Zyvn left," I say. "Of his own accord. I didn't even hit him. He just left."

"I've never heard of Zyvn doing that either."

"Umbra, you've got to keep this a secret," I beg her. "If the Houses find out about what happened, it's over for me. And if that happens, then Balthazar will be upset. Right? He won't be happy if the Houses find out. So please, you'll keep this a secret, right?"

"I will say this only once," she says as she takes a step towards my spot on the couch.

A cold chill darts down my spine and I prepare myself for the worst. *She's going to tell me the second she has an opportunity to kill me, she'll take it. She'll take it and damn the consequences that'll follow.*

"Your purpose is to give Lord Balthazar exactly what he needs. For now, he wishes you to be alive. That makes you worth protecting in my eyes. There will come a time when that will change, as all things change over time, but as long as you give Lord Balthazar what he requires, you and I won't have any problems."

She expects me to screw up sometime in the future and lose Balthazar's favor. I'd be lying if I said I never entertained that idea. But hopefully by then, I'll be strong enough to defend myself from him. What's *really* telling is how determined she is to make sure Balthazar gets what he desires. She's protecting me because that's what Balthazar wants. That says a lot about her... *and* her feelings.

"You... care a lot about Balthazar," I say in a quiet voice, knowing that what I'm about to ask might not be well received.

I can't *not* ask it though. This is the most Umbra has ever spoken to me and it's all because she's looking out for Balthazar. Despite the fact that she's soft spoken, that her voice is barely above a whisper, she speaks confidently. There's no doubt in her eyes, no hesitation in her words, only pure conviction in her mind, body, and soul. She's wholly dedicated to Balthazar and that's a terrifying thing for me to be aware of.

"Are you... in love with him?" I ask.

All things considered, it's a stupid question, but I need to know. Jealousy, envy, greed... these feelings make people do atrocious things, especially if it's in the name of love. If she loves Balthazar, she might possibly be my greatest threat. Even more of a threat than Zagon.

"No," she answers without hesitation. "I owe him."

"For what?"

"My salvation," she replies just as quickly.

"Umbra–"

"So long as Lord Balthazar wants you alive, I will protect you, your secrets, and any other foolish whims you have. But rest assured, you will not get in our way of achieving what we've set out to do."

"I got it," I whisper as I sink a little further into the sofa. It's like being chastised by your mother, except a million times worse.

These plans she's talking about are overtaking Zagon. I want that as well because it'll make my life easier in the long run. That means we're all on the same page. She doesn't have to worry about me and I don't have to worry about her.

Sure, Umbra and I are never going to be best friends, but I can live with that. Hopefully over time, I'll secure my own Shadow Seer or at least my own allies I can be somewhat friendly with. For now, Balthazar is enough. I don't need to be friends, or even friendly, with Umbra. We can be cordial and civil.

Black shadows creep up her calves towards her waist, signaling our conversation is over, and the words fly out of my mouth before I even realize what I'm saying.

"Thank you."

Thank you for showing up today.

Thank you for bringing me home.

Thank you for protecting me even if your sole reason is because of Balthazar.

Thank you for being straight with me and always answering honestly.

Her eyebrows pinch together for the briefest of seconds, the shadows creeping up her torso. A moment later, the shadows cover her completely, but I hear that one word full of judgment and disdain before she disappears for good.

"Humans."

To her, I'm still human and the thought makes me smile.

I T'S NEARLY 4PM and I'm snuggled up in bed reading a fantasy romance book to help me decompress after the crappy day I've had. I've calmed down a great deal since nearly being killed. Thankfully, it's pretty easy to do so long as I don't think about what happened. Hence, the fantasy romance novel.

Balthazar appears without any warning and my entire body jolts in surprise, but it can't be helped when 1. I've almost been killed and 2. He arrives without notice or warning.

"You're here early," I say as I glance at the digital clock next to my bed, ignoring the rapid pulse twitching in my neck.

He usually arrives in time for dinner, hangs out for a bit, then leaves to go make more deals or head back to Jeznia. Dinner is usually between 6pm and 6:30pm. For Balthazar to be home two hours before dinner only means one thing. Umbra told him what happened and he came as soon as he could.

Balthazar says nothing as he stands at the foot of our bed. He hasn't once looked at me and my stomach coils. His lack of attention is a little concerning.

Quietly, I grab the bookmark beside me, put it in place, and set the book on the nightstand. The book thuds lightly against the nightstand, but Balthazar doesn't react as his eyes glare holes into the floor. His hands are tucked into the pockets of his pants, but I imagine they're curled into tight fists. He doesn't move, reminding me a great deal of a statue.

"Balthazar," I say his name gently, hoping to lure him out of whatever trance he's in.

He doesn't flinch or appear like he's heard me. Tossing the covers off me, I slink out of bed and walk to where he stands. My approach doesn't draw his attention. He's lost in whatever thoughts are running through his mind.

Balthazar's entire body is corded tightly, ready to snap at a moment's notice. I tentatively reach out, gently running my hand up, then down the expanse of his back. That snaps him out of his trance as he turns to me, his hand clenching my wrist like I have no right to be touching him.

"It's me," I say in a soft voice, having already expected that he might react this way.

I expect his scowl to soften as he realizes it's me he's talking to, but it doesn't. Instead, the enraged look on his face only deepens as he turns to fully face me.

"Zyvn will pay for what he did," Balthazar growls, steam slowly rising off him as his eyes bleed red. "No Beastial will take from me."

He's teetering on the fence between remaining somewhat cool and collected versus going berserk. I need to calm him down before he goes up in flames. Literally. I'm not sure how I'll be able to deescalate the situation if his humanoid appearance melts off him.

"Ok," I say in a calm, quiet voice. "You'll make Zyvn pay."

Balthazar moves fast as his hands come up to hold my face, his thumbs brushing against my cheeks. Steam continues to billow off him, thicker and heavier as the seconds pass. His eyes slowly begin to glow red and the heat that radiates off him increases as his ice cold fingers press into my scalp.

"Sloane, I can't – I *won't*," he says but the rest of his message dies on his lips as he stares at me, a snarl grabbing hold of his mouth.

"Ok," is all I say, my hands coming up to gently hold his burning hot wrists. I try to hide my wince as I offer him a reassuring smile. "Ok."

My reaction thankfully settles him as he inhales deeply, his eyes sliding shut, and he breathes out the words, "Peccatum meum."

"I'm here," I whisper as my hands drift to the base of his neck, my fingers scratching against his scalp. "I'm here, Balthazar."

If I had any lingering doubts about Balthazar's feelings towards me, they would be obliterated into the sun after this desperate display of *needing* me to be safe. But perhaps more importantly, his reaction solidifies how grave a situation I had been in. I've never seen him so worried.

He didn't react this way even after Chad shot me. Granted, we still had an ace up our sleeves with my wish, but today's reaction is drastically different. When Chad shot me, Balthazar was angry that Chad had overstepped. Despite that, the death Balthazar gave Chad was merciful.

This, on the other hand... Balthazar is teetering on the edge of losing his composure and unleashing raw, feral anger that throws logic to the wind. I've never seen him behave like this.

The anxiety I've worked so hard to bury is threatening to break through. So, I do the one thing that consistently squashes my anxiety. I dive headfirst into questions.

"Have you had altercations with Zyvn before?" I ask, grateful Balthazar takes a few more deep breaths to calm himself down.

"We've crossed paths in my time as a Contract Liaison," Balthazar answers as his hands drop away from my face, his arms curling around my body. "He killed the devil who used to work my territory."

"Why?"

"The devil killed a human for personal reasons. When The Tribunal found out, they assigned Zyvn to take care of the problem."

"I've heard The Tribunal, like, five times now and have absolutely no idea what it is," I tell him as my hand rubs up and down his back, my tone light as I do my best to calm us *both* down, to help us focus on the aftermath while ignoring the danger I had been in.

He softly chuckles, a small smile on his lips as his black and red eyes connect with mine. Gently, he pushes hair behind my ear.

"The Tribunal rules Odantha. It's made up of five Heralds who oversee all of Odantha. They're similar to the seven Lords of Jeznia.

"The Tribunal has also taken upon itself to govern Ephiri, though it's mostly passive governing. Since Jeznia lost the war, there hasn't been much objection. There are some whispers here and there, but for the most part, Jeznia has accepted the way things are.

"Odantha's government also has The Magistrate that works outside of The Tribunal, but they occasionally work in tandem together when necessary."

"And The Magistrate is...?"

"They determine which souls gain entry to Odantha."

"But The Tribunal doesn't?"

He shakes his head. "The Tribunal governs their world and inhabitants. The Magistrate decides the human souls who make it into Odantha."

My eyes shift back and forth between his as I process what he's told me. He always has an answer for every question I ask. I figured he'd know some things about Odantha since they're enemies and all, but Balthazar knows *a lot*. It seems unusual to know so much about a world he'd only survive in for twenty four hours.

"How do you know so much about Odantha?" I ask curiously.

"We weren't always forbidden from existing on each other's planes," he confesses and my eyebrows go up in surprise. I knew the cold and the heat weren't always in existence, but it seems strange that they'd let each other into their worlds. "There are old texts containing information on how Odantha operates. There's always a possibility that things are different now, but I suspect most of the governing is still the same."

"I see," I reply.

It's a surprisingly straight forward response. Hopefully, the data isn't too out of date. Then again, he does work with The Magistrate if he finds a soul worthy of entering Odantha. That's what he did with Sarah. He blacklisted her from making bargains with other devils and informed The Magistrate of her pure soul. He may dislike them, but he willingly works with them when necessary. I should operate on the assumption that his information is mostly correct.

My eyes trail down Balthazar's front as another question forms on the tip of my tongue. I'm not sure if this question will upset him all over again, but I need answers. I need to know why I was attacked today and if it'll continue to happen.

"Do you know why Zyvn attacked me?"

"Two reasons come to mind," Balthazar answers as his arms drop away from me and he takes a couple steps back. He combs his hand through his thick hair before he answers. "The first reason might be they're upset that you're practicing magic in Ephiri. There aren't any definitive rules against devils using magic in Ephiri since devils must use magic to grant the wishes of humans, but Odantha may not approve of your specific usage of magic when it doesn't involve wishes. The Tribunal may have decided to take action against you for that.

"The second reason is you're a devil that isn't affected by the cold. As I mentioned previously, the cold wasn't always in place. Devils used to roam freely between the three worlds.

"The story goes that Hapshein, a previous High King of Jeznia, got too greedy. He wanted to conquer the three worlds. Ultimately, he lost the war and the Creator decided it was in the best interest of everyone to be segregated. Though you and I know that you pose no threat to Ephiri, you're breaking a rule the Creator imposed and The Tribunal is very strict about upholding those rules."

He sighs heavily as he runs a hand through his hair again, his eyes concentrating on the floor as he speaks. "I knew Odantha would become involved eventually, but I didn't anticipate it would happen this quickly."

No response leaves my lips as I mull over what he's said. Technically, I'm not breaking any rules that we know of by practicing magic in Ephiri. However, I *am* breaking the rules by living here full time. It hadn't crossed my mind that the cold doesn't affect me despite being topside for three weeks. I'm still getting used to the idea that I'm no longer human. The cold has been far from my mind other than when Balthazar spends too much time with me.

His answer creates a plethora of other questions. Why am I the exception to the rule? Did Balthazar do something when he granted my wish? Or maybe it's my own magic that did it?

"Do you know why the cold doesn't harm me?" I ask.

"It's the way I granted your wish," he confesses as he refuses to meet my stare.

He's fiddling with his middle finger and it dawns on me that he's uncomfortable about answering the question. My stomach drops. Why? What information is he withholding from me now? Everything just keeps going from worse to worse.

"I need you to elaborate on that, Balthazar. How, exactly, did you grant my wish?" I demand to know, my voice leaving no room for rebuttals or refusals.

I don't want him beating around the bush, which he's probably tempted to do. Whatever he's done, I need to know the whole truth of it because it's affecting my life. He should have told me weeks ago when he turned me into a devil. It's infuriating that he omits things or doesn't bring them to my attention. I hate how I'm constantly learning about things *after the fact*.

If I had known about the cold, I would have made different decisions. For example, I'd only practice magic in Jeznia instead of on Earth. That way I'd give the illusion that I needed to go back to Jeznia to survive. We could have fooled Odantha if I had known about this, but instead he kept it from me. Why? Why did he feel the need to withhold this information from me?

Balthazar huffs out an irritated breath as a stoic expression befalls his face. His black–red eyes are guarded as he stares at me. His defenses are falling in place as he prepares for me to flip out on him. My heartbeat stutters as he opens his mouth to answer.

"I gave you seven years per your contract."

My eyebrows pinch together as my eyes dart back and forth between his gaze. *What the hell is he talking about?* If my voice is a little more tense than usual, it's not my fault that my patience is running out when he answers in roundabout ways.

"I don't know what you're talking about. *Explain* to me what you're saying."

His jaw juts back and forth, eyes narrowing as he meets me head on.

"When I granted your wish I made it so the cold would be delayed by seven years. When your contract expires, you will be forced to live by every rule the devils live by, but for now, you have time to adjust, to mentally prepare for your future. Afterall, Jeznia is an acquired taste," he says as he glances away from me.

The words he speaks next are forced out of him as if it physically pains him to admit such a truth.

"I didn't want to overwhelm you. I wanted to give you the opportunity to slowly acclimate to Jeznia instead of being forced to dive in headfirst. That is why the cold doesn't affect you… because of the choice *I* made."

My mouth hangs open after hearing his words. I don't know what to say. Balthazar is constantly surprising me. I'm so hung up on the big bad powerful Lord of Jeznia, heir to House Primis, that I often overlook how thoughtful and considerate he is.

His answer shows me how much care, thought, and attention was put into granting my wish. Without hesitation, he gave me a *grace period* to adjust to my new life, to prepare for my future of living in Jeznia for eternity. He thought and reflected on how my life was going to change, how it was going to affect me mentally, emotionally, personally… he put himself in *my* shoes and showed me a kindness he shouldn't even have when he granted my wish.

In a world that is cruel, unforgiving, and so different from the one I grew up in, Balthazar granted me the opportunity to *adjust* to Jeznia simply because he didn't want to *overwhelm* me.

Damnit, I'm gonna cry.

"Balthazar," is all I can say as tears blot my eyes and emotions warp my voice.

How has such a kind soul such as him survived in Jeznia? How did he make it through all the horrific bullshit to find his way to me?

"It was foolish of me, I know," he says, irritation laced in his voice as his hands curl into tight fists. His face shifts into clear outward anger as he keeps his gaze focused on the bed. "If I had simply done my job the way I was supposed to, Zyvn would never have been assigned to kill you. I knew the risks when I granted your wish, but I selfishly did it anyway."

His eyes snap to mine, the depth of his gaze full of anger and regret as he quietly utters the words, "I did this to you. The blame is solely mine."

"No," comes out of my mouth before he even finishes his sentence. "You did nothing wrong. I can't thank you enough for what you've done. I'm at a loss for words, but *thank you*, Balthazar. Thank you."

He inhales sharply, clearly uncomfortable with my gratitude, most likely because he's unaccustomed to receiving it, but I don't care. I'm on the verge of telling him I love him because I'm overwhelmed by how grateful I am, but that confession would probably scare him so I bite back the words desperately trying to leave my mouth.

"You shouldn't be thanking me, Sloane. You should be cursing me. I knowingly put your life in danger."

"I will *never* curse you for this, Balthazar. I don't think you understand the gift you've given me," I tell him as I take his hands in mine. "If anyone else had granted that wish, I wouldn't have the chance to get closure from my old life. I would have been thrown into Jeznia without any help. If my wish had been granted that way, I wouldn't have survived. I can't... I can't thank you enough for the gift you've given me."

Tears descend down my cheeks as I hold his gaze. I can't believe how lucky I am to have met him. The circumstances under which we met were horrendous. I will never deny that. But I can't deny all the good that has come from meeting him. The way Balthazar treats me, respects me, views me as his equal, how he does these hidden acts of kindness... it's more than I ever hoped for in a significant other. It's hard to believe that because a human wished me dead I've found an incredibly thoughtful and considerate partner.

Balthazar looks undeniably uncomfortable from hearing my words, but he's doing his best to meet me head on. He loosely holds my hands as he maintains eye contact, but the frown that's pulling down his lips gives away his true emotions. He doesn't want or like my kind words; he'd prefer to hear me say I hate him.

A light laugh tumbles out of my mouth before I have the wherewithal to suppress it.

"You look like you're constipated," I say because it's true but I also say it in an attempt to liven up the mood.

"I feel like it too," he replies as his lips pull down even more, but his actions speak louder than his words. He continues to hold my hands and look me in the eyes even if he's dying to create physical space between us.

"You may hate it and try your best to get rid of it, but you have some good in you," I declare. He grimaces and I lightly whack his shoulder as I laugh. "That's not a bad thing!"

"I assure you that it most definitely is. Being good only makes me weak."

I roll my eyes, but internally, I'm grateful for how quickly we can bounce back from such a serious conversation. I'm sure he appreciates it more than me.

"You're so dramatic."

"That's what makes me fun," he replies with a sly smile as he sits down on the chair in the corner of the room.

"Uh–huh, keep telling yourself that."

"I will," he quips and I openly roll my eyes at him as I sit down on the bed. My right leg is crossing over my left leg when Balthazar abruptly declares, "They're calling a House meeting."

He snaps his fingers as he stands up. His three piece suit has been replaced with the outfit he wears to Jeznia.

"What, why?" I ask as I quickly get up from the bed, only briefly surprised my outfit has been changed as well.

The timing of the meeting is too coincidental. They must know about what just happened at The Commons today.

Still, I venture to ask Balthazar if that's what he think. "Do you think they know what happened with Zyvn?"

He clenches and unclenches his jaw as he stares at me with a guarded expression. That can't be good. "We'll find out once we get there."

Nerves get the better of me as I suddenly feel very sick to my stomach. What'll happen to me if they know? Will they hold another trial and order me dead? Do they know Zyvn attacked me but not the reason why? There are too many questions and no one to supply me with the answers. I hate this. If I knew anything, I could prepare. Going in blind is too much for me to handle.

Balthazar beckons me towards him, extending his left arm so I can take my place by his side. My legs are shaky as I make my way over to him. Thankfully, Balthazar does me the courtesy of pretending he doesn't see. He confidently slides his arm around my waist, securing me in place as he pulls me flush against him. As he raises his other hand to snap his fingers, he glances at me, his eyes and voice cold.

"Be prepared, Sloane."

With that, we disappear from sight.

VIII

WE ARRIVE IN his office a moment later before quietly
making the walk down to the throne room. The doors open,
creaking against their hinges as Balthazar enters the room
with me trailing behind. For once, we're not the last to show
up. House Lupus and House Aranea have yet to arrive.

"Lord Balthazar, it's unlike you to show up so early,"
Meik of House Anguis states from his seat to Balthazar's
right.

"The timing happened to work out. Don't get used to it,"
Balthazar casually states as he climbs the steps to his throne.

However, he surprises me as he grabs my hand on the
fourth step, yanking me past the fifth step where my seat
resides, and pulling me up to the seventh step with him. He
sits down on his throne before tugging me into his lap, arms
securely wrapping around me despite appearing like he's
lazily holding onto me.

What are you doing? I ask as I settle into a more
comfortable position, leaning into his embrace.

Securing a safe getaway should we require it, he
answers effortlessly and I realize just how dangerous this
House meeting might turn out to be. My heartbeat shoots into
overdrive as tension bunches my shoulders towards my head.

I keep reminding myself we don't know what the meeting is about so there's no sense in getting worried, but there's no denying the timing of it. What else could this meeting be about if it isn't about me?

"How much longer are we going to wait for the others to arrive?" Balthazar asks as he trails his hand up and down my thigh. "The meeting shouldn't be held up merely because they can't afford to make it on time."

Someone scoffs at Balthazar's hypocrisy, but no one openly objects to his statement. Barely a moment later, both Lord Priscilla and Lord Taron appear in their thrones.

"High King Zagon is making important moves and it is our duty as Lords to ensure we're ready for his call," Taron declares as soon as he arrives.

A quiet hum surges through the room and Balthazar's body tenses beneath me. He's not happy about Taron's declaration. Probably because he wants to overthrow Zagon but I'm over the moon that this news isn't about me. It's about High King Zagon.

All my tension and anxiety immediately vacates my body. I practically slump against Balthazar. There's no need for me to be on edge anymore. I can lazily listen to what everyone's saying and not worry I'm one vote away from being sentenced to death. This is good. I can deal with this kind of meeting.

"Lord Taron do not mistake convenience for extraordinary," Balthazar states in a threatening tone.

Goosebumps dart down my arm at the dark timbre his voice has taken on. Heat settles low in my belly as Balthazar commands the throne room. He may be the youngest Lord in this room, but he owns the room, owns *them*. No one dares to challenge him and, despite what Balthazar claims, it's not because of his big scary dad. It's because of him, his magic, and his strength. They follow him because *he's* the big bad wolf, not because of who is father is.

The way he so effortlessly tore Taron down without a second thought contrasts so violently against the devil I know within the privacy of our own room. They lack his respect while I have all of it. His arrogance, his rudeness, his distaste for them is clear as day, practically a physical entity standing beside him. Yet he showers me with love, kindness, and a thoughtfulness I didn't know existed. Seeing the contrast *excites* me knowing I'm the one who holds all the cards.

I can't help it. Seeing him in his element with the Lords, how he leads them and commands the room while putting them in their place *does* something to me. I love having his submissiveness, I love the power he willingly hands over to me but seeing him be the dominant devil Lord that he is in a room full of powerful devil Lords is sexy as Hell.

My hand has a mind of its own, sinful thoughts filling my head as my fingers slide down his torso, ghosting a little too close to his crotch. He flinches, his hand expertly grabbing that wandering hand of mine. He lazily inspects my fingernails as he speaks.

"High King Zagon may be in possession of one of your Blood Reapers, but only a fool would ever forget his place."

His voice is nonchalant, like he cares way more about the status of my fingernails than the rest of the people in the room. My eyes snap over to Taron. His face flushes red, most likely due to anger and embarrassment. His hands clutch his armrests as murder fills his eyes. Taron's pride has been wounded.

"*You* forget *your* place, Lord Balthazar," Taron states, unable to hold back his rage. "It's only a matter of time before you wind up dead. High King Zagon's children *never* last."

"I shall deliver that message to him," Balthazar hums out as he fiddles with my fingers, handling them as if they're delicate and could break at the lightest touch. "I'll let him know you believe he's incapable of siring a fitting heir. I'm sure he'll be pleased to hear that."

Before Taron can respond, Meik interrupts the argument. "What do you know of High King Zagon's business, Lord Taron?"

"He's making moves—"

"Yes, you've already stated that," Balthazar cuts him off. "A vague notion that our beloved High King is making moves. Tell me Lord Taron, do such undefined plans normally get you this aroused? Did High King Zagon even utter those words to you or are you speculating what he might be doing with one of your Blood Reapers?"

Oh, Balthazar is *not* holding back. He's really going for the throat with these questions.

Maybe let up on him, yeah? I suggest. Lord Taron already has it out for us after what we did with Finthorn. Humiliating him in front of the Lords won't do us any favors. If anything, it'll only motivate him to look further into him, myself, and House Primis.

"Such arrogance for someone who knows so little," Balthazar stabs the metaphorical knife deeper into Taron's gut.

"Do you know of High King Zagon's plans, Lord Balthazar?" Carmilla asks before Taron can get a word in.

It seems no one has the patience for him and I don't blame them. Who calls an urgent meeting just so they can deliver vague intel? *Zagon is on the move. Be ready.* What the Hell can they do with that kind of information? Be ready for what? How should they be ready? Should they be fortifying their Houses or preparing to vacate Jeznia and bring war to Earth and Odantha? He's wasted everyone's time calling this meeting.

"I haven't a clue," Balthazar replies as he finally drops my hand and looks out at the throne room. "High King Zagon doesn't trust anyone. He won't share what brilliant plan he's working on, not even with the heir to his House."

There's a brief silence as he shifts his gaze down the circle of Lords. "However," he states loudly. "Lord Taron is right that we should be ready for his call when he makes it. I trust whatever he's working on will create massive shock waves within the three worlds."

The excitement is palpable as it spreads throughout the room. I watch as spouses and heirs make eye contact with each other while the Lords shift within their thrones. I'm missing something in what Balthazar said. He didn't say anything particularly illuminating, yet something resonated with them. What was it? What did I miss?

"Is there anything else for us to discuss?" Balthazar asks in a bored manner.

No one answers and after a few seconds, Balthazar stands from his throne, causing me to stand with him. He holds my hand as he walks down to the landing where I should technically be seated. Fire ignites his horns, darting down his neck and back as he stops at the edge of the landing.

"Lord Taron, the next time you waste my time will be the death of you. I do not care how deeply your loyalty for House Primis runs. You waste my time a *third* time and you will be dead for it."

A cold chill blows through the room as Balthazar makes a physical show of just how angry he is about the situation. He means business. He *will* kill Lord Taron should he waste Balthazar's time again.

The heat low in my belly sparks to a fierce flame. I'm finding there's almost nothing sexier than Balthazar striking fear into the hearts of the Lords of Jeznia. *He* is in charge. Despite their rage, they keep themselves in check because they know Lord Balthazar Primis is not one to be trifled with. He may be the youngest, but he is the most powerful devil among them. And what they fail to see is that he is *mine.*

That thought ignites the flame to a burning desire. My hand squeezes his tightly as my body presses into him. The words cannot be tampered down as I think them in an instant. *I* want *you.* The thoughts must echo loudly within his own head because his body stiffens for the briefest of seconds before he directs his attention to the rest of the room.

"Do not test my patience because of my youth or inexperience. I am the son of High King Zagon Primis. I am the Lord and heir to House Primis. I will not hesitate to slaughter each and every one of you—"

"You are *nothing* without your father's namesake," Lord Priscilla hisses.

My fingers dig into Balthazar's hand, a hardened glare upon my face. I couldn't suppress it no matter how hard I tried. She's a fool for entertaining the thought that Balthazar would hide behind his father's name. He doesn't need Zagon. His skill and strength at magic proves that. He would eat her alive. Maybe he should. If only to prove a point.

Balthazar chuckles low and deep, his hand slipping from mine before he slinks his arm around my waist and pulls me tight against him.

"Lord Priscilla, it is not my father's namesake that I rely on to keep you in line. It is my father's magic. No matter how far I fall within the ranks," he says, his voice dropping low as his tone loses all amusement. His grip tightens around me as he speaks, "I will *always* have Primis magic. Never forget that."

He snaps his fingers. An instant later, Priscilla is encased in a layer of ice with only her head exposed. A murderous glare settles on her face. She shifts in her seat, most likely to push against the ice and break it, but she visibly winces. Her eyes narrow at Balthazar, her lips pulling back in a snarl before she inhales deeply and pushes all her strength into breaking the ice. Red stains the broken shards as ice clatters around Priscilla's feet. Tiny spikes are imbedded in the ice. So small yet sturdy enough to break through her skin.

My eyes snap to Balthazar as awe and envy wash over me. He's so precise and detailed with his magic. It truly is like breathing for him. I can't help but wonder if I'll ever get that way.

"Each and every one of you is free to challenge me," Balthazar booms as he glances around the room.

"I wouldn't dream of it, Lord Balthazar," Meik hums from his throne.

"Lord Taron has wasted *all* of our time," Carmilla states, restrained anger in her voice. "I might fight you, Lord Balthazar, for the honor of killing Lord Taron should he waste our time again."

Meik chuckles as he shifts forward in his seat, placing his chin in the palm of his hand. "I couldn't agree more, Lord Carmilla."

Taron's entire demeanor changes as he sits stiffly in his throne, face frozen. I don't miss the way the two Lords sitting on either side of him shift to the opposite side of their thrones, creating more distance between them and him. If I were in their shoes, I'd do the same. The three most powerful Houses in Jeznia have allied themselves against Lord Taron. He might stand a chance against one of them. Balthazar did say brute strength and power aren't the only ways to kill someone. But being forced against three Houses... Taron *and* his House would be obliterated.

"It won't happen again," Taron curtly states before disappearing from sight.

"My patience is thin," Balthazar declares to the room. "Don't waste my time. I'm not feeling very lenient."

"I second Lord Balthazar's sentiment," Carmilla chimes in and the remaining four Houses agree with her.

Balthazar says nothing else before snapping his fingers. We transport out of the room and back into his office. I barely have time to gather my bearings before he pounces on me, pinning me on top of his desk.

"You want me?" he asks as he nips and sucks my neck.

A sly smile pulls at my lips, my left hand coming up to comb through his hair as my right hand drags down his bare back.

"I do," I hum. His lips are a tease against my neck. I crave more of him. "You're sexy when you threaten the Lords."

"Tell me more," he says as he slowly moves his way down my torso, his hand lifting my leg up to give him access to me.

My breath hitches in anticipation for what's to come. He's taking his time as he works his way down, but I know where his target is and I get wet in anticipation. That expert tongue of his is the best I've ever had. I'm practically squirming from the memory recall from the last time he used it.

"Your confidence and arrogance when you speak to them, your display of power and magic, never getting provoked by the insults they throw your way," I say as my breaths come out heavy.

His mouth latches onto my clothed crotch as he drags his tongue with enough pressure to drive me wild. Irritation zings down my spine. I want all barriers removed. I want us skin on skin.

"I love it," I whisper. "I love watching it happen. You put them in their place so effortlessly. You display your power so beautifully. And yet… if I ever demanded you to bow down to me in front of them, I know you'd do it in a heartbeat. All of it makes me so horny."

He rips the fabric of my clothes away and plunges his tongue into me, that sinful appendage doing God's work as he laps me up. His fingers brutally grip my legs as he buries his face into me like he can't get enough. His tongue flicks against me so sure and firm, the pleasure building inside me as my hips hump against him. My hands clench against the edge of the desk, using it as leverage to thrust my hips against his mouth.

"Balthazar," I breathe out and can't keep myself from looking down at him.

He's buried his mouth and nose into me as he eats me out, his fingers digging painfully into my thighs. My skin has turned pink beneath his fingertips. He continues to eat me like I'm a drug he can't get enough of, growling his satisfaction as his tongue flicks and swirls against me. It's sinful how good it feels and I drown in the sensations.

With my head still propped up, I watch as his right hand disappears from my leg and slinks down the front of him. My head falls back onto the desk, but I don't miss the way his arm moves. He's masturbating while performing oral sex on me. He's enjoying himself so much he needs to receive his own pleasure. It drives me wild.

My hips rock violently against him as I look down at him with his mouth latched onto me and his hand vigorously jerking back and forth as he pumps his cock. *What a sight.* I'm on the verge of cumming, I just need a little more–

My orgasm crashes into me so perfectly, my legs tightening around his head as his tongue continues its work. It hits me hard and fast before I'm slumped against the desk, more than sated with the result of his eager work. I blink slowly as I stare up at the ceiling, my chest heaving up and down. My legs loosen their grip around his head as my body falls further into those satisfied, relaxed endorphins coursing through me.

Balthazar doesn't stop his ministrations, his tongue lapping up every last bit of liquid I have to offer as he continues to masturbate. When he finally obtains his release, his bites – hard – on my inner thigh. I hiss as I smack his head, mildly irritated he has a biting problem, but he doesn't let go. He grunts through his orgasm, teeth sunk into the meaty bits of my thigh, eyes flashing white before he finally releases my flesh from his teeth.

Blood dribbles down my leg onto the desk and I glare at him.

"Fix that," I order.

His reply is to lick the blood and, although it's a beautiful sight to see, I'm still rather annoyed.

"Balthazar, *stop* the bleeding," I order him.

He snaps his fingers and the blood is gone, but not the mark. It's red, slightly inflamed, but thankfully pain free. I contemplate telling him to remove the mark but decide against it. I like that it's in a place no one can see, that we're the only two people who know it's there, and *how* it got there. It's a consolation prize in a way and I want to keep it for as long as possible.

"Thank you," I say as I sit up.

My eyes glance down where Balthazar is still crouching on the floor and I don't miss the white cum splayed across the front of his desk or that he still clutches his dick in his hand. My lips purse to the side of my face, a little disappointed with the turn of events.

"I don't remember giving you permission to get off, Lord Balthazar," I say as I place my index finger beneath his chin and lift up.

He rises onto his feet but places his hands on either side of my body as he leans down towards me. His mouth is hovering over my own and irritation flits down my spine. He's testing my boundaries and I don't appreciate it. Perhaps I've been too lenient of an owner. I need to remind him of his place.

"My deepest apologies," he murmurs, but I don't miss the smirk ghosting across his lips.

"Send me home," I whisper against his lips. "I want you to stay here and think about what you've done."

"Sloane."

He practically growls my name, his displeasure dripping off him like soured wine. I instinctually lean away from him, my eyebrow arching up as annoyance grabs hold of my face. Is he seriously *challenging* me right now? *That won't do.*

"You heard me, Lord Balthazar," I say, a cutting tone to my voice. "*Do not* make me repeat myself."

A harsh glare rests on his face, the red within his eyes bleeding into the black. He's angry I'd dare turn him away. *You should have thought about that before going rogue.* His entire body has gone stiff while he stands in silence. As if the longer the silence prevails, the more likely I might change my mind.

My lips twitch to curl into a smile. The urge to say 'The Hell with it' and continue our fun clashes against my need to assert dominance. Then there's the enjoyment from torturing him and riling him up. Each and every time I'm always amazed that he submits to me, especially during times like this where he *hates* it. His pride is at odds with his lust. It's a magnificent thing to watch someone as powerful as him obey and submit to someone as weak as me.

My fingers reach out, gently wrapping around his limp cock. His eyes flash red as he waits to see what I'll do. A coy smile surfaces on my face as I speak.

"I *own* your pleasure, Lord Balthazar," I say, tone low and sultry and intended to entice. The smile on my lips widens as he bites his lower lip. "You don't get to cum without my say so. Do you understand?"

"I understand," he breathlessly replies, his muscles contracting as he holds himself back from doing whatever ungodly things he's thinking of.

"Good," I reply as I release my grip on his cock. "I'll see you later tonight."

His face morphs into irritation as his eyes dart back and forth between mine. I can see the question lingering in his gaze. *Are you seriously leaving right now?* I smile sweetly at him, loving every second of this encounter. Oh, if only the

Lords could see him now and how easily he comes undone because of me.

"I want to kiss you, Sloane," he grinds out, his biceps flexing as he leans forward, but doesn't close the distance. He's aware that would only make his situation worse. *Damn, I love how well he listens.* "I need to have my way with you."

I peck his lips, laughing a little viciously as I pull away. "It's time I go home, Lord Balthazar. I'll see you when you finish up your business here."

He's clenching and unclenching his jaw, eyes narrowed in anger. He's probably rethinking this whole submitting and ownership dynamic of our relationship. Afterall, he has more power than me. Being dominant comes more naturally to him than it does to me. Yet, he surprises me by leaning forward, his hot breath ghosting against my ear as he whispers in a threatening, sinful tone.

"I'll have you *begging* for my cock, Sloane," he growls out quietly. "We both know no one can fuck you the way I do."

He snaps his fingers, teleporting me out of the room, leaving me hot and bothered and entirely all alone.

IX

I'M HALF TEMPTED to telepathically reach out to him, to demand he come back to the apartment and deliver on his promise, but I manage to hold myself back. As much as I would like to have my way with him, Balthazar has important stuff he needs to do. There are also other things I need to concern myself with. Like a shower.

It's nearly 6:30pm when I finish washing myself down, my hair thrown up in a towel while I'm dressed in a baggy cotton T–shirt and black leggings. I venture out to the kitchen, surprised to see steaming hot food already on the island. I'm even more surprised to see Umbra standing roughly a foot from said island with two folders in her hands.

"Uh, thank you for the food," I say as I grab an empty plate and start dumping food onto it.

It's a good mixture of Mexican food and the delicious aroma awakens my hunger, making me impatient to eat.

"It's from Lord Balthazar," she answers in that even, dead tone. *She literally could give zero fucks.* "He wanted me to relay that he's busy securing important deals and won't be joining for dinner."

That makes sense. His normal schedule was thrown off when he came to the apartment around 4pm instead of 6pm.

Plus we had the House meeting and then a little bit of fun afterwards. I imagine if I see him at all tonight, it won't be until it's closer to the time I go to bed. It's a bummer, but sometimes that's just the way things go.

"Would you like any food?" I ask as I sit down at the island.

I feel a little more relaxed around Umbra after our last conversation. She's made it explicitly clear that as long as I give Balthazar what he needs and I don't fuck up their plans, I'm not a problem in her eyes. We won't ever be the best of friends, but it's a huge weight off my shoulders to know where I stand with her. I don't feel the need to walk around on eggshells anymore. It's nice.

"Study up on this," Umbra orders as she tosses the folders down onto the island, ignoring my implied question about eating together.

"What is it?" I ask even though I'm already reaching for it.

She says nothing as I open the contents of the top folder. It's information about the Houses. Shocked, I quickly thumb through all the documents. It's information on the current Lords, their heirs and spouses, their House Aides, which circle they're in charge of ruling. I discard that folder for the other one. It contains information about Odantha, about The Tribunal, The Magistrate, the types of titles and jobs they have and what their duties entail.

"Are these your notes or his?" I ask as I read the names of the five Heralds who make up The Tribunal.

"Both."

My attention is split between the conversation with Umbra and reading the materials in my hands. This is a goldmine of information. I'm grateful Balthazar is sharing it with me. I won't have to constantly ask him for basic information anymore.

If I get this stuff memorized, maybe it'll help me with learning my magic. At bare minimum, it'll prevent me from looking like a fool in front of the Houses and Zyvn if I should ever see him again.

"Are these mine to keep?" I ask.

"Yes," Umbra answers.

"Thank you. This is incredibly helpful."

"You are Lord Balthazar's spouse," Umbra says in that signature monotonous tone. "It's time you start acting like it."

What the Hell does that mean?

I have to wonder if she knows the truth. That Balthazar and I aren't *really* married, that he didn't originally grant me a wish, that my wishing to be a devil was the ace up the sleeve.

Balthazar heavily relies on her for his House obligations but within that same breath, he treats her like she's dirt beneath his shoes. Would it benefit him to tell her the truth or would he keep her in the dark? The urge to ask her what she knows teeters on the tip of my tongue but I bite it back. In asking any questions along those lines, I risk revealing a truth she might not know. Instead, I ask a different question. One that she's equally as likely not to answer.

"Is there any information in here about you?"

As expected, she remains stoically silent. Barely a moment later, she disappears in a cloud of black smoke. My eyes roll skyward but I can't say I'm surprised. In a way, it was a dumb question. I can just look through the Jeznian folder to see if she's in there. Still, would it have killed her to give me an answer?

With Umbra gone and Balthazar busy buying the souls of desperate humans, I quietly eat my dinner as I idly read through the documents. There's a lot of information to take in, but at the same time so little. I don't immediately notice any damning facts or pieces of information I can use. It seems rather basic, but having basic knowledge is one step up from where I was a minute ago. What Umbra gave me is something I can build on. It's a jumping off point that I know will prove to be useful.

"You know what I need?" I ask the empty room as my fork clatters against my plate. "Index cards."

After a quick search on which local stores sell index cards, I head out to purchase some with the credit card Balthazar gave me. The next several hours are me pouring over the documents and transferring the most important information onto the index cards.

Yes, it's redundant writing the same information from one piece of paper to the next. But writing notes has always been the quickest way for me to memorize data. I could throw the notes away the second after I finish transferring information onto them and still be able to recall the information I wrote down. It's a useful skill I'm grateful to have.

A nostalgic feeling washes over me as I continue writing important information onto the cards. I'm reminded of high school and the many hours I spent studying to get an acceptable grade. I was a lot more relaxed in college, learning how to balance the responsibility of school and a social life. But high school? Every little thing had me stressed and thinking it was the end of the world.

I can't help but wonder if I had known where my life would take me, would I have wasted countless hours stressing over a B–, grieving breakups with boys not worth my time, and trying so hard to fit in with my friends instead of just focusing on finding people who liked me for me? Honestly, sixteen year old me would be losing her shit over a real life devil romancing me.

A snort falls out my mouth, my pen slipping a little as I mess up the letters. To be fair, twenty six year old me still loses her shit from time to time when I actually sit and think about it.

High school me would call me a liar if I told her I played the dominant role in our relationship with the devil. I lacked so much confidence in high school. I was easily intimidated, pushed into doing things I had zero comfort doing. All to make my friends happy and pray they wouldn't abandon me.

My thoughts wander to Balthazar. What was he like at sixteen? Was he more arrogant than he is now or more unsure of himself? If I had to wager a bet, I'd say more arrogant and incredibly entitled. He probably felt on top of the world as a Contract Liaison under his mother guidance. Six years experience at sixteen years old. Primis magic. Father under the belief he's dead. *He was probably an annoying little shit.* I can't help the smile grabbing hold of my face.

The pen rolls against the table as I finally finish writing the last card about the Houses and place it on the island next to all the others. It's kind of crazy how many index cards there are when all the information is rather basic. Still, basic information is better than no information. And if I study these cards just a couple minutes a day, I'll have everything memorized in no time.

My attention moves to the folder containing knowledge about Odantha. Anxiety creeps up my spine as I open the folder and begin to read what's inside. Odantha is the opposite of Jeznia. Heaven to Hell. That simple fact unsettles me for one reason: that means I'm being *hunted by Heaven*. The place where all the untainted human souls go… or at least souls with very minimal stains on them.

That means Odantha is *good*. I always thought I was, but it turns out I'm not. I'm *bad*. I'm *evil*. I'm a devil now. Horns and all. My soul is and always has been a red Jeznian soul. I was never good to begin with.

It's hard wrapping my head around that. How am I supposed to just accept that I've always been bad and that my evilness was predetermined before I was even born? It's unfair. None of the good I did mattered in the end. I was evil since conception. I never had a choice about who I was even despite how much good I did. And now I'm being hunted for things entirely out of my control.

Honestly, it's on par with how my life has been going these past three weeks.

With a heavy sigh, I refocus my attention on the reading I need to be doing and away from the spiral into a self—pity party. There's no sense in feeling sorry for myself. It won't do me any good.

Wiping a piece of lint off the paper, I read the information before me.

The Tribunal. Consists of five Heralds. They rule Odantha, making all important decisions regarding the world.

The Magistrate. Consists of three Wardens. They monitor and declare which souls gain entry into Odantha and where they'll spend eternity. There are two places a soul can go. Live within the city or in the Fields of Prosperity.

That sounds pretty similar to Jeznia. Jeznia has The Wastelands. I assume the Fields of Prosperity is the counterpart to The Wastelands. And just like Jeznia has the city where all the Lords live and the tortured human souls go, Odantha has a city too. That must be where the Heralds, Wardens, and angels live. *I wonder if Odantha has pearly white gates and a golden city?* Balthazar did mention TV didn't have everything wrong when he told me we had to seal our deal with a kiss. Maybe Odantha really does have pearly white gates and a city made of gold.

A light smile touches my lips at that thought as I flip the page to continue reading about Odantha.

Guards monitor entry of souls into Odantha per The Tribunals order. Defenders are assigned by the Magistrate to protect certain human souls to guarantee entry into Odantha upon their death.

"Wait a second," I say as I read that last sentence over again.

If I'm reading this correctly, it's basically saying that Defenders ensure a devil can't make a deal to purchase that human's soul. How and why do they decide which soul is worth protecting? Why wouldn't every human soul be worth protecting?

People aren't *born* bad. They grow up to be bad. I'm sure Chad wasn't a little shit when he was a baby. He must have fallen off the beaten path at some point. So if Odantha really wanted to ensure good souls went to them, they'd be more involved in helping our world be a better place instead of leaving it up to circumstances and environments. They're using a passive approach and only defending super special souls that they deem worthy.

My fingers curl tightly into my fist, crinkling the paper in my hand in the process. *Odanthians can only be bothered to show up when something goes wrong* Balthazar's voice rings through my mind. He had said that back in Paris when I'd been prodding him for information, hoping to get out of my deal somehow. He also said that if real angels existed, they would care more about humans than Odanthians do. I get it now. I get why he said that. Odantha cares about what goes on in Ephiri, they just don't care *enough*.

Odantha only cares about Jeznia staying in line and taking the purest souls from Earth. Everything else is nothing to them.

My jaw clenches tightly as I smooth out the crinkled paper in my hand. I don't understand how Odanthians are better than me. They have the power to make real change on Earth but they don't do anything. They sit back and watch our slow descent into oblivion.

The rage simmering within is reaching its boiling point. I need to concentrate on the paperwork and forget about Wardens and The Magistrate who don't make a difference.

My eyes focus on the next job title directly beneath Defenders.

Transcribers.

Transcribers report the happenings and goings on Ephiri. They tend to stay hidden, never involving themselves in incidents. They merely record what happened and report back to The Tribunal. That essentially means they're spies, keeping tabs on humans and on Jeznians and Odanthians visiting Earth. *Is that how they discovered me? A Transcriber was watching me?*

My eyes snap up, instantly searching the apartment but there's nothing amiss. The hair along the back of my neck prickles at the thought that someone could be lurking around, watching my every move, and reporting it back to Odantha.

I'd much rather meet them head on and come to a conclusion quickly without dragging it out.

"Hey Transcriber," I shout out into the empty apartment. "If you're here, let's do this. Stop spying on me like a perverted old man. You've got a problem with me, do something about it instead of crying home to Mommy and Daddy."

"Transcribers are trained to be elusive," someone declares in a calm tone as a blindingly bright white light invades the apartment. "Even I do not know when one is around."

I jolt from my chair, already anticipating exactly who is behind that voice. My magic rushes forward at my command, the purple smoke and gold lightning wrapping around me in a protective layer. I don't know how good I'll be able to intentionally fight him off, but I know my real magic will keep me safe.

The white light clears. Zyvn stands in the apartment with his arms loosely at his sides. He wears a light grey cloak. It doesn't hide the armor underneath or the sword clipped to his waist, but he exudes an air of peace instead of conflict.

His steel grey eyes inspect the apartment while I keep all my attention on him as I look for any small movement that will give me an edge. He seems taller than I remember. Beefier too. Will I stand a chance against him again? *I have to.*

"If you attack me, I'll make you regret it," I declare and I hate that my voice cracks towards the end. It trembles as I speak, giving away just how scared I am of the current situation I'm in.

He technically shouldn't be able to get into the apartment. Balthazar warded it to prevent magic users from gaining entry, which he *should* have done before Finthorn kidnapped me but he hadn't. Now that it's been officially warded, Balthazar has assured me no one can get into the apartment except for me, him, and Umbra. So how is it that Zyvn teleported himself inside? *Probably because he has the ability to neutralize magic* bitterly runs through my mind.

"I haven't come here to attack you," Zyvn states as his eyes slowly slide over to mine.

He hasn't moved an inch from his spot, keeping his distance of about eight feet from me. My heart beats loudly within my ears, my chest tightening as fear edges its way closer to the surface. I have to keep myself as calm as possible. I can't think clearly when I'm too scared.

"Come to murder me instead?" I ask.

My voice doesn't waver this time as I remain in my defensive stance. To be honest, I don't know if it's a good stance, but it's all I've got. I'm going on pure instinct and I pray it helps.

"The Tribunal surely wants you dead," he replies, his voice detached and cold as his hand shifts to rest on the hilt of his sword.

My body stiffens at that small, simple act. If it were anyone else, I wouldn't think anything of it. But Zyvn has proven deadly with that sword. I need to be prepared for an unexpected attack.

"Aren't you The Tribunals bitch?" I ask, not sure if I want to provoke him into an attack. "If they want me dead, doesn't that mean so do you?"

"Usually, yes."

He glosses right over my insult. I'm clearly too far beneath him to be insulted by. Irritated by that fact, my words hold a little more bite to them as I speak.

"But what? Today's my lucky day?"

"Yes."

A few seconds pass by before I grow too irritated to wait for him to elaborate. He clearly isn't going to. God, he's too much like Balthazar in that sense and it drives me up a wall. The familiarity of it all gives me more confidence. I relax a bit in my stance, the fear ebbing away as I speak.

"Are you going to explain why you're here then? Jesus, I swear, it's like all of you are incapable of giving more than the bare minimum."

His eyebrows pinch together as he openly frowns. "I forgot how fickle humans can be."

"Fickle? You're calling *me* fickle? You were the one who tried killing me earlier today, but have changed your mind and *I'm* the fickle one? Okay asshole. Sure."

"How did you obtain your magic?" he asks as he steps forward.

I instinctively raise my arms in front of me. Fear flits down my spine as my magic slowly starts to drain from me, the lavender cloud turning into a thin mist. It's nearly gone. *This must be what his powers do.*

"Stay back," I order as I take a few steps away from him and immediately sigh in relief as my magic fills me up again.

He must use a radius around himself that neutralizes the magic. Can he make it bigger than it currently is or is that his limitation? Is there a way I can safely figure that out? *Probably not,* I think grimly.

"That's not the magic you were using earlier today," he states as he tilts his head sideways while studying the lavender cloud with gold lightning streaking through it. "Show me the other one."

"No way! I'm not doing anything you ask. You tried *killing* me today. I'm not going to pretend that didn't happen."

"What is your name?"

"Sloane," I answer without hesitation because apparently I'm Pavlov's bitch.

"Sloane, you will either answer my questions or I will kill you. Those are your only two options. It was not my intent to come here to kill you but if I am not given the information I seek, I will carry out The Tribunals orders. Now... Show me the magic you used earlier."

"Why should I trust you? You say you won't kill me, but what if the second I bring my magic forward you make a move on me?"

The right side of his lip ticks up in mild amusement, but it doesn't meet his eyes. "I intend to do exactly that."

"You just said you weren't going to kill me," I shout as a gold lightning streaks angrily towards him but fizzles out of existence three feet from him.

"Bring forward your magic," he orders.

"No!"

"Very well then."

A moment later, he moves too fast for me to react. Except I'm already reacting as a painful tingle engulfs my body like a thousand pin prick needles covering every surface. The lavender smoke and gold lightning magic disappear completely, but an explosion of apple scented smoke consumes the room as I teleport and end up directly behind Zyvn as he swings his sword down on the spot where I used to be standing.

"How are you doing that?" he asks as he turns on his toes, swinging his sword towards my head.

My hands instinctively come up to protect me and as they do so, I feel the magic burst out of my arm towards the impending blade. I know the moment the magic hits the blade because the hand that Zyvn uses to hold his sword gets violently thrown off its trajectory, missing me by a mile.

"I don't know," I confess as my heart rapidly beats against my chest and my breath comes out in big gulps.

I'm terrified, but I also feel *alive*. The magic thrums inside me like a living, breathing entity. But this time it feels a little different, like my psyche is scratching at its doorstep trying to get in to gain control of the magic. It's almost as though my nails are scratching against a steel door. No matter how hard I try, there's no way I can gain access to the old, deep magic when my attempts are weak and feeble.

Zyvn moves quickly, drawing my attention back to him. He swings the sword towards my gut and I'm teleported to the other side of the kitchen. Zyvn's grey eyes look alert and eager as he spins around, using parkour moves as he launches himself over the kitchen island towards me.

"How did you obtain this magic?" he asks and he's not even out of breath.

Meanwhile, I can't get a full inhale in and I'm starting to feel sick to my stomach from the smoke–apple infested air. I sprint around the kitchen island, away from him, but my foot stupidly gets caught on a stool and I tumble to my hands and knees.

Before I can get up, a painful burst of magic covers the expanse of my back as the sword comes bearing down on me. I cry out, mostly shocked by the impact, but I won't deny the pain I feel. Zyvn pushes his weight into the sword and I *feel* it slice into the magic that's protecting my back.

How is he doing that? How is his sword creating a *tear* in my magic? Is that normal? Horror grips me as I realize if I stay in this position, that sword will eventually cut through the protective layer and sever my spine in two.

"Stop," I cry out because it's the only thing I can think to do in my current situation. He said he didn't come here to kill me. Hopefully he was telling the truth.

Zyvn doesn't let up, his sword pressing down onto my back as I remain on my hands and knees. The pain of using my magic and his sword cutting through said magic is making me lose focus. My vision warps as I'm overwhelmed by nausea. I genuinely might pass out if he keeps going.

"*Stop!*"

A burst of magic expels from me at the same time I shout. Zyvn's sword flies off my back, embedding into the ceiling as my body collapses onto my stomach. Rapid panting echoes within the apartment. It feels as though I've run a marathon I had no training for.

Sweat coats my entire body. I have no energy to move, no energy to lift even my pinky finger. Any attempts to do so are met with an empty void so vast and dark, I briefly wonder if I have arms and legs.

If Zyvn wants to kill me, now is the perfect time to do so. I'm completely vulnerable and unprotected.

My vision distorts as my chest tightens. Air rapidly passes through my airways but it's constrained. Am I going to die? After I worked so hard to prevent Chad's wish from coming true?

It's not fair. I haven't done anything wrong. I'm not killing humans or even hurting them. Is the cold seriously worth killing me over? I haven't made any attempts to go to Odantha. I've stayed in my lane, I've mostly kept to my old lifestyle, I don't interact with anyone except Balthazar, Umbra, and any customer service people. That's it. I shouldn't be killed merely for existing the way I do.

"What do you want from me?" I pant out as I try to flip over onto my back.

My attempts are not going well when my body is completely spent. My only option right now is to distract him with conversation. If I can keep him talking long enough so that feeling comes back to my body, I'll have a chance at surviving.

"How did you obtain this magic?" he asks.

"I don't know," I answer honestly. There's no point in lying anymore. "I've had it ever since I was turned."

"Turned?" Zyvn asks and it's the first time I hear true emotion in his voice.

My line of sight is limited due to my position on the floor. I can't see the expression on his face, but I imagine he looks confused based on how his voice sounds.

"Yes," I reply before groaning loudly as I finally manage to shift onto my side. I glance up at Zyvn as he hovers over me.

Just as I expected, his eyebrows are pinched together as he scowls at me in confusion. He's trying to make sense of what I've told him, but judging by the look on his face, it's not going well.

"What do you mean by 'turned?'"

"My wish," I answer. "I asked to be turned into a devil for all eternity. This is the magic I got with it."

He's quiet for a few moments as he processes what I've said. I watch him carefully, looking for any sudden moves, but his stance is rather relaxed. Despite me being a sitting duck, he doesn't appear to care how easy it would be to kill me. At least, not yet.

My nerves calm as I take a deep inhale. For now, I can relax too.

"If you've worded your wish correctly," he says as our eyes connect, "that means you've found a way to avoid soul collection."

"I'm hoping so," I confess from the awkward position on my side. "If you're not going to kill me, will you bring me to the sofa?"

"Your magic has drained you of your energy."

It should be a question but he says it as a statement.

"Yeah, so will you help me to the couch?" I ask.

"It would be so easy to kill you."

Terror stabs through my calm demeanor, but I do my best to remain unruffled by what he's said. I don't want to give him any ideas. Instead, I need to remind him what he told me earlier before our fight.

"You said you weren't here to kill me. Are you telling me you're a liar?"

"When it suits me," he answers simply.

My blood turns cold as I realize I'm not out of the woods yet. Why didn't it cross my mind that he might have come here to find a weakness in my magic? That's such a basic yet smart thing to do. And I stupidly let him goad me into it.

I'm not sure if my magic will still work, if it'll protect me from an attack when I'm this spent. I've never been in this kind of situation before. Everything's still too new to me. What should I do?

Call for help.

Right! Balthazar will be able to save me. Hopefully, I can reach him telepathically. If he has that turned off, there will be Hell to pay.

Balthazar, I need you. I need help, I think as strongly as I can while Zyvn crouches beside me. *I'm in danger.* Zyvn's studying me as his gaze roams over me like a predator with a slight furrow to his pronounced brow.

"Your magic is like nothing I've ever seen in Jeznians," he states more to himself than to me.

"They say you're over 3,000 years old," I venture to say, testing out on how much he's willing to depart with.

I just need to keep Zyvn preoccupied long enough for Balthazar to swoop in and save the day. That's it. But where the Hell is he?

Balthazar! Help!

"Indeed, I am," Zyvn answers airily, most of his attention on my body and not on the conversation. "Yet, I have never bore witness to this type of magic within a Jeznian or an Odanthian. This magic is… old," he says as he reaches out a hand to touch me. "Older than it has any right to be."

His hand is calloused against my skin as he grabs my arm and inspects it. "There are two forms of magic within you," he murmurs, turning my arm over and over like he'll find what he's looking for by inspecting it. "A devil should not be capable of such a feat."

"Yeah, well, devils aren't usually humans first," I quip as he rolls me onto my back, his eyes studying me like a science experiment. It's starting to freak me out. He might legitimately slice me open in an attempt to get to my magic.

Balthazar! Zyvn is here! I need help! I can't move!

"Yes, you are the first of your kind. I suppose that leaves room for these kinds of unexpected outcomes. I am curious…

Why would you make the mistake of selling your soul?" he asks casually as his eyes flick up to meet my gaze.

"Excuse me?" I balk at his question.

"I have always wondered what would possess a human to make such an erroneous decision."

"Fuck you," I spit out and I actually manage to pull my arm away from his hands. He does nothing to stop me.

Zyvn stares at me devoid of emotion, but I can see the judgment in his eyes. He thinks I'm an idiot for selling my soul, like I'm the same as all the other humans who sold their souls for wealth and greed. It's insulting.

I sit up onto my elbows, my arms shaky due to lack of strength, but I glare at him with all the anger I possess.

"I sold my soul because *assholes* like you don't give a shit about collateral damage. Balthazar showed up at my apartment to kill me and I did the only thing I could think of to save my life. Where were you, huh? Where was a Champion ready to fight Balthazar off and protect my life? I was left to my own means so I solved the problem the only way I knew how. 3,000 years old and you're *still* a judgmental ass. Prick."

His jaw pulses as his fingers curl into tight fists and a glare settles on his face. The glare is more pronounced due to the silver paint highlighting the wrinkles and furrows of the muscles in his face. If I wasn't enraged, the look on his face would worry me, but right now all it does is piss me off even more.

"A devil is not allowed to kill a human. It is a violation of ordinance 15.17 section A."

"Even if he's fulfilling the wish of another human?" I challenge. I don't miss the shift in Zyvn's demeanor as he realizes what I've said.

He sits back on his feet as he silently regards me. I can see how deeply he's mulling over everything I've told him. Maybe he's trying to find a flaw in what I've said, but even if he does find one, there's nothing I can do to change it. I've already made my decisions. There's no turning back time.

"You could have simply let him kill you instead of clinging on to life," Zyvn states. "There was a possibility your future would have been Odantha."

"Odantha was never in the cards for me," I tell him as I push up into a fully seated position.

Little by little, my energy is returning. My legs feel like jelly, but they should be back to normal within the next ten or so minutes based on how my recovery is going. Thank God it happens quickly or else I'd *really* be screwed.

"Are you saying you are a bad person?" Zyvn asks.

It's a fair question but it still angers me because I honestly don't know. I never considered myself a bad person, but at this point, what do I know? I was born with a Jeznian soul. I was destined for Jeznia before I took my first breath. Maybe my entire life I was uselessly fighting against the current.

"I was a human born with a Jeznian soul," I answer, my voice barely above a whisper as my eyes cling to his.

"That is impossible," he argues, brows furrowing together as his eyes dart back and forth between mine.

"No, it isn't."

Zyvn's brow deepens even further as he shakes his head. "It *is* impossible. The Creator would never allow such an occurrence to happen. It is unnatural. The devil is lying to you."

"He's not–"

"He is–"

"*But he's not,*" I snap at him.

"The Creator would never allow such an anomaly to occur," Zyvn insists, his voice angered and offended that I would suggest such a thing.

"Yet Balthazar pulled out a red orb from me when I sold him my soul," I reply back just as angered and offended as Zyvn. "He triple checked to make sure I was human. *I was there* when the Records Keeper confirmed it was *my* soul.

"Balthazar doesn't understand how it happened either, but it's a fact. I was a human born with a Jeznian soul. You weren't there, you didn't see what I saw."

"It does not matter that I was not present. The Creator follows strict rules to help balance out the three worlds. Giving a human a Jeznian soul goes against everything the Creator stands for. The devil has deceived you. He must have procured a Jeznian soul to trick you into selling your soul."

I understand Zyvn's distrust towards Balthazar but it's starting to grate on my nerves. Saying the same thing over and over again isn't going to change my reality. I *was* born with a Jeznian soul. Balthazar *isn't* lying to me. He's worried about the fact that I have old, deep magic. If Balthazar had it his way like he originally intended, I'd be a weak devil who could easily stay under the radar. But that's just not how things worked out.

"I get it," I tell Zyvn. "I really do. It's hard to wrap your head around something so life shattering, but Balthazar isn't lying. The Creator isn't as noble as you believe it to be."

"This is not possible. You have allowed yourself to be duped by the devil, but I cannot say that I am surprised. Humans are irrational creatures who lack the foresight and intellect required when dealing with the other worlds. It is why your world remains cut off from the others. You should be embarrassed by how easily you have been deceived, but you would first need the awareness to acknowledge your gullibility."

I open my mouth to tell him off, but someone else beats me to the punch, voice dripping in venom as a lowly growl reverberates within the condo.

"That's my wife you're insulting."

X

B ALTHAZAR STANDS DIRECTLY behind Zyvn, a
dagger pressed against his throat while the other hand grips
Zyvn's wrist. Balthazar looks infuriated as his eyes snap to
mine, the black gone from his irises.

"Are you harmed?" he asks as his gaze roves over my
body looking for any wounds.

"No, I'm ok," I answer. "My magic physically exhausted
me so I can't fully move around yet, but he didn't hurt me."

"I wasn't trying to," Zyvn states calmly, completely
unbothered by the knife pressed against his neck. "I only
wanted to see her magic in action."

"What makes you think I'm going to buy your bullshit?"
Balthazar sneers as he dips his head forward so his lips are
near Zyvn's ears.

He digs the dagger into Zyvn's skin and I'm not shocked
to see a trickle of blood at the tip of the knife.

"If I wanted her dead, I would have killed her before you
arrived. She was incapacitated with no way of defending
herself, yet she lives. You may keep the knife on my throat if
it'll make you feel better but be assured you will not be
killing me today."

"Is that so?" Balthazar asks before he plunges the knife forward into Zyvn's neck before pulling it back out.

Blood gushes out of the hole he's created and my jaw drops, a gasp flying out of my mouth. Is it really easy to kill Zyvn? A stab to the throat and he's gone after 3,000 years? He'd been so difficult for me to pin down. Yet, Balthazar struts right up to Zyvn and kills him like it's nothing.

"It takes more than that to kill a Beastial," Zyvn unsurprisingly states as he lifts his hand to the wound in his neck.

He grips his neck tightly and when he releases it, the wound is gone. There's not even a scar to show where he had been stabbed. His blood soaked clothes are the only piece of evidence Balthazar ever stabbed him. I can't say I'm surprised he has healing abilities. He has the power to cut off a devil's magic. Of course he'd be able to heal himself from a stab wound.

"We're not as easy to kill as you devils," Zyvn says in a threatening tone and Balthazar noticeably bristles.

"Yet, you were unable to kill Sloane," Balthazar retaliates as he walks around Zyvn and lifts me to my feet.

Most of my feeling and control has returned now. Painful pins and needles flood my feet as all my weight sinks into them. I'd much rather be sitting down as the feeling comes rushing back.

"Can you take me to the sofa?" I ask Balthazar.

He hoists me up in his arms bridal style and, to my utter shock, turns his back to Zyvn as he walks me over to the couch in the other room. Zyvn wordlessly follows us, his eyes surveying the room as he enters.

It happens quickly. Just as Zyvn walks through the threshold of the room, Umbra descends from her spot on the ceiling. She holds a sickle scythe gripped firmly in her left hand as she aims for Zyvn.

He reacts expertly, using his forearm armor to deflect her attack and they brawl. She's lithe and quick, using the walls to help her stay just out of his reach, yet he seems to anticipate her every move, dodging her attacks with ease.

"You have a rather sloppy Shadow Seer," Zyvn states in an almost bored manner as he dodges another swipe of Umbra's dagger.

"Shadow Seers are not known for their hand to hand combat," Balthazar replies as he places me on the couch. "But from where I'm standing, she looks like a decent opponent."

"Are you going to stop them?" I ask from my position on the couch. "What if he really kills Umbra?"

"Then she's not worthy of being my Shadow Seer."

"Seriously?" I ask, anger clipping my tone. "After everything she's done for you, you won't help her out even a little bit?"

"Sloane, if I intercede in her fight then I'm stating I have no confidence in her abilities. If she dies, it's because she is unworthy by *both* our standards. I'm letting her handle this because I have the faith that she can."

When he puts it like that, I feel bad I insulted her. But at the same time, *two* against one is always better than one against one. What's so wrong with accepting help every now and then? Wouldn't it be better to kill Zyvn and not have the threat of him looming over us forever?

I know if I said that, Balthazar would just say the same thing he's already told me. Interfering would be the same as him telling Umbra he has no trust in her. He won't do it.

Sighing, I sink a little deeper into the couch as I watch the fight.

Umbra manages to nick Zyvn on his jaw, somersaulting over his arm, before she does a back handspring to land beside Balthazar. She expertly twirls the sickle scythe before clipping it to her waist. Balthazar smirks at Zyvn as if he's gloating. A small trickle of blood trails down Zyvn's jawline.

"Given enough determination, Zyvn, we *will* kill you. You can count on it."

"I look forward to the duel," Zyvn states but he doesn't look entertained in the least bit.

He's slightly out of breath. Envy creeps up my spine as I realize just how much of a workout Umbra gave him. Umbra, a Shadow Seer who has no formal hand to hand training, same as me. Yet she was able to get him slightly out of breath while he treated me as if I were a toddler.

I hate that my competitiveness is rearing its ugly head over something so stupid. Umbra and I are on the same side. A win for her is a win for me. I just hate that I prefer *I* was the one to get the win.

Suddenly, a bright light consumes the room and when it clears, Zyvn is nowhere to be seen.

"Should we move her to a different location, Lord Balthazar?" Umbra asks as soon as Zyvn is gone.

"It won't matter," he replies. "His powers will allow him entry no matter where we go. The Transcribers will make sure to keep track of us if we move. We can't escape him. We have to kill him."

"Hold on a second," I say, my attention turning to them as something vital dawns on me. "What took you so long to get here? I asked for your help *three* times. If he wanted me dead, I *would* be dead. You're lucky you're not talking to a corpse right now."

"It's difficult transporting into a room that doesn't allow magic," Balthazar states. His eyes avert elsewhere as he quietly states, "And... I don't have the keys to the condo."

The shock is instant but is quicky replaced by rage. Did I hear him right? I couldn't have. There's no way I heard him correctly.

"Come again," I say, unable to hide the fury raging within.

"It won't happen again," he opts to say instead of repeating himself.

Red floods my vision as the anger takes over.

"You bet your ass it won't happen again," I shout, jumping up from the couch as I whirl around to glare at him.

Lightning streaks across my chest as lavender smoke curls around me. "I almost *died* because you don't have keys to *your own apartment!*"

The smoke thickens as the lightning activity increases. My hands tremble as I try to reel in my emotions, but all I want to do is hit him into oblivion. How could he not have his keys? If Zyvn had wanted to kill me today, I would be dead right now. No more wishes to save me, no more loopholes to keep me out of the walls of Jeznia, nothing. I'd be dead. All because this asshole doesn't have keys to his goddamn apartment.

"I can't," I say, my eyes sliding shut as I shake my head. I need him to leave before I do something I regret. "I can't deal with you right now. I need you to go."

"Sloane—"

"Go!"

Lightning strikes across the room, narrowly missing Balthazar's feet. He swats his hand before turning his attention to Umbra. With a nod of his head, she disappears into black shadows. He, however, still remains.

"I told you to leave," I scream. "I'm too mad at you and I don't know what I'll do!"

I've never been so out of control before. Then again, I've never had magic at my fingertips before. Yes, I'm mad at him, but I'm also scared of what I might do. What if the old magic comes out? Will Balthazar be able to protect himself against it?

"You need to go," I order him, body trembling as the lightning continues to streak around me.

Instead, Balthazar pulls me down onto the couch as his arms curl tightly around me. My body falls into his and his forehead bumps against mine.

Instantly, I struggle against his tight hold. "Let me—"

"No," he breathes out, his voice quiet and gentle as he holds me against his chest. "Fight me if you must. Stab me, punch me, do whatever you believe I deserve. I almost lost you twice today due to my own shortcomings. Punish me however you see fit."

"Punish you…" I trail off because his abrupt admittance barrels into me and I'm at a loss for words.

He had kept his composure pretty well while Zyvn and Umbra were here, but now that we're alone, I can't miss the way his body trembles beneath mine or how the tightness of his hold borderlines painful or the slight quiver to his inhales. He's *scared* and he probably doesn't know what to do with it.

It dawns on me that the more danger I get into, the more used to it I become. I have an easier time compartmentalizing it, blocking it out, and moving on from it. But Balthazar…

the more danger I get in, the harder it is for him to manage his fear, anxiety, and worry. He's never cared for anyone this way before. He's never had his heart walking outside his chest.

And now, he's asking for his punishment, a *physical* and *painful* punishment probably to replace the emotional turmoil he's in. What do people say? It's easier to handle physical pain than it is to handle emotional pain. Balthazar probably has no idea how to process all this.

A heavy sigh expels from my mouth as my arms finally wrap around him. He shifts us around, causing me to fall backwards onto the couch. He sinks into me, lying completely on top of me. His forehead presses into the side of my neck, his cheek resting against my collar bone as his arms slide underneath me.

The full weight of his body falls on top of me almost as if he means to protect me with his body. If Zyvn were to suddenly come back, Balthazar would be in the perfect position to take the brunt of any attack.

My vision blurs as I stare up at the ceiling, tears sliding gently down the side of my face. All the rage dissipates from me as I envision the terror he must have been feeling when I called for help desperate and afraid, when he knew Zyvn was attacking me but he had no way to get inside, when the fear became too much, clouding his mind and judgment. I can't imagine how he must have felt while unable to use his magic, being forced to use rudimentary means to get inside the apartment, all while being terrified out of his mind that he'd find me dead.

My arms squeeze tighter around him, a few more teardrops sliding down my face.

"Zyvn isn't going to kill me, Balthazar," I tell him gently, my fingers threading through his hair. His grip tightens around me as his body fully envelops me in a bear hug. "He had the chance to do it today and he didn't take the opportunity. He won't kill me."

"He didn't kill you *today*, Sloane, that is all. The next time you two cross paths, he won't be so honorable."

"I don't think so," I breathe out in a quiet voice, my eyes studying the white ceiling as I play with the thick, soft strands of his hair. "The whole point of today's visit was to figure me out but in the end, all I gave him were more questions than answers. I told him I was born with a Jeznian soul and he couldn't wrap his head around it."

"You shouldn't have told him that," Balthazar instantly chides me. He lifts his head high enough to offer me a small glare. "The Tribunal will insist upon your immediate death once they hear that."

"Zyvn doesn't seem to care about what they want," I say. "They already want me dead. He told me so. And he said normally he'd do what they wanted, but I think I'm a mystery he wants to solve."

"And once that mystery is solved," Balthazar says as he lies his head back down, "you will be out of luck."

"Thanks for the vote of confidence," I gripe.

He sighs heavily, arms squeezing me a little tighter. "I mean no offense, but Zyvn has perfected the art of killing devils. *Powerful* devils. I fear even with your special magic you may not be a match for him."

"Not now, but I will be," I say.

"I like your confidence, Sloane."

There's a gentle lull of silence and I swear Balthazar's drifting off to sleep. I almost let him but I'm not entirely done with the conversation. Zyvn had been so convinced it was impossible for me to be born with a Jeznian soul. Balthazar must think it strange too. I can't help but wonder if he's searching for answers and not telling me.

"Are you looking into why my soul is Jeznian?" I softly ask, fingers still playing with his hair.

"Admittedly, Sloane, my attention has been pulled elsewhere."

When he doesn't expand upon the statement, I give his hair a slight tug. "Are you going to tell me what *does* have your attention?"

He heaves out a loud sigh, his body relaxing even more and I feel the true, deep weight of him on top of me. I revel in the feeling as I wrap my legs around his hips, hooking my feet underneath the inner parts of his thighs. Just three weeks ago he declared the devil didn't cuddle yet now look at him.

"Zagon is up to something and I suspect no good will come of it," Balthazar states and my thoughts immediately race back to the House meeting we attended a couple hours ago.

Taron made a big stink, saying Zagon was making important moves yet had nothing to show for it. Still, Balthazar backed up that claim, saying whatever Zagon is working on will create shock waves throughout the three worlds: Jeznia, Ephiri, and Odantha. That can't be good.

"Why do you think whatever he's doing is going to affect the three worlds?" I ask.

"I presume he's grown bored, Sloane. Usually when that happens, immortals go to war or they die."

"Go to war?"

"Yes," he breathes out. "War is the only way to overturn rules put forth by the Creator. For instance, if Zagon wishes to no longer be constrained by the cold, he would need to defeat Odantha and make an appeal with the Creator. From what I know, the Creator often sides with the victor."

"So, basically whoever wins gets whatever they want no matter how damaging it'll be to everyone else," I say as the impact of what Balthazar's saying hits me full force.

"Precisely," he hums out as he snuggles a little bit deeper into the crook of my neck, completely unaware of how life shattering that piece of information was to me. "It is why Odantha fights so hard to keep Jeznia in check. They prefer the mediocre yet delicate balance of the three worlds."

"And you?" I ask, heart in my throat as I wait for his answer. "Do you prefer it that way too?"

His head rests atop my chest. He can probably hear how fast my heart is racing. Anticipating his answer has my stomach tightening into knots. What if he says something I don't want to hear? What if he wants to wreak havoc on Ephiri because he's also bored? I can't support that – *I won't*. Even when the time comes when everyone I know and love is deceased, I would never want to subject the people on Earth to the likes of Jeznians. I can only imagine the kind of diabolical torture Jeznians would bring upon humans.

"Frankly, I don't care what happens," he answers with a deep exhale. "The lives of Ephirians means so little to me."

"So, what happens when your father and I are at odds?"

He lifts his head to stare me in the eyes, his eyebrow cocked up as mild offense grabs hold of his handsome face. "Are you genuinely asking me that question?"

"I need to hear you say it," I tell him.

His head dips for the briefest of moments before he looks at me with a seriousness that lets me know there are no lies in the words he speaks.

"I choose you, Sloane. Always."

That's probably the closest he'll ever get to saying he loves me and I couldn't ask for more even if I wanted it. But I don't care about that. I care about his answer.

A soft sigh of relief blows out my mouth as a smile spreads across my lips. My hand lifts to gently caress his face as I reply in kind.

"I choose you too, Balthazar. Always and forever."

TWO FULL WEEKS manage to pass by without any hiccups or further attacks from Zyvn. Balthazar has cautioned me to be careful whenever I practice my magic but hasn't outright suggested I stop. The urgency for me to become stronger outweighs Zyvn's unannounced attacks. The gruesome reality is both sides are now against me. We're forced to risk sound judgment in favor of quicker results. It can't be helped. I *have* to practice magic.

Little by little, I become better and gain more control. I can now change the color of anything I want to my heart's desire. I can levitate objects the same size as a large mixing bowl and move said object smoothly around a room. My magic control and strength are nowhere where they need to be, but the improvement has given me hope that I'll get where I need to before I'm killed.

I've also spent the past two weeks studying up on Jeznia and Odantha. I've learned quite a bit even with the minimal information I've been supplied with.

For instance, Zagon prefers brute strength and power above all else despite being the House of Shadow Seers – House Aides who aren't well trained in hand to hand combat and instead focus on stealth and obtaining secrets. Zagon's love of brute strength is a particularly intriguing fact considering that Taron implied Zagon has requested the support of House Aranea, the House of the Blood Reapers.

From what Balthazar's reports state, Blood Reapers have no need for strength when their power allows them to control the body of the victim whose blood they drink. It would be most useful to train Blood Reapers in speed and stamina, *not* strength. Knowing what their specialty is, it begs the question: who is Zagon trying to control and why? Unfortunately, neither Balthazar nor I have any ideas.

As it currently stands, all we can do is keep our heads down and continue on our determined paths.

Rowers glide by on the Charles River while I sit on a bench with a hot pumpkin spiced latte within my hands. Cool weather has settled over Boston despite tomorrow's forecast of mid 70s. It's comfortable weather, requiring pants and a sweater for the relaxed and shorts and a T for the active.

As I sit gazing out at the water, I lazily practice my magic, changing the color of the bench railing every couple of minutes. It requires so little effort now, but I won't ever forget what Balthazar told me. The Lords fear him despite how young he is because they became complacent. Magic weakens if it's not used regularly. I won't ever make that mistake. No matter how easy it becomes, even if it's as easy as breathing air, I will always practice.

There have only been three House meetings since the one Lord Taron called two weeks ago, which Balthazar has admitted is odd. He's convinced something is going on behind the scenes and they're explicitly leaving him out of it. He doesn't say much, but I can see the worry in his eyes. He's afraid they're working with Zagon to target me.

There's nothing I can say or do to comfort him, which just makes me feel utterly useless. Besides, he might be correct in assuming everyone is working against him. The Houses don't like Balthazar and it's not like there's any familial love between Balthazar and his father.

A heavy sigh blows out my mouth as I analyze everything I know. It's not much. We have more unknowns than answers.

We need to know who Zagon's targeting. We need to know if the Houses are working together without Balthazar. We need to know why my soul is red. We need to know how and why I have old, deep magic. We need to know if there's anyone else who knows I have old magic. We need to know what Odantha's doing in all of this.

There's too much stuff we *need* to know and not a lot of ways to safely figure it out.

"You are more refined with your lesser magic," Zyvn's voice interrupts my thoughts as he suddenly appears a few feet in front of me.

He blocks my view of the river, but at the moment, I don't care. I chuck my drink at him at the same time I bolt from the bench. If he's back again, it's safest to assume he's here to kill me. Even though he had the chance to take me by surprise and didn't, it's safer to assume I'm in danger whenever he's around.

Problem is… I'm not as fast as Zyvn. I take only three steps before his calloused hand curls around my wrist and he yanks me backwards. I anticipate the painful tingles of my magic to flood my system but they never come. Zyvn has either found a way to nullify the old magic or he isn't attempting to kill me.

"Let me go," I yell as I tug my hand from his but his grip is too powerful.

"Settle down, Sloane. I am only here to talk."

"You don't need to be holding my wrist to talk, Zyvn," I snap as I glare at him.

"You are ignoring the fact that the only reason why I am holding your hand right now is to prevent you from running away. Or was that *not* what you were doing just a moment ago?"

"I'm not running now, am I?" I ask rhetorically.

Yet despite that, he answers. "No, because I am holding you in place."

My glare deepens as irritation courses through my veins. He seems like the kind of guy who *always* has to get the last word in. That doesn't surprise me much. It's an ego thing and to be 3,000 years old *without* an ego seems impossible. He also probably thinks he's always right, has lost his sense of humor, and probably uses mind games as a way to torture someone to death because where's the fun in stabbing someone?

"If I promise not to run away, will you let me go?" I ask and it can't be helped that my tone is a little too haughty.

He's seriously annoying.

"I would have to trust you for your promise to carry any weight."

"Fine. What do you want, Zyvn?" I ask in a clipped tone as I try my very hardest not to roll my eyes at him.

"We need to talk. I have news about your supposed red soul."

XI

I OUTWARLDLY SIGH as I shake my head. "I already told you Balthazar isn't lying about my soul."

"I agree with you and that makes this all the more troubling," Zyvn replies as he finally releases my wrist. "A human should not have a Jeznian soul. Perhaps that is why your magic is so old."

My fingers rub my wrist where he grabbed me as I contemplate his words. It makes sense a human having a Jeznian soul would end up having different magic. It's the simplest answer to a complicated scenario. Still, it's a little embarrassing to think I haven't connected the dots on that.

"Have you found anything out about why a human might be born with a non—human soul?" I ask.

"I have informed The Tribunal about the anomaly," he answers instead, completely ignoring my question. "They have ordered I ensure your death."

That's exactly what Balthazar said was going to happen. It doesn't surprise me that The Tribunal's doubled down, but it does piss me off. I'm literally not doing anything. I'm not making deals with humans or killing them. I'm not hunting or killing Odanthians. All I'm doing is existing *exactly* as I was prior to being turned a devil. The only difference now is that I have *magic*. So why are they so adamant about killing me?

My gaze shifts to Zyvn, taking in his stance and readiness for a fight. He appears mostly relaxed but I know the kind of fighter he is. Even his calm, unassuming stances are dangerous. He could unsheathe his sword and cut my head off my shoulders in seconds if it weren't for my magic. Even my own ego can admit that The Tribunal sent their best killer to sentence me to death.

My eyebrows furrow together as my anger simmers. Enemy or foe, Zyvn?

"Is this a courtesy notice or something?" I ask, haughtily, a glare forming on my face as we lock gazes. "Have you come to warn me that the next time we meet, you'll be trying to kill me?"

A little smile pulls at the edges of his lips but he quickly squashes it. "I would not be *trying* to kill you, Sloane, but no. This is not that. I have spent the last two weeks in our library looking for any hint of information regarding this topic. I stumbled upon a reference to keys and the souls, but the scripture was faded, making it illegible. I have come to request if Balthazar has any insight or if he is looking into why your soul is red."

"Last we spoke about it, he didn't have anything new to share with me," I answer honestly. "He's been a bit preoccupied between his job and trying to figure out what his father is up to."

Zyvn's expression immediately sours, a scowl forming on his face as the atmosphere around him darkens. "Jeznia's High King?"

"Yup, that's the one," I answer as I watch him as nonchalantly as I can for any miniscule reactions. He doesn't give much away. "Balthazar thinks his dad might be bored."

"A bored king is a dangerous thing," Zyvn declares, mirroring Balthazar's sentiment two weeks ago.

It's a little off putting and yet, jolts me into the realization of how similar the two of them are. Not with how they speak, but rather with how they draw the same conclusions and how they hold themselves with an air of confidence so strong, it's pungent.

I haven't met Zagon or any of the Heralds who rule over Odantha, but no one else I've met from the other worlds exudes as much confidence as Balthazar and Zyvn do. They walk around as if nothing exists in the three worlds that could hurt them, let alone kill them. It's fascinating and strange how similar they are.

I try to squash the smile that begs to be let free at the idea of telling Zyvn and Balthazar they're more alike than they'd like to admit. I'm pretty sure they would lose their shit if I told them that. It's tempting. *Really* tempting, but I bite back the words. Pissing Zyvn off won't do me any favors and I need as many favors as I can get from the Beastial sent to assassinate me.

"Inform me of anything new you learn," Zyvn orders me. "Merely call my name and I will arrive as soon as I can."

Before I can make any request of my own, he's engulfed by a white light. When the light clears, Zyvn's gone.

A heavy sigh blows out my mouth as I stare out at the Charles River. Staring at it but not really seeing the boats and rowers going by. My thoughts turn over the little information Zyvn shared with me. It really isn't much, but it's more than what I had five minutes ago.

He said he found references to keys and souls. Keys to what? Are they literal keys? Could there be a key tucked away within my soul?

My best guess would be if my soul *had* a key, it would be the whole thing. If I've learned anything from cinema, it's that keys can take any shape or size when it comes to the supernatural and fantastical.

But what if my soul isn't a key? Is there a key and my soul is a lock or companion piece to the key? Zyvn quiet literally gave me useless information. It's created more questions than insight. Still… I'm grateful he shared it with me. He didn't have to do that. It's not like I knew he found new information. He gave that to me unprompted. Which means he's desperate to figure this puzzle. That's good. Until that answer cures his curiosity and, subsequently, my protection from him.

"Lord Balthazar won't like learning you've joined forces with the enemy," Umbra's voice startles me.

I spin around on my toes to see her staring at me with harsh amber eyes. She wears her anger well and, if we hadn't already discussed it, I'd be convinced she was in love with Balthazar. She's very protective of him and whatever agenda he has. Why? Why is it so important to her?

There's no mistaking the betrayal within her eyes. She believes I've thrown Balthazar under the bus for my own selfish reasons. A pit forms in my stomach. I need to smooth things over in order for our team to work efficiently. With everyone else gunning for me, I can't afford to have someone so close to Balthazar working against us.

"Balthazar will learn to like it once he hears Zyvn and I have entered a truce of sorts."

"I heard no such dealings," she hisses at me, her anger growing as it consumes her entire body. I've never seen her so expressive before. Allying with Zyvn has really tipped her over the edge. "Only a fool would believe such a thing."

"Then I'm a fool, Umbra," comes my petty reply, "but I'm trusting my gut. Zyvn won't kill me, not until he figures out what I am. Also, let me remind you that he *can't* kill me because of my magic."

"He need only tire you out before the opportunity presents itself."

Shit. She makes a valid point. I pinch the bridge of my nose in aggravation.

"Just trust me, alright?" I demand because I don't have a counter argument for what she's said.

I know how stupid and pathetic I sound, but I can't explain logically why I know he won't kill me. He just won't. I *know* he won't. He *shared* that information with me *willingly.* I guess he could be setting up a trap. I certainly don't know him well enough to spot a trap, but it's a risk I have to take. I'll do my best to play him while he plays me, but in the meantime, I'm going to collect information.

"You have no trust of mine," Umbra harshly states. "Lord Balthazar overexaggerates your intellect. He offers you too much leniency. Believing you've entered a truce with Zyvn is naïve and going to put our goal in jeopardy. It will bring me great pleasure to take your last breath once Lord Balthazar finally realizes your incompetence."

I hate to admit it but she's a good second–in–command. One Balthazar deserves. Even so, she has no right to speak to me like I'm a *child.* I'm not as stupid and naïve as she believes I am. My instincts have gotten me far in life. I know Zyvn won't harm me. He'll be a good resource for us. He can get us information from the other side. *Current* information, not something that's outdated.

The rage that was simmering within explodes to a burning inferno.

Good second–in–command aside, she forgets her place and who she's talking to. I am the *wife* of Lord Balthazar while she's the employee. She can't keep walking over me. I need to remind her of my position and power. If I don't, she'll continue to see me as less than and treat me as such.

She doesn't have to agree with what I do, but she has to respect it.

I step towards her, my shoulders pulling back as I give her my best glare. "You speak to me like that again and I'll gut you."

The words drip like venom from my mouth, burning me on their way out, but the release is euphoric. Taking charge is empowering. I need to shed this pathetic victim mentality where all these horrible things are *happening* to me. Not anymore. People want to fuck around with me? Then I'll fuck right back. I've got *magic*. I'm not human anymore. I need to stop pretending that I am. I'm a *devil* and Lord Balthazar's *owner*. I'm stronger than how I behave, stronger than Umbra, and it's about time I owned it.

"I am going to do things *my* way," I tell her as I close the distance between us, only allowing for about half a foot between us.

She doesn't back down, doesn't cower from me, but I wouldn't expect her to. She's a hardened badass who has probably seen things I can't even dream of. She's not scared of me. *But one day she will be.*

"If you have a problem with the way I handle things... scratch that, I don't care. It's my way or the highway. You're either on board or you're out. So, what'll it be, Umbra?"

"Til death do us part," she says but there's no ounce of kindness in her voice. Only pure hatred.

I recognize the message for the threat that it is. If I don't deliver on my attempt of being this scary new person, I'm dead by her hands.

My anger bursts from me, igniting as fire along my horns. The fire crackles loudly, whooshing in the wind as my eyes narrow into an unforgiving glare. Everyone thinks they can kill me, that it's their *right* to kill me. I'm sick of it. I might not be able to do anything about the others, but Umbra is part of House Primis. She is Balthazar's Shadow Seer and, by default, an ally of mine. She can't and she *shouldn't* be treating me this way.

"Watch your tone when you speak to me," I order darkly. "I may be new at this, but I'm a quick learner."

A smirk darts across Umbra's face as she sizes me up and down. "There it is. Peccatum suum. You won't disappoint."

"Excuse me?" I practically shriek in surprise as the flames quickly die out, taking all my rage with them.

What is she going on about? I won't disappoint? About what?

"Your helpless human act is no longer useful," she states in a low tone. "Lord Balthazar is coddling you, giving you time to adjust, but that will get you killed. If not by me, then by Zyvn. If not by Zyvn, then by another House. You need to awaken the hate in your heart."

"You said Balthazar's heart made him stronger," I argue.

"*Your* heart makes you weak," she states, eyes narrowed. "You and Lord Balthazar are not the same. If you indulge that heart of yours, you'll never amount to anything. Where is the anger that had you attacking Chad in broad daylight? That had you kill Finthorn? Without it, you are nothing. Even with your magic."

"Fuck you," I snap at her, the flames coming back alive as I shove her. I hate that she lets me. "I'm going to prove you wrong, Umbra, and when I do, you'll regret ever provoking me."

"No. I won't."

"What is your problem?" I ask as I step away from her to angrily pace. Words fly out of my mouth and I'm embarrassed to admit I'm grasping at straws. "Why do you hate me so much? Are you *lying* about loving Balthazar?"

Her upper lip sneers as she levels me with a look of raw anger. "I have no feelings of love towards Lord Balthazar. I'm pushing you because Lord Balthazar won't. Your power is the piece that's missing in our plan and he's letting you squander it! The stronger you become, the greater the chances of our success. I'm done watching the two of you piss it away. I will kill you myself before I watch you ruin what Lord Balthazar and I have aimed towards."

Her outburst stops me in my tracks. This is important to her. Whatever she and Balthazar are scheming is greater than life and death. It's something she *cares* about. That's unusual for a Jeznian. No wonder she's so desperate to kill me. I'm a liability.

I inhale deeply, a strange calmness coming over me. My anger's gone and when I speak, my voice is level. She practically flinches at the difference.

"Duly noted," I say. "But know that sometimes in order to become stronger, you have to gain more knowledge. Zyvn will prove his usefulness to us. I know it.

"Trust me or don't," I say as I hold her gaze, "but if you go up against me, know that you will lose. I don't care how new to this I am. I don't care that you were born Jeznian. My power supersedes yours. Fall in line or get snuffed out. It's your choice."

She stares at me for a long hard moment, anger and smugness mixed together upon her face, before she vanishes in black shadows. My eyes roll skyward at her dramatics before I flop down on the bench.

Just what exactly are Balthazar and Umbra doing? And why hasn't he told me about it? It's unsettling. I've been stupidly so blind in my trust with him. I always think I have all the information but then he drops these bombs on me.

The cold doesn't affect you.

It's because of how I granted your wish.

I cannot express how much I appreciate what he's done for me, but I can't help but wonder why he didn't tell me. And now, with these incessant comments about a plan, I'm starting to wonder just how much he is holding back from me. I should talk to him, ask him what she meant. But what will he say? Will he say nothing? Will he threaten to kill her? Will he even bother with a warning?

Her words cut through my building doubts.

Lord Balthazar is coddling you.

I'm pushing you because Lord Balthazar won't.

Your power is the piece that's missing in our plan.

My power is the piece that's missing in their plan. What does that even mean? It sounds like I'm just a tool for them, a weapon to help them win whatever game they're playing at.

But what about the person beneath it all? What about what *I* want? I never agreed to their plan. I don't even know what it is!

A deep sigh falls out of my mouth as my head falls forward into my hands. My elbows rest on my thighs as I study the intricate concrete beneath my feet.

Balthazar cares about me. I know that. But to what degree? He *said* he'd follow me to the ends of the universe but that's because I'm destined to rule and take what's mine. What if I'm not those things he says I am? Before we met, I never would have described myself that way. He brought that out in me. But does that mean he only sees a small part of who I am instead of the whole picture?

Lord Balthazar is coddling *you.*

It never crossed my mind that Balthazar would do such a thing. I didn't even know he was capable of it. But with the facts laid bare, I guess he has been. He gave me seven years to adjust to Jeznia so I wouldn't have to dive head first. He's not super on top of me learning magic. Honestly, he works more than he helps me.

I guess he has been coddling me and I've been too naïve to notice. But what does Umbra expect from me even if he was pushing me to my limits? I'm not going to be a seasoned magic user just because she wants me to be. It took Balthazar five years from when he started using magic before he was strong enough to become a Contract Liaison.

Five long years of daily practice under the harassment of his mother.

My eyes squeeze shut as the raw truth slams into me.

I don't have that same luxury. I don't have five years to waste practicing magic. Not with whatever Zagon's doing. Not with the Houses curiosity about my powers. Not with

Odantha wanting me dead. I need a way to speed up the process. And since Balthazar clearly isn't going to be the one to do it, I need to take it into my own hands.

I need something challenging. Something Umbra would suggest if only Balthazar wouldn't chop her head off.

It pops into my head the moment I think of Umbra. I lean back against the bench, my head resting on the bar behind my shoulders as I stare up at the clear blue sky. Air blows uselessly out my mouth. The idea is dangerous, reckless, wild. Unhinged, even. But it's the only plausible way I see myself advancing my magic. *Truly* advancing it. The only problem is Balthazar won't like it.

He won't like it one bit.

XII

I SPEND THE next couple of hours formulating a speech with counter arguments for any resistance I might receive from Balthazar. I can't think of every scenario, but by the time Balthazar arrives at the condo, I'm confident he won't be able to deny my logic. Still, my stomach tightens into knots as anxiety threatens to get the better of me. He's going to *hate* my proposal.

Shortly after 6pm, Balthazar arrives without a sound. His eyebrows immediately furrow together when he sees no food on the kitchen island. I stand off to the side of the island, my fingers fiddling with each other in front of my waist. It's the only clue that gives away how anxious I feel, but Balthazar spots it instantly.

"If this is about the little deal you struck with Zyvn, I admit I'm not pleased with it," Balthazar states as he shifts his entire attention to me, resting his hand lazily atop the kitchen island.

I'm not surprised he already knows about the deal. Umbra probably told him as soon as she left me.

"But you've made several valid points," he states. "I'll go along with it for now. However, the moment he steps out of line, I will interject."

"Oh, that's good," I reply, my breathing somewhat shaky because that's actually not why I'm so nervous right now. "I'm glad to hear you're on board."

His confusion deepens on his face as he takes a step towards me. "Sloane... what has you so tightly wound?"

My stomach bottoms out. I knew he'd cut straight to the point and, despite how long I prepared for it, I still don't feel ready for the argument that's about to happen. *Just rip off the band aid, Sloane.*

"It has come to my attention that you're coddling me," I rush out before quickly moving on to the rest of my speech. "That I'm not being pushed to my full potential.

"Normally, I'd love to be given the time, space, and freedom to learn at my own pace, but unfortunately, we don't have that luxury. The Houses are snooping around to figure me out, Odantha has ordered me dead, *twice*, Zagon's a huge problem if he ever finds out about my real powers... There are too many threats around every corner. I don't have five years to learn magic. I'll be dead by then. I need to get better faster and the only way I can see that happening is..." I trail off before taking a deep inhale.

I can't get a full breath in. My back is too tight and tense. I bite my lower lip before forcing the words out. He's *really* not going to like this.

"I want to go train in the seventh circle," I declare.

"*Absolutely not,*" he bellows, flames instantly igniting on his horns and darting down his back.

I understand his objection. I expected it. But I still flinch at his tone and reply.

He's objecting because the seventh circle is the most brutal of all the circles. They're the bottom feeders and *revel* in it. Jeznia doesn't have merits that far down. Even if they did, the inhabitants wouldn't aspire to own any. They *like* it in their circle. They feel no need to move up higher in the circles.

Case in point, there are never any attempts to break into the sixth circle. They're happy where they are because there's no oversight. They can do whatever they please whenever they want.

Technically, Lord Ruulin of House Scolopendra is in charge of the seventh circle, but according to the notes Umbra gave me, he doesn't involve himself with it. The inhabitants essentially govern themselves and it's vicious. But not having Lord oversight in the circle means I'll be able to practice my magic undetected. No whispers of my presence will be uttered into Ruulin's ears. He'll be none the wiser and so will the rest of the Lords. It's a perfect plan.

Or rather it *would* be perfect if the summary of what goes down in the seventh didn't make my stomach churn. It's no place for a human or a newly minted devil, but I have to progress faster than I currently am. The only way I see myself achieving that is constantly being put into a life and death situation.

"Balthazar, I need to learn my magic at a rate faster than I currently am," I tell him.

"You don't need to go to the seventh circle to achieve it," he snaps as steam billows off him.

The flames of his horns burn bright and hot. Heat rolls off him in waves, filling the five foot gap between us as I'm bathed in his anger.

He's raging on the inside and doing everything he can to keep from lashing out, but I'm not an idiot. I know anger hides the true emotion of whatever a person is feeling and I know Balthazar well enough to know his anger right now is hiding his fear. I don't blame him. Without my magic to protect me, I wouldn't survive the seventh circle. But I've seen my magic in action against a 3,000 year old Beastial. I *can* and I *will* survive. It'll test my weaknesses and force me to grow quicker than I can ever imagine. I *have* to do this.

"I won't die–"

"You don't actually know that Sloane."

"My magic will protect me."

"Have you forgotten how vulnerable you are when your magic depletes your strength?" he practically snarls.

"No, I haven't," I answer him in a quiet but firm voice. "I know the risks, but I also know I won't die. Doing this will only make me stronger."

"*You do not know that Sloane!*"

I rush forward, my arms encircling him as I pull him flush against me. It burns but I don't let go. He needs me in more ways than one. I can endure a little pain to comfort him, to let him know that even if I go somewhere, I'll always be there.

"Trust me, Balthazar," I whisper into his ear as the flames lick down his neck.

The heat of his fire burns my face. My eyes automatically slide close to protect themselves, but I refuse to let him go and create distance. He needs all the reassurances I can give him, even if it'll cost me a few burn scars.

"I'll survive. Do you want to know how I know that?"

He says nothing as he stands there motionless, his arms draped by his side. As his silence drags on, I pull my head back far enough so I can look him in the eyes. He's frowning as the rage slowly disappears, but his fear doesn't go away. His eyes drown in it and my heart twinges. I'm the reason for all his fear right now. I'm the reason he's feeling this way and it eats me up inside.

I offer a smile to hide my own pain. He doesn't smile back.

"I have to come back to you," I answer my own question as I tenderly caress his face. "I take pride in my ownership of Lord Balthazar, heir to House Primis. I won't abandon you. I'll survive."

"There's another way for you to achieve what you desire."

"If we had the time, I would take it, but you know that I'm right. This is the fastest way to get me to learn magic. It'll take me decades to advance if I stay on Earth. I have to go to Jeznia."

His eyes slide shut as the fire on his horns finally dissipates. A moment later, he slumps forward, forehead resting on my shoulder as his arms curl around my waist.

"I do not want to sanction this," he confesses quietly.

"I know," I whisper as I comb my hand through his hair. His thick tresses are hot from where the fire burned.

"There are other ways," he murmurs.

"Not as fast as this. We don't know what your father's doing. We don't know what the Houses know. Odantha will send another Beastial after me when Zyvn doesn't deliver. I'm the weakest link. I have to do this, Balthazar."

"A week," he says. "I give you only one week."

"When I survive the first week, you can come visit me," I confidently tell him. "But I'm not leaving until *I* feel I'm ready."

"Sloane," he growls as he squeezes me.

"You said that if you interjected during Umbra's fight with Zyvn it meant you had no confidence in her abilities. Does that mean you have no confidence in me?"

He scoffs as he pulls his head away from mine, a soft glare upon his face as his jaw juts to the side. I smile at him, proud of myself for cornering him.

"Cat got your tongue?" I ask, my voice full of mirth as I dare to lighten the mood but it only causes his glare to deepen.

"If you die, Sloane—"

"I won't," I cut him off as I hold his face in my hands, all the playfulness erased from me. "*I won't.* I promise you, Balthazar."

He sighs heavily, his forehead coming to rest on mine again.

"Very well," he whispers. "Umbra will take you to the seventh circle."

My arms wrap around his shoulders as I lean into him for a kiss. "I'll make you proud, Balthazar. When I return, the Lords will cower at my feet."

"I don't care about any of that," he confesses against my lips. "Just come back to me, Sloane."

My heart twinges in my chest, threatening to break in two at the broken vulnerability of his voice and words. I won't fail. I won't allow myself to cause him that sort of pain.

"I will," I tell him. "I promise."

We speak no other words as he seals his lips over mine. The kiss is languid and sensual as his hands slowly roam over my curves. I sink into him, surrendering myself over to him as our tongues curl and twirl together. A slow heat begins to consume me.

His scent of smoke invades my nose as he takes my lower lip in between his teeth and gives it a tug. His left hand grips my ass cheek firmly before slipping around and in between my legs, pressing against the core of me.

I open my stance, giving him easier access and he purrs his thanks as our tongues continue their sensual dance. The mood between us is different than our normal trysts. There's no power play between us right now. Only pure desire. Mine of gratitude for supporting my decision and his of desperation for letting me go to train on my own in a world that will likely chew me up.

His left hand continues to rub me over my jeans while his right hand ventures beneath my shirt. I flinch at the coldness of his fingers, but excitement blossoms in me as he trails that hand up towards my breast. He pops my boob out of the bra before lazily rubbing his thumb over the nipple. It hardens and peaks quickly, his cold thumb an intense contrast against the warmth of my skin.

I shiver against him, my hand sliding down the front of him to his restrained cock. I mold my hand to it the best I can as it remains within his pants before I slowly rub up and down. It hardens in my grip. He growls his appreciation before snapping his fingers. In an instance, we're left completely bare in the kitchen and he takes the opportunity to slip his finger inside me as his mouth encloses on my breast.

A moan of approval tumbles out my mouth as I hike my leg up to wrap around his waist, my hips grinding against his hand as he pumps me. His erection presses against my stomach, his tongue flicking my nipple as his right hand plays with my other breast. He's an expert when it comes to my body and I shamelessly surrender myself over to him as the sinful pleasure builds within me.

He curls his finger against my inner wall as he pulls out, the finger hitting the backside of my tender nerves, and I audibly gasp at the sensation. He strokes me over and over as his mouth moves on to the other breast. My body arches against him as I edge closer to my release, a whimper falling out of my mouth as my hands grip his shoulder firmly. I'm close and he does nothing to stop me from reaching it.

The orgasm breaks in an explosion of a delectable release, a deep moan of satisfaction escaping me as my body jerks through the orgasm. Balthazar doesn't stop his teasing of my nipples or lets up on stroking me from the inside. I ride out my orgasm far longer than I ever have and then slump against him, satiated and breathing a bit labored. He holds me in his sturdy arms as he hoists me up before walking us to the bedroom. His hardened cock rubs against my bare ass with each step he takes and the sensation makes me desperate for him to fill me up.

Balthazar gently places me down on the bed, trailing kisses down my body before he climbs onto the bed. His actions are unhurried as he reaches out, spreading me open with those tantalizing cold fingers. His greedy black–red eyes drink in the sight of me, how wet I am for him, how I throb and ache to be filled by his cock.

"I will gladly drown in you, Sloane," he breathes out before lowering his mouth to me.

I'm already sensitive from my post orgasm. His licks are slow and purposeful, yet they lack the usual build up. He's not doing this for my pleasure. He's doing it *for his.*

The awareness of that fact slams into me hot and hard and I lay my legs against the bed as best I can so he can feast better on me. Balthazar hums his appreciation as his arms tuck under my legs, his freezing hands pressing into my ass cheeks as he lifts my hips up higher for him to better enjoy himself.

I sigh as I relax into it, thoroughly content with sitting back and enjoying the consistent, steady pleasure he's giving me. It feels good. Especially with how sensitive I already am.

I feel the dull ache begin to creep in, my core throbbing to have its void be filled by something bigger than his tongue, but I keep my mouth shut. I let Balthazar indulge, knowing that this will be the last time we have sex for at least a week, maybe even longer. If he wants to engrain the way I taste into his brain, I won't deny him that.

My ache intensifies despite my determination to let him enjoy himself and I can't refrain from teasing myself as my fingers drag over and around my nipples. Balthazar must catch on to what I'm doing because his tongue picks up its pace. He licks me strong and fast as I play with my breasts. As I reach closer to my second orgasm, he lifts off me, lips wet from me.

Before I can utter a protest, he's sliding into me, his cock hot and firm as it fills me to the brim. I groan, my head coming off the mattress as I reach for him. My nails dig into his hips as I drown in the sensation. He pulls out only to slide in so smoothly, curling those hips expertly and causing the tip of his cock to press against my inner wall as he slides in. I gasp at the delicious sensation, my legs clenching around him as my hips do their best to match him.

"Peccatum meum," he says in between his languid, sensual thrusts. "The seventh circle will destroy you, but you'll come out a Queen on the other side."

"I'll come back to you," I reply as we look at each other.

"I know you will," he says, sliding back in smoothly, hips connecting against mine.

"Kiss me."

He leans down without hesitation, his lips capturing mine as he takes his time with the kiss. He expertly moves his hips as he kisses me deeply, conveying all the unsaid words he's unable to express. It overwhelms me. I realize just how much faith he's putting into me despite his fears of losing me.

I wrap my arms around him, pulling away from our kiss to whisper into his ear. My voice warbles as tears blot my vision. "I'm coming back."

"I know you are."

"I won't abandon you."

"I know you won't."

"I'm going to master my magic and come back to you."

"I know you will."

He kisses me as he changes his tempo, slamming his hips into me hard and rough. I tighten my grip on him as he pulls back so he can ram forward. The pace is relentless, violent, and everything I need to get me out of my thoughts. I moan in ecstasy with each exhale I have, my breath stuttering with each ferocious thrust of his hips. The impact sound of our bodies bounces off the walls.

Slap.

Slap.

Slap.

I hold on to him for dear life as he coils his magic around me, using it to tease my most sensitive parts. I bite down on his shoulder, *hard*, as my orgasm hits me like a landslide. So hard it knocks the wind out of me.

Balthazar's grunting and moaning as his hips quicken their pace. His movements become unsteady and he's quickly spilling his seed. His hips jerk before he completely stills, our labored breathing mingling together as he rests on top of me.

He shifts his head so our foreheads touch and our eyes slide shut while his cock remains buried inside me.

"You will come back to me, Sloane."

"I will," I quickly agree through heavy breathing. "I promise."

"I have your word."

"You have my word."

He says nothing else as he kisses me. I eagerly return the gesture. I'd be lying if I said I wasn't scared. I'm about to do something crazy. The seventh circle is essentially the most brutal war zone I could go to and I'm an untrained civilian willingly entering such a dangerous place. I'm scared I'll die, but I trust my magic to protect me... so long as I don't overuse it in one go.

I've got this, I think as Balthazar pulls out of me to lay down beside me on the bed. No matter what happens, I'm coming out of this alive.

I glance over at Balthazar as he pulls me close, worry etched onto his face but he keeps his thoughts to himself. My hand reaches up, playing with strands of his black hair before I kiss him on the forehead and force a smile on my lips.

I'm making it out of this alive.

I have no other choice.

XIII

THE NEXT DAY after breakfast, Umbra takes me to the seventh circle.

Balthazar and I said our goodbyes shortly after I woke up. He rushed through it. He was barely a whisper upon my lips before disappearing to go buy souls. No words exchanged. He simply left with a snap of his fingers. Because he didn't want me to go? Because he hated how vulnerable he was feeling? Because he wasn't sure if he'd see me again? I honestly don't know.

To say I was disappointed by his behavior is an understatement. I don't know how long I'll be gone. I don't know what dangers or trouble I'll run into. He could have offered me more than a barely there kiss. But a small part of me understands. Balthazar isn't used to having his heart outside of his chest. He probably doesn't know how to deal with the violent storm of emotions barreling through him. Honestly, the fact that he stayed long enough to kiss me goodbye is a miracle in and of itself.

Umbra says nothing upon her arrival at the apartment. Merely grabs me by the wrist and transports us out of the condo in Boston and straight to the seventh circle of Jeznia.

As soon as we surface, wind whips wildly around us, threatening to knock me off balance. My hands shove their way into my hair, quickly tying it back as best I can. As soon as I do, my stomach drops at the sight before me.

Lightning streaks across a bleak, rainless sky as thunder booms so loudly it reverberates down to my toes. My head tilts backwards as I stare up at the massive mountain before me. The top of it disappears into black clouds, only to be highlighted by sporadic streaks of yellow lightning.

Lava flows freely down the top of the mountain before it suddenly disappears. I assume the lava is diverted elsewhere so as to not destroy what looks to be the first circle of Jeznia.

Enormous, looming walls create a boundary, sectioning the first circle off from the second circle beneath it. Light from the circle spills up into the open sky and I quickly realize as my eyes scan down the mountain that there are monolithic walls barricading each circle. Impenetrable, unscalable walls to prevent those from lower circles gaining access to the higher circles. Balthazar's statement rings through my mind. *The circles are kept separate because a divided world is easier to control.*

The walls tower into the sky. Even from the distance at which I stand… they are glorious, intimidating structures. Without proper magic, it would be impossible to climb them. They're too smooth for picks. There are no foot holdings. There is nothing to grab onto to use to climb up. The walls do their job perfectly.

My gaze slowly descends the mountain, taking note that each circle is darker than the one before it. The sixth circle, the one that stands in front of me, has only two lights. The expansive circle before me is shrouded in darkness before a brief flittering of lightning illuminates forests and open plains. We must be near the base of the mountain if there are plains within the sixth circle.

My eyes snap back up to the highest and smallest circle. The first circle. Home of the Lords. Where all the rules get made and enforced.

Sharp, pointy rooftops poke over the walls. I'm instantly reminded of massive looming black doors with House mascots and weeping souls carved into them. They would require buildings of great stature, ones that would compete with the grandness of the walls that encased each circle. And since Balthazar said the second circle doesn't attempt to invade the first circle, they can afford to have massive buildings eclipsing the tops of the walls.

The volcano booms so loudly the ground beneath my feet shakes. Massive boulders explode out of the volcano. My breath hitches as I watch the flying, burning rocks sail through the air. They're on a collision course with the first circle when all of a sudden the rocks slam into an invisible wall, an electric crackle echoing out into the sky as the rocks slide down the forcefield and out of sight.

I exhale a large breath, my shoulders sinking in relief. Balthazar is safe.

I should have excepted the first circle to be protected. The Lords wouldn't risk their lives so carelessly.

My attention diverts away from the first circle as I soak up the colors of Jeznia. Bright yellow, vibrant orange, and fiery red. Muted reds, oranges, yellows, browns, and dark greys. The color palette screams Hell through and through. There is nothing inviting about an erupting volcano, walled cities, and a blackened sky.

But what of the world outside of the mountain?

Cautiously, I turn around, balancing myself as best I can against the violent winds. I look beyond the wall that encages the seventh circle and out into the wild. A barren wasteland as far as the eye can see.

My eyes squint as I see something in the far distance. Lightning cuts across the sky. Is that another mountain range? The light disappears before I can make out much detail. My attention drops back to the barren wasteland. It must be hundreds of miles of pure nothing. I don't see any wandering souls, but I can't be certain I would be able to. The magic that entraps the souls could also hide them from our view.

"Is that The Wastelands?" I ask Umbra and she turns her attention to where I'm looking.

"Yes."

"Does it encircle the entire base of the mountain?"

"Yes."

That would explain why no one from the seventh circle attempts to break out. Unless they are truly desperate for freedom.

Butterflies swarm my stomach, a cacophony of nerves and fear. Despite the unsteadiness of my legs, I force myself towards the edge of the wall. Wind whips up from the ground, creating an invisible barrier that prevents me from falling over the ledge. Tingles shoot to my toes as I stare down the wall. It's a long way down. My mouth goes dry as my tongue licks my lips.

"How high up are we?" I ask, afraid to hear her answer.

"Half a mile."

"How wide is the circle?" I ask as my thoughts race on how I'm going to survive here.

"The seventh circle is roughly ten miles wide."

I glance out towards the wall opposite us, protecting us from The Wastelands. Ten miles from here to there. And yet the wall ten miles away still looks daunting, impressive, and invincible.

My eyes snap back down the wall to the blackened ground beneath us. My stomach drops. How am I going to get down there? Was there a reason why Umbra brought us to the top of the wall and not to the ground?

"Umbra, how are we getting—"

A searing hot hand shoves me against the middle of my back and I begin my quick, windy descent. For the first few seconds, I feel weightless. Then the fear barrels in as my brain understands what's happening. I'm falling. The ground is rapidly approaching. *Think, Sloane. You can't die before your training even begins.*

Instinctively, I'm reaching out to my magic. I'm familiar enough with how my magic moves, how it feels, and how it sometimes resists my commands. I know how to levitate objects. I should be able to levitate myself and stop my descent.

Tampering my fear as best I can, I draw forth my magic, but the wind flooding my ears is too distracting. Fear threatens to overwhelm me. I don't feel my magic as I reach for it.

The ground continues to come up fast. If I don't do something soon, I'll splatter against it, nothing more than blood, bones, and guts spread out against a barren plain.

Focus, Sloane, you've got this. Except, maybe I don't. There's not even a whisper of magic inside me and I'm almost out of time. I *am* going to die. I'm going to die even though I promised Balthazar I'd come back to him. Not even an hour since I left our home and I've already broken my promise.

Then all too suddenly, an explosion of pain rips through me as I come to an abrupt stop mere feet from the ground. The smoky apple scent suffocates the area as I drop to the ground rather ungracefully. The impact hurts, but I don't care. I'm happy to be alive.

A moment later, Umbra appears beside me as she steps out of her shadows. I glare at her. She's not looking at me, though. She's looking out towards the roving hills in the distance. Her fingers curl into the palm of her hands as a gust of wind blows through, carrying with it the scent of death, rot, and blood. I hold back my gag as I stand to my feet.

"There are creatures here you won't find in the other circles," Umbra says, her eyes scanning the landscape.

"How do you know that?" I ask.

I've read all there is to know about the seventh circle, but there was nothing about the creatures within the circle. Admittedly, there wasn't much on the seventh circle. The Lords never visit and most of the intel appears to be based off reputation instead of fact.

Umbra inhales deeply, her body corded in tension as she glares out at the seventh circle. Her words hit me like a ton of bricks.

"I was born here," she states evenly, no hint of emotion within her words.

No one born into the seventh circle ever leaves it. Whether it's because they don't want to or because they can't, they *all* stay within the seventh circle. If what Umbra is saying is true, she is the *only* Jeznian to climb her way to the top from the absolute bottom. To have started at the seventh circle and work her way up to Balthazar's House Aide is unheard of. Even with the limited knowledge I have of Jeznia and how it's run, I know what she's done should be impossible.

"How did you survive?" I ask because she has now become the most vital piece of knowledge I could gain access to.

Umbra was *born* here. How does an infant survive in a place this brutal? According to the notes on the seventh circle, children aren't off limits. There's no such thing as innocence to them. They treat children the same way they treat full grown adults. It's cruel, sickening, and unforgivable, but what can one expect from the bottom feeders of Hell?

"I don't know," she answers as her golden eyes turn to me. "Be on guard at all times. While the Houses may be powerful, they rely too heavily upon politics. The seventh circle has no governance. You will be raped, tortured, and killed for amusement. They don't threaten you with pretty little words like the Lords do. They act first, process later."

She pauses only for a moment before she continues speaking, her words detached. "I've been instructed by Lord Balthazar to bring you food once a day. You won't see me. I won't give you a chance to beg for your freedom. You stay here until you die or you master your magic."

My heart stops for a moment as I realize the true danger I'm putting myself in.

"U–understood," I somehow manage to say.

Bile sits at the back of my throat as the walls around me close in. I've bitten off more than I can chew. What was I thinking coming here? My magic may protect me but it doesn't make me invincible. It drains me of my energy and completely immobilizes me. I'll be an easy target to torture and kill.

Even now, I feel the aftereffects of using my magic. It saved me from becoming a splattered mess on the ground, but at what cost? My body is tired and lethargic. How will I survive?

I shouldn't be here. I should be back home.

"Umbra, I was thinking–"

She's gone from sight, abandoning me to the seventh circle of Hell. *Fuck.* I am truly and utterly alone. The severity of my situation weighs down on me like a ton of bricks. My previous confidence can no longer be found. My bravado was only that. My magic has limits. I knew that and I *still* volunteered to go to the seventh circle.

My knees give out as I sink to the ground. I can't telepathically call Umbra. She'll ignore me. My only other option of leaving this place is calling Balthazar. He'll come get me in a heartbeat. He may tease me for calling him not even an hour into leaving Earth, but I don't care. Feeling ashamed and embarrassed is better than being dead.

Inhaling a deep breath, I focus on connecting with him telepathically.

Bal–

Something hard and heavy collides into me as it drops from the sky. Sulfur and decay invade my nose as we tumble down the slope. Rocks dig into me with each roll we take as my vision disorients from all the spinning.

Whatever I'm entangled with bites and claws me. I attempt to shove it off me but our tumbling keeps us together. Pure luck has me landing on top with the creature beneath me. As quickly as I can, I push off it, scrambling to my feet.

It screeches as it lunges for me. I sidestep it as best I can as I soak in the creature's appearance.

It's roughly four feet tall with a frail and bony body. Leather wings protrude out of its back as it stares at me with a head shaped like a pterodactyl. It's long, gangly limbs are disproportionate to its body.

The creature is fast as it lunges for me a second time. I have to rely on my magic to remain safe. Painful, violent tingles shoot down my arm as a blast of concentrated fire shoots out of my palms. My aim is off and I miss my target.

Adrenaline pumps ferociously through my veins, my heart beating a mile a minute as I'm hyper focused on my opponent. Magic vibrates throughout my entire body, lashing out viciously at the creature any time it gets too close. I'm painfully aware that too much of my magic is being uselessly drained.

It has a mind of its own, intent on protecting the body it inhabits, but I need to pull it back. It's unnecessarily aggressive and wasting my strength. If I could use only a portion of the power its letting out, I can win without losing my ability to move once the fight is over.

I sidestep the creature's attack, but my leg gives out as exhaustion seeps in. I narrowly miss being skewered alive. *Come on, Sloane, you've got this.* I concentrate on wrapping my fingers, within my mind's eye, around the magic and when I feel it within my grip, I yank it back as hard as I can. It hurts.

It hurts *a lot*.

Each time I grab at the magic, it feels like thick, long talons are piercing through my hands. A cry of pain explodes out of my mouth as my right hand grips the magic. Fire shoots out of my left hand, successfully hitting its target. The fire concentrates into a laser, burrowing its way through the skull.

The creature plops to the ground, dead. With the threat now gone, my magic disperses from me. I fall forward, face first, into the unforgiving, hard ground. My right hand throbs in time with my rapidly beating heart. I breathe heavily into the dirt, but my mind is already assessing my situation.

I can't remain lying here. I'm vulnerable to another attack. I need to get up. I need to move.

Arms as heavy as a boulder shift forward. I plant my palms against the ground. With all the energy I have, I push up onto shaky limbs. Too much magic has been used. I need time to recuperate.

My eyes dart around the surrounding area for any threats. I don't see anything in the sky or scaling the wall. My attention turns to the roving hills in the distance and my heart drops. Something is heading this way, a cloud of dirt kicking up behind it.

It looks big even from this distance. My eyes squint as I try to take in more details. Is that… an elephant? *Shit.* I don't think I have the strength to take on an elephant. I barely survived the pterodactyl like creature.

I need to get up. I can't continue to be easy prey for these assholes. The whole reason why I came to the seventh circle was to learn how to properly use my magic, not die. I promised Balthazar I would come back to him. He *needs* me. I gave him my word so I have to survive. Screw dying. I'm going to make the seventh circle my bitch.

Pushing through the exhaustion despite how much my muscles cry out against me, I get to my feet. I scan the area again, this time looking for an escape route. The wall looms behind me, to my left, and to my right. I have to go forward, but I want to avoid colliding with the elephant running my way. I can't waste any more magic on a fight. Not until I've gained a little more strength back.

"Come on, Sloane. You've got this. You can do it," I hype myself up as I take an unsteady step forward. "That's it. There you go. Now, take another step."

Sure enough, one by one, I take more steps forward. I keep a watchful eye on the predator heading my way. Thankfully, the elephant lacks the speed the pterodactyl possessed. My eyes shift forward and settle on a spot about a football field's length away. If I can just get within those rocky hills, I'm confident I can lose whatever's chasing me.

Push, Sloane. Push like your life depends on it! My legs resist every attempt I make at lifting them faster, but I force through it. I push my legs faster and faster until finally, I'm running. The elephant–like creature continues to chase after me, slowly closing the distance between us. Faster. I need to be faster. There's only a little further left before I make it to the hills. *Come on!*

A rush of energy *whooshes* through me. Suddenly, I'm sprinting. My body feels alert, aware of every direction with no exhaustion to be found. I run faster, my feet pounding against the rocky terrain. I reach the hillside in no time.

An angry roar bellows behind me as the elephant notices my newfound speed.

Heart in my throat, I scale up the hill as quickly as I can. When I reach the top, I take a moment to pause. My chest heaves as I greedily drink in gulps of air. Rotten, stale bitterness lingers in the wind, coating my tongue and mouth. I ignore it as best I can as I spare the elephant a glance

It still chases me, but I've gained distance between us. I'll easily lose it within the terrain. As long as I continue to make smart choices, I'll survive.

I can do this.

I will conquer the seventh circle.

No one is going to stand in my way.

With one last look at the Hell elephant, I disappear down the other side of the hill, never to be seen by the elephant again.

XIV

COUNTLESS HOURS GO by as I walk through the valleys of the hills, climbing over rocks and decaying bodies. There's little light to show me the way with thick, grey clouds shielding any sun from view. *If they even have sun here*, I think bleakly.

I'm forced to walk by the light of lightning bursts. Each flash lasts only seconds, but I do my best to study my surroundings each time. There's a forest up ahead which offers me two choices. Remain in the hills or venture into the trees. Judging by the number of bodies within the hills, I might have a better fighting chance within the forest.

My foot slides over a skeleton, it's bones warped and cracked. I can't discern the shape of the creature and quickly move on from studying it. I'm no longer phased by the morbidity of it all. Instead, I seize the opportunity presented to me. I study each body as best I can in the fading light, estimating the size, shape, and appearance of these creatures so I can know what to expect.

Thankfully, my energy is back. The recovery time was much quicker this time around. I have to assume it's because I attempted to control my magic by pulling it back. It was horrifically painful, but what else can I do? If I let the magic do what it wants, I'll be a sitting duck.

Next time I'll need to pull it back quicker. I know I should be focused on learning the other magic I have, the devil magic Balthazar gave me, but at this point it's useless. The more powerful magic within me rears its head in every life and death situation. And since I've inserted myself at the center of a life and death situation by willingly training in the seventh circle, that apple smoke scented magic is going to come out every chance it gets.

So… if I'm to come out of this *alive*, I need to gain *control* of the old, deep magic.

A heavy sigh expels from my mouth. Controlling it will be the hardest part. The magic fought me tooth and nail when I grabbed it. It's determined to protect the host, but at what cost? I have to wonder does the magic even know how vulnerable I become after its use? Does it care?

My assumption is that it doesn't know. Which would mean the magic has enough awareness to protect me from external threats, but not enough awareness to know it's making me vulnerable to attack. And because of the way it behaves, I have to assume that on some level, the magic is sentient. Could I find a way to speak to it? To let it know giving me access to its power will not harm it?

I wince as a sharp pain shoots up my ankle. I've rolled it on the uneven terrain. It's difficult to maneuver in the dark light. My feet are killing me. I'm not used to walking this much in a single day, let alone over rocky and uneven grounds. I wore the best shoes I could think to wear, but even still I can feel the effects of my inexperience.

I need to take a break before I enter the forest. With no idea what lingers within the trees, it would be best to rest. For all I know, I could get attacked the moment I cross the tree line. If that happens, a little rest beforehand will do me some good.

With a grunt, I plop down unceremoniously in between two large boulders. The relief is immediate. My feet beg me to remove my shoes but it's a risk I can't take. I can be attacked at any moment. I can't risk running away barefoot. The shoes will remain on at all times unless they're destroyed or a foot has been injured.

My body slumps against the boulder on my right and I realize the tiredness consuming me is from physical exertion, not magic depletion. I've been walking for hours, sticking low the valleys instead of the dips and crests of the hills. Still, the constant walking, jumping over dead bodies, and scaling large boulders has been taxing.

Just three weeks ago, I spent forty plus hours sitting at a desk. I squeezed in a workout wherever I could, but I didn't train for this kind of steady, physical exertion. My body is spent. I'll sleep deeply tonight and that worries me. Will I even hear an attacker approaching?

My stomach growls. My mouth is parched. I should've come better prepared. I was so focused on training my magic that I didn't think about bringing any necessary supplies like food and water. Eating a meal once a day isn't enough. At the bare minimum, I should've brought a backpack, a change of clothes, and a medical aid kit. More weight to carry, but it could be the difference between life and death.

As if my injuries know what I'm thinking of, they flare to life. I glance down at the scratches lining my arms. The pterodactyl creature got a few good hits in, but thankfully none of the wounds are deep. But my arms look red and inflamed. They could get infected. Or worse, the pterodactyl nails could have been poisoned.

Balthazar will kill me for dying, but the disappointment he'll feel in finding out that I died in such a lame way will be brutal. I have to survive. Regardless of any poison and infection. I will not die.

Besides, if my magic is so determined to protect the host, perhaps it will rid me of deadly diseases. The thought eases my worries as I slump a little lower against the boulder.

Time passes by indefinitely and, before I know it, I drift off into a slumber.

SHARP, SHOOTING PAIN consumes me as fire bursts out of my chest. A shriek not belonging to me echoes out into the sky. My eyes snap open and dart around, rapidly taking in the situation.

Fire blows out of my chest like a flame thrower, a constant feed of heat and pain. It singes the creature in front of me before the creature has the opportunity to dodge. Another shriek escapes its mouth. It darts out of the path of my fire, a low growl tumbling out of its fang infested mouth.

I scramble to my feet, heart in my throat, as I internally reach out to my magic. I envision my hands clamping down on it and I'm startled as the magic thrashes against my hold. Brutal claws tear and shred at my hands, forcing me to let go, but I quickly latch back onto it. I *need* to gain control. It can't be using magic so carelessly. I'll die if it does.

Meanwhile, the creature regards me carefully, mindful of the flames that don't appear to be disappearing anytime soon. I'm reminded of a bat as I stare at the shape of a furless head, shriveled up nose, and no eyes within its sockets. It's tall, but I can't discern its true height due to it being hunched over onto its knuckles. The limbs are long and lanky, but this bat–like creature doesn't have any wings.

Bones protrude out of its emaciated body. My assumption is lack of food and nutrition are a running theme in the seventh circle. They kill to eat. They're no different than wild animals, except with a more intelligent mind, their killings might be crueler, sometimes less about killing and more about enjoying the violence of it all.

Wrinkly, dry skin the color of ashen grey fits tightly over the bony, tall body. The creature paces back and forth, its sharp nails on its hands and feet scuffing the ground with each step it takes.

It sniffs the air as it paces while I struggle to turn off the fire raging out of me. My magic refuses to listen, convulsing wildly within my grip. My palms tear, hot blood coats my skin, yet in reality, I'm still as a statue in front of the creature. The fight for control over my magic is internal, the pain imaginary, but it takes all my willpower to silence my screams.

Despite the pain I feel, I know I need to move. I'm trapped between two massive boulders and my attacker. Unfortunately, I can't scale the boulders. I need to walk around them and somehow scoot by the bat creature.

Hesitantly, I take a step forward. The creature's head snaps in my direction, its arm lashing out confidently and fast. My magic rips its way out of my hands, bursting out of my chest as an invisible force slams into the bat's arm. It screeches as it lunges for me. My magic bursts out again, but I yank back on it as hard as I can.

I'm unable to suppress the ungodly bellow that leaves my mouth as agony like no other overwhelms me. I glance down at my hands, afraid of what I'll see. They feel shredded to bits but look completely normal. I pray that whatever is happening internally is not real damage or long lasting.

The bat slams into me while I'm distracted checking the state of my hands. The creature pins me against the boulder, its maw opening wide as it intends to bite down on my head.

My stomach bottoms out, my heart stalling as a shrill scream leaves my mouth.

"No!"

Instincts take over. My hands give way to the magic, releasing it from my grip. With a feral whoosh, the magic surges forward, a beam of concentrated fire expelling from the palm of my left hand. I move without hesitation, latching my hand onto the creature's head. It howls in pain, instantly retreating backwards. A moment later, it slumps to its knees and my hand releases its head.

The creature cradles its head, but it's pointless. There's a gaping wound caused by the fire. It's brain is exposed to open air. Blood pulses out in a steady stream, sliding down the bat's face. White bone contrasts against ashen grey skin.

I keel over and vomit at the grotesque sight. Dead bodies are easier for me to handle, no matter the state of their decay. They're no longer warm and still bleeding. They're carcasses. But this… it's more than I can handle.

The creature somehow gets to its feet despite whatever pain and symptoms it might be feeling. Even with its brain exposed and injured, the creature still wishes to fight. *Fuck.* I was hoping a blow to the head would kill it. But it's staggering on its feet. I can use this opportunity to get out from the boulders.

I don't hesitate. I run.

I only managed to get a few steps in before a cold, firm grip curls around my wrist. With a yank as if I weigh nothing more than a doll, I'm slammed into a boulder. The air is knocked out of my lungs as my head throbs from impact. My whole body aches and my vision warps.

Somehow, or by the grace of god, I see through my hazy vision. The creature pulls its free arm back to swing forward. Without really thinking, I latch onto my magic, envisioning an impenetrable wall blocking the creature's attack.

Bones crunch in midair as the hand slams against the invisible force. There's a split second before I realize my plan worked. *It really worked!* My achievement is short lived as the creature sinks its teeth into my shoulder. The wall I had created was only large enough to block the trajectory of the arm. I mistakenly left the rest of my body vulnerable to attack.

A yell of anger and pain expels from me as sharp tingles consume my chest. Fire bursts from my chest straight into the creature, piercing it all the way through. A moment later, its teeth go lax before the creature plops to the ground, lifeless.

My hand reaches up to the bite wound I received. Warm blood coats my hand, squelching between the gaps of my fingers as it pumps out of me like a faucet. If I don't do something soon, I'll die. I have no aid to use, no tools to makeshift into a thread and needle. All I have to rely on is my magic. Magic that won't fully obey me. Magic that resists my hold. Magic that may only understand a physical body barreling at me and not poison lurking within my veins or me bleeding to death.

My eyes slide shut, my heart in my throat as blood spills out my shoulder and down my side. I concentrate as best I can, reaching out to the old, deep, resistant magic. *Heal me*, I practically beg over and over within my head. Despite the heat of Jeznia, coldness seeps into my body. If the creature has punctured a major artery, I don't have long before I die. I need to heal as fast as magic, as fast as a snap of the fingers. *That's it!*

I do it on instinct. At the same time my index finger and thumb snap together, I imagine the wound being gone. My hand is still slippery and wet with blood, but my fingers poke around my shoulder for any holes. *Did it work?* I yank off my shirt and wipe away the blood. There's nothing but smooth skin.

A cry of relief bubbles out of my mouth, tears blurring my vision. I used my magic on *purpose* and it *worked*. For a few moments, I sit there, a shit eating grin upon my face as my breathing and nerves calm. I did it. I used my magic to heal myself. It obeyed. It listened. It healed me when I ordered it to.

Suddenly, wind blows through the valley, carrying with it the putrid smell of the bat creature's blood. Even to my human senses, it smells *fresh*. It won't be long until it attracts attention. I can't be here when it arrives.

Forcing myself to my feet, I stumble around the corpse as I exit the shelter of the boulders. My head throbs in pain in tandem with my heart. My body aches along the muscles in my back and shoulders, but I am not exhausted. I successfully held back my magic, only letting it out when absolutely necessary. It didn't uselessly drain me of all my energy, making me vulnerable to attack. I still have my stamina and strength.

A smile breaks out on my lips as I walk towards the forest. I've achieved a lot in the short time that I arrived here. It was smart to come to the seventh circle to train. If I had remained on Earth, it would have taken me months, or even years, to see this same kind of growth. I had no challenge while practicing on Earth. Here, the blood thirsty, brutal way of living will *force* me to improve or die. It's exactly what I needed.

As I approach the tree line, my eyes dart around every possible surface I can see for any visible threats but I don't expect I'll be able to catch sight of one. The trees are *massive*. They could give the Redwoods a run for their money.

Black leaves about the size of my torso cling to branches the same thickness of a bus. Dark grey mossy vines drape down the branches but never reach the forest floor. The forest is dense, stretching on for miles as it curves around the mountain base. It's possible the forest completes a full circle, but that doesn't matter. Right now, I need to find a safe place to rest. Preferably *off* the ground.

My head falls back as I glance up at the impending trees. I'm not sure how I'm going to climb one of these things, but I have to do everything possible to keep myself safe.

I turn around to face the mountain, surprised at the distance I've managed to create. The wall looms tall and intimidating even as far away as it is. Yet it is the mountain that commands all of my attention. It towers unimaginably high as vicious lava spews from it. Lightning cracks across the sky as dark grey clouds hide the top of the mountain from sight. From this great distance, I can finally appreciate the sheer size of the mountain the inhabitants call home.

My eyes slowly drift down the mountain, counting each wall I see until at last, I reach the wall that separates the sixth and seventh circle. The wall that Umbra pushed me off of. It's a long way up the mountain from the seventh wall. I won't be able to ascend the mountain without magic. For now, I'm trapped within the seventh circle until I gain enough power and control to scale the formidable walls.

Blowing out a loud breath, I turn back towards the forest and the impressive trees. I've survived two attacks and escaped a third. I commanded my magic to heal me and it did. I can do this. I will survive this. I will come out the other side stronger and better. I won't break my promise to Balthazar.

Trust in yourself, Sloane.

With a shake of my hands and renewed confidence, I disappear into the trees.

XV

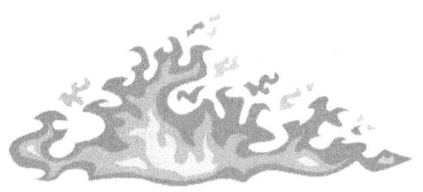

Dᴀʏ ᴛʜʀᴇᴇ.

Three vicious, agonizing, exhausting days. If it weren't for the daily meal Umbra brings me, I would have no idea how many days have passed. It's impossible to tell when there's no sunlight. The looming, grey clouds never disappear. I fall asleep to muted darkness and wake up to muted darkness. It *never* changes.

Umbra's visits are the only way I'm able to keep track of the days. Her delivery is unannounced and unexpected. There's no whisper of her arrival and no sounds of her departure. One moment there's nothing, the next, I have food.

The first day my meal arrived, I lunged for it and nearly got my hand bitten off in the process. A creature had been lurking near the bag. It was a savage thing. Roughly six feet long, three feet wide, worm—like, and a mouth lined to the brim with sharp teeth. If it hadn't been for my magic's ability at sensing danger, I would have lost my hand.

Since then, I've been cautious whenever I approach the bag of food. In doing so, I've managed to thwart off burrowing critters that were a little too curious about the bag and probably very dangerous to my life.

As if my stomach knows I'm thinking about the bag of food I've yet to receive today, it growls angrily. Only a few short moments pass before my stomach rumbles again. I look around hopefully for the bag but find nothing.

A heavy sigh blows out of my mouth. Umbra shows up whenever its most convenient for her. She could show up at 3pm on Wednesday, 8am on Thursday, and 5pm on Friday. I don't know when my next meal will show up but I *do* know it will come. And that has been a saving grace for me.

My hands rest against my torso, my fingernails fiddling with a stiff part of my shirt as I remain tucked away within the giant roots of the trees. I barely remember what the shirt used to look like, having gotten too used to the blood, mud, and sweat covering it. I had contemplated requesting new clothes on my second day here but couldn't figure out how to make the request. Now, I know better.

New clothes would be a death sentence.

Too many creatures rely on scent to find their prey and I *finally* smell like the seventh circle. New clothes would smell too pretty, drawing too much attention from curious inhabitants. It's best to continue wearing my dirtied, bloodied clothes. They allow me to move around more freely, blending in with the rot and decay of their world.

Yet, despite knowing all that, I would give up my left arm to wash my hair. Three days is too long for my scalp. It itches. It's tender. The hair is starting to knot. I've done my best to comb my fingers through it and braid it, but there isn't much I can do to treat my scalp. I can't imagine the state my scalp will be in when I finally finish my training. I might have to use magic to repair it back.

A large thud echoes within the forest and barely a second later, a vibration trembles through the ground and up my spine. I push back further into the roots, my breathing clipped and quiet. No roar or shriek follows the thud. With that little information, I can gather it's not a fight, but it could be a number of other things.

My heart pulses in my throat as I strain my ears to hear anything else. My fingers curl and uncurl within my palms as my body tenses to move into action. I refuse to let someone sneak up on me. That's a lot harder to accomplish when the creatures hide so well within their surroundings. They were born here. I'm the foreigner come to invade their home and it shows. I've been caught unaware far too many times.

Thankfully, over these past three days, I've gotten better at sensing an attack before it happens. My magic still acts on its own, though, lashing out to protect me whenever I've miscalculated or misjudged my safety. It still struggles against me each time I attempt to control it, but I've noticed it's beginning to *listen*.

It's only been three days since my first attempt at controlling the magic but I can already see a difference in how I interact with it. I'm confident I'll be able to master it so long as I stay alive long enough to do so.

A scuffling towards my left has me springing to me feet, hurtling myself over the large root and towards the sound. I won't allow them to get the drop on me. I'll attack first, force them on the defense. I've learned the hard way that it's harder to gain the upper hand when you've been taken by surprise.

As I reach the top of the root, my stomach bottoms out at the sight before me. My momentum has my ghosting over the curve of the root and descending towards the ground. Exactly what I *shouldn't* be doing. I made the wrong choice jumping over this root.

The creature's head snaps to me, four large, bloodshot eyes zeroing in on my considerably smaller frame. I land with a small thump and there's that split second where we assess each other before making our moves.

It stands roughly two feet taller than me, but that's misleading when it walks on all fours instead of on its two hind legs. It's beige skin sags towards the ground, covered in open sores and scabs. Large wings protrude out of its back while a tail curls and whips behind it. A vague familiarity washes over me as I stare at the creature's face before I'm suddenly hit with the realization.

Gargoyle.

It's a living, breathing gargoyle.

A low growl emits from it as a snarl morphs onto its face. The tiniest tightening in its body has me flying into action. *Attack before it attacks you.* I move forward with intent, calling forth my magic. Smoked apples smother the air as I grab hold of the magic inside me, barely wincing at the pain of being stabbed through the hands. Forcing the magic to my command, I use it to launch myself into the sky.

The gargoyle's fast, its clawed hand reaching out and swatting me down before I can clear it. Air leaves my lungs as I slam into the unforgiving ground. The gargoyle attempts to trample me but I roll out of the way. I can't catch my breath as I maneuver around the creature, avoiding the sharp claws aimed at me.

I need to find an opening.

My fingers curl tighter around the magic, using it to make me faster. The magic obeys, propelling my legs faster and faster. A loud roar of frustration leaves the gargoyle's mouth before it rears up and flaps it gigantic wings. The wind the wings create is powerful, knocking me off balance. The gargoyle jumps at the opportunity.

It swipes at me, but I raise my arm up for impact, pushing the majority of magic into that arm. The gargoyle's hand collides with the invisible wall, but instead of retreating, the gargoyle pushes *into* the wall. It's weight is incredible. The wall, and my magic, strain against the gargoyle. I'm faced with the bleak reality that the wall will break. My magic is going to give out at some point.

Somewhat alarmed, I force more magic into my arm, the air drowning in that smoky, sweet and tart smell. The gargoyle roars as it pushes all its weight into the magical wall. There's a crack. I can practically *feel* the crack splicing across the surface of my magical wall.

And then all too suddenly, the wall shatters. The gargoyle comes tumbling forward onto me, pinning me against the ground.

Air escapes my lungs at the weight of the gargoyle sitting atop me. It's too heavy. I'll suffocate to death if I don't get it off me soon. Either that, or I'll die from compression.

Desperate, I push as hard as I can, but the gargoyle doesn't budge as its greedy eyes bear down on me. Its lips pull back into a snarl, drool escaping its mouth and coating me.

I can't breathe.

I can't move.

I need more magic. Thankfully, it lingers within my hands, but it's not enough. I need more of it.

Yanking as hard as I can, I maneuver the magic towards my chest, but it fights against me. The magic is trying to escape, pulling in the opposite direction of where I want it to go.

My vision distorts, a warbled cry dying in my mouth. I'm seconds away from actually dying. I can *feel* it.

As if to prove my point, the gargoyle opens its massive maw and aims for my head. I'm going to die.

I'm going to die.

My hands yank on the magic again, my face turning beet red as my hands shred against the nails of the magic. My heart stops beating as fear overloads my system. I do my best to ignore it. Fear will do nothing but hinder me. *Push through it, Soane.* Take ownership of the magic. It's *mine.* It belongs to *me.*

So, it better stop resisting me.

A rage filled roar leaves my mouth as I yank on the magic as hard as I can. It crashes into me, its thorny tendrils wrapping tightly around me. Sharp, long thorns dig into my muscles, my bones, my organs. I'm going to die. Not because of some creature from Jeznia, but because of my own magic.

The pain is too much. My vision blurs and warps as I feel faint. The magic doesn't let go as it burrows deeper into me, shredding me to bits in its wake.

I'm going to lose consciousness.

I'm going to die.

My body heats up too fast. My skin bubbles from the heat and I shriek in pain. Any tears I might cry dry up faster than I can produce them. I'm *burning.* Literally burning from the inside out.

There's a roar in the distance and I'm vaguely aware of the weight pressing down on me disappearing. But I'm in too much pain to be relieved. The bubbles along my skin pop, oozing liquid that smells rotten. The magic claws and scrapes its way further into the core of me.

I vomit from the pain, my consciousness fading in and out. The magic rips through me, throwing bits of flesh and blood and organs into the air until suddenly, it settles, curling and cocooning into the deepest parts of me. As it sinks comfortably into place, it slowly fades from my mind before blinking out like a spark.

Not a moment later, my entire body bursts into flames and I lose consciousness.

XVI

W HEN I COME TO, I'm peering up at the black canopy of the forest. My body, weak but not exhausted, feels strangely foreign. As if it isn't entirely my own. Will it even work if I attempt to use it?

Bracing myself for failure, I push up into a seated position. My accomplishment isn't celebrated as I quickly access my surroundings. The gargoyle is nowhere to be found. Relief floods me. I have no desires to fight that thing again.

My hand lands in something wet and squishy, drawing my attention to the ground. Instant disgust fills me and I can't withhold the gag. I'm sitting in a puddle of guts, blood, and skin.

I rise up to my feet, intent on wiping my legs down as best I can, but I'm startled into immobility.

My white skin is gone, replaced by dark charcoal skin cracked with golden veins scattering along the surface. My stomach drops as I lift a trembling hand, turning it this way and that as I stare at charcoal fingers, sharp onyx nails, and golden light peering up through the cracks. This… this is what Balthazar looks like beneath his humanoid appearance. Am I… am I like him now?

Heart hammering wildly against my chest, I inspect my entire body. Why do I look like this? Long, silver hair drapes around my shoulders and I'm ashamed of the shriek that escapes my mouth. *Calm down, it's your hair, Sloane.* Tentatively, I thread my fingers through it, giving it a tug. Sure enough, the hair is attached to my scalp.

My eyebrows pinch together as I continue studying my new look. Again, why do I look like this? The last thing I remember is fighting a gargoyle. It pinned me to the ground. I couldn't escape. I was running out of time and desperate. I reached out to my magic and it... it tunneled its way into me. I passed out and now I'm... this.

Is my magic gone? Is that why there was a burst of flames? Maybe that explosion was the magic leaving my body and now I look like this as an after effect. Maybe I was always meant to look like this due to my wish but the magic allowed me to still look human. If it's gone now... what does that mean for me?

Inhaling a shaky breath, I hesitate to reach for it. What if the magic's not here? Will I be able to survive the seventh circle?

Taking another deep inhale, I call the magic forward. It races to the tips of my fingers as fast as the speed of light, jolting me backwards from the shock of it. It doesn't hurt anymore. The tingles are just that. *Tingles.*

My eyes snap down to my fingers and my lips part at what I see. Magic glittering like a thousand stars bloom at the tips of my fingers, fading out as they descend down the knuckles towards my palm. I rub my thumb over my fingers, watching as the stars brighten when my thumb presses into them. It's beautiful, like nothing I've ever seen.

I'm transfixed by the sight, watching as the magic brightens and fades at my touch, when suddenly, I realize that's *my* magic. It's *listening* to me. I should try using it to see how much control I have over it.

Quickly standing to my feet, I glance around the area. Empty. There is absolutely no one withing the vicinity. No one to test my magic on.

Then I'll just do something else with my magic. Anything else.

Taking a few quick breaths, my thumb presses against my index finger before a *snap* echoes into the forest. Not even a millisecond after the snap is made my appearance changes. I'm back in my original skin and I can't help but revel in the freckles scattered along my arms. A moment later, I pull my hair outwards, sighing in relief at the familiar brown color. I'm *me* again.

A laugh bubbles out of my chest. It worked. Without hesitation, without resistance. The magic *obeyed*.

I nearly cry tears of gratitude as the magnitude of what I've just accomplished barrels into me. The magic has been fighting me tooth and nail, shredding my hands, wrists, and arms as it resisted my every attempt at using it. But now it listens.

In some messed up way, that fight with the gargoyle helped me and the magic bond. When I reach for it now, it doesn't feel foreign. I can't discern where I end and the magic begins. We are one and the same. The revelation leaves me shocked.

"Holy fuck," I breathe out as I lift my fingers up, bringing the magic forward once more.

The glittering stars consume my fingertips. My eyes shift over to the mess of skin, blood and organs on the forest floor before I snap my fingers. Instantaneously, the gore is gone. My jaw hangs open.

Is it really this *easy* to use magic? I mean sure… all I had to do was shed my entire body and go through the most excruciating pain that I've ever experienced in my life. But… is it really this easy?

"There's only one way to find out," I mumble to myself.

With one last look around the area, I disappear from sight.

DAY SEVENTEEN.

I've walked a full circle around the mountain. It would've taken me much longer to accomplish if I hadn't been practicing teleportation. The seventh circle is far larger than a ten day walk.

It was difficult to tell the distance I traveled while teleporting. The forest is practically identical to itself. Every new area I popped into looked exactly the same as the last. Same tall trees, same chittering creatures, same rot scented air. I started leaving magic infused marks to ascertain whether I had visited the place before or not.

Ten full days later, I happened upon a fading mark.

The teleportation training was not without its obstacles. I lost count of how many times I appeared in an area only to be inches from an inhabitant. They ranged in size, strength, and swiftness. Each creature had their challenges that tested my mettle. One creature was so strong it nearly severed my spine in half.

Other opponents were too fast for me to keep up with. The delay it took my brain to get a message down to my magic was more than enough time for the quick opponents to stab me, punch me, bite me. One stabbed me right in the heart. If it hadn't been for my magic's ability to act fast and cleanly, I would have actually died.

The fighting was not for nothing, though. With each new fight, I gained more control over my magic. As well as an understanding of how to fight. I started anticipating moves better and counter attacking with more intelligence. I could think ahead three steps of the fight, sometimes challenging my understanding by withholding the use of my magic. I trained myself both in physical fights and usage of my magic.

Ever since that horrible incident with the gargoyle, my magic no longer acts out without my say, even when it feels danger is too close. It swirls beneath the surface, curling deep inside me, always alive and waiting. There are times a zing of irritation bursts from within whenever I've made a particularly stupid decision, a scratching beneath the surface as the magic requests to be let out.

The more familiar with the magic I become, the more I realize that it's not actually *my* magic. It's old. Truly ancient. And it is sentient in some way. It has its own awareness of what happens around me. Another pair of eyes lurking within the shadows of my existence. I'm not sure how I feel about it.

At first, the magic had been my saving grace. Zyvn would have killed me if it hadn't been for the magic. But the day I fought the gargoyle... the magic *challenged* me and I almost died because of it. Did it *want* me to die only to begrudgingly surrender to me when I didn't cave in? I'll never know. I've tried asking it several times but I always receive no answer. It may be sentient, but its limited in how it communicates. Perhaps even how it thinks.

Having sentient magic complicates things. For now, it cooperates. Maybe in a week it won't. I'm also no longer human. I'm immortal. The magic might play by my rules for one hundred years, two hundred, three hundred. But at some point down the line, it might not want to cooperate anymore. What if it wants to separate itself from me? Or worse? *Take over?*

I come to the same conclusion every time. I'll deal with the problem *if* it arises. There's no guarantee I'll run into those issues and I'm not going to waste my time on what if's. The matter I'm choosing to focus on right now is returning to Balthazar.

I've learned all that I can from the seventh circle. It nearly killed me, but I came out the victor. I know my magic better now than when I first arrived. The seventh circle did its job. Now, it's time to return home.

Quietly, I walk towards the wall that divides the sixth and seventh circle, exiting the massive forest that keeps me mostly safe from aerial attacks. It looks like about a two mile walk from the forest to the wall. I *could* walk that but I don't see the point. I need to figure out how far I can teleport myself in one trip. My goal is to be at the top of the wall. I don't think I can get there on the first try, but it's worth a shot. I might surprise myself.

Calling the magic forward, it swirls to life as it lights the tips of my fingers. Inhaling deeply, my thumb and index finger snap together. Almost instantly, the magic yanks me down through the muck and mud as I speed through the empty space at lightspeed. A second later, I ricochet out of the void and back into Jeznia. I'm not on top of the wall. Not even close. I'm about halfway between the wall and the forest. A mile and a quarter, maybe?

Honestly, that's not bad, but it certainly won't allow me to travel between the worlds. I'll have to continue to rely on Balthazar until I master teleportation at its fullest.

My lips pull downward as I glance at my fingers, my magic sparkling along the ends. Over the past couple weeks, I've noticed some areas of magic are easier to use than others. The thought that my magic might have limitations *has* crossed my mind. It's too early to tell if the one with limitations is me or the magic, but it's entirely possible I may never be able to teleport between the worlds.

Still, I have to at least try.

Taking another deep inhale, my fingers snap together a second time. When I pop up, I'm at the base of the wall. It towers above me, tall and foreboding. My lips pull downward as I assess the situation.

Teleporting vertically has been a challenge. The trees were great places to hide and sleep with their many thick branches and massive leaves but it always took me a couple of tries to reach the first branch. And that's the difference between the trees and the wall. Trees have branches. This wall is as smooth as glass for the entire half mile. There's no way I'll reach the top in one teleportation.

Thankfully, snapping my fingers and using my magic is as easy as breathing. I'll have to continually teleport upwards until I reach the top of the wall and pray I won't fail at any point.

I snap my fingers together and a moment later, a pickaxe is in my hand. I slam it as hard as I can into the wall. Absolutely no damage is made within the wall. I slam it again. The pickaxe vibrates violently within my grip, nearly flying out of my hand in the process.

My head tilts back as I stare up at the towering wall. Smooth, black surface. No bumps or dimples to be seen. Half a mile. Umbra climbed half a mile without magic, without an ability to dig into the wall, without any safety measures put into place. How the Hell did she do it?

It doesn't matter. I *need* magic to make it to the top. No point in comparing the two of us.

Shaking out my arms in anticipation, I gather enough courage to tackle my teleportation trip. *I've got this,* I assure myself as I squint up at the wall. *I can do this.*

Three quick inhale—exhales fill the silence before my fingers snap together. I disappear into the void before emerging about one third way up the wall. For a split second, I'm weightless. Then gravity pulls me down.

The wind lifts my hair as it billows through my clothes. The drop hits my stomach a second later and anxiety swarms through me like a hurricane.

I hate this. I hate every second of it. *Concentrate, Sloane.* Forcing my eyes shut, I concentrate on pulling the magic forward and snap my fingers. I enter the void before resurfacing. I glance up just as I begin falling. *I'm close.* One more time and I'll be at the top.

The sickening feeling of falling shoots up my legs, racing towards my heart. I can't help it. My eyes snap downward. The ground is so far beneath me. I wouldn't survive the fall if my magic fails me.

My fingers snap together but nothing happens. My heart skips a beat as I snap my fingers again, but I continue to fall. *Concentrate, Sloane!* I tug my magic forward, fighting off the terror as best I can. The magic races down my arm into my fingers and I snap them together. A breath of relief rushes out of my mouth as I enter into the void. When I resurface, I'm about ten feet above the wall.

A shriek of surprise flies out of my mouth as I fall. The landing is rough but I manage to stay on my feet. My heart pounds mercilessly against my ribs as I stare around in shock. I did it. *I did it.*

"Fuck yeah," I shout out towards the seventh circle.

I beat it. It promised to chew me up and spit me out, but I refused to give in. I fought tooth and nail and came out the other side.

"You've done well, Sloane."

I whirl around, surprised to see Balthazar standing about five feet from me. My heart thumps against my chest as I soak him in. He's more handsome than I remember.

"Balthazar," I breathe out his name like a prayer upon my lips before rushing to him.

He chuckles, arms opening wide to embrace me. There's about three feet of distance between us when the wind shifts suddenly. Two feet between us when the smell of sulfur hits my nose. One foot from him when I realize the sulfur is coming from him. Not his familiar scented smoke. *That isn't Balthazar.*

On instinct, my fingers snap together and I teleport to the other side of him, a solid ten feet of space between us. Fury courses through my veins as my heartbeat thunders in my ears. I spin around to glare at the imposter. How *dare* he embody all that I love.

The fake Balthazar looks confused as his hands drop to his sides.

"What's wrong?" he asks in that sensual voice and I want to rip out this creature's vocal chords for impersonating Balthazar.

I don't know much about the actual inhabitants of Jeznia but I do remember one House owns Shifters as their House Aides. House Anguis. Per Balthazar's notes, Shifters can change their appearance and voice to perfectly match their target, however they cannot change their scent.

To come to me when the wind is too unpredictable only means one thing. Whoever the Shifter is knew I'd figure it out and didn't care. He doesn't plan on me leaving alive. *We'll see who survives this fight.*

Before either of us makes a move towards the other, metal singing through the air cuts through the violent sounds of the wind. My entire body goes rigid. I act before I find the source of the sound. My fingers snap and I barely manage to teleport out of the way.

The sound of metal clanging against the wall greets my ears when I resurface from the in between. My eyes dart over to the creature holding the weapon and my breath stalls in my chest as my stomach drops at the sight before me.

A tall, muscular scythe wielding creature stands between me and the Shifter; its back is to me. It's adorned in a tight, deep burgundy hooded leather vest that drapes down to its ankles. Its biceps bulge as it lifts the scythe off the wall and slowly, it turns towards me.

Eyes are sewn shut and its lower jaw is missing as if it was ripped off. The wind's direction changes again and the scent of thick, coppery blood assaults my nose. My heart's in my throat as the creature takes a menacing step towards me.

Executioner.

Of House Vespertilio.

That means the second and third Houses have teamed up to have me killed. The news doesn't shock me. They must have figured out what I'm doing down here in the seventh circle. It's not surprising they figured it out given how much time I've been gone. It's been 17 days. The Lords of Jeznia stipulated I must attend House meetings since I'm Lord Balthazar's wife. It's impossible that there hasn't been a single meeting since I left. Balthazar could come up with an excuse or two but after the third missed meeting, there would be no denying our separation.

My absence would have them sending spies after me to figure out *why* I've been neglecting my duties. Now that they've found me secluded and unprotected in the seventh circle, they're taking the opportunity to get rid of me. I can't say I blame them.

Meik and Carmilla may have sided with Balthazar during his trial, but I'm no fool. That had more to do with Zagon Primis than Balthazar. I'm not stupid enough to think my questionable family relation to Zagon would protect me from the other Houses. I'm fair game to them. They're willing to risk the wrath of Balthazar if it means knocking him down a peg.

Fuck that.

I'm not here to weigh Balthazar down. I can hold my own and I'm going to show these assholes exactly that.

The Executioner takes calculated steps towards me. My heart jumps a beat at its approach. I need to assess the situation and figure out my best plan of action.

Executioners are trained in close combat, using the scythe as their choice of weapon. Their specialty is destroying a soul out of existence. Which means that even when an immortal dies, its soul goes somewhere. Unless, of course, that immortal is killed by an Executioner. According to the notes Balthazar gave me, the magic exists in the scythe, *not* the Executioner. So as long as I avoid the scythe or Hell, even break it, I'll be ok.

My eyes dart over to my second opponent. The Shifter is a bit of a wild card. If I remember correctly, they're not usually trained in combat, but Umbra made a note within the margins saying she thinks that's a ploy created by Lord Meik to undersell the Shifters talents.

Shifters are difficult to spot since they can assume the identity of their targets. If you don't know what the target smells like, it makes it impossible to tell a Shifter from the original person. If Meik implies the Shifters aren't good at fighting even though they are, it's an ace up his sleeves. The smartest thing for me to do is assume the Shifter knows how to fight.

My weight bounces back and forth on my feet as the Executioner approaches me. I expect it to rush at me but it doesn't. It's slow approach puts me on edge. An Executioner has to be able to move swiftly if it ever intends to hit a target with a scythe. The slow approach must be an attempt to trick me into thinking I can outrun it and when I least expect it, it'll strike true and fast without a moment's hesitation.

The beat of my heart thunders rapidly in my ear as my stomach clenches in unease. My opponents are not simple citizens of the circles of Jeznia. If they were, this fight would be a cakewalk. Instead, I'm going up against two *House Aides* from the most powerful Houses outside of House Primis. I might actually lose if I'm not careful and smart about this fight.

My weight shifts back and forth on the balls of my feet as my hands shake out my nerves. *You've got this, Sloane.*

My magic is badass. It's old. It's powerful. It knows what the fuck it's doing. I got this. I can do this. If I lose a limb, I'll just give myself another one.

I can do this.

My resolve slides into place, a calm washing over me. My fingers snap and a moment later, a gun appears in my hand. Acting quickly, I shoot the Executioner. The creature jerks with each impact but doesn't stop its approach. The bullets appear to be only a minor inconvenience. I need to change tactics.

I change targets, quickly aiming the gun at the Shifter and shoot. It yelps as it rolls away. Good, the bullets are a threat to it.

BANG

BANG

BANG

The Shifter evades each bullet. The gun may be a threat to it, but it appears to have no problems evading death. I toss the gun to the ground, mindful of how close the Executioner has gotten. It still moves at a snail's pace, but any moment, it could disappear from sight. I need to eliminate the Executioner.

My fingers snap together and a sword appears in my hand. I have no idea how to use this thing, but it can't be that hard, right? Just swing and stab. If I can get the Executioner through the heart or chop off its head, I win.

My breaths come in and out in rapid succession as my brain finds the courage I need. My hands grip the sword tightly before I dart off into a full sprint at the Executioner. I don't know how to fight, not really, but I've managed to survive *seventeen days* in the seventh circle. That's worth something, right? It may not be enough to win a fight against an Executioner, but at least I won't die a crying, sniveling mess.

Magic, work with me here, I beg as I sprint towards my looming target. The Executioner pulls the scythe back in preparation of swinging forward and, within a singular second, it disappears from sight. *Fuck.*

I throw out a Hail Mary, spinning in a circle as I extend the sword outward, hoping against all hope that it'll connect with the target once the Executioner reappears. The air is suddenly drenched in copper so thick that it coats my tongue and threatens to suffocate me. A scream mixed of surprise and fear falls out of my mouth as my magic floods my body, putting up a shield at the last second.

The scythe clangs against the invisible shield, confusing the Executioner as its head tilts sideways. I take the opportunity of the stunned Executioner to lash out with my magic. I imagine an invisible slithering spear wrapping around the Executioner's neck before piercing through its skull. To my utter surprise, the Executioner uses the scythe to slice its throat. Blood gushes out of it and I feel the magic that's wrapped around its throat break.

Shock paralyzes me as the Executioner pulls the scythe back. No one has ever managed to *break* my magic before.

My eyes snap to the dark metal of the blade and light gleams against the smooth surface. That blade is more dangerous than I gave it credit for. I knew it had magic within the blade, but is the magic old magic like mine? Is that why it's able to cut through mine?

I teleport out of the Executioner's reach just as it swings the scythe forward. Why is the Executioner moving so slowly when just a second ago it was moving fast?

Arms wrap around me from behind and I feel the cool blade of a dagger slicing across my throat, splitting it open.

"You forgot about me, my wife," Balthazar's deep, familiar voice fills my ears but the smell of sulfur makes me gag.

Blood spurts out of my neck in time with my heartbeat. My hand instinctively rushes up to my neck but the Shifter has my arms trapped against my sides. It's too strong against my strength.

I teleport, attempting to transport out of the Shifter's arms, but since he's holding onto me, he teleports with me. Fear rampages through me like an unforgiving tsunami. I'm bleeding to death. I need to heal my wound but I've never healed an injury by thought alone. I've always touched it, channeling my magic from my hand to the wound.

I stumble on my feet, dizziness making me imbalanced, but the Shifter keeps me standing. The Executioner approaches us with steady footsteps. The wind whips wildly around us, almost as if it's directly linked to the whirlwind of emotions swirling inside me.

It's not enough for me to be dead. The Lords want my soul obliterated. But if I don't have a soul inside me, will the Executioner's magic still work? Am I connected to my soul in the Record Keeper's vault? If the Executioner slices me with that blade, will the blade's magic slice through my soul in the vault?

Terror grips my body in a vise–like grip, the rapid pumping of my heart gushing blood out of my wound faster than it should be. I'll die from fear before the Executioner's blade touches me.

The wind changes directions again, making me downwind from the Executioner. Its coppery, rotten body odor rams into my nose. I watch in slow motion as the Executioner scrapes the blade of the scythe against the ground, bringing the weapon into an upward swing in preparation of swinging it down on me. Lord Carmilla and Lord Meik want to be absolutely certain that I'm removed. Not just dead, existing on another possible plane for fallen immortals. They want me to be obliterated *out of existence*.

The thought infuriates me, destroying any fear I'm feeling. I'm not some easy target they can take down with minimal effort. I am Lord Balthazar's *owner*. My magic is old, powerful, and deep. It's about time I unleash it and show these fuckers just how outmatched they really are and I'm *not* talking about the Shifter and Executioner. After I dispose of them, I'm going after the Lords.

I can't hold back the words as I growl out in a low, menacing voice, "I'll make them pay."

XVII

"WHAT DID YOU say?" the Shifter asks as he leans his head forward to hear me better.

I don't bother to repeat myself. Instead, a rage filled scream explodes out of me, violent and powerful. The Lords want to kill me to eliminate a threat. They want to kill me to weaken Balthazar. They want to kill me because they hate my origins. *Fuck. That.*

Without warning, my body goes up in flames. Skin bubbles and pops before sliding off into big plops. The Shifter shouts in surprise as he let's go of me. He's unprepared for me whipping around at the same time he let's go and wrapping my arms tight around his middle, securing his arms against his sides. I have him trapped. *Good.*

He instantly fights against my hold, desperate to free himself from the burning flames. Pain ravages through me, hot and blinding, but I hold on as tight as I can. The flames burn me as if the fire isn't coming *from* me. The only difference between me and the Shifter is that *he* will die from these flames. They may harm me, but they won't kill me.

Gritting my teeth through the excruciating pain, I pump magic into my arms to make me incredibly strong. The Shifter won't be able to free himself from my magical hold. I refuse to let him escape. Discounting the fact that he's here to literally kill me, this Shifter deserves to die for the simple act of impersonating Balthazar.

Agonized screams expel from the Shifter as the fire burns through him. His useless fidgeting does nothing to save him from his death. The flames eat him alive until finally, his screams stops. He slumps against me, lifeless.

Heavy pants pass through my mouth as I finally release the Shifter. The corpse thuds against the ground and slowly, I turn towards the Executioner. Quietly, it stands on a pile of my melted skin. My stomach churns at the sight of the large clumps. It's disgusting and my stomach threatens to eject what little food I have in it, but I don't have the time for superficial luxuries. Not when the Executioner moves with such dizzying quickness.

The Executioner swings its scythe up, its speed significantly faster than it originally showed me. In this moment, it's clear to me it had been holding itself back, wanting to let the Shifter kill me. The Shifter would get all the glory for killing me… and subsequently, all the blame. *Lord Carmilla probably ordered it that way to keep her hands clean. 'I didn't order Sloane killed, Lord Balthazar. It was a Shifter that killed her.' Smart, but pointless now since I won't be the one dying.*

The Executioner moves fast, closing the distance between us in a heartbeat. My magic shoots out, our intent linked, as it creates an invisible shield around me. The Executioner swings its scythe forward in an elegant arc and the blade bangs against the invisible shield. A smirk pulls at the corner of my lips as I stare into its sewn shut eyes.

"You've fucked with the wrong devil," I say, my voice multi–layered as the magic flows through me freely, uninhibited by my boundaries.

It's a new level I've reached in using my magic. The magic hurts as it courses through me. Almost as if I'm rolling over a bed of sharp nails, but I grit through the pain. I won't pull back now. Not during a fight with the Executioner. This bastard is going to die, not me.

Deep magic vibrates within me. My eyes flicker up, catching sight of the scythe's blade vibrating in time with my magic. Familiarity washes over me as the blade and my magic call to each other. They're begging to touch, to shed the distance between them and merge as one. I nearly laugh at my luck as the realization cuts through me.

My magic and the blade's magic... They're of the same origin. Perfect.

The Executioner doesn't seem to notice or care that its scythe is behaving erratically. It pushes forward, leaning its weight into the scythe in an attempt to pierce through my shield. The Executioner's biceps bulge as it grunts against the resistance.

A loud, audible crack echoes through the air and I wince as a tear is physically cut through the shield. The tip of the blade pushes forward, breaking through the shield. I react on instinct, praying my assumption is right. My hand reaches for the blade.

Instantaneously, the blade and I magically connect seconds before the shield breaks and the scythe comes barreling at me. In that short amount of time, I use the magic to rotate the blade towards the Executioner. As the Executioner's weight bears down on the scythe, the backside of the weapon slams into me and the blade goes straight through the Executioner's chest.

We fall to the ground in a heap. Blood sizzles against the fire that continues to consume my body. The Executioner's heavy weight nearly crushes me as it remains motionless despite the roaring flames. Using magic to fuel strength into my arms, I push the large creature off me.

It rolls onto its back, the scythe still embedded in its chest. I rush to my feet, falling into a defensive stance as I watch the Executioner for any sudden movements. Desperate clawed fingers ghost over my neck to check for the life ending wound the Shifter gave me. I find no evidence of being cut. The angry burst of magic that burned off my humanoid appearance must have healed my neck. *I got lucky*, I think as I lean down, grabbing the hilt of the scythe. Things would have ended very differently if my wound hadn't healed.

I give the scythe a tug, only semi–surprised by the weight of it as it remains embedded in the Executioner. Pushing magic into my arms and core, I yank the blade out. The Executioner grunts but does not move.

I lift the scythe over my right shoulder as I stare down at the bleeding, dying Executioner, debating on what I should do now. This asshole was sent to kill me. It was following *orders*. House Aides are *bound* to their Lords. If the Executioner had gone against Lord Carmilla's wishes, it would have probably pulled out its own heart as punishment.

My lips pull down into a frown. Still. It tried to kill me. I can't afford to give it leniency. Not if I'm to protect Balthazar. Not if I'm to show the Lords I'm a true threat, not someone to be trifled with. If I let the Executioner live, it'll show them I'm weak, that I don't belong here. I should kill it. I have to kill it.

The Executioner doesn't move. It lies motionless on the ground as the rise and fall of its chest begins to slow.

My fingers curl tightly around the hilt of the weapon as I question my resolve. It's dying on its own. Do I truly need to kill it with the blade? It would be a mercy kill, ending the suffering immediately, but the blade would destroy the soul. Can I live with that?

No. I may be ok with killing to survive, and I fully support a mercy kill, but I won't do this. I don't know what kind of life this Executioner lived or why it made the decision to become a House Aide. All I know is if things were in the reverse, I'd want mercy shown to Umbra. I wouldn't want her soul destroyed into oblivion. Lord Carmilla doesn't deserve that mercy, but her House Aide does.

My hands release the scythe and it clatters loudly against the ground. A deep sigh whooshes out of the Executioner's mouth and I can only hope it's in relief of receiving my mercy.

The Executioner parts its lips and utters out a couple words in a rasped, wet whisper.

"Descendere in fla…"

The rest of whatever the Executioner planned on saying dies on its lips as it exhales its last breath. Its head slumps to the side and, for a few moments, I simply stand there, staring at its corpse and the burnt corpse of the Shifter a few feet from us.

In that moment, the weight of what just happened hits me full force. Two Houses attempted to murder me and *failed.* They've *earned* an enemy in me. I won't take this lying down. It's time I show them who's the real boss. It's not Balthazar they should fear. *It's me.* It's time they learned that.

Quietly, my fingers curl around the scythe and I sink the blade into the dead Executioner's chest. I grab a firm hold of its forearm and teleport over to the shifter.

Fingers curl around the Shifter's forearm and my eyes cast up towards the mountain. Each individual wall stares back at me. Sixty miles. Sixty miles with dead weight. Literally.

The flames that continue to burn my body flicker and sway in the wind as I contemplate the logistics of my situation. Simple horizontal travel I can teleport about a mile. Straight vertical travel I can teleport about a quarter mile. I have yet to attempt teleporting both horizontally and vertically at the same time, but I need to do so in order to *ascend* the mountain. I have to assume the distance I'm able to accomplish will be similar or less than traveling vertically. Quarter of a mile, give or take several hundred feet.

My eyes glance down at the two corpses. Make that significantly less with all the added extra weight.

I contemplate leaving the bodies but immediately squash the idea. I have to bring them back with me. I have to prove to them I'm a threat. Without these bodies, my words mean nothing to the Lords. I *need* these corpses.

"You've got this," I exhale loudly as my fingers grip their forearms tightly. "You just killed an Executioner and a Shifter. You can teleport your way up to the first circle."

My breath comes in and out in quick, short bursts before I embrace the insanity of what I'm about to do. A split second later, the three of us teleport off the wall. We emerge about an eighth of the way towards the next wall. Wind violently whips around us as we descend towards the impending ground.

I teleport again and emerge a little closer to the wall but notably a little lower to the ground. That's not good. So not only do I have to concentrate on crossing a ten mile distance, but I need to make sure I don't lose altitude while doing it. Fuck.

I teleport a third time. Nearly halfway there but I'm still losing elevation.

A frustrated yell erupts out of me as I teleport a fourth time. *Higher, Sloane, HIGHER.* I can't afford to lost altitude and land in the sixth circle. If I do, another House will discover my whereabouts. And it won't be just any House. No. It'll be House Aranea. Lord Taron. He won't take the intrusion lightly. There will be consequences for me trespassing into his circle. I *have* to make it to the wall that divides the sixth and fifth circle.

The next time we emerge, we're higher than the wall, but not close enough to land. Relief washes over me at the height I've gained. We'll make it. One more teleportation should do it.

We blip out of sight before reappearing and landing roughly on the sixth wall. I tumble over the bodies, narrowly missing getting cut by the scythe. I refuse to leave it behind. This scythe belongs to me now. Lord Carmilla will have to pry it from my dead hands. Only a fool would leave behind this kind of power. Next time I land, I just need to be more aware of the blade to avoid any mistakes.

I take a few moments to plan out my trip to the fifth wall. Five teleportations is all it takes. Easy enough. I can do this. I did it once. I can do it five more times.

My gaze travels up the mountainside and a frown mars my face as I study the top three walls. Their ascension rate is astronomically severe in comparison to walls four, five, six, and seven. I might actually run into trouble. Whatever. I'll think about that when I get there. For now, I should focus on crossing the fifth circle.

Standing to my feet, I grab the Shifter and Executioner by the forearms again. After a large inhale and exhale, we disappear from sight. Now that I know what I'm doing, it's easier to accomplish. As expected, it takes me five teleportations to reach the fourth wall. I nearly miss it, though, almost overshooting the width of the wall.

We come crashing down in a heap, rolling towards the edge of the wall. As we come to a stop, the Shifter's legs drape over the edge. Gravity begins to pull the body down the wall and I leap in desperation to hold it back. I refuse to lose these bodies. They're my only proof that the Houses attacked me.

Once the corpse is secured, I flop down on my back, my chest heaving. I can feel my magic draining me. It's been a while since I've exerted this much magic in such a short amount of time. I have to conserve it as best I can if I want to be able to walk into the throne room.

Shit.

The throne room.

It'll be empty upon my arrival. The Lords only go there when a meeting has been called. I need to get them in that room before I get to the first circle. How can I prove my worth and power to them if they're nowhere to be found?

"Umbra," I yell into the wind. "I need you to call a meeting."

Barely a moment later, black shadows swirl above me before Umbra descends from the mass. She wields a dagger, poised to strike, as she falls from the sky.

"Oh shit," expels from me as I roll out of the way.

Her dagger clangs against the ground, but she's already moving into another attack. I draw my magic forward, creating a shield between the two of us. I keep it focused and small, not wanting to exert too much of my magic. I still have a long way to go from here to the throne room. I can't afford to deplete my magic.

"Umbra! What the hell?" I yell as she continues her onslaught.

She's fast and uses the shadows to her advantage, disappearing one second only to return in a completely different direction. She's forcing me to broaden the shield to cover my entire body. The dagger stabs the shield over and over again but doesn't penetrate it. Yet I can feel the magic weakening and the whole situation infuriates me. What is her problem?

Wait.

What if this isn't Umbra but a Shifter? Fury explodes through me as I focus my magic to my hands and a beam of concentrated fire shoots out directly at Umbra.

"Enough," I demand as she disappears into the shadows.

I whirl around, already anticipating her to show up behind me, and whip out my hand just as she exits the shadows. My hand connects, fingers curling tightly around her throat, as I yank her close so we're almost nose to nose.

"I don't have time for this," I growl out, my anger amplifying my magic as I hold her in place.

She's trying to stab me with the knife but it can't break through the magic that protects me.

"Prove to me you're the real deal, that you're really Umbra, or I'll fucking slice you with the scythe. *You hear me?*"

The glare on Umbra's face hardens but she stills all movements. "I'm not so easily fooled, Shifter. Lord Balthazar will punish House Anguis for impersonating his wife."

"You think *I'm* the Shifter?" I ask in bewilderment.

My eyes flit down to the hand curled around Umbra's throat. Charcoal skin, similar to the appearance of when molten lava cools down. Cracks dart across my skin, illuminated by the color in the exact shade of hot magma.

It takes me far too long to connect the dots, but I eventually get there. I don't look like me. I burned so hot during my fight with the Shifter and Executioner that my humanoid appearance melted off.

No wonder she thinks I'm a Shifter trying to impersonate me. I look nothing like the Sloane she knows. Never mind the fact that a Shifter pretending to be me would get access to a lot of conversations Meik would benefit from. Umbra probably assumes I'm still in the seventh circle, learning to control my magic.

"You told me Balthazar was coddling me," I tell her, the words falling out as quickly as I can think them, "that my heart makes me weak, and that if I indulge my heart, I'll never amount to anything. It's me, Umbra. I went through a metamorphosis in the seventh circle. Now, it's your turn. Prove to me you're really Umbra."

She's glaring at me and for a moment, I think she's not going to answer, but she finally says, "My favorite way to kill an opponent is a dagger to the top of the spine, severing all central nerve connections to the brain."

"Right, 'cause then they lose their mobility and can't fight back."

"Yes. The death is quick and quiet—"

"Both very important for a Shadow Seer."

"Precisely," she agrees.

I stare at her for a few seconds before finally releasing my hold around her neck. She takes a step back, her amber eyes flitting to the corpses a few feet from us.

"An Executioner and a Shifter."

"Yeah," I breathe out as I sit down on the ground, finally allowing myself to relax in her presence. "I'm on my way to the throne room. That's why I need you to call a meeting. I need the Houses to be present when I walk in with the corpses of two House Aides."

She smirks as she nods her head. "I'll notify Lord Balthazar. It'll be a treat to see the look on their faces when you present them their gifts."

I can't help but smirk back. "My thoughts exactly."

Shadows start to curl around Umbra's ankles and ascend her frame. I lunge for her, my fingers curling around her calf.

"Wait! It, uh, it might take me awhile to get there," I admit and she frowns. I shrug my shoulders as my hand lets her go and I sit back. "I haven't fully mastered my magic. It takes me five transportations to get from one wall to the other. Just let Balthazar know so he can wait outside for me. They won't start a meeting without him, especially if he's the one who called it."

She says nothing but gives me a curt nod in response. A moment later, she's gone.

"Alright. Let's do this," I breathe out before grabbing hold of the corpses and teleporting to the next wall.

I'm honestly not sure how much time passes before I finally reach the wall separating the third and second circles. I've exerted a lot of magic and I'm starting to worry I won't be able to make it the rest of the way up. At least I have a last resort in asking Umbra or Balthazar to help me, but I want to do this on my own. I worked hard to be this advanced with my magic. I killed an Executioner and a Shifter *on my own*. I don't want Umbra or Balthazar swooping in at the last minute to help me get to the throne room. I can do this. I *will* do this. To prove not only to the Lords and Houses how strong I am, but also to myself.

I take a few moments to let my body recuperate. The more I use my magic, the more drained I become. I haven't built up substantial stamina yet despite being in Jeznia for seventeen days. To be fair, though, *three* House Aides challenged me within an hour and I'm still alive. On top of that, I'm still able to use my magic *and* I'm not a sitting duck waiting to be slaughtered. That's really impressive if I give myself a moment to take it in.

I can feel my energy replenishing as I take some time to rest. I'm perched on the edge of the wall, my legs dangling down the side of it as I stare at the city that occupies the second circle. My attention is drawn to the black gothic style buildings that are built into the mountainside. Yellow–orange light illuminates the city, breathing life into it.

I estimate the closest building to me is roughly three miles from the wall, giving the city plenty of a buffer from the third circle that apparently tries to break into it every couple hundred years. They've created a mine field of traps and weapons from the wall to their precious city. It's smart. I wonder if these tactics were from the mind of Lord Carmilla and House Vespertilio or if these actions were put in place by the second circle inhabitants. Just how involved are the Lords in their circles?

Balthazar has never made any mention of circles, but I don't imagine the first circle requires much oversight. It's the top of the barrel. It probably operates quite well on its own because everyone wants the same things. The first and seventh circle must be very similar in that aspect.

My feet kick against the wall as I admire the scenery. It's morbidly beautiful. The buildings, even from this distance, are breathtaking in their arches, sharp edges, and elegant curves. The dark black of the buildings contrasts beautifully against the magma yellow–orange and deep reds of the mountain. The city looks like it's slowly burning, as if the buildings are coal waiting to ignite. It's stunning.

Maybe if the rest of the circles were as nicely maintained as this one, there wouldn't be an issue with uprisings. The lower circles are wilderness. I didn't come across a single outpost or shack in the seventh circle. The inhabitants merely lived in the trees or underground. The higher up the mountain, the thinner the trees get until there aren't anymore. I saw a couple of sparse buildings in the fourth circle. The third circle…

I glance behind me, down the side of the mountain. There's a small city built into the mountainside not too far from the wall. My guess is they settled there to make it easier to try to invade the second circle when the desire arises. At least, that's what I would do if I were in their shoes.

Still, their small city is nothing in comparison to the second circle. There isn't much light in their circle and most of their roads look like dilapidated bridges over sheer drop offs. Roofs have caved in. Buildings are leaning. Foundations are crumbling. The city looks weathered and worn.

My attention shifts back to the second circle. Their buildings look well kept. There's plenty of light. Their roads are a healthy mixture of mountain terrain and bridges.

I get distracted by the intensity of the city as I stare at it. Despite there being roughly ten miles between the walls, the city can't grow from wall to wall. The mountainside is too steep. Instead, the city has to grow parallel to the wall in limited space.

Maybe the backside has more favorable conditions for the city to grow outwards. Or maybe they're just as limited in their space. Despite its lack of terrain to spread out on, the city looks beautiful. I can't help but wonder if the first circle will be even more beautiful than this. Just how large or small is the city? I don't imagine it has a high population. Maybe it contains one per cent of Jeznia's population. Maybe there's only one spot in the entire circle that has buildings and the rest of the circle is wilderness.

Admittedly, I'm excited to find out.

Huffing rather loudly as I get to my feet, my eyes drift over to the corpses. A frown pulls at my lips as I stare at the burnt corpse of the Shifter. It's too burnt to be identifiable. It's no wonder Umbra thought the corpse was me. I look nothing like my human self right now and the Shifter is roughly the same height as me. Will Meik and the other Lords believe me when I inform them it's a Shifter? I suppose if it were me, I might think it's a corpse from the seventh circle and that I'm lying about it. But then my eyes shift to the Executioner. The other Lords may not believe me about the Shifter, but there's no denying the Executioner.

Without hesitation, I grab a forearm in each hand before teleporting. It's trickier now. The incline is steep but the harder part is the buildings. Their height eclipses the wall height. That means I have to dodge them while making sure I'm not losing height while also making sure I'm traveling the distance between the two walls. It's going to be hard.

Case in point, my third teleportation has me emerging *inside* one of the buildings. I drop to the floor in a heap before I'm able to teleport a fourth time. By the grace of God or the Creator, the room is empty. I don't stick around long enough to be discovered by the owner.

I quickly teleport out of the room, concentrating on traveling higher than the buildings. It works, but I lose distance horizontally. It's going to take me more than five teleportations to get to the first circle. Exhaustion is starting to creep in. I just want to sleep, but I can't. I need to make it to the throne room. Inhaling deeply, I teleport a fifth time.

When I pop out again, I come up short on the wall. I estimate I need one more jump and I'll have made it to the first circle wall.

"Come on, come on, come on," I whisper to myself as the corpses and I disappear into the space in between.

When we emerge, we've overshot the wall by quite a distance.

"Shit."

What do I do? Turn around to the wall or keep going? I don't know where I am nor do I know where I need to go. I should go back to the wall to rest and gather my bearings. That seems like the best choice to make.

I teleport again and this time, we appear about three feet above the wall. We've almost landed when I register a substance coating the wall. As we approach, it becomes abundantly clear the wall is covered in spider webs. My heart and stomach bottom out as we land with a thud. The stickiness of the webs hold us in place.

Panic immediately sets in as I struggle against the webs.

"Fuck, fuck, fuck, fuck, fuck," I mutter repeatedly, fear overloading my senses.

These cobwebs are insane. Try as I might, I can't yank myself out of them. Every little struggle seems to make the cobwebs even stickier. I'm practically glued in place.

My chest heaves violently as my imagination starts to get the better of me. Every movie I've ever seen with spiders in it floods my brain. Their massive ungodly size, the swiftness of them despite how large they are, how they spin their prey in spools of webs before sucking them dry… I'm going to die. I'm going to die and it'll be because of these wretched, terrifying spiders.

I can't hold back my desperate shrieks and whimpers as I fight as hard as I can against the webs. Balthazar said the spiders are worse than the bats. I don't want to find out whether he was speaking the truth or not.

"Come on, come on, come on," I scream while tugging against the webs, tears streaming down my face as I imagine coming face to face with a spider.

I worked too hard to die this way but my fear overloads my brain. I can't think straight. All I can think about is a spider crawling its way towards me and I'm stuck, unable to escape.

"*Please*," I yell to no one and my magic surges through me just as I see a spider eclipse the wall.

My heart stops beating at the sheer size of it. It's as big as a *minivan*. Long, thick legs, white hair and skin, and fangs as long as my thigh.

"No, no, no, no, no," I cry as I shake against the webs that hold me.

Eight beady eyes bigger than my head peer at me before it begins its approach towards me.

"NO!"

I tug against the spider webs, my magic vibrating within me as terror grips my heart. The spider is fast and I can't. I fucking can't. Fear drowns me of all rational thought.

My magic suddenly bursts into flames, covering my entire body. It's excruciating, but the cobwebs burn away in the process.

The spider hoists up onto its back legs as it uses its front ones to shield it from the flames. I desperately reach out to the Executioner and Shifter, pushing through the pain that consumes me. The fire hurts me but it won't kill me. I can take the pain if it means living.

My hands clamp down around body parts of the corpses before I teleport away. The flames don't die down as we travel through the in between. If anything, they burn hotter and brighter.

A grunt of pain passes through my lips. My tears evaporate as soon as they appear. My lips shrivel and crack from the heat. I try not to concentrate on the pain, instead focusing on getting back to Balthazar.

When we emerge from the in between, we slam into the mountain side, immediately sticking to more cobwebs mere feet from another massive spider. It screeches at our sudden, burning appearance, rearing up and away from the fire. I can't hold back my own scream at seeing another spider and my flames burn brighter and hotter from the intensity of my emotions.

Ashes drop from my arms and I glance down. The cracks darting across my skin widen and I realize with horror that the magical fire *is* harming me. If it goes on long enough, will it actually kill me?

The spider shrieks, drawing my attention back to the issue at hand. I can't think about what the fire is doing to me. Not right now. My first priority is getting off this god forsaken mountain and away from these spiders.

Despite the burning, raging pain, I muster enough energy to teleport again. My fingers remain tightly curled around the corpses. When we surface again, we stick to more cobwebs. The higher we ascend, the more populated the mountainside becomes with spiders. My flames never die down, the pain rampaging through me intensifying the longer I stay aflame. My vision begins to warp and I fear I might pass out and die from the pain.

We emerge from the space in between after I don't know how many teleports and abruptly land on top of a spider. It shrieks as it rears up, bucking us off. The corpses and I tumble to the ground, landing on smaller spiders. They squeal and shriek as the flames burn them. A few lash out in their pain, sinking their fangs into us as they fight us the best way they know how to.

Pain explodes with each bite and my will to live disintegrates into the flames. I can't do this anymore. It's too much. I should just let myself die. The pain would be gone. I could finally rest *peacefully*. I wouldn't have to prove a point to anyone anymore.

My life is nonexistent anyway. There's only Balthazar. I have no family or friends, no job or responsibilities. No one would miss me but Balthazar. And even then... I'm a walking liability to him. I may be strong now, but his father is still stronger. Besides, everyone is out to kill me. The Lords, any

Jeznian I meet, Odantha and its rulers… There are more people who want me dead than people who want me alive.

Who am I to stand in their way?

Who am I to say no to the majority vote?

Who am I among the rulers of literal *worlds*?

With a shuddering breath, tension releases its strong hold on me and my body slumps against the ground.

XVIII

THE LARGER SPIDERS shoot their webs at us. *Smart*, I think. Cover me in enough webs and the fire will suffocate. Hopefully.

The spiders attempts are not thwarted by any attempts from me. I lay motionless, pain ravaging every molecule in my body. Just end. Please let it all stop. I just want it to stop.

"You've done well," a soothing, deep voice whispers into my ear as arms scoop behind my neck and knees.

I'm hoisted effortlessly into the air. Somehow, I find the strength to open my eyes. My gaze shifts over to the face of the person who holds me.

Burning, glowing red eyes. Skin the same charcoal color as mine. The same yellow glowing cracks dart across the skin's surface. The only difference between the two of us is the black ooze dripping down their face. Their horns are the same shape as mine. They're also are on fire. Smoke wafts up my nose, so unique and familiar that I nearly weep from joy.

Home.

I'm home.

"Balthazar," I breathe out his name as I slump against him, relief overwhelming me.

"You did well, peccatum meum," he repeats before we disappear into the in between.

A moment later, we appear inside his office. As if I were the finest China dish in all the worlds, Balthazar gently places me down on the floor. He hovers over me, a hand stroking my face.

"Sloane, you need to turn off your magic," he says.

My head shakes weakly. I'm too far gone. The magic is too powerful. I just need to die. That's the only way the pain will stop.

"Sloane, turn off your magic."

"I can't," I weep, tears evaporating as soon they appear.

Balthazar presses his forehead against mine, not once wincing from the intensity of the flames.

"Yes, you can," he states firmly before whispering in a soothing, cold voice. "Turn off your magic."

His words wash over me cold like ice, easing the pain rampaging through me. I desperately seek out more of that relief. Gingerly, the cold slowly encases me from head to toe. My tears now flow freely down the sides of my face. Finally, *finally*, the pain is gone.

"Good job," Balthazar whispers as he strokes my face tenderly. "You did well, Sloane."

"Are you really here?" I ask, my voice warbled as I raise up my hand to touch his face. His human appearance stares back at me, black–red eyes darting back and forth between mine.

"I am," he answers. "I've called the meeting you requested. The Lords are all waiting."

A weak smile graces my mouth as my hand plops back down to the ground. "Good. Do you know where the bodies that I was carrying are?"

"Here with us."

"Good, good. Thank you, Balthazar."

Silence drapes us as my eyes flutter close. Gentle fingers caress my face, pushing strands of hair behind my ear. Fingers ghost down the length of my jaw, over my lips, before firmly settling around my jaw and neck as a thumb caresses my cheek.

"I've been eagerly anticipating your return," he says in a soft voice as his thumb brushes against my lower lip.

My eyes peer open and I'm immediately met with his intense stare. He's soaking in everything about me; the slant of my nose, the shape of my lips, the curve of my cheeks. His eyes linger over my face, burning every feature of me in his mind. I can't help but do the same. Seventeen days. It's been seventeen days since I've seen his face. I want it etched behind my eyelids.

I finally register what he's confessed and a small smile adorns my face. "Is that your way of saying you missed me without directly saying it?"

He chuckles, deep and low, as he leans down and presses his lips oh—so—lightly against mine. "Perhaps."

"I missed you too," I reply openly, not at all bothering to mince words. "I was hoping to have a badass entrance, but I wasn't anticipating the spiders."

"Mm," he hums as he lays down beside me on the ground, pulling me onto him.

Barely a moment later, his fingers thread through my hair, nails scraping against my scalp. I contemplate telling him I haven't washed my hair in seventeen days but I don't think either one of us really cares.

"The spiders can't survive in the lower altitudes," he says.

"We should take up residency in the seventh circle then," I weakly declare.

He chuckles, the sound like a hot bath on a rainy day. "We'll go wherever you desire."

My arm curls around him as I snuggle deeper into his chest. I inhale, nothing special about the simple action, but that smokey scent fills my senses. My heart clenches in my chest as my vision distorts. A sudden deep and vicious longing overwhelms me.

Seventeen days. Seventeen days *without* Balthazar. Without my *home*. How did I go so long without him?

"I missed you," I whisper, unable to speak any louder for fear of my voice warbling.

His grip tightens, his nose brushing against my head before he speaks so softly I almost miss what he says.

"You have no idea the torture I went through in your absence, Sloane. Never again will you leave my side."

My breath hitches in my throat at the severity of his words. He must have been out of his mind with worry the entire time I was gone. He had once a day when he knew I was alive and that was when Umbra delivered my food. Any other time of day, he had no idea if I was alive, if I was suffering, if I was dying, or if I was already dead.

Guilt gnaws at me as we embrace each other in a comfortable silence. I don't regret my decision to train in the seventh circle, but that doesn't mean I don't feel bad for what I put him through. I can't imagine how horrific it would have felt if our positions had been swapped. I'd worry about him every second of the day. Is he safe? Is he hurt? How is he progressing? Did he *die* today? What would I do if he did? It's the worst kind of torture to be put through.

"I'm sorry," I whisper as I curl into him.

"There is nothing for you to apologize about," he replies firmly before swiftly changing the topic. "How are you feeling? I don't imagine the Lords will wait much longer."

"I should be good enough," I say as I sit up and glance around the office.

It's exactly how I remember it. Minus the two corpses near the door.

Balthazar rises to his feet and extends a hand down to me. I gladly take it and he hoists me up. His eyes dance down my frame, then back up and he smiles, wide and handsome.

"You're absolutely stunning."

My eyebrows pinch together in confusion as I glance down. I'm still in my devil form; charcoal black and cracked skin. I have no idea the color of my eyes. I'm still a little confused about how I have hair, especially when my body keeps going up in flames, but I'm doing my best not to question it. I'll consider it a small win and move on.

"Come, we need to get to the meeting," Balthazar says.

Wordlessly, I follow after him. He uses his magic to bring the bodies with us as we walk down the hallway to the throne room. The doors are closed but their size no longer appears daunting. Especially in comparison to the size of the walls that encase the circles of Jeznia.

"Would you like to enter together?" Balthazar asks and I blink in surprise.

I hadn't thought about that. I just assumed we'd enter together but entering alone will deliver a more severe message. It'll make a statement that I'm strong enough on my own, that I am no longer a weakness to Balthazar, that I'm a formidable opponent on my own. I killed two House Aides today. I may be a newly turned devil, but I am *not* someone they'll want to fuck around with.

"Alone," I answer him.

He smirks wide and vicious. "As you should."

Balthazar moves fast, hand gripping my face possessively as he hungrily kisses me. I surrender myself to him, my arms eagerly wrapping around him as my body leans into him. I've missed his kisses. I've longed for his touch. I want to forget about this meeting and go back to our apartment and just *be together*. Whether we're making love or snuggled up in bed. I don't care which one it is. I just want to be with him.

I open my mouth to tell him that but he pulls away, almost as if he knows what I'm about to say.

"Wait five minutes before you enter," Balthazar states in a low, sensual voice. He wants to disappear to our apartment just as badly as I do. "I'll let you know when to enter."

"Ok," I breathe out as my hands gently cup his face and I speak without thinking. "I love you."

Shock courses through me at the words I've spoken. I hadn't meant to blurt them out but we haven't seen each other in so long and I had been fighting for my life every day that it seems so silly to be worried about saying three little words. But still...

I hadn't meant to say those words. At least not yet. What if it freaks Balthazar out? Emotions like these aren't well received in Jeznia. Caring for someone else is only good for getting yourself screwed over. Or worse, betrayed and killed.

I shouldn't have said it.

I part my lips to apologize, to do my best to take it all back when Balthazar suddenly grips my face in both hands and presses his forehead to mine.

"Peccatum meum, the word love does not even begin to encapsulate the depth of my feelings for you, but it will have to suffice," he states, fingers threading into my hair as he creates enough distance between us to lock gazes. "I love you, Sloane."

Shock nearly paralyzes me as my mouth drops open in surprise. "Are you... really Balthazar? Because I don't know if he's actually capable of saying 'I love you.'"

"Only for you," he states gently, dual colored eyes darting between mine. "I have every confidence in all the worlds that you'll keep yourself safe. I don't need to fear what the other Houses will try to do. You'll put them in their place; you'll have them whimpering on their hands and knees, begging for your forgiveness. I have no doubts."

"At least one of us doesn't," I say, a small laugh tumbling out of my mouth to hide my insecurities. "Alright, go now before we ditch this meeting entirely."

He growls but he tears himself away from me and snaps his fingers. The doors creak and groan as they slowly open. Balthazar casts me one last look before strutting into the room with all the confidence in the world.

"Greetings, my Lords," he says as he disappears into the room and the doors close behind him.

I'm left by myself with the two corpses as I wait for his signal to enter the room. The five minutes feels like a lifetime, but finally, the time arrives.

Come in now, Sloane, Balthazar's voice floats through my mind. I inhale deeply, my eyes sliding shut as I envision the throne room, envision each Lord sitting in their chair, the hatred upon their faces when they see me, but more importantly, the shock on Carmilla and Meik's faces when they see me dragging the corpses of their House Aides behind me. They certainly did not expect me to survive their attack. I can't wait to see the fury wash over them once the shock dissipates.

My eyes open. With a snap of my fingers, the doors creak open. I feel the strain as they resist me but I flood my magic forward and it breaks whatever seal is wrapped around the room. Confidently, I grab the wrists of each House Aide and being my walk into the room.

Ruulin and Taron, the two Houses closest to the entrance, immediately act. They use their magic to create a shield at the entrance, but Balthazar's voice echoes throughout the circular room.

"That won't be necessary," he declares loudly and full of pride. "My wife would like to make an appearance."

A hush falls over the room as I walk forward in my devil appearance with my head held high. I'm halfway across the room when I imagine my magic filling me to the brim. It cascades down me in glittering ripples. My human appearance descends from my head to my feet in the same path my magic takes. Three silver circlets adorn my horns. A circlet for each death I've experienced.

The day I met Balthazar.

The day Chad shot me.

And the day of the gargoyle attack when my transformation nearly killed me.

The clothes I had worn during my training in the seventh circle are gone, replaced by a beautiful, fantasy inspired black wedding gown. A long, tulle black cape is clipped around the front at my collar while dainty silver chains drape down my shoulders. I walk confidently across the room, not at all bothered or worried about the lava channels in the ground. There's no need to worry when I use my magic to let me walk over them as if there was plexiglass caging the lava in.

No one speaks a word as I ascend the stairs to Balthazar, the bodies I drag behind me thudding against each step I take. I don't look at anyone but Balthazar, at the smug, proud, gloating aura that captures his entire presence.

I smile, malicious and proud, as I surpass the fifth step and continue my way up to his throne. His eyes flash white as his smirk deepens. He doesn't move from his chair. Not until I've reached the top step.

There's no hesitation in his actions. He stands as I let go of the wrists of the House Aides and he easily steps out of the way as I move to sit down on the throne. There's an audible gasp, I imagine from Ivy, but I can't pinpoint exactly where it comes from as I sink into the chair.

My hands rest on the armrests of the throne as I cross my right leg over my left. Slowly, I scan the room, my eyes pausing on each stunned and angered face. I find it interesting that Carmilla refuses to meet my gaze while Meik's eyes look ready to murder me.

A pleased smile spreads across my lips as I speak, low and steady, "My Lords."

I've achieved exactly what I set out to do. There's no doubt about who holds the power. *Perfect.*

No one says anything in response to my greeting. Balthazar remains standing to the left of the throne, his face devoid of any emotion as he watches the room. I take a slow inhale, allowing myself to embrace the dominating woman I know I can be. The one Balthazar sees in me. It's easy to welcome it now that I'm so much stronger.

Two of the most powerful Houses tried to kill me today and *failed.* They might not have sent their best House Aides, thinking I'd be an easy target, but becoming a House Aide is no easy feat. Even the lowest ranking House Aide is worthy of being feared. Feared by everyone *except* House Lords and their heirs. And me.

My smile disappears as I glance around the room again, the words dripping out of my mouth like poison. "I apologize for the delay. I know you've requested my presence at these meetings but I've been rather... preoccupied. It would appear, Lord Meik and Lord Carmilla, that your House Aides have gone rogue."

Carmilla bristles upon hearing the words while Meik grips his throne armrest so tightly that it cracks. Neither one is pleased about the fake mercy I've shown them. Their anger is understandable. I've given them only two choices in how to respond. Either go along with my lie and admit their Houses don't have all their House Aides on a short leash or admit they willingly attacked Lord Balthazar's wife and suffer the consequences of such actions. It's not a good place to be in.

"Yes, it would appear so," Carmilla relents as she finally lifts her gaze to mine.

Her face is completely flat. I can't figure out what she's thinking or feeling. Even her eyes don't show any emotion. It's like she completely shut off any and all emotions.

It unnerves me, as I suspect it's meant to. A calm and collected enemy when faced with a surprise is a dangerous enemy. Carmilla isn't the second most powerful House for no reason. I need to proceed with caution; provoking her too much will likely cost me my life.

"I feel I must apologize for killing your investments," I say as I glance down at the corpses, my heart hammering inside my chest.

My stomach churns and clenches. It takes everything in me not to lean over and dry heave. Every single Lord in this room is hanging onto the words I speak. The awareness of that fact is equal parts exhilarating and terrifying.

There's no going back. From this day forward, I'll be a target on their radar *not* as a way to hurt Balthazar, but as a *threat* to them and their livelihood.

"It's my understanding that becoming a House Aide is pretty difficult and therefore, Houses are rather limited in their numbers of House Aides," I address the room. "If my life hadn't been endangered, I wouldn't have taken such extreme measures."

Meik clicks his tongue as he sits back against his throne. "Such benevolent words, Sloane of House Primis."

His tone doesn't match the words he's spoken. His voice is filled with malice and hatred, perfectly matching the sneer on his face, yet his words are kind and gracious. There's no denying how he truly feels, though. He wants my blood spilt across the floor. Or maybe dripping down the stairs. Whichever one is gorier, I'm sure.

Balthazar's hand reaches out to squeeze my shoulder. "Indeed," he hums. "She's far more lenient than I am. I fully expect a Shifter and Executioner gifted to House Primis to placate our anger or there will be retaliation."

It's not lost on me that Balthazar's eyes drop to where Ivy sits upon speaking the word retaliation. Carmilla doesn't miss the look either and her fingers curl into her hand as her lips press into a thin line.

Unfortunately, Meik has no heir and no spouse for Balthazar to go after. I'm not sure what kind of retaliation Balthazar could take on a House that only has a Lord. Judging by the smug look on Meik's face, he must be thinking the same thing.

"What can you expect to achieve without your father's support?" Meik asks, amusement dripping in his voice as he leans over in his chair to taunt Balthazar.

One moment Balthazar's holding my shoulder, the next, his hand is wrapped tight around Meik's throat as he slams the Lord against the back of his throne.

"Would you like to find out?" Balthazar growls.

"Lord Balthazar let's give him the opportunity to comply first," I say and the room visibly shifts as Balthazar releases Meik's throat, disappearing from Meik to reappear beside me again.

Interestingly, it's Ruulin of House Scolopendra that bursts out in laughter. It's loud and piercing as it echoes off the walls of the throne room.

"That must be some magical pussy," he muses through his laughter.

I raise my hand to stop Balthazar from whatever vicious actions he has running through his head. Balthazar says nothing, but a low growl vibrates out of him as his hands form tight fists.

"It's more than that, Lord Ruulin," I state in a low voice as I lean forward and smirk at him across the room. "It's about knowing how to *control power*. Considering the standing your House has among this room, I wouldn't expect *you* to understand."

I watch as the fury washes over him and I don't miss the amused looks House Lupus and House Felix share across the room with each other.

"You dare speak to me, a Lord of Jeznia, that way?" Ruulin asks as his voice trembles in his rage.

"I do dare," I reply as I sit back in the throne, showing off a relaxed pose despite how on edge I feel. "It's your move, Lord Ruulin."

He huffs indignantly as his eyes scan the room for any type of support. None is given. I imagine the Houses are biding their time. Balthazar said no Lord would attack a devil they don't truly understand. It's probably why they're showing such restraint right now.

It's clear I killed two House Aides on my own. Considering the shape and size of my horns, they probably suspect Primis magic runs through my veins as well. But even I know Primis magic means nothing if I'm incompetent. The corpses at my feet prove how competent I really am. I've made it clear I'm not an easy opponent.

When Ruulin makes no attempts of retaliation, I scan the room once more before lazily rising to my feet. I'm trying to give off a cocky air of indifference and I hope it's delivered well.

"House Vespertilio. House Anguis. You may have curried favor with Lord Balthazar when you voted in his favor during his trial, but making moves against his wife is a quick way to sour that relationship," I state, walking to Balthazar and dragging my hand up his arm before leaning my entire body against him. He holds me without hesitation as he pulls me tightly against him. "I trust you'll keep your House Aides in check."

I smile sweetly at the Lords as I run my fingers through Balthazar's hair. "Have the day you deserve."

Not a moment later, Balthazar teleports us out of the room.

XIX

WE ARRIVE IN the condo a moment later. It feels surreal to be back after such a long time away. Everything is exactly how I remember it, yet it feels so foreign. Seventeen days isn't a long time, but the constant fighting for my life made those seventeen days feel like years.

Balthazar whirls around, scooping me up into his arms as he growls low in satisfaction. "You were *exquisite*."

I thread my fingers through his thick hair as he captures my lips. He's pulled me flush against him and I'm not ignorant to the stiff erection pressing against me. He reveled in every second I commanded that room. It must have taken him a lot of willpower to keep his composure amongst the Lords, *especially* when I ordered him around in front of them.

I greedily kiss him back, having desperately missed his warmth, his comfort, his presence. I want to burrow myself into him and not come out until at least a week later, but I know that's impossible. Too much has happened. The Lords know I'm a threat now. That Lord Balthazar may hold the title but *I* hold the power.

It's only a matter of time before Zagon gets wind of things. How will he react? Surely he'll hate the idea of his heir submitting to someone else. Especially someone who used to be *human*. Will Zagon even consider me a devil? Does he have the power to undo Balthazar's wish and make me human again?

Balthazar's hands grope me as he holds me close, interrupting my thoughts. He can't get enough of me, can't get close enough. It feels like he wants to eat me alive. I want to let him. I really do. But there are more urgent matters that we need to deal with first. Like how will we respond to any potential House retaliation?

"Balthazar, wait," I breathily order as I push against him.

He snarls his disapproval and even ignores my demand as his lips attack my neck. Conflicting emotions swarm me as my head drops back, giving him better access. I hate that he's ignored my plea but I want this just as badly as he does. I've *missed* him in every way imaginable. This isn't just some mindless fuck. It's a reconnection we're both desperately in need of. Would it really be so bad to indulge now and deal with everything later?

No. It wouldn't be bad at all.

I allow my dominant demeanor to sink into place. My hand grips his hair and I yank back as hard as I can. Magic floods my veins and Balthazar's eyes flash in surprise at my new strength. I sneer at him as my hand releases his hair so I can grip his horn. I tug it towards the floor.

"I see I'll have to retrain you, Lord Balthazar," I state in a low voice. "I'm not too pleased about that."

I pull him all the way down to the floor so his cheek is resting against the cool surface. He doesn't lay flat, choosing to stay on his hands and knees. I release his horn as I stand to my full height, my gaze harsh as I stare down my nose at him. He peers up at me from his spot, refusing to move an inch despite having the complete freedom to do so.

His physical submission is always such a wonderful sight to behold.

"Did you misbehave while I was away?" I ask as I slowly circle around him.

It's a little different now that I know how to control my magic. I'm not completely helpless or weak against him anymore. If he really hated this, would he have the strength to resist me?

The realization has a different kind of enjoyment thrumming through me. He honestly might not be strong enough to break free from me and the thought delights me. Not because I would deny him his safety, whether mentally, emotionally, or physically, but because it means we have *trust* in each other to *not* hurt one other.

Submitting to me, even when I might be the more powerful one, shows me just how much trust he has in me to respect his wants and to keep him safe. He would never show this side of him to anyone else; only ever me. *Because he loves me.*

The thought nearly has me crumbling into a heap of sobs. This beautiful, powerful Jeznian Lord who has only known cruelty and darkness has given himself to me. Wholly, completely, and indefinitely. Without wanting anything in return.

My vision warps as I drop to my knees. My hands grip his face firmly as I lift his head from the ground. He raises up, his red speckled eyes lock onto mine, and the words flow easily from my mouth.

"I love you," I whisper in sincerity, my eyes darting back and forth between his.

His hands ghost over mine, like he's suddenly afraid to touch me. His breathing comes out clipped as his eyes memorize my face.

"Peccatum meum, you have my heart, body, and soul," he whispers, voice trembling.

In that raw moment of our vulnerability, the play ends. Not because he asked for it but because I'm not strong enough to do it right now. Because I need him to know so many other things. Because now isn't the time for play. It's the time for our connection.

Tears descend my cheeks as a large smile breaks out on my face. "It's scary, isn't it?"

"Terrifying," he agrees as a grin graces his face.

"I don't know what I'll do if they ever target you," I confess in a shaking voice.

His face darkens for a brief moment before he leans forward, pressing his forehead against mine and stating confidently, "We'll destroy Jeznia."

A light laugh tumbles out of my mouth. "It's a good plan."

Balthazar moves swiftly, arms encircling me as he nearly crushes me to death within his embrace. His hand gently cradles the back of my head as his head leans into mine. His longing bleeds off him and I realize truly how much he missed me.

"I thought of you every day," he says as if he can hear my thoughts.

I melt in his arms, loving everything about it. The way it feels, the way it smells, how it is simply *home*.

"Me too," I breathe out as my arms wrap around his waist. "You kept me going. I couldn't break my promise to you."

"I knew you wouldn't."

"It was Hell," I confess, my eyes sliding shut as I enjoy the warmth of Balthazar. "I don't understand how anyone in the seventh circle survives. They have no food, no shelter, no support system. They attack without provocation. If I didn't have my magic to protect me, I would've died. It was brutal. Relentlessly brutal."

Balthazar doesn't say anything, probably because there isn't anything he can really say. He simply holds me against him and the comforting smell of smoke washes over me.

The exhaustion of the past seventeen days slams into me and I suddenly don't have enough strength to hold myself up. Balthazar feels me slump against him and pulls away just enough to inspect me.

"I need a nap," I sleepily tell him.

The hidden worry eases out of his gaze as a small smile touches his lips. His fingers brush hair away from my face as he effortlessly lifts me from the floor. Carefully, and with all the tenderness he holds, he walks me down to the bedroom and tucks me into bed.

"Rest, peccatum meum," he says as he brushes his lips against my temple.

I fall asleep before he leaves the room and it's the first time in seventeen days that I sleep completely undisturbed.

HOURS PASS AND by the time I wake up, I'm feeling refreshed. Like an entirely new person. I had forgotten how amazing a good night sleep felt. My thoughts are finally clear. I hadn't even realized how foggy my brain had become by operating with such little sleep. It had become so normal to me that it's actually a little unsettling that the brain fog is gone.

Tossing the covers off me, I head straight to the bathroom for the longest shower ever known to man. The water is scalding hot, leaving my skin red and raw but that's exactly what I need. The seventh circle filth clings to me like a glove and the viciously hot water is the only way to get myself clean.

I shampoo my hair four times before using a hair mask, twice. I lose count how many times I scrub and soap myself down. No matter how many times I do it, I don't feel clean enough. Eventually I give up and exit the shower.

It's incredibly overwhelming looking at all the products lining the counter. I'd forgotten these small little luxuries. Seventeen days is not a long time, especially not to an immortal, but it had been brutal and unforgiving. I had been consumed by my survival. The levels I was forced to stoop to in order to survive… hair product and makeup seems so silly now.

Puckering my lips to the side of my face, I force myself to put on some mascara and a little blush. Something reminiscent to my old life. Hopefully, it will help me find my way back. Yet at the moment I can't control the pounding of my heart, the clipped inhales while I breathe, the slight trembling to my hand. The smell of the shampoo and conditioner, the smell of the soap, Hell even the smell of the makeup, has me completely on edge. I never should have showered. It'll draw attention. Any moment now, someone will attack.

I whirl around in anticipation and, for a moment, I truly believe I'm back in the seventh circle. But something's off. It's too bright. Too clean. It takes me a few moments to remember I'm back home. I'm in Boston. There aren't any Jeznians here. I'm safe.

The realization feels like a trick but I do my best to push through it. *You're in Boston. You're safe.* I repeat until my sprinting heartrate settles.

Embarrassed, I force myself to finish the routine. I dry and style my hair. I dress in comfortable but cute clothes. I attempt to wear jewelry but the idea of someone ripping an earring right off or strangling me with a necklace has me putting the jewelry back.

Once my outfit is complete, I give myself a once over. The woman I stare at looks cute but it feels as though I'm staring at a stranger and not my reflection. This woman in the mirror is who I *used* to be. I'm no longer her. The problem is I'm not quite sure who I am anymore.

My gaze shifts around the large bedroom and I'm suddenly overwhelmed by the foreignness of it all. I had become accustomed to sleeping on tree branches and in burrows. And, try as I might, the *smell* of everything puts me on edge. The room smells too clean. There's no rot or decay. My instincts *scream* at me that someone is seconds away from popping out from around a corner, ready to kill me or die trying.

I glance back at the mirror, hoping to find something that will ground me, but my eyes settle on the pretty woman staring back at me.

She's not me anymore. *She's not me anymore.* The hair, the makeup, the clothes…

The person I was seventeen days ago is no longer who I am today. I'm more powerful now. I know how to control my magic, make it do exactly what I want. Yet now I'm riddled with scars, bruises, and unhealing wounds. Was the physical strength really worth the mental cost? Did I bluff my entire way through that meeting with the Lords earlier today? Are they aware of how fragile I truly am?

My eyes squeeze shut as my heart pounds violently against my ribcage. The flowery scent of my hair nearly has me hyperventilating. The hairs along my forearm rise up in anticipation of an attack.

"You're not there anymore, Sloane," I force myself to say out loud. "You're in Boston. You're safe."

I open my eyes and take in every small detail of it. There is nothing about this condo that resembles the brutalness of the seventh circle. I'm safe. It's ok for me to be clean and to smell nicely. I won't attract anyone's murderous attention.

Still, the walls feel as though they're caving in. I need to get out of here before I have a full magical meltdown.

In a rush, I barely remember to grab my purse and wallet, the strange weightiness of them throwing off my balance. Expertly countering the added weight, I quickly take the elevator to the bottom floor, reveling in the cold, crisp air as I step out onto the sidewalk.

The familiar smells and sounds of Boston wash over me, pulling me more into reality and away from the seventh circle. There's no lingering scents of decay or sulfur in the air. The *sun* is out, shining so brightly I have to squint. Birds chirp and squawk while people shout and honk their car horns. It's familiar yet foreign.

I focus my attention on the familiarity of it, on how it makes me feel. Maybe if I do something I'm used to do, it'll help bring me mentally back home. There's a café nearby and indulging in a hot latte is probably what a therapist would recommend I do. Without allowing myself the time to hesitate, I walk off towards the café.

It's second nature anticipating the moves of the people around me and even still, as I turn the corner down a new street, I collide firmly into someone. My body acts on pure instinct. The punch is thrown before I even realize what I've done.

Burning hot fingers grab me around the wrist, yanking my arm down and around. The action causes me to spin. My leg flares out as I twirl, but my attacker evades it. I'm shoved roughly away. I turn around on my toes, fully ready to launch into another attack when I finally get a good look at my attacker.

Zyvn.

"What the Hell?" I ask, more surprised than angered.

A scowl consumes his face as dark grey eyes rage a storm within their gaze. His lips press into a firm line.

"Where have you been?" he demands to know.

"Training," I answer simply as my body begins to relax.

"You were not training in Ephiri. I have looked for you."

"No, I wasn't. Very observant of you," I quip, irritation coating my tone as I sidestep him and continue down the sidewalk.

My heart is racing a mile a minute. I'm trying my hardest to reacclimate to being home and this asshole ruins that in literally one second. I can't calm down. My body keeps telling me it needs to fight, that my opponent isn't dead yet which means there's still a damn good chance *I'll* end up dead. But that's not how things work up here and Zyvn said he'd give me a warning before coming for my head. Against *everyone's* judgment, I trust him. He won't kill me without letting me know first.

I'm safe. Just calm down.

Zyvn effortlessly follows me, his strides easily keeping pace with mine. Irritation digs into my gut and I decide to lean into that. Better to be irritated than scared shitless.

Although, there's only a couple reasons why Zyvn would be following after me and since he hasn't offered any warnings of coming to kill me, there's really only one reason. He probably has something to share about my soul.

"Have you discovered anything new while I was away?"

"The scripture does not make much sense," Zyvn confesses as we enter the coffee shop.

The scripture? It takes me a moment to remember what he's talking about. Before I left to go training, he mentioned a scripture from his library that referenced keys and souls. I remember him saying most of it was illegible but it sounds like he's translated some of it if he's here talking to me now.

"What does it say?" I ask curiously as I step in line.

It's crowded but not overwhelmingly so. People mind their business, completely unaware of who and what stands in their presence. A devil and a Beastial. How would they react if they knew? Would they care? Would they call me a monster? They wouldn't be wrong. The things I've done... I had to do what was necessary to survive. Jeznians wouldn't bat an eye at what I've become but humans would. I've taken a step away from humanity while simultaneously taking a step closer to being a devil through and through.

"The little sense I can make of it translates that there are two keys," he answers, drawing my attention back to the conversation. "They are in link to a void."

"What?" I ask, eyebrows furrowing.

That doesn't make much sense at all. The word choice is weird. He has to have mistranslated something.

"That is the exact translation," he states as we walk up to the counter. "It does not make sense."

I offer a restrained smile to the cashier as I step up, my attention split between not being rude to the cashier while wanting to ask Zyvn questions.

"May I…" My eyes aimlessly glance around the menu before I decide on something familiar, "May I have a medium hot vanilla latte?" After a moment of silence, I glance at Zyvn. "Do you want anything?"

He arches an eyebrow despite the scowl on his face. He offers no answer, merely allows the silence to become awkward. Rolling my eyes, my attention returns to the cashier.

"He'll have a medium hot coffee. Dark roast please."

Zyvn walks away from the counter towards an empty spot near the back as I pay for our drinks. I join him a few moments later, sitting down at the table he stands next to. A visible frown mars his face as he watches me sit but eventually, *reluctantly*, he takes the seat across from me.

"What is the exact translation?" I ask. "Word for word."

"Two keys are in link to a void."

That really doesn't make much sense.

"Are you sure the translation is accurate? It sounds… off."

"That is because the real translation doesn't make sense to your human language."

Honestly, that's fair. I snap my fingers and offer him finger guns in agreement to what he's said but who am I kidding? A 3,000 year old Beastial isn't going to understand that.

"Well… did you find any information about the void then?" I ask as I ponder over the sentence *two keys are in link to a void.*

"It exists where no one exists."

A frown blooms on my face. Isn't that kind of what voids are? A place of nonexistence. To say it exists where no one exists is kind of redundant. Isn't it?

"Right…" I trail off, tapping my fingers uselessly against the tabletop. "So… last time I spoke with you, you said you find reference to keys and souls. How am I connected into all of this with the void?"

Zyvn allows the silence to drag on and my gaze, naturally, wanders as I wait for his answer. I know he'll answer. He may not want to, but he needs my help as much as I need his.

I glance out the window, assessing for any threats that might be lurking. All I find are a bunch of clueless humans who wouldn't know what hit them if my humanoid appearance evaporated. I don't see any threats but that doesn't mean they aren't out there. I remain alert in case someone tries to get the drop on me.

"You are a human with a Jeznian soul," Zyvn states casually, tone monotonous as he continues spewing information. "Putting aside the absurdity of your existence, logic dictates there must be a counterpart to your red soul. There should be a blue soul within a human body somewhere on Ephiri.

"Humans should not have Jeznian and Odanthian souls," he continues, "yet there is one so we must assume there is another. There must be a reason it has happened. I believe it is because these abnormal souls are keys to this void."

His reasoning tracks but he could still be wrong. The keys could be something else for all we know. Still, I can admit it's strange that I have a Jeznian soul as a human. I agree with him on the Odanthian soul. In theory, a human out there *should* have an Odanthian soul. Otherwise, I'd be one Hell of an anomaly and that just doesn't sit right with me.

"Odanthian souls are blue?" I ask because it's new information I'm learning.

"Correct."

Who could have the Odanthian soul? Could it be the same person?

That seems like a security risk. Why put both keys in the same place? Then again… who would go rummaging around for *two* souls in one body? Putting the souls together *could* be the smartest thing ever. No one would think to check the same body twice. Not when there's over seven billion humans alive at any given time. It's actually a little bit genius if I really think about it.

"Could I have it?" I ask without hesitation. "Could I hold both the blue and red soul?"

"I do not know," he confesses. "The scripture does not tell me if a human can possess both souls."

"Well… how can we find out?"

I ask the question even though I already know the answer. Just the thought of Balthazar rummaging through my chest cavity again makes me want to hurl. Having him retrieve my soul, to this day, was one of the most painful things I've ever experienced. And that's saying something considering the shit I just went through in the seventh circle.

"We search inside your body for a secondary soul," he answers.

I huff out an annoyed breath, not at all enjoying the answer I expected to receive.

"I don't want to do it," I confess, arms crossing over my chest.

"Having that bit of information will help me translate the scripture better," he states with no room for argument.

"True, but…" my voice trails off as my gaze eyes him up and down.

Just why is Zyvn working so hard to figure this all out? Last I remember he was still my enemy. Helping me understand my soul better isn't exactly the best enemy tactic to have. If I gain more knowledge, I'll most likely become more powerful. Why would he want that?

"Zyvn, why do you care so much?" I ask just as a barista walks over to hand us our drinks.

He regards her for a moment, watching her walk away before his attention turns back to me. His face hardens as determination fills his gaze.

"I must understand what you are before I kill you."

"That shouldn't surprise me, but it does," I mumble to myself as my hands curl calmly around the base of my drink.

"You are an anomaly," he continues speaking. "If I kill you without understanding what purpose you serve in the greater plan, the consequences could be catastrophic. The Tribunal believes your existence might bring the end of times, but I know the Creator would not bring you into existence without purpose," Zyvn states. "Perhaps you *are* meant to bring the end of times, but if that is true, it is because that's what the Creator wants."

"You can't seriously buy into that crap, can you?" I ask, anger flitting down my spine at his words.

He's basically saying I have zero choice in how this all plays out. That's bullshit. A person *always* has a choice. I don't have to bring the end of times if I don't want to.

Zyvn's eyes narrow, causing the silver face paint to highlight the small wrinkles forming around the edges of his eyes. "You were created with a purpose, Sloane Kensington. I will find out what that purpose is and make my decision accordingly."

A *tsk* falls out of my mouth as my eyes roll skyward. "No, you won't. You literally said you'll sit back and let me bring about the end of the world because the Creator wanted that to happen. You're going to do whatever you believe the Creator wants you to do, not what you *should* do. How am I the one with an evil soul when you're the one willing to let the world to end?"

"The world is due for an ending and being reborn," he answers through clipped words. "Your human lives are too brief to understand—"

"Bull. Shit. If that were true, why the hell would The Tribunal care if I bring the end of times?"

"Every time it ends, it resets," he states plainly as his gaze shifts away from me and out the window. "Everything resets. Jeznia will be given opportunities they currently do not have access to. We cannot— The Tribunal will not allow Jeznia to gain power. It will reshape the world as we know it. That is why The Tribunal has done everything they can to postpone a reset."

Silence drapes over us as I digest what he's said. I agree with The Tribunal that Jeznia can't gain power. They would destroy everything that is good and beautiful on Earth if given the chance. The average human wouldn't survive the brutality of Jeznia. I barely did and it was only because of old deep magic. Humans would be slaughtered, raped, and tortured all for the amusement of Jeznians.

"You would really let the world end just because it's what the Creator wanted?"

My voice is barely above a whisper and yet, the quietness of it draws his attention back to me.

"I might," he answers honestly and tears burn hot within my eyes. Our world as I know it irrevocably changed because he'd rather obey the Creator than give a damn. "But that is not the point of this visit. Your Jeznian soul might be the key to a void. If that is true, we must discover what this void is. Protect it, destroy it, do what we must to keep everyone safe. If your soul is the key, we must find the second key."

"The Odanthian soul," I reply quietly.

"Yes."

"Ok," I whisper as I huff out a breath of resignation, wiping my unshed tears as discreetly as I can. Zyvn is right. We need to find this Odanthian soul. I'll deal with the end of the world bullshit later *if* it even comes up. Because it's just an assumption made by some asshole Beastial who doesn't know shit. "Poke around my insides and see if I have a blue soul too."

"That I cannot do," Zyvn answers. "A Defender or The Magistrate will have to do it."

"Absolutely not," flies out of my mouth. "If you can't do it, Balthazar will. There's no way I'm letting a Defender, The Magistrate or whoever else anywhere near my body."

Zyvn's eyes narrow, his fingers curling into his fists. I can see the protest on his face before he speaks, but I don't give him the chance to verbalize what he's thinking.

"That's non—negotiable, Zyvn. If you can't do it, Balthazar does it."

"You are a fool for putting your trust in him."

Fury flashes hot and wild within my veins as pale white fire ignites my hands. My entire demeanor changes as murderous intent fills me to the brim. How *dare* he speak so poorly of Balthazar? He has no right. Balthazar has done more for me than Odantha ever will. I'd be a fool for trusting an Odanthian. Balthazar has earned my trust. Odantha hasn't.

Zyvn quickly shifts to attention, his body poised and ready for a fight as he assesses me.

Magic coats the air, thick and heavy, as we sit across from each other, silently daring the other to make the first move. My lips part, my voice calm and steady as I speak the words evenly.

"Balthazar saved my life while your people left me to die. My trust in him is not without evidence, Beastial. It would be wise to hold your tongue the next time you see fit to insult *Lord* Balthazar."

A beat of silence passes between us before Zyvn relaxes a little.

"It appears your training was a success," he states as he rises from his seat. His hand curls around the hilt of his sword as he glares down at me from his staggering height. "If you put the peace at risk, devil, I *will* kill you. Your purpose be damned."

"I'd expect nothing less from you," flows easily from my mouth as my jaw juts back and forth. "Until then, Beastial."

Zyvn nods his head once, but his attention is drawn towards the entrance of the café as Balthazar's voice interrupts our meeting.

"You don't want to stick around?" Balthazar asks, a forced grin upon his face. "You're going to miss all the fun."

XX

Zyvn WHIRLS AROUND, hand popping the sword out but not fully withdrawing it from the sheath. He glares openly at Balthazar walking towards us. The sight is so unusual. Balthazar doesn't typically walk across the room. *Why doesn't he just transport himself over here?* It takes me a moment to remember why.

Zyvn's magic cancels out devil magic. All devil magic except for the magic that exists within me. It was why Balthazar couldn't teleport into the apartment and why he has to use his legs to walk across the café instead of appearing out of thin air.

He looks so out of place weaving between tables and bodies as he makes his way over towards us. It's strangely human. A small smile works its way to my mouth. He must hate it.

Judging by the fire in his eyes, he does. Balthazar may have used friendly words, but the look on his face says otherwise. He's livid.

He may have agreed to overlook my team up with Zyvn, but his hatred for the Beastial appears to run deep. Judging by the way his body is tensing, I can easily surmise he intends to deck Zyvn in the face. That is, if Zyvn hasn't already anticipated it himself.

"Balthazar," I breathe out as the amusement eases off of my face. "You said you were fine with my arrangement with Zyvn."

"I said I would go along with it until he stepped out of line," Balthazar states as he finally arrives at our table.

"He hasn't done anything wrong yet," I tell him.

"Did I or did I not just hear him threaten to kill you?"

My eyes roll as a sigh falls out of my mouth. "A meaningless threat. You have nothing to worry about."

"Sloane—"

"No, *enough*," I snap at him. I just spent the last seventeen days in Hell and survived. I can handle Zyvn. Even if Balthazar doesn't think so. The question is out of my mouth before I can pull it back. "Do you think I can't handle myself?"

"Of course I do. That is not the issue—"

"Then why are you making such a big deal out of this?" I ask and don't miss the irritation flitting across Balthazar's face. *Good.* Now he's as irritated as I feel. "Zyvn is simply doing his job of keeping the balance between the three worlds. That's fine because I have no intention of messing that up. He has no reason to kill me."

"So he says," Balthazar quips, eyes narrowing in Zyvn's direction.

"I believe him. So, are you saying I have horrible judgment or something?"

Balthazar arches up an eyebrow as he turns his attention back to me. "If you have to ask, Sloane, then the answer is yes."

"Fuck you," I spit out, my head shaking to and fro as angry tears burn my eyes. I refuse to look at either of them. "I'm doing my best here, Balthazar. I'm making the best decisions I can with the information I have."

"Peccatum—"

Always with that nickname whenever he gets himself into trouble. It's infuriating he thinks it can calm down any situation. He doesn't know me half as well as he thinks if he believes a silly nickname is going to sidetrack me from him being a jerk.

My eyes snap to him as a harsh glare takes over my features. "You don't get to call me that when you're being an asshole."

He inhales sharply, like my words physically wound him, but I speak again before he can say anything else.

"I need you to look around inside me to see if you can find another soul."

"Why would you be in possession of another soul?" he asks.

"The same reason why I had a Jeznian soul to bargain with instead of a human one. We need to rule it out. Zyvn hasn't come across anything that says two souls can't be in one human. So, take a look. See what you find."

Balthazar clicks his tongue as he glances between me and Zyvn. "What aren't you two telling me?"

Zyvn remains silent, gazes locked with Balthazar as his temple pulses from the clenching of his jaw. It doesn't appear he'll be answering Balthazar anytime soon. Which means it's up to me.

Inhaling deeply, I answer him. "The scripture said something along the lines of two keys that are in link with a void. He also read within the scripture mention of these keys and souls. So we think the Jeznian and Odanthian souls are the keys to the void."

"A void," Balthazar speaks as his eyebrows furrow together.

"Yes."

"Such as the space we travel while teleporting?"

"Perhaps," Zyvn finally speaks, ears perking up in interest at Balthazar's proposed idea.

Balthazar barely spares him a look before directing his attention to me. "We don't require keys to enter that space."

"There's something in there, though," I state, vividly remembering the first time I traveled with Umbra and how something tried crawling up my leg. "Maybe there's a doorway that requires the keys."

Neither one of them says anything to dispute what I've said, which means there's a very real possibility our void we're looking for is in there.

I suddenly sit forward, my hands clapping together and their eyes flit to me.

"Balthazar, take a look around in me for another soul. Zyvn, see if you can find more information in the scripture about the void's location. I'm assuming the space we travel through is vast since it connects all three worlds. We're basically looking for a needle among needles. I doubt we'll get lucky with the scripture, but you never know."

Zyvn's scowl deepens and I imagine it's because he doesn't enjoy taking orders from a *devil*. But he remains silent because what I've requested of him is logical and reasonable.

"What exactly do you intend to tell The Tribunal when they realize your target has not been taken care of?" Balthazar asks.

It's a good question. One I should have asked but failed to think of. I don't imagine they'll take it lightly. They rule Odantha and probably expect blind obedience. Would they send another Beastial after me?

"I will not withhold the truth from them," Zyvn answers.

"But you will not readily offer it up unprovoked?" Balthazar challenges.

Zyvn's eyes narrow as he stands a little straighter, squaring up against Balthazar. "No, I will not."

"Do you intend to inform us should The Tribunal work around you?"

As much as Balthazar's original hostility towards Zyvn had irritated me, I'm grateful for him now. He's asking questions I haven't thought to and, quite frankly, don't have the mental capacity to think of. My mind is overloaded with everything else. I can't think of Odantha or how The Tribunal wants me dead. Thankfully, Balthazar is more than willing to pick up my slack.

"If I am able to, yes, I will," Zyvn answers.

"Even if you decide to kill me?" I ask, knowing that at any point in his research he might deem me necessary to kill.

"Though you do not deserve it, I will give you a warning first before I make my attack."

"Much appreciated," I dryly laugh out. At least he's honest.

"Inform me as soon as you know whether you hold the blue soul or not."

Balthazar bristles at the command but I couldn't care less. This working relationship is full of animosity and a lack of trust. I order Zyvn to do something. He orders me to do something. There's no pleasantries or respect involved on either side. There's no point in getting offended by his behavior when I dish it right back to him.

"Aye, aye, Captain," I lazily reply, offering him a salute.

His temples pulse as he glares at me, but a moment later, he disappears in a bright white light. It's truly blinding and I hate him for it. It's still an adjustment being topside. The seventh circle had been pitch—black with only bouts of light from the lightning scattering across the sky.

"I don't trust him," Balthazar states as he finally sits in the chair adjacent to my own.

"You don't have to trust him," I reply, fingers digging into my eyes as I try to get rid of the annoying white blotch now blinding my vision.

"He is a Beastial, Sloane."

"I'm well aware, Balthazar."

"You're not understanding," he snaps before clarifying. "He's a *soldier*. Soldier's take orders. They do not defy their superiors and start an investigation on their own. He may be withholding information from us."

"Would you expect him to be completely transparent?" I ask, unable to suppress the haughtiness dripping in my voice. "Let's be honest for a moment. Do you expect *us* to be transparent with him?"

"Not in the slightest. Which is precisely why—"

"We proceed with caution," I interrupt him as my eyes reopen. The white blotch is still there, but I can see Balthazar through it. "The fact of the matter is we need his help. But let's not be stupid about it, yeah? We have to work together to figure this out. If my soul really is a key to some void and there's a counterpart out there, we'll need his help in finding the Odanthian soul."

Balthazar huffs indignantly, eyes refusing to meet mine as he glares outside the window. "Sloane, I—"

His voice cuts off, his jaw clenching so tightly I nearly see a vein popping. His fingers grip his biceps as unspoken words rampage his mind. At a quick glance, he looks angry, livid, and outraged but the more I study him, the more I see fear running through him.

My hand reaches out, fingers curling around his forearm as I speak gently, "Hey, what's wrong? Why are you so upset?"

His gaze snaps to mine, the red in his eyes slowly suffocating the black out. "He cannot kill you."

"He won't," automatically spills from my mouth and Balthazar inhales sharply.

"No, Sloane," he breathes out. "I cannot—"

He can't finish his statement and my chair scrapes against the floor as I slide over to him. He visibly winces, eyes squeezing shut as he clenches his jaw again.

"The seventeen days you were gone were Hell enough," he whispers and I notice a rip in his clothes from how tightly he grips his arms. I barely hear him as he states, "I will not survive your death."

His whispered admission overwhelms me, tears pooling within my gaze. My training in the seventh circle really did a number on him. When I made the decision to go, I never anticipated how deeply it would affect him. Why would I? He's Lord Balthazar Primis of House Primis. He's heir to the most powerful House in Jeznia. He's been fairly open about his feelings towards me, but still. I think to some degree I thought there would always be a distance between us and that distance would be his upbringing in a cold, cruel, and unforgiving world.

I never thought he would come to love me more deeply and passionately than any human man ever could. I never thought he'd become so codependent upon me and my survival that he would die without me. I never *thought*. And that's where I went wrong.

My fingers grip his forearm as I blink away the tears.

"You won't have to survive my death, Balthazar," I tell him, my voice quiet and gentle. "The whole reason I went to the seventh circle was to get stronger. My magic *is* stronger. *I'm* stronger. Zyvn couldn't kill me before and he can't kill me now. No matter how hard he tries. You're not going to lose me, Balthazar. I promise."

His eyes open and the tension eases out of his face as his hand slides up to cup my cheek.

"Peccatum meum," he breathes life into the words as his eyes dart back and forth between mine.

The air is heavy between us. Full of unspoken emotions too intense for either one of us to say. The grim look upon his face hurts my heart and I want it gone. I want that pain to never exist.

Before I can stop myself I ask, "Who knew you'd be such a clinger?"

It's stupid and a bit callous but Balthazar can't suppress the laugh. I'm grateful to see the smile on his face. Balthazar snorts as he shakes his head, his hand falling away from my cheek.

"Only for you," he confesses.

When the silence falls on us again, it's not so heavy. Yet as we sit there, unease crawls its way up my spine. I can't help how quickly my eyes shift around the room, looking for invisible threats. It's unsettling being back on Earth where the sun's too bright, the air's too crisp, and the space near me is too crowded. I need something to distract myself. And as much as I don't want to do this, it'll help distract me *and* we'll get an answer.

"I need you to check if you can locate the blue soul inside me," I say, cutting straight to the chase.

Balthazar hisses an inhale as a deep scowl forms on his mouth.

"I don't like it either, but it needs to be done," I say to his silent objection.

"It's not there."

"You don't know that. Yes, hiding two souls in the same body is risky, but even you have to admit that it's also smart."

A low growl rumbles in his chest. "Sloane, you cannot ask me to do this."

"To do what?" I challenge, mild annoyance brewing under the surface.

"To *harm* you," he states so plainly I almost miss the meaning of what he's said.

I assumed it would be no big deal to him. Looking for the soul won't kill me. It'll certainly *feel* like it'll kill me but I know it won't. *He* knows it won't. But admittedly, it never crossed my mind that he wouldn't want to do it simply because it'll hurt me.

Instinctively, I lean over towards him, filling up as much of his view as I can. "I can handle it."

He refuses to meet my stare.

"It's not about *you* handling it," he hisses and I can't help it.

I close the distance between us, lips searing over his as my fingers dive into his thick hair. He responds in kind, neither one of us caring that we have an audience as we kiss each other like it's our last breath.

I can't explain into words or thoughts what this moment means to me. The devil who came to kill me all those weeks ago now refuses to hurt me in any way, shape, or form. He cares too deeply about me to even consider harming me. I don't know what good or bad I did in the world to deserve him, but I'm too selfish to feel guilty about having him. He's mine and I'm going to do everything possible in my power to ensure he's kept safe and well loved.

As we pull away, my forehead rests against his. Our breathing is labored as it mixes together. My eyes remain shut as I hold his face gently within my hands.

"You can handle this," I whisper and I feel his face scrunch against mine.

He *really* doesn't want to do this. I'm honestly surprised how resistant he is to it. If the shoes were reversed, I wouldn't want to do it either but some things just have to be done. We need to know if I have the Odanthian soul.

I know it won't bring much comfort but I say it anyway. "It'll be over before you know it."

"Fine," he grumbles.

With a snap of his fingers, we're back at the apartment. I assume he'll dive right in to get it over with as soon as possible, but he doesn't. He gently grabs me by the arms and guides me over to the bed. Wordlessly, he pushes me to lie down. I follow his lead, kicking off my shoes in the process as I get as comfortable as I can on the bed.

Worry etches its way onto his brow, his eyes rapidly scanning over my body. My stomach clenches for him and for me. This won't be pleasant for either one of us.

He spends a few moments just staring at me until finally he does it. He moves swiftly, sliding his hand into my torso in a matter of milliseconds. The pain is excruciating. My magic activates on instinct. I have to fight it while also being in the worst pain of my life.

It thrashes and lashes out at Balthazar, slicing him across the face. He grunts but doesn't retaliate as he continues searching my body for another soul. I'm fighting my magic tooth and nail but can't get a handle on it. The pain is too much. My magic wants to destroy Balthazar for hurting me the way he is. But I refuse. I won't let it kill him.

His hand turns upwards towards my chest cavity and my vision blurs white. I can't hold it in. My head turns sideways and I expel the contents of my stomach.

Balthazar says something to me but I can't hear him over the thundering of my pulse. My hands grip tightly around his forearm and lamely, I try to yank him out. It's pure instinct. I want the pain to end. I don't care about finding the damn blue soul. I just want the pain to end.

Instead, he pushes his arm forward.

I scream in utter agony.

Magic violently bursts out of me, filling the room with its rage. It targets Balthazar, fully intent on destroying him into oblivion if I don't gain control of it soon. How am I supposed to gain control when the pain nearly blinds me?

Balthazar grunts as my magic lands a hit but he doesn't withdraw his hand. Instead, he turns his hand downward, going south towards my navel. The screams that rip out of me are ungodly. My vision goes completely blank and I try yanking his hand out of me once more. Fingernails dig into his forearm but he continues his search. It makes my magic angry.

It attacks Balthazar again, hitting him so hard that blood splatters against the sheets. The warmth of it coats across my chest but I barely register it amongst the pain and misery.

Balthazar doesn't retaliate. Quietly, determinedly, he takes the abuse. Even as another smattering of blood splays across me.

Balthazar says something again but I still can't hear him. I've lost all control of my magic. The blinding pain is too close to the metamorphosis pain I went through during my fight with the gargoyle. I genuinely don't think I'm going to survive this. The pain might actually kill me.

Then all too suddenly, it's gone. Like a light switch flicking off.

Heavy breathing fills the room and belatedly, I realize it's not just me. My head rolls to the side, exhaustion nearly having me unconscious, but fear and worry zap energy into me as my eyes settle on the scene before me.

Balthazar is shredded to bits, blood pooling at his feet and staining his clothes. He slumps to his knees, a dazed look upon his face as he stares at me. It's as if he's never seen his blood outside his body before.

It takes too much effort, every muscle within me protests my actions, but I manage to get off the bed and kneel beside him.

"Balthazar, heal yourself," I demand, voice wavering as tears blur my vision. "Why haven't you healed yourself?"

"I can't," he says simply before falling forward onto the bed and sliding off as he lands with a heavy thud on the floor.

XXI

MY HEARTBEAT THUNDERS in my ears, shock
paralyzing me as I stare at Balthazar's unconscious body. The
silence in the room is deafening. He continues to remain
motionless. I can't even tell if he's breathing. Bile sits at the
back of my throat as I stare down at him.

I don't know what to do. My hands tremble as
uncertainty mixes with fear. Is he dead? Have I killed him?
He can't be dead. He's Lord Balthazar of House Primis. He
can't *die*.

But what if he did?

"Oh god," I breathe out, the tears sliding down my face.
What if he's really dead?

With a trembling hand, I reach for him. He's completely
limp in my grip. Dead weight and my heart twinges painfully
within my chest. For a moment I truly fear he's gone. But
then I quickly refuse to accept that fate and push what little
magic I still have within me to help roll him onto his back.

A gasp flies out of my mouth as my eyes scan his body.
There's so much blood everywhere. Muscle and bone are
visible through the deep lashes on his torso. If he can't heal
himself, wounds like these will definitely kill him. I look for

signs of his muscle and skin mending itself but find none. *Why* can't he heal himself? Fuck, I'm going to lose him.

A gargled sob fills the room as my hand comes up to suppress the sound. I thought I had my magic under control. Ever since the gargoyle attack, I've been able to control when I use it. It hasn't gone against my will. Not since that day. But this…

"Balthazar," I whisper his name, fear coating my voice.

He says nothing. He does nothing. He just lies there, motionless. I quickly shove my finger in my mouth, soaking it fully to the knuckle, before placing it underneath Balthazar's nose. It takes far too much time for a huff of air to hit my wet finger but it does. He's alive. He's alive but I don't know for how much longer.

I need to heal him. I need to fix his wounds but I've never healed anyone before. What if I accidentally kill him? *It's a risk I have to take.* The thought has me viscerally recoiling. A risk I have to take? This is his *life*. My magic clearly still doesn't listen to me. What if it decides to finish the job while I try to heal him?

Blood continues to soak the carpet beneath me. He won't stop bleeding. He won't heal. If I do nothing, he'll die. I have to at least try, consequences be damned.

Another warped sob escapes my mouth. There's a moment of hesitation, of me contemplating if there are any other options, before I regrettably plunge forward. My hands lay flat along his chest, fingers slipping into crevices that shouldn't be there.

I concentrate as hard as I can on my magic, on it being healing energy, and it filling my hands before entering into Balthazar's body. This magic will *heal* him. Because if it doesn't, I'll find a way to get rid of it once and for all.

Magic flows down my arms and into my hands, that familiar tingle and warmth spreading to my fingertips. When my hands are full, I release the magic into Balthazar. I feel it leave as my hands get colder. Balthazar doesn't react. He doesn't grunt or groan, doesn't hiss or snarl. He stays quiet. I don't know whether that's a good sign or not but I continue pushing my magic into him.

"Please work, please work, please work," I chant over and over again. "You can't die on me, Balthazar. You can't."

I don't know much time passes. Seconds stretch into minutes that feel like hours. And in all that time, Balthazar doesn't wake up. He doesn't move. I can barely tell if he's breathing.

It's impossible to keep the tears at bay. I break down crying as I shove more magic into him.

"*Please,*" I beg. "Please wake up. You can't die."

My stomach clenches as a sob explodes out of me. I won't survive his death. He's all I have. There's no point in any of this without him. I need his laughter, his relentless teasing, his strength and fortitude. I can't live without him the same way he can't live without me.

"You have to wake up," I beg him, tears staining my cheeks.

He doesn't respond. Desperation floods me and my actions are no longer my own.

"Wake *up!*" I scream, my hand slamming down on his chest.

A burst of magic expels out of me, latching onto Balthazar. He jolts into a seated position, a violent, gargled inhale filling the silence of the room. His chest heaves as he looks around the room with a dazed expression upon his face.

Without hesitation, I jump into his chest as my arms encircle around him. Sobs pour out of me, desperate and loud and full of gratitude. His arms weakly wrap around me, his blood dampening my clothes but I don't care. I don't care because he's *alive*.

"What happened?" he asks, voice gruff.

"Do you remember looking for a blue soul?" I ask as I pull away far enough to look him in the eyes.

He nods his head. "Yes. I couldn't locate any soul within your body."

"After you removed your hand, you lost consciousness. I tried healing you," I confess and I finally inspect his body.

My fingers pull away the shredded fabric of his clothes as my eyes study the lacerations. Most of them are gone without even a scar to remind us of what nearly happened today. There are a few slowly stitching themselves back together, the magic a glittering gold as skin molds to skin. It's fascinating and grotesquely beautiful.

My fingers ghost gently down a cut that's being mended. Balthazar flinches underneath my touch, drawing my eyes up to his face. A grim expression meets my gaze and I frown.

"Why couldn't you heal yourself?" I ask.

"I don't know," he answers. "When I called for my magic, it wasn't there."

"Is it..." I bite my lip before forcing the question out. "Is it there now?"

He snaps his fingers and instant relief ripples through his body. All the tension exits out of him in a single exhale and he sinks down onto the floor, flat on his back, as he blows out a deep breath.

"Yes. It is."

"Good," I whisper, eyes coasting down his chest.

His body is nearly mended but there's still so much blood. I grab the blanket off the bed and wipe away the blood as best I can and that's when I notice it. The tattoo… the pointed tip near his navel… it glitters golden.

My eyes squint as I wipe away more blood. The glittering gold piece is so small I nearly miss it amongst the black ink. I bend down to get a better look.

"Sloane, as much as it grieves me to say this, I'm going to need a few moments to switch gears—"

"Shut up, I'm not trying to go down on you," I interrupt him.

He pauses only for a moment before saying, "I find I'm insulted you aren't."

"You're such an asshole," I laugh out and poke the spot that shines. "This looks new. Am I wrong?"

He lifts his head to inspect what I'm looking at. Confusion etches its way onto his face and he props himself up onto his elbows to get a better look.

"What in the seven circles?" he mumbles to himself.

It takes me a moment to realize what he's said. Then all too suddenly, laughter bursts out of me. The image of five year old Balthazar attempting to use magic for the first time and every time he fails, his cute little five year old voice says, "What in the seven circles?"

If I didn't know Jeznia was made of seven circles, I wouldn't have a clue what he's talking about. It's cute he has a phrase to say when he's completely and utterly confused. I think my favorite part about it is how un—Balthazar it is.

Tears streak down the sides of my face as the laughter continues. It gets funnier the more I think about it. Through it all, I see Balthazar roll his eyes even as my stomach begins to cramp.

"Laugh it up all you want," he grumbles, coming into a fully seated position on the bedroom floor.

I'm giddy, unable to calm down. Every time I think of him saying those five words, I lose it all over again. The release is euphoric and desperately needed. The fear of him dying has shot my nervous system. But the laughing… it's bringing me back to reality.

I don't think about the way he looked all cut up and bleeding to death. Or how terrified I was that I was going to lose him forever. I focus on those five little words and how silly he sounded and let myself laugh until my tears dry up.

Minutes pass by before I've calmed down. The whole time Balthazar sits there silently, patiently waiting for me to get my shit back together. He's smiling, though. And it warms my heart.

I wipe the tears from my eyes before I lean forward to look at the tattoo again. I can't help but poke the area where the golden glittering bit of magic is. Despite the stark contrast, it's easy to miss amongst all the black swirls. That's how small it is.

My lips purse side to side as I study the rest of his tattoo. It takes up most of his torso. It swirls in a way that text only does, telling a story I can't read. The text follows the shape of an inverted triangle, all coming to a point where the glittering magic now resides.

My finger traces the tattoo, curiosity getting the better of me. Slowly, my eyes slide up to meet his gaze. "What does your tattoo mean?"

He arches an eyebrow, gaze flitting down to his stomach consumed in black ink, a slight frown pulling at his lips. Silence consumes the air as I wait for him to answer me. It drags on to the point that I'm not sure he's going to tell me.

There are some things about Balthazar he doesn't like sharing. This might be one of those things. But then he inhales a heavy breath before answering.

"It has to do with House Primis," he says, his eyes fixated on the black swirls of his tattoo. "It's stupid, foolish words of putting the House above any and all other things. The House *must* come first. If someone is ever found to have not kept the House's best interests front and center, death is their punishment."

"How would someone find out you didn't put the House's best interests front and center?" I ask.

Are there Shadow Seers peering through the words of his tattoo? Does Zagon know what's going on with me? With Zyvn and Odantha? The thought terrifies me. If Zagon does know what's going on with me, that means he's waiting for an opportunity to present itself. And when he strikes, it'll be at the perfect time. Because how else do you stay the High King for as long as him? You move only when you're absolutely certain to win.

Balthazar sighs again, hand threading through his hair. "Magic," he answers simply. Then he taps his chest. "Magic has been inked onto me and binds me to House Primis."

"But who decides if you've done something against the House? Is it Zagon?" I ask, unable to hide the urgency within my tone.

"It's the magic," he answers simply.

My hand pinches the bridge of my nose, frustration and fear lacing my every words. "How does that work?"

A moment later, Balthazar snakes his arm around my side and pulls me into his lap. With a snap of his fingers, the bloodied clothes, blanket, and blood splatters disappear.

We're in comfortable clothes, *soft* clothes, and instinctively, I sink into him. *Home.* I am home.

"It's magic, Sloane. You give it a command and it obeys it."

That makes no sense though. Magic isn't a living thing. And figuring out if someone is doing something with good or bad intentions requires actual thought, reflection, and analyzation. How can the magic determine that Balthazar keeping me from Zagon is in the best interest of House Primis or not? There's too much room for error.

"But there's room for interpretation of whether or not someone is doing something in the best interest of the House or if they're trying to sabotage it. How can the magic know—"

"It's *magic*, Sloane," Balthazar repeats himself as his finger hooks beneath my chin and he raises my face to look me in the eyes. "It *feels* what my intentions are. It doesn't have to understand them. It only needs to know the feeling and, if my intentions are bad, the feelings are bad."

"That's too easy to manipulate."

He scoffs, eyes rolling in such an uncharacteristic way as he shakes his head. "No one can fake their feelings, Sloane. *No one.*"

He has a point. In the beginning, I tried denying my attraction towards him but deep down I always knew I was drawn to him. He's too charismatic for his own good. Even when he owned my soul and I wanted to hate him. The magic would know that, wouldn't it? It'd know I was lying to myself because no matter how hard I tried to logic my way out of not being attracted to him, my feelings of attraction were always there.

My eyes drift down to his chest to where his tattoo resides. The tattoo is now hidden behind the clothes he wears but I imagine it easily enough. The way it swirls and molds together into a beautifully intricate and inverted triangle.

A frown pulls at my lips as I think about the meaning of the tattoo. *Stupid, foolish words of putting the House above any and all other things.* He probably didn't even want it. It was most likely forced upon him by order of his father and to refuse it would mean death.

My heart twinges as I realize his whole life has been doing what others want of him. His mother wanting him to learn magic and better their lives. His father wanting him to rule House Primis and give up being a Contract Laison. The Lords wanting him to bend to their whim. When will he be able to do what *he* wants?

The answer is simple.

When *I* come into power.

The thought is chilling. I've never thought of myself as being in a leadership position of any kind. I never minded being a simple employee, meeting monthly quotas and getting a livable wage. I never strived for more, but I was ok with that. My social life and hobbies fulfilled me.

But now I have deep and old magic inside me. Magic that's probably more powerful than the great High King Zagon. If I become High Queen Sloane with Balthazar at my side, he won't have to answer to anyone. He can do whatever he wants.

Balthazar's cold finger presses against my forehead. "What are you thinking about?"

My eyes snap up to his. I debate telling him and decide against it. He doesn't need to know. He'd only think I was pitying him. Instead, I ask a more important question. "Will I ever get a tattoo like that?"

His eyebrows shoot up towards his hairline. I've surprised him with that question. I'm not sure why, but it's clear that I have.

"If you become a true Primis, yes," he answers, his tone quiet but firm.

My eyebrows pinch together. What the hell does that mean? How does one become a *true* Primis?

Balthazar says nothing else, clarifies nothing about what he's just said. He's going to make this tough on me. Like pulling teeth without numbing the area first.

"Ok so what would make me a true Primis?" I ask.

He huffs out a deep breath, eyes shifting away from me to focus on the nightstand beside us. He doesn't like where this conversation is going.

"A ritual," he answers quietly. "It's not a marriage ceremony, at least not like your human ones, but it has the same effect. Once complete, you would be viewed as a Primis in the eyes of Jeznians, your origins be damned."

"Then doesn't that mean I'm already a true Primis if everyone thinks we're married?"

"No," he answers simply. "Being married does not mean we participate in the ritual. The only reason why we would go through with the ceremony would be so that House Primis can acquire your power. You must be someone *worthy* of House Primis. If you are, the High King will make you a pawn to his House so as to not risk giving you the chance to rise above."

If I became a true Primis, based on what Balthazar just said, it would give Zagon *zero* reasons to hunt me. I'd be a part of his House, I'd be a pawn, I'd be *bound* to put the

House's best interest above all else. That would make Zagon happy, right?

Maybe that's exactly why Balthazar doesn't want us to do it. I'd be bound to the House and to his father. Why would Balthazar want that when he *hates* Zagon? His hatred of Zagon is probably why he never offered doing the ritual in the first place. But that hatred might be blinding him to the easiest solution of keeping me safe.

If I become a real Primis, I will be protected by House Primis. Zagon will have no reason to come after me, to hurt me, or to even kill me. He'll acquire my power, I'll become his pawn, and I'll be *safe*.

And besides… Balthazar and I will still be able to overthrow Zagon. As long as our actions are in the best interest of House Primis, the binding magic won't stop us. We can ensure my safety while also getting rid of his father.

We should do it. We should perform the ritual.

"Balthazar—"

Umbra abruptly arrives in the room. My instinct takes over as I jolt to my feet ready to defend myself. It takes a few seconds to realize who she is and that she isn't a threat. The barest smirk flits across her lips, like she's proud I jumped into action, before she gives her attention fully to Balthazar.

"I trust this couldn't wait," Balthazar states. It's impossible to miss the hidden threat in his voice.

But even I know Umbra wouldn't be stupid enough to disturb him like this unless there was something he needed to hear right away.

She nods her head once and says, "I've located the Blood Reaper."

XXII

THE BLOOD REAPER'S been located? What is she talking about?

My lips part to ask for clarification but Balthazar snaps his fingers. An instant later, our comfortable clothes are replaced with new ones. A fall plaid skirt, a soft rustic brown sweater, black tights, and black platform shoes. Balthazar wears a tight black turtleneck shirt, a rustic brown jacket, black fitted pants, and black shoes.

He matched our outfits. The asshole matched our fucking outfits. My lips purse together in a lame attempt to hide my smile. He smirks, throwing a wink in my direction as a playful look fills his gaze. *I thought you'd like it,* he telepathically sends my way.

A short laugh bursts out of my mouth. "Me? You must mean you."

He shrugs his shoulders, his smirk widening with each word he speaks. "What can I say? I'm a romantic."

"Uh—huh."

"What? It's only fitting they know who I belong to."

"And what? Your turtleneck is your collar?" I ask, fully joking but the heated look Balthazar sends my way tells me I hit the nail on the head. "You're joking."

"I would never joke about such things," he purrs.

Before either one of us is able to get lost further into the conversation, Umbra makes a quiet noise. If it were anyone else, I'd assume it was unintentional but as Shadow Seer, her whole purpose is to never make a sound. So, if she makes one, it was wholeheartedly done on purpose.

Balthazar knows that as well and directs his attention to his Shadow Seer.

"The Blood Reaper is targeting a human," she states, her full attention on Balthazar.

"Evidence?"

"It's been lingering around her the past three days. There is a Defender protecting her."

I recognize the word Defender from the studying I did before heading to the seventh circle. They're assigned to humans by The Magistrate. They make sure a devil can't bargain a deal with that human, ensuring their safe entry into Odantha. Why would a Blood Reaper be targeting a human protected by a Defender? Something feels off about this.

Just what the Hell is going on?

"Three days but it hasn't made a move?" Balthazar asks.

Before Umbra can answer the question, I cut in. "Care to fill me in on the details? What's going on? What are you two talking about?"

If there's a bit of snark to my tone of voice it's really not my fault. Balthazar should have clued me in earlier. It gets frustrating being left out of what he does behind the scenes.

Balthazar shifts his attention to me. His hand drags up the side of my body before settling comfortably around my waist. His red speckled black eyes study me for a few moments, a slight purse to his lips before he finally hands over the information.

"As you recall during one of the House meetings, my father has employed a Blood Reaper. I've tasked Umbra with finding out who the Blood Reaper's target is. If this human has a Defender protecting it, I'd say Umbra has indeed found the correct target."

"I thought Defenders just made sure a devil couldn't make a deal with that specific human," I say as I wrack my brain again through the information I studied before my jaunt in the seventh circle. Maybe I missed something?

"Correct," Balthazar hums. "It's rare for a human to require more protection than that, but devils are not the only Jeznians who venture topside. It's the Defenders duty to protect their human from *all* supernatural threats."

"And who protects the humans who don't have Defenders? What if a Feral Monger attacks a human. Who's protecting that human?" I ask, eyebrow arching up as I anticipate he'll say no one.

"Champions protect your average human," he answers, a slight sneer on his face.

I click my tongue at the word, remembering our conversation in Paris all those weeks ago. *"You ever wonder why it was only me who showed up at your apartment and not a Champion?"* he had asked me. At the time I hadn't understood. Now, I do. Balthazar's notes were very clear on that.

Champions lazily do their jobs, often losing battles and costing humans their lives. Champions don't see it as some high honor but more of a burden. Someone to be babysat, wasting the Champions skill. Balthazar's notes, unfortunately, had substantial evidence to back it up. And a lot of snide comments written in the margins along the lines of *if you accept a job, then do it to the fullest*.

"I see," I hum. "And what would Zagon want with a human?"

"I haven't the faintest idea." His eyes cut over to Umbra. "Any information on Zagon and Caelum?"

"The Blood Reaper is always alone," Umbra answers. "To my knowledge, Zagon has not left Jeznia."

"And Caelum?"

Umbra remains silent, her jaw going taut as her fingers curl tightly into her palms.

"You can't track him," Balthazar surmises in a dead tone.

"No," she admits.

Damn. Just who is this guy if he can manage to stay out of Umbra's radar?

"Who's Caelum?" I ask. It's the first time I've heard his name.

"Zagon's Shadow Seer," Balthazar answers. "One would expect he'd lose his edge after a couple hundred years, but Caelum is as diligent as the day he was turned. No matter. Take me to the human."

"Us," I clarify. "Take *us* to the human."

Balthazar smirks. "It was implied."

"Uh—huh. Sure it was," I reply and a bark of laughter comes out of him, loud and full of life.

I smile despite myself. There was a brief moment I thought I'd never hear that sound again. It's overwhelming to hear, nearly bringing me to tears.

As his laughter dies down, he catches the expression on my face. He must understand the emotions running through me because his hand tightens its grip around my waist. Gently, he kisses my forehead. When he pulls away, he offers a curt nod to Umbra.

She says nothing as she touches Balthazar's shoulder. His hand remains firmly around my waist and the three of us are quickly enveloped by her shadows. The trip is violent as air whips around us, yet she expertly travels it with ease.

I've never understood why her in between is different than Balthazar's. His feels as though we're trekking through sludge while hers is like we're in the middle of a tornado. Even more confusing is the fact that her magic *comes* from Balthazar. So why isn't her in between the same as his?

A few moments later, we emerge, our feet crunching against a gravel driveway. The sun burns brightly but a canopy of leaves protects us from it. My eyes cast down the gravel driveway to the two story colonial house.

An elegant porch wraps around it's left side, disappearing towards the back while lush green grass begs me to lay down and forget why we're there. Crisp, cool air blows through as birds sing loudly in the tall, old trees.

Suddenly, the screen door swings open, clattering against the frame. Out steps a petite woman, no taller than five foot three. She wields a gun in her hands. Her pale skin is nearly as white as snow which makes the color of her moles and freckles that much darker. Her curly dark brown hair has natural red highlights and she stares at us with frightened but determined light brown eyes.

"Stay back," she orders as she holds the gun firmly in her hands. "I'll shoot."

Balthazar takes a step towards her as he scans the area. "Where is the Defender?"

"Second floor window on the left," Umbra answers effortlessly, like she clocked the Defender as soon as we arrived.

My eyes immediately go to the window. There's someone standing there, hidden behind the curtain. Why is the *human* out front while he hides away? That doesn't seem very Defender like.

Balthazar disappears only to reappear a moment later, hand curled tightly around the Defender's neck. The Defender doesn't move, his entire body still as a statue. He's of equal height as Balthazar with gorgeous dark brown curls and flawless sepia skin.

While Balthazar is lean and cut, this man is built like a warrior. The broad expanse of his back strains against his cotton gray shirt. His pants look a little too snug around his thighs, like he's clearly not wearing his own clothes. His dark brown eyes stare straight ahead but there's something odd in the way he stands.

Balthazar's head tilts sideways, eyebrows furrowed as he releases his hold on the Defender.

"Where is the Blood Reaper?" Balthazar asks the woman. "Why has he left the Defender behind?"

"I—I don't know," she stutters, the barrel of the gun tipping towards the porch. "Erij jumped in front of the Reaper to protect me. Next thing I know, the Reaper is screeching bloody murder before it disappears."

Balthazar's eyebrow arches before he nods his head towards his Shadow Seer. "Umbra."

She disappears and reappears holding a Jeznian bat. My jaw drops open. I knew they were big but seeing the size comparison between Umbra and the bat is *crazy*. What's even crazier is how easily she handles the bat despite its massive size.

The bat shrieks in her hold but she's clamped its wings down. It can't reach her with its bite but the fight is strong.

Wordlessly, she brings the bat over to Balthazar and shoves the poor thing towards the Defender. It reacts the way any stressed animal would. It bites the Defender. It swallows the blood greedily, but not thirty seconds later, it starts writhing in pain.

Umbra lets go, but the bat doesn't fly away. It flops onto the ground, miserable and in agony.

"I've never heard of a Defender with poisonous blood before," Balthazar hums as he watches the bat writhe before snapping his fingers.

Its head explodes in an instant and the creature dies. A mercy kill, but it never would've needed killing if they hadn't force fed it the Defender's blood. I bite back the words I want to say. Now isn't the time. It's more important we figure out what's going on.

"I must say," Balthazar continues, his voice a low thrum as he studies the Defender, "I find it hard to believe the Blood Reaper was in so much pain that it failed to kill the Defender or take him with it. Lord Taron may be an idiot, but his Blood Reapers are lethal, cunning, and smart."

Balthazar's eyes cut to the woman before stalking towards her. Fear grabs hold of her entire body and she lifts the gun without hesitation, firing off two shots. It happens so quickly no one has time to react. The bullets don't miss their target, Balthazar's blood splaying across the air. My heart lurches into my throat. I've only just saved him and now I'm going to lose him to this crazy lady? No. I won't. I can't.

My magic hums beneath the surface, demanding I take action, and I almost do. But then Balthazar keeps walking as if he wasn't shot. He doesn't even slow down. Instead, he quickly walks up the three steps to her porch, grabs the gun, and bends the barrel before tossing it to the side.

A split second later, he shoves his hand inside her. Her agonized scream echoes off the trees, sending birds flying to the sky. She fights him as best she can but I know that pain too well. It's almost impossible to move, to think, or to function. I'm honestly surprised she's able to fight him. Most people crumble to their knees. Some even faint from the pain. It's astonishing she remains on her feet.

Balthazar rummages around inside her for a few more moments before yanking his hand back. When he does, he's holding a tennis sized ball that shines a deep and majestic blue. My mouth drops open in shock as the woman slumps to the ground, chest heaving as she does her best to regain her composure.

Balthazar's eyebrows pinch together as he cradles the blue soul and he mutters more to himself than anyone else, "What is the Blood Reaper playing at?"

"Give—give that back," the woman groans.

"You know what that is?" I ask in shock from my spot on the gravel driveway.

"It's mine," she simply replies.

Maybe she doesn't know it's her soul, but she does know it came from her and that's all she needs to know to demand for it back. I can't help the miniscule smirk on my lips. I like her. She's got more spirit in her than anyone I've met.

"I fear it is not," Balthazar states. "You are merely a keeper of a key."

The words sting even though he doesn't direct them at me. He's summed up my entire existence into eight words. I am merely a keeper of a key. Zyvn basically got at the same thing. There's a purpose and reason for why the Creator created me. My wants, my desires, my goals? They mean nothing. I am a key. I am a potential bringer of the end of time. Both have the same meaning. I have no say in how my life plays out or the kind of person I could have grown into.

Balthazar steps down from the porch, the heavy sound of his shoe snapping me out of my thoughts. He walks straight over to where he left the Defender. The Defender remains unmoved as Balthazar approaches him. Balthazar's brows furrow as he walks closer to the Defender. He hesitates in his steps before turning his attention away from the Defender and towards our surroundings. Balthazar's intense gaze scans the trees, the backyard, the road at the end of the driveway, looking for something.

"What are you looking for?" I ask as he comes to stop beside me and the Defender.

"How is it that the Defender is still immobilized?" he asks quietly enough that the wind nearly muffles his words. "If the Blood Reaper has truly left, the Defender should be free from its powers."

"So, you think it's hiding somewhere within range," I say.

"Yes, but why?"

"For that," I state, head nodding to the blue orb within his hand. Zagon must want the blue orb just as much as we do. "I assume a Blood Reaper can't extract souls from bodies, right?"

If Zyvn as a Beastial couldn't go looking around inside me for the blue orb, I'd assume House Aides are unable to do the same thing. There must be a certain level or type of magic required for soul extraction and only a limited amount of Jeznians and Odanthians have that power.

"It would be unwise to try and steal from me," Balthazar replies in that low voice of his, upper lip pulling back in a snarl.

"But who does the Blood Reaper work for?" I remind him because we're not actually here for the Blood Reaper. We're here because this Blood Reaper is only doing what Zagon has ordered it to do.

Balthazar curses as he realizes the answer.

"What I want to know is," I trail off as I glance around our surroundings. "Why hasn't Zagon shown up yet? If he's targeting the keys, why would he let you take the soul? Isn't that too risky? He doesn't know what you'll do once you have the soul. Shouldn't he be here by now?"

Balthazar's gaze slowly turns to mine, his eyebrows furrowing as he wonders the same thing. His black—red eyes dart down to my feet before snapping back up to my face. His eyes widen for the briefest of moments as something dawns on him. Then all too suddenly, rage grabs hold of his face as his eyes narrow and his temples pulse rapidly while he clenches his teeth.

The hair rises on the back of my neck. His entire demeanor has shifted to urgent and worried. It immediately puts me on edge.

"What? What do you know?" I ask as I step closer to him.

He ignores me, his eyes snapping over to Umbra.

"Get her out of here, *now*," he barks out a demand, leaving no room for arguments.

The urgency of his order startles me, my heart jumping to my throat as a bolt of fear zaps down my spine.

"Balthazar, what—"

Before I can ask for any clarifying information, cold fingers wrap around my wrist. A split second later, shadows consume me in a violent swirl of maigc.

"No," I shout as I fight against Umbra's magic. "I won't leave him!"

My magic pushes against hers, demanding it bring us back to the location we were just at. Her magic puts up a good fight and the two of us tumble through the space in between like tumbleweeds out on the open prairie.

Her fingers dig into my wrist but I feel them slowly starting to slip away. She's losing her grip. If I can just push her a little more, I'll be free of her and able to get back to Balthazar. I can't let him face his father alone... or whatever he thinks is about to happen. We're partners, a team. I spent the last seventeen days in Hell so I wouldn't be a weakness to him anymore. I won't let him do this on his own. We're stronger together.

The shadows toss us viciously left, then right and I use that momentum to push Umbra's fingers off my wrist. The darkness of the shadows make it impossible to see her. I pray she's ok, that she makes it safely to wherever she was planning on taking me, before I focus my magic on returning to Balthazar. I concentrate on the feeling of him, of the distance between us and destroying that distance into tiny pieces. I have no idea where the woman with the blue soul lives, but judging by her lack of accent, she lives in America. I can find them. I can find *him*.

Something grabs hold of my ankle, cold and sticky. I can't suppress the shriek that bursts out of my mouth, but I regain my composure quickly. Afterall, I have magic. I'm stronger than I've ever been before. I can defeat whatever is in here. I *have* to.

Without hesitation, a blast of fire shoots out of my palm towards my foot. The light from the fire barely illuminates the space in front of me. I'm unable to see what's grabbed me, but it cries as the fire singes it. A moment later, it releases its hold on me and I pop out of the space in between.

The landing is rough as I fall to my hands and knees. Tiny rocks dig into my skin, eliciting a hiss of pain out of my mouth. I stand as quickly as I can, eyes darting around the area to gather my bearings. A breath of relief whooshes out of my mouth as I recognize the house. I've made it back.

A second later, my heart drops as I take in the vacant yard. Where is everyone? The woman, the Defender, and Balthazar are all gone. My eyes dart around as I look for any signs of a scuffle or fight. Everything looks oddly serene and calm.

Wind blows through gentle and soft. Leaves sing their delight as they dance in the wind. Sunlight finds its way through the thick canopy, its light swaying across the lush, green lawn.

Where is Balthazar?

My heart hammers inside my chest, its pulse a thundering mess inside my ears. I take a tentative step forward, the hairs along my arm rising up. Something doesn't sit right with my instincts. It's that familiar feeling I'd get in the seventh circle right before a creature would attack the living shit out of me. Something is terribly wrong here.

My hands tremble as fear rampages my senses. I can feel the threat hurtling towards me, but I haven't the slightest clue where it's coming from or when the attack will happen. I'm a sitting duck. Do I leave? Do I try to find Balthazar another way? But what if he needs my help?

I spin around on my toes, my breath coming out clipped as my eyes dart around for an unknown threat. Is it the Blood Reaper? It's probably waiting for the perfect moment to strike. I should put a shield up.

My loud breathing echoes in the quiet of the yard as I quickly throw up a shield around my entire body.

Balthazar. I attempt to reach out to him telepathically, but I'm not sure what the limitations are. Can he even hear me if he's back in Jeznia? *Balthazar, where are you?* Silence is all I receive in response. My stomach drops. I *know* something is wrong, but I can't figure out what it is.

The hair on the back of my neck rises up as if electricity lingers in the air. I whirl around, heart in my throat as I anticipate an attack but there's no one there. Then all too suddenly, the impending doom weighs down on me all at once.

Thunder booms despite the cloudless blue skies. Wind whips wildly around me as the space in front of me begins to visibly split in two. Something is emerging from the space in between.

I jump back ten feet just as a foot steps through the opening. The rest of its leg comes through a moment later. Its skin is a deep burnt burgundy color. Its leg is corded in thick muscle, its thigh as wide as my waist, and its knee at the height of my belly button. I can't even see its body but I can already tell. This creature is *huge.*

My eyes lift skyward as it fully steps through the split and my lips part at the familiar horns. *Primis* horns. Is this monster standing before me *Zagon Primis?* He wears a gladiator style skirt, the leather pleated slates gently blowing in the wind. There's no shirt, only his bare chest on display. He's entirely all muscle. While Balthazar is muscular, he is also toned and slimmer. Zagon, on the other hand, is pure muscle and brute force. A literal mountain.

His thick, square jaw perfectly houses the fangs protruding from his top lip. A deep, scowling brow, black, endless eyes with no white to be seen, a scar running down his cheek to his jaw, monstrous horns probably twice the length of my arms, and braided black hair reminiscent of Viking braids.

Zagon's mere presence bears down on me, threatening to buckle my knees under the weight of it. A crack splinters in my shield and my heart nearly stops beating as his head turns to me. With all black eyes, it's impossible to tell if he's looking dead on, left, or right, but when his lips peel back into a sickening smile, I know it's because he's staring right at me.

"Sloane Amelia Kensington," his voice booms and the gravel driveway vibrates in response.

The blood in my veins freeze upon hearing my middle name coming from his mouth. He's done his homework if he knows my full name and the thought terrifies me.

"What a pretty little thing you are," he muses to himself before tilting his head towards his right. "Rather fortunate for you, hmm?"

Balthazar stands confidently beside Zagon, hands in his pockets, shoulders pulled back, and his head held high. My heart threatens to beat itself into cardiac arrest as my eyes dart between him and Zagon. Balthazar doesn't look displeased next to Zagon. In actuality, he looks rather smug.

No.

My gut twists into painful knots. This isn't right. Whatever Zagon is playing at right now... It's not reality. It isn't. Balthazar wouldn't betray me. He wouldn't lie to me.

The connection we have is *real*. No matter what this version of Balthazar claims about our relationship, what we have is real. Besides, how can I even be sure it's him and not a Shifter?

Inhaling deeply, I square my shoulders up as best as I can while directing my gaze into Zagon's endless eyes.

"To what do I owe the honor, High King Zagon?"

He chuckles, deep and low. The vibrations bounce through my chest and it takes everything in me to appear as calm as possible.

"Caelum always spoke so highly of you," he states.

My breath hitches in my throat. Caelum... Zagon's Shadow Seer? He *spoke* of me to Zagon? He's been watching me, but for how long? Zagon must know about my red soul. But does he know of the old, deep magic?

Zagon shifts his weight onto his left leg, the gravel crunching beneath his massive size, and I blurt out the first thing that comes to mind.

"I trust his assessment was accurate?"

I have to think of a way out of this. Create an opportunity for me to teleport away. But no matter what I do, the grim reality is that Zagon will always have a way to track me down. There's nowhere safe for me to go. He'll find me in Jeznia and on Earth. And if I flee to Odantha, The Magistrate will have me killed. I can't escape.

"Extremely, wouldn't you agree, Balthazar?"

"Indeed," Balthazar hums, the smugness slowly easing off his face to be replaced with open candor. My stomach churns, an irritating tenseness grabbing hold of my shoulders causing my head to twitch. "Caelum has always—"

"If your Shifter could kindly shut the fuck up, I would greatly appreciate it," I interrupt him, not wanting to hear the lies that'll be spewed from his mouth.

Zagon openly laughs as Balthazar scowls.

"Though I appreciate your animosity," Balthazar says in a low voice, any love and familiarity completely gone. "It really is me, Sloane."

He raises his hand and snaps his fingers only to reappear inches from me. My body nearly jumps back but something grounds me in place. The hairs along my neck and forearms stand to attention as I stare into the face I love but it's all wrong. All of it. The slant of his nose, the shape of his eyes, the smoothness of his cheeks... it all *looks* like Balthazar, but something's *off.*

Balthazar leans into my space, our noses practically touching.

"Go on," he urges, his red speckled eyes challenging me as his brows furrow. "Take a whiff."

I can't pass up the opportunity, inhaling deeply and nearly feeling relief upon smelling the familiar smoke that I've come to associate with Balthazar. Except... if he's a Shifter, he's supposed to smell like sulfur.

My eyes snap up to his and he gleefully smirks down at me.

"We had such good times together, didn't we?" he asks, his eyes glinting as he leans forward to press his cheek against mine. His whispered words are a knife to the heart. "I even called you High Queen."

My vision blurs as he disappears before reappearing beside Zagon. The tears can't be held back as my lower lip and chin tremble. Balthazar has only called me High Queen once. The day he asked my permission to train me in normal devil magic. There's no doubt this man is my Balthazar. But why?

My eyebrows furrow as I desperately think of any and every excuse. How could this have happened? I know those moments between me and Balthazar were real. He wasn't faking his sincerity or his vulnerability. So… how can both be true? How can Balthazar be so madly in love with me *and* be the devil currently staring at me with such disdain?

I can't… I can't make sense of it.

My eyes drift to Zagon, to the pure arrogance and entitlement of his entire demeanor. *Caelum always spoke so highly of you.* He said it so callously. He wanted to instill fear in me, to make me afraid of being watched at every waking moment, to never know if I'm truly alone. My eyebrows pinch together as pieces start to slide into place. But if Zagon was always going to throw Caelum in my face, why would he require Caelum *and* Balthazar to watch me? Surely he didn't require his two most powerful men to babysit little old me. That *actually* doesn't make sense.

"Why…" I trail off as I desperately blink through my tears.

"Because you're unique, Sloane," Balthazar answers and I shake my head, directing all my attention to Zagon.

"Why would you need Caelum to spy on me if your son was already doing it for you?"

"See?" Balthazar asks, as he calmly walks back to his father, as if to punctuate what he says. "I told you she was smart."

"They can only safely stay in Ephiri for 36 hours," Zagon answers. "They rotated their time."

"No," I huff out, my hands hastily wiping my tears away as determination has my spine straightening.

He wouldn't do that. He wouldn't waste Balthazar's time like that. Not when his Shadow Seer had it completely covered. If Zagon really is allied with Balthazar, he'd be using him in a much more strategic way.

Zagon wouldn't be able to stay High King of Jeznia if he made stupid decisions. Wasting manpower on a silly little girl would be a stupid decision. He needs his allies to keep him strong, to keep him powerful, to keep him High King. Because no matter how much brute strength he has, if he doesn't have the brains to back it up, the other Lords of Jeznia would eat him alive. So no, I don't believe him. And I don't believe that's really Balthazar betraying me right now.

Besides, Zagon has powerful magic. He could be tricking my senses. He could have trapped me in an illusion. This could all be a dream while Balthazar is fretting over my unconscious body. All I know is that the devil standing before me isn't my Balthazar.

"I don't know how you're doing it," I say, eyes locked on to Zagon's pitch black gaze, "but that's *not* Balthazar."

Zagon's eyebrows pinch together, the first indication that his amusement is disappearing. This is about to get serious fast. I need to be ready for it.

"How can you be so sure, Sloane?"

"Because," I answer as I hold my head high. "You can't trust a devil."

He dryly chuckles. "No. You can't."

"That is true," Balthazar replies, the right side of his mouth pulling up into a smirk. "You certainly can't trust me."

"Balthazar is the *only* one I trust."

"An erroneous decision, I assure you," he says. "I was only ever after your soul, Sloane. Never you."

The words hurt coming from his mouth, his voice, his face, but I refuse to believe them. Even if it makes me delusional. The *only* way I'd ever believe he betrayed me is if we were alone. Just the two of us, privately, together. *That* is the only time I'd ever believe it was all a lie.

"Then why didn't you just take it when you first had it?" I challenge. "That day when the Records Keeper balanced it with Chad's soul... you could have just taken it then. Why didn't you?"

Balthazar laughs loudly but there's no amusement in the sound. "And have a Champion hunt me down?"

"We were in Jeznia—"

"I would have been *chained* to Jeznia had I taken your soul without your consent," Balthazar violently spits out, his face contorted into such an unfamiliar rage it nearly has me taking a step back. "Anytime I set foot in Ephiri thereafter, a Champion would. Hunt. Me. Down."

"But you would have had the soul," I argue, trying to poke holes in his argument at every chance I get. "Your *father* would have had the soul. It would only be a matter of time before Zagon found the second one. It would have been worth the risk. You're *not* Balthazar."

"*I am.*"

"It doesn't matter," Zagon cuts in, voice sharp. "We have your soul. We have the Odanthian soul. You're smart. I will only offer you this opportunity once. Bind yourself to House Primis."

"No," I breathe out quietly before he can get another word in.

Rage washes over Zagon's face. "You will."

It was never a choice. Zagon wants me bound to his House. He must know about the kind of magic I have. He must want a way to control it if he can't physically possess it.

My head is shaking back and forth as I take a step away from him. His lips pull back in a snarl, a low growl reverberating in his chest as he advances towards me.

"I won't," I breathe out, eyes snapping over to Balthazar.

He remains motionless, face stoic as he watches the rage overcome his father. He does nothing to protect me, makes no moves to show me he's on my side. *That isn't Balthazar*, I remind myself. It's not. Balthazar would die for me. He'd freeze to death in Odantha if it meant my survival. He may look and smell and sound like Balthazar, but I refuse to believe it's him. It doesn't *feel* like him.

The ground shakes beneath Zagon's weight as he suddenly rushes me. The color drains from my face as I stare like a deer caught in the headlights. The realization slams into me like a ton of bricks. He's going to kill me if I don't bind myself to House Primis. If he can't have my magic, he'll make sure no one else can. Not even me.

My eyes snap to Balthazar. His jaw is clenched tight, temples bulging as he stares at me with his dual colored eyes. Our eyes lock and the smallest, quietest whisper echoes within my mind.

Run.

I don't think. I react.

My magic activates and I'm yanked down by my feet. Zagon's roar cracks like thunder as he desperately reaches for me while I sink through the ground. He misses, his hand swinging over my head just before I disappear into the space in between.

Magic rushes through me, pushing me through the space faster than I've ever travelled. It's impossible to breathe as the invisible muck passes over my nose and mouth. My hands reach up to my face, covering it from any potential threats within the space.

A short moment later, I'm violently ejected into the air, arms flailing as I try to assess where the ground is. Up, down, or sideways? I have no time to figure it out. The air is knocked out of my lungs as I land flat on my back.

Lightning streaks across the pitch black sky. Sulfur burns my nose. My fingernails scrape against compacted dirt. The air is stale and drowning in rot. More lightning scatters across the sky, illuminating my surroundings for mere seconds.

Hastily, I rush to my feet, my heart rapidly thumping against my chest as I turn on my toes looking for any attackers. Despite being out in the open with no cover, there are none I can immediately pinpoint.

Glowing light in the distance catches my attention and I abruptly stop all movements as I make out what it is I'm staring at.. My stomach bottoms out as my mouth drops open in shock. My blood freezes. My heart stops.

I am so *fucked*.

My eyes drift up the volcanic mountain, stopping at the first circle before descending down towards the base. My chest heaves as my breaths come out clipped. I spin around, praying that the seventh circle's outer wall is behind me, but only a fool would believe that. The mountain is too far away. I can *see* the outer wall from here. That only means one thing.

I'm in The Wastelands.

My knees buckle and I drop to the ground. No one who enters The Wastelands ever leaves. Not even Zagon Primis will venture into The Wastelands. It's not a risk worth taking. Not when deep, old magic rules the terrain.

Wait.

My head snaps up as I look at the city of Jeznia. I *have* deep, old magic. If anyone can break out of The Wastelands, it's *me*. I once told Balthazar that. Now, I get to put my money where my mouth is.

It won't be easy. Nothing about deep, old magic ever is. But I refuse to give up. I fought to save my life against Chad's wish. I fought to save my life against Zyvn's orders. I will fight to save my life from The Wastelands. I have to because I can't leave Balthazar to whatever fate Zagon has in store for him.

In the one moment he was able to break free from Zagon's control, he told me to run. He wanted me to be safe. I knew it. I knew that Balthazar would never betray me.

I need to get back to him. I need to help him break free from Zagon and take the fucking bastard *down*.

I don't know how I'm going to do it, but I *will* break get out of The Wastelands. Zagon's a dead devil walking. *No one* messes with Balthazar and gets away with it.

"I'm coming for you, Zagon Primis," I whisper to the mountain.

Nothing he does will save him. He cemented his death the moment he used Balthazar for his own gain. Zagon doesn't stand a chance against me. I'm Sloane fucking Kensington. Lord Balthazar's owner and wielder of deep, old magic. But more importantly...

I'm the future *High Queen of Jeznia*.

Epilogue

ZAGON SWIPES FOR Sloane, but her head disappears
beneath the earth before he can reach her. He bellows to the
skies, causing the ground and house to shake in his anger.
She's escaped. The relief washes over me, slowly calming my
pounding heart. *She's safe*. It might only be for a moment,
but Sloane's smart. She'll evade Zagon. I know she will.

Just as I knew she wouldn't be fooled by Zagon's
impersonation. His illusionary magic may work among the
Lords of Jeznia, even on myself, but not Sloane. Never
Sloane.

Zagon was smart in using my actual body as a stand in,
but with the Blood Reaper keeping me immobilized and
unable to speak, his magic had to do all the heavy lifting.
There was no way he'd be able to trick her. And
unsurprisingly, he didn't.

Because Sloane is more powerful than him.

She may not understand it, may think she's crazy for
believing so strongly I was false, but her magic can see what
she cannot. I finally understand it after all this time. Her
magic is *born* from the Creator, old and experienced. It
makes the most sense. It explains why she's so powerful, why
the magic is so old, why it's eerily reminiscent of the magic

that possesses The Wastelands. It's because it comes straight from the Creator.

Our devil magic is but a baby in comparison to hers.

Her magic must have seen the threads of Zagon's magic working tirelessly to fool her human eyes. And because she's smart, she trusted her instincts even if she didn't fully understand it. She's brilliant on so many levels and powerful beyond imagination.

There's no question. She *will* become High Queen. Or something entirely new and more powerful. Zagon doesn't stand a chance against her. No one does.

Zagon whirls around to face me, his fury grabbing hold of his entire being. Instinct has me wanting to back away but I'm held in place by the Blood Reaper's magic. The bite mark along my neck throbs in time with my racing heart.

I was unaware Blood Reapers had venom to help nullify their preys magic. An oversight I won't make again concerning House Aides and their many hidden talents.

Pain flares to life within my body as I fight for control. My bones ache and my muscles strain, yet I refuse to give up. Even as my body continues to refuse all my demands, even as my body only listens to the Blood Reaper's command, I will *always* resist. The pain is nothing compared to the alternative of submitting.

Bitter acid burns the back of my throat as Zagon takes steps towards me. I should have known I was his target all along. Going after Sloane would have drawn my attention. Zagon *had* to come after me if his goal was her in the end. I put all my attention into securing Sloane's safety. I never once considered my own. Because why would I be the target? Yet the Blood Reaper did not hesitate to swoop in as soon as it saw an opening.

It waited for Sloane and Umbra to leave. It waited until I was alone. And just as I was going to face my father head on, it struck. My guards were up for Zagon but not for the Blood Reaper. My own carelessness did me in. I was too focused on protecting Sloane, on making sure she was beyond his grasp, and in doing so, I left myself wide open.

I'd do it all over again.

Sloane is the air I breathe. Without her, there is no point in anything. I'm nothing but bones and dust. If my life must forfeit so that hers may remain alive and well, I have no reservations or hesitations. I will always choose Sloane.

Zagon's hand slides under my jaw before he effortlessly lifts me off the ground. Air struggles to pass through my windpipe as he raises me to his disgusting face. I wish for nothing more than to see him dead. Begging, tortured, degraded… it means nothing to me. I want his motionless heart in my hands, his mouth agape, eyes wide. No pulse. No breathing. Simply dead.

"I *will* have her magic," Zagon states. "It belongs to me."

Fuck you. Her magic belongs to no one but herself. It's a shame he doesn't understand it yet. Doesn't understand that she *owns* him. And every ungodly Jeznian within the seven circles. In time they'll know. But by then it'll be too late.

"But we have more urgent matters to attend to than Sloane Amelia Kensington. She'll come in due time."

Without warning, we rapidly spiral down through the earth as if sucked in by a vortex. Zagon holds me tightly around the neck, uncaring that he might suffocate me to death without access to my magic.

When we resurface, he tosses me harshly to the ground. My back collides against a straight hard edge but without the use of my body, I can't discern what I've hit. I'm forced face first into the cold, unforgiving floor.

"Blood Reaper, stand him up," Zagon orders.

My joints feel stiff as I'm forced into a standing position against my will. The Blood Reaper stands behind Zagon, almost completely hidden within the shadows. But I see it. The piece of blood red cloth draped over its head and down its entire body. It's humorously reminiscent of a child throwing a sheet over their head to play ghost except this cloth helps hide the Blood Reaper from its prey. It moves swiftly in the wind without making a sound. The cloth drowns out all sound.

And when the Blood Reaper is ready to bite, the magic of the cloth forms the mouth. Hands suddenly appear all over the cloth, overwhelming you as they hold every possible inch of your body in place. Once the Blood Reaper has you within its grasp, it's nearly impossible to escape. I was so close to escaping, to using magic to free myself but it bit me just in time. Venom spread through me like literal wildfire, shutting off all access to my magic.

The Blood Reaper warps in and out of my view as the cloth billows against its frame. I think of all the ways I'm going to make it suffer before gradually turning my attention away. The Blood Reaper is not important right now. My surroundings are.

I glance around, a little surprised at the familiarity of it all. Of all the places he could have taken us, I hadn't expected Zagon to take us here.

A lone fire chandelier thirty feet up illuminates the dark space, causing the odd glitch in the Blood Reaper's disappearing act. Massive bats dive down towards the circular counter. Sharp spires line the aisles, all heading towards the circular center where a desk, a magical creature, and scales await.

I try to glance towards the edge to ascertain how close I am to it, but my eyes don't move. The Blood Reaper even controls those. I may not be able to see the sheer drop off from where I stand, but I'm well aware of it. The drop from the bridgeway would kill even a seasoned Jeznian who lacked magic. Someone such as myself. If I'm not careful, I might be one accidental shove away from certain death.

"Records Keeper," Zagon booms, his voice echoing off the walls. "I've come to collect Sloane Kensington's soul."

"The soul is not yours to collect," the Records Keeper screeches, it's multi—layered voice grating even to my ears.

It may abide by the rules set forth by the Creator and Death but even then, it answers to no one. Only they could possibly persuade the Records Keeper to bend the rules, but that's not a guarantee. The Records Keeper will *always* do what it was created to do. It cares not for some pointless High King who will be replaced by the next powerful devil thirsting for power. A hard lesson I learned early on as a Contract Liaison.

Zagon clicks his tongue. "Ah, but it is. You can either hand it to me or I will take it by force."

"Your magic will do you no good here."

"I don't require magic when all I need to do is kill you."

A mere second later, Zagon severs the Records Keeper's head from its body. The skull clatters against the ground but it's not dead. Something so simple would never be enough to kill the Records Keeper. I've seen Contract Liaisons decapitate it, burn it, stab it, cut it off at the torso… any and everything but it always puts itself back together again. A simple decapitation will do nothing to the Records Keeper.

Case in point. It slowly bends over to pick up its head. But then Zagon moves. Faster than light. He grabs the body before eviscerating it. Over and over again he stabs the body, shredding it to ribbons as if that will somehow make a difference. It won't. How on earth has Zagon remained High King all this time if he wastes his energy in such a way?

A glint catches my eye. Something shimmering and iridescent flies out of the Records Keeper. I nearly miss it amidst the blood spewing and innards bursting from the frail body. The object lands in a puddle of blood, more blood splattering across it, but it still shimmers against the firelight.

Zagon notices it too as he carelessly discards the Record Keepers' body. It lands with a hollow thud and I yearn to wince but my face remains deathly stoic. Zagon, covered in rotting blood, plucks a gem from some intestines and holds it between his fingers. A smirk forms along his face.

"Everything living can be killed," Zagon states calmly as he examines the gemstone before crushing it in one smooth motion. "You merely need to find the way."

Air swirls around us, vicious and untamed, as the Records Keepers' magic vacates its body. A wind vortex rises from the body, wild and brutal as it instantly snuffs out the chandelier. The wind gains traction and power as it grows. I realize with horror how abnormal the vortex is as the strength of the wind starts to push me *away* from the body instead of sucking me in.

My feet slide against the floor towards the edge. The edge that has a sheer drop off to certain death. Panicked, I attempt to use my magic but nothing responds. I try to move backwards but it's no use. Not while under the Blood Reaper's control.

Zagon doesn't care to notice my impending death as I approach the edge. He wordlessly disappears behind the counter, his ginormous size too heavy to be moved by the wind. I, however, am not as fortunate as my toes kiss the edge of the bridgeway. Without access to magic, I won't survive the fall.

I strain against my confines, veins bulging in my neck as I fight to lift my arms up, but they remain glued to my sides. My feet slowly skid over the edge. This is it. This is the end. I'm going to die and Zagon will eventually have Sloane. He'll steal her power and discard her for nothing. I *cannot* die. I *will* not.

As if by divine intervention, the wind stops just as the balance is about to turn against my favor. But it's not over yet. I'm still teetering on the edge of death while I wait for Zagon or the Blood Reaper to make their next move.

The bats screech and wail as they realize their friend has been murdered. The noise is tortuous. Their high pitched screeching threatens to burst my ear drums. Yet pity bubbles beneath my chest at their distraught screeching. I don't think they've ever known life without the Records Keeper. It's sad, really, to think the Records Keeper no longer lives. We were never friends but I'd grown accustomed to its presence with every soul drop off. We never exchanged more than business words, but we respected each other and our place within the game.

Now, it's dead without so much as a goodbye. Who will fill its place? Will the Creator create a new Records Keeper or leave us floundering to figure it out on our own?

My thoughts are interrupted as Zagon emerges from behind the counter. He snaps his fingers and, a moment later, I'm turned to face him. A red orb the size of a tennis ball sits comfortably in his oversized hand. I'd recognize that orb anywhere. The smooth surface, the deep rich red, the hum of power, the vibration of the unknown. It's Sloane's soul. Without a doubt.

My upper lip twitches as a low growl rumbles through my chest. Murderous intent consumes me. Red bleeds into my vision. If he so much as *scratches* her soul, I *will* have his heart.

Zagon tosses the orb carelessly in the air before catching it easily and I want nothing more than to tackle him to the ground. Yet with this damn venom running through me, I can't do shit. Not until it runs its course. That is, if the Blood Reaper's magic doesn't hold it indefinitely.

Zagon snaps his fingers a second time and the blue orb manifests next to the red orb. The Jeznian and Odanthian souls. *Keys to the void.*

My heart drops at the realization. I'd forgotten what Zyvn had told us. Forgotten that Zagon had an entirely different agenda aside from taking Sloane's magic. He wants whatever is locked away in that void. And if he were to get it…

I have to assume it's powerful. After all, why else would the Creator lock it away? It wouldn't go through such pains to keep it hidden and protected if it were mere sentiment.

Zagon *cannot* have whatever it is.

Zagon glances at the Blood Reaper and nods his head. A moment later, my body slumps to the floor. The pain and exhaustion are immediate, but my body is my own again.

I glare up at Zagon, at the smugness in his disgusting eyes, and murderous intent consumes me all over again. It takes everything within me to squash it. I'm free now and Sloane will require my help. I can't carelessly attack Zagon when the odds are embarrassingly stacked against me. She *needs* me. I need to stay alive for as long as she requires my help.

Zagon snaps his fingers and the orbs disappear to a place only he knows. With one powerful swat, the bats are silenced into death with a single hit. Their bodies drop like flies, some thudding against the floor while others slide off into the abyss.

Zagon slowly turns to face me, his lips splitting into a wicked grin. Chills dart down my spine as it takes everything within me to not react. I can't deny it. Zagon is more powerful than I am. I have to tread carefully if I'm to survive long enough to help Sloane.

"Your girlfriend's power will have to wait," he says. "The void awaits."

I force my face to remain blank. He watches me as intently as a predator. He's looking for any small reaction that might give away my true intentions. *So that's why he gave me my body back.* He wanted to see how I'd choose.

Sloane.

Or him.

Will I put the House first, put *him* first, or choose the woman he believes to be nothing more than a cockroach?

My shoulders pull back as my head tilts so I can properly look at him. There is no doubt within his gaze. He believes he knows exactly how I will choose. How I will be *forced* to choose. *He has another thing coming for him,* I think bitterly.

Confidently, I step towards him, all emotions devoid from my face. He watches in glee as my right fist comes to press into my chest directly above my heart. Effortlessly, I bow at the waist a full ninety degrees. An obvious sign of my submission to him. He grunts his approval, too stupid to notice the magic thrumming through my right hand now hidden from his view.

He doesn't notice as my magic weaves its way through the binding magic tattooed on my chest. He doesn't notice as my face winces in utter agony. The pain is unbearable. Binding magic is powerful. More powerful than Zagon's magic. Someone who is bound *cannot* betray whatever they're bound to. Ever.

Yet Sloane gave me a gift when she nearly killed me earlier today. Remnants of her magic now live within me. She's given me a work around on my binding oath to House Primis. *Her* magic is stronger than this oath, than House Primis, than High King Zagon Primis. He won't know what hit him until it's too late.

The old magic weaves between the binding magic, painfully snipping all the way through one measly line. When the binding magic breaks from that small incision, I nearly faint as sweat falls off the tip of my nose. I might genuinely vomit. I might even fall face first. The pain is too much.

Yet when I speak, my voice is nothing but light and firm. The words leave my mouth effortlessly because betraying Zagon Primis and the House is the easiest decision I will ever make.

"Indeed," I hum out, faking every ounce of pleasantry I can despite the agonizing pain of breaking my binding oath. "The void awaits, my High King."

I will *always* choose Sloane.

Preview

Bargain with the Devil series – Book 3

Releasing September 5th, 2026

I

Balthazar

MUCK AND SLUDGE threaten to drown me. No matter how hard I fight, the thickness of the in between presses down on me, pushing me further and further away from the three worlds. My magic aches to dispel the sludge, but it's useless. I've tried countless times to mold and move the muck, but nothing's worked. Magic… at least *my* magic cannot penetrate whatever magic is used within the in between.

My lungs beg for air which makes no sense. I inhale and exhale with ease but it feels as though I'm suffocating. Panic begins to bubble deep within my chest. *I'm going to die here.* Countless times that thought has passed through my mind and I haven't died yet.

I push forward, shoving the panic down to the deepest depths of my soul. There are only so many times I can come back empty handed before Zagon actually kills me. For weeks I've been sent to the in between to find some sort of gateway to the void. But with no real frame of reference, I'm flying around blind. I'm forced to constantly shove my hand into a puddle of mud, praying I'll find the damn needle.

Meanwhile, time passes on and I have no fucking clue where Sloane has disappeared off too. It's been four weeks since she escaped Zagon's murderous, greedy hands yet I'm no closer to finding her than I am to finding this cursed gateway.

Burning in my lungs jolts me out of my thoughts. I'm not breathing. I *can't* breathe. I inhale as deeply as possible but no air passes through my lungs. I'm *drowning* in air. Instinctive panic flares to life, my magic taking over as I transport myself back to Jeznia. My body is thrown to my hands and knees upon arrival in Jeznia as I gulp down deep, dry breaths of sweet, sweet air.

The heat of Jeznia scorches my body. A strange oddity that I've become used to after leaving the in between from my prolonged visits. It's as though the longer I stay in the in between, the less accustomed I become to Jeznia's harsh environment.

"Any luck?" Umbra's whispered voice asks me.

Luck. Such a peculiar word. One I've never believed in. Nor has Umbra. But things change and she only ever uses words she means. Luck. I will need luck to find the gateway *and* Sloane.

"None, I fear," I answer honestly as I push up onto my feet.

Her dehydrated skin has tightened around her joints and the curves of her bones. Thinner. Frailer. The task I've assigned her is taking its toll, but I fear I cannot have her let up. We *must* find a way to kill Zagon and if that means she forfeits her life in exchange, so be it.

"Any news on your end?" I ask as I walk over to my desk, snapping my fingers.

A glass of water appears and I gulp it down. If she's noticed that the Jeznian heat is getting to me, she says nothing.

"Zagon caught me," she confesses.

My eyebrow arches as my eyes slowly slide to hers. He caught her? If that were true, she wouldn't be standing here.

"You're sure it was him?"

It would be bold and idiotic for a shifter to cosplay Zagon, but so few Jeznians have a strong survival sense that it wouldn't surprise me. I suppose it could be a devil practicing their magic, holding random appearances for extended periods of time. A skill that's required if one were to make Contract Liaison. But Umbra nods her head. She's sure it was him. If I were to doubt her now, there'd be no point in having her as my Shadow Seer. Umbra knows how to spot a fake better than me. If she says it was Zagon, it was Zagon.

"And yet... he simply let you go?" I ask, curious and confused.

Again, she nods. My eyes narrow. Zagon would never let anyone spying on him go. He wouldn't bother with torturing them for information either. He'd simply behead them in one clean slice. What is he playing at?

I snap my fingers, my cup of water refilling before I take a couple more deep gulps as I mull over the situation.

Zagon let Umbra go. He knew she'd run straight to her lord. He knew she'd tell me what transpired. He caught her sneaking around, caught her looking for a way to kill him, and he let her go. He let her come running back to me to *tell me* that *he knew*. He knew I was looking for a way to kill him and he doesn't care.

A sharp laugh bursts out of my mouth. He doesn't believe we'll find a way. He truly thinks himself invincible. And you know what? Good. The Record's Keeper believed itself invincible but Zagon was right. Everything living can be killed.

"He underestimates us, Umbra," I say as I walk around and sit down at my desk. "And that will be his downfall."

With a snap of my fingers, a map lies flat on the surface. Red ink crosses out areas and circles others. Lame guesses of where the void might be. A deep sigh blows out my mouth as I cross out yet another one of the many locations.

Weeks.

I've been at this for *weeks*.

"Any news on Sloane?" I ask as I mull over the next location I should search.

I try to sound as if I don't care about her whereabouts but it's useless. Umbra already knows Sloane is peccatum meum. No matter how distant I sound or how unphased I appear, Umbra knows not knowing where Sloane is eats away at me day and night. Her absence painstakingly carves a chasm through my soul, slowly threatening to split it in two. Umbra must sense the shift in me, the misery and pain, or else there'd be no point in having her as my Shadow Seer.

I huff out a heavy breath as I focus on the map while I await her answer. Perhaps I should choose something closer to the worlds. I've been searching the farthest reaches from the three worlds but maybe the Creator kept it close. It would certainly be unusual.

My pen *tap, tap, taps* against the desk, my lips pressing side to side of my face.

"I cannot locate her within Jeznia," Umbra answers plainly.

"She'll be masking her magic," I remind her.

"She's not here."

My hand comes up to the bridge of my nose, my eyes squeezing shut as I pinch the spot between my eyes. "You're positive?"

"No."

I knew she'd answer that way. If Sloane truly has mastered her magic, if she has full access to the deep, old magic running through her, no one will be able to find her. Not unless she let's us. But if that were the case, why the radio silence? Surely if she's able to mask herself to such a degree, she'd be able to open a telepathic channel to me.

I've been trying every damn day. Countless times a day. Calling her name. *Shouting* her name. But nothing. All I receive is emptiness. An emptiness so vast and bleak I fear it will freeze me from the inside out.

Inhaling deeply, I circle a random spot on the map, snap my fingers, and the map disappears. I glance up at Umbra, at her sewn shut eyes, at her elongated ears, at her ashen colored skin. Her body may be small, but it is built for strength. Still, the wear is there. Her sleuthing around the halls of House Primis has taken from her. She dares not complain. Dares not speak out against my orders. But if we are to succeed, if we are to find Sloane and kill Zagon... I'll need Umbra to be more akin to a partner than a bound employee.

"Speak freely," I order as I sit back in the chair, my arms crossing over my chest. "Do you think this is wise?"

"No," she answers without hesitation, without remorse or fear.

"Do you think I should join Zagon and forget Sloane?"

Umbra's head tilts heavily to the side and the muscle where hair should be for an eyebrow cocks up. Odd. I've never seen her make such a face.

"Speak freely, Umbra. I may be telepathic, but I'm no mind reader."

"What Hapshein did was unwise," she states and a snort tumbles out of my mouth.

Hapshein the Destroyer. He nearly eviscerated the three worlds during his reign. He's the whole reason the Creator created the cold and the heat. If he'd been successful, I imagine the human species would be extinct and Odantha on its last leg.

Hapshein sought out to destroy all that there was after some strange experience in The Wastelands. Before The Wastelands were what they've become now. Back when we could supposedly roam The Wastelands without it becoming our tomb.

"Am I to take your statement as to mean I've gone mad?" I ask and, despite my best efforts, I cannot hide the bite in my tone.

"Hapshein made Odanthians fear Jeznia. Hapshein dragged the Creator out from where It slumbered. Hapshein forever changed the worlds," Umbra says reverently, her whispered voice shouting at me in refrained rage.

She's never shown me such emotion before. My instincts have me sitting to attention, anticipating an attack from every direction. She's a skilled fighter, which is unusual for a Shadow Seer, but she has to be. There was no other way to crawl her way up from the seventh circle. In a fight, she'd never win against me, but she'd certainly maim me.

"What he did was unwise," Umbra says, "but thousands of years later, he still remains."

"Who gives a flying fuck about legacy?" I growl, fire igniting between my horns, hot and fierce, as it descends down my spine.

Legacy is all Zagon strives for. To overshadow Hapshein the Destroyer. He will not stop until he's crowned Zagon the Undefeated, Zagon the Ruler, Zagon the *God*. It is why every one hundred years he rapes any mediocre devil he can find, spawning as many offspring as he can, before throwing them to the wolves and seeing who will survive.

Primis magic is strong. Our lineage was the first to wield magic. Year over year, we've manipulated it, made it stronger, faster, harder to defeat. The Primis name was built far before my father came into existence yet he prances around as if he gifted Jeznia with magic. He wants worship, song, and praise. He wants frightened followers, fanatic loyalists, and an obsession of his name and power.

He will do anything and everything to create that legacy, to become known as the most powerful devil in all of Jeznian history. *I* do not care if people recall my name thousands of years after my death. *I* do not care if Jeznians and Odanthians fear me. *I* do not care to change the three worlds forever. I only care about two things.

Finding Sloane.

And killing Zagon.

"You will as soon as you realize it's the only way to achieve what you want," Umbra snaps at me, hairless eyebrows furrowing over sewn shut eyes.

I react on instinct, my magic lashing out as I break her bicep bone. She doesn't even flinch. Pain is nothing for a seventh circle inhabitant. Bitter shame burns through me down to my core. She got under my skin. She got me to lash out. She made me *emotional* and *out of control*. That's unacceptable. I'm Lord Balthazar Primis, heir to House Primis. If she can get under my skin in such a way, the Lords will be able to do it too.

I *need* to find Sloane. Before it's too late. Before a House sees the opportunity I've given them and my head is removed from my neck.

My hands vigorously rub my face, the stress coiling too tightly around my spine and shoulders. I need to get out of here.

With a snap of my fingers, I heal the broken bone I caused. I don't bother looking at her as I speak.

"Find me if you have any other news," I order.

I disappear without waiting for a reply.

Thank you for reading!

If you enjoyed Becoming the Devil, please considering taking a moment to leave a review!

Also by Alessandra Vu

Bargain with the Devil series
Paranormal Fantasy Romance
Bargain with the Devil – September 2024
Becoming the Devil – September 2025
Book III – September 2026

Standalone
Dark Romantasy
The Wolf and His Prey – June 2025 novella

Acknowledgements

Honestly, special shout out to Britt aka @brittsbookbabblings and Manogna aka @booksbymanogna for ARC reading every single one of my publications. I know 3 (2 books and 1 novella) isn't a large number, but it has really warmed my heart and meant a lot to me to see you two continually show up and come back for more of my stories. Thank you so much. ♥

Zoë. Zo-bo. At this point I don't know what else to say other than thank you. My gratitude can no longer be expressed in words. I will never stop appreciating you continually making time for me and my stories. Even when I haven't even edited them, you still happily read the gritty, raw, and grammatically incorrect stories riddled with spelling errors everywhere. Your enthusiasm literally is the encouragement that helps me keep my head down and writing. Your support fuels my motivation. You make this possible. Thank you so, so, so, SO fucking much. I love you girl. I love that your my cousin, but I can't put into words how much it means to me that we're friends.

KIMBERLY FUCKING [withholding last name for privacy reasons]. I may come up with the worldbuilding but you're the person that fleshes my worlds out. Being able to text you at any point in the day to bounce off ideas and ask for flaws within those ideas is absolutely CRITICAL to my writing and storytelling. I may not always like hearing the fatal flaws in my grand plans (lol) but without your critical eye and brain, my worlds wouldn't make any fucking sense. Honestly, you write these books as much as I do. Thank you so much. Thank you for your support, your encouragement, and your brain even when you're dead tired from working long shifts. I couldn't do this without you.

Mackenzie! My emotional rock star! You let me keep my head in the clouds and dream big for my future. I never feel silly or judged when I share my grandiose future with you. I feel *free*. If it were anyone else, I don't think they'd know how much it means to me to have that, but it's you. You get it. You know what it means. Thank you. And thank you for always making time to read my stories, squeezing them in during studying and tests and work. Your texts as you read always put a big ass grin on my face. I live for them. So never stop. Thank you so much for your endless support, for believing in me when I don't, for always telling me to "stay the course" and "keep writing".

Brianna thank you for showing up in my life in ways that are incomprehensible. You take your role as older sister very seriously and I can't thank you enough for that. Your my shelter when I need it, my sustenance when I'm low, my partner in crime when I'm feeling feisty. Thank you for always having my back (even when I'm bat shit crazy). You allow me to fall back into my old self and keep me protected. Thank you. You're the best big sister I could ever ask form.

My children. You fill my life with joy and light despite also bringing some of the hardest days I've ever had. The joy you bring me keeps me motivated to make this dream come true. I don't ever want you to give up on your passions and that means I can't either. I love you two so much and I hope one day to look back on these days with pride at where I ended up. You keep me motivated, to try harder, to show up for myself. I love you. Thank you for everything.

Meet the Author

Alessandra Vu is a stay-at-home parent of two. She started writing reader insert fanfiction when she was 16 years old and gradually shifted over into original stories. Her favorite genres to read and write are fantasy romance (romantasy), paranormal romance, and urban fantasy romance. Her favorite book series is The Hidden Legacy by Ilona Andrews and her favorite comfort series is The Lunar Chronicles by Marissa Meyer.

alessandra03330

Want to learn more? Use the QR code to view Alessandra's website, socials, and more!